David S. Jones was born in London during 'The Blitz'. Upon leaving school at fifteen with nothing more than a cycling proficiency certificate he tried various jobs. At eighteen he joined the Middlesex Fire Brigade serving three years until eventually leaving for Australia on the ten pound assisted passage scheme.

Returning some years later he joined the Household Cavalry and served in Malaya with the Armoured Reconnaissance Squadron. Back home in the UK after his tour of duty overseas, he became part of the Mounted Ceremonial Squadron, based in Knightsbridge, riding on several prestigious events, including the investiture of Prince Charles at Caernarvon. Upon leaving the Army he worked at various jobs, mostly as a carpenter but also driving trucks.

Eventually he found unlikely employment as a personal bodyguard to an American millionaire and entrepreneur, travelling throughout Europe. Upon reaching Portugal he left this employment, (fired) met and married his Portuguese wife. David has four children from that marriage, three living in Portugal and one in the UK.

He later returned to London and joined the London Fire and Rescue Service, serving for a further eleven years. It was during this time that he had the idea to develop the children's character *Fireman Sam*, now an international success as a children's TV series. After sustaining a back injury David had to leave the Fire Service. It then became necessary for him to make a living by doing something which did not require physical involvement. This led to him developing his writing skills.

Upon his departure from the fire service he returned to his beloved Portugal, eventually building and managing a highly successful bar/restaurant complex in the Algarve. He formed a construction company and built some stunning villas. Life then took a sadder path when his marriage failed. Following his divorce and having custody of the children he concentrated on bringing them up until they had flown the nest. This was a dark and difficult period. Once the children had gone he decided to raise some money and live his life to the full. After selling his shares in *Fireman Sam* he obtained a skippers licence, bought an ocean going sailing boat, which he named *"Thankusam"*, and sailed it from the UK to Portugal and later to North Africa.

He has continued to develop as a writer over the past years, and several of his ideas have been considered for TV and film both in the UK and America. His latest venture *'Trevelyan'* is the result of a chance re-union with an old Guards colleague who visited him at his Algarve home. His style of writing and ability to develop a good story line makes his work hard to put down. *'Trevelyan'* is a story, which is a compelling read with many twists and turns that keep the reader guessing until the final chapter.

Read more: http://www.david-s-jones.com/

David S. Jones

TREVELYAN

WELCOME TO THE WORLD OF
NICK TREVELYAN

AUSTIN MACAULEY
PUBLISHERS LTD.

A CIP catalogue record for this title is available from the British Library.

ISBN 978 14963 648 3
2nd Edit

www.austinmacauley.com

First Published (2013)
Austin Macauley Publishers Ltd.
25 Canada Square
Canary Wharf
London
E14 5LB

Printed and bound in Great Britain

I am delighted that you have taken possession of a copy of my novel. It is my greatest desire that you will enjoy the story. This work can be described as a book full of facts into which is woven a fabric of fiction or alternatively a work of fiction that is studded with fact.

It is for you to decide which is which.

David S. Jones

Contents

1
The New Recruit

When the limping electric train finally slowed to a halt at Camberley station and the doors opened, Nick knew immediately that the tall, upright, barrel-chested military figure standing on the platform was waiting for him.

The figure was wearing an immaculately pressed uniform whose creases looked as if they might have been carved from mahogany. A crimson sash crossed the huge chest. On his upper arms were three chevrons denoting his rank. Sergeant? His red and blue forage cap had a small shiny black peak edged with brass, shielding the black marble eyes and practically touching the bridge of his Romanesque nose.

Nick, pulling himself up to his full height, and putting on his most winning smile, walked hurriedly up to this imposing figure, whose eyes were barely visible shielded by the severe angle of the peak of his cap. The sergeant, Nick thought, was built like the proverbial brick convenience with a broad, jet-black clipped moustache and a square jaw that jutted forward in a commendable imitation of Desperate Dan.

Nick extended his right hand, but the sergeant ignored it. 'Good morning, Sergeant, I'm Nicholas Trevelyan. I'm so sorry about ...' but he was interrupted by a tremendous roar that made him take a hasty two steps backwards.

The ferocious Glaswegian accent was like a blistering wave of heat from a bomb blast. 'Colour sergeant! That's what I am – Colour Sergeant McGarrigal and don't you forget it!'

'I'm really sorry but ...'

'Mr Trevelyan, you're late!'

'But the train was ...'

'SHUT UP, MR TREVELYAN! Join the other recruits waiting for you in the car park by the minibus. I'm surprised they haven't died of old age by now! Just start praying I let you come to Sandhurst, and don't decide to send you back to Waterloo on the next train. Because I might, I just might!'

Nick attempted a reply.

'I'm...'

'Be quiet, Mr Trevelyan! Fortunately for your future health and career, I don't happen to be your particular troop's colour sergeant, but should I ever have the misfortune of bumping into you again, you will address me as '*Staff*' and nothing else. Is that clear?'

'Yes.'

'Yes, what?'

'Yes, Staff.'

Nick hurried with his case to the nearby station car park. A regulation Sandhurst minibus stood waiting there, surrounded by seven other, apprehensive-looking potential officer cadets. Nick climbed aboard; looking as nonchalant as he could – which at that moment wasn't very nonchalant at all – hoping no one had heard the frantic exchange, which had taken place on the platform.

Nick couldn't help thinking, though, that with the colour sergeant's penetrating roar still ringing in his ears, there was little doubt that most of Camberley had been privy to the tongue-lashing that he'd just endured.

That morning, when Nick's real life began, he was twenty-one years, five months and a few days old. Six feet two, sturdy and athletic, he'd played scrum half for his university's rugby team. His dark brown hair was thick and grew fast; on the morning he left for Sandhurst he knew he needed a haircut, but he also knew that Sandhurst would soon be dealing in its traditional efficient way with that particular requirement.

If you got up close to Nick you noticed that his that his left eye was green and the right one a clear blue. Something that Nick didn't think about very often.

He could hope to be a second lieutenant in the British Army at the end of the forty-four week Commissioning Course he was about to embark on at Sandhurst, if he could stick it out to the end.

Becoming an army officer had been his dream ever since he was eight. Back then, he'd been living close by Windsor Castle with his mother Annabelle and younger sister Sophie while his father George had been away on military service. Windsor was the venue for many military parades and Nick's mother had taken him to see them whenever she could.

The soldiers, with their perfect marching formations and splendid scarlet and gold ceremonial uniforms, had all made an indelible impression on Nick's younger incarnation.

That impression had led to Nick boarding a train that Monday morning in August at 09.36 at London's Waterloo station. This was the delayed 09.18 from Waterloo to Camberley.

The English summer was proving as unpredictable as ever and the grey sky above was heavy with rain.

'What's the matter?' a voice said, Didn't your mummy wake you up on time?' The other cadets fidgeted nervously. Nick cast a quick glance at the rearview mirror where he spotted his smirking protagonist at the back of the coach. The smirk gave way to an irritating nasal laugh.

Some inbred Hooray Henry with more money than sense, Nick thought. He felt like telling this aristocrat that it was hardly his, Nick's, fault, if London Regional Railways couldn't get its act together and its leaves off the line, but with a now cap-less and fairly terrifying shaven-headed McGarrigal driving as if the vehicle had personally offended him, Nick was certain that saying anything at all to the aristocrat would be a seriously rash plan. The nasal laugh assaulted Nick's ears again as the minibus pulled out of the car park and headed for its destination Sandhurst, the world-famous Royal Military Academy.

'If this is the way you are intending to behave then you would do better to turn around right now and go home,' added the aristo.

A second, strangely affected voice, added support to the complainant.

'Disgwaseful, just disgwaseful.'

They arrived at the entrance to Sandhurst a few minutes later. McGarrigal nosed the vehicle up to the main gate security barrier, carefully placed his treasured cap back on his head, meticulously adjusted it and got out of the vehicle. He walked over to the security cabin, had a quick word with one of the soldiers on duty, and waited until a bomb search of the vehicle had been completed. Then, sticking his head into the minibus, McGarrigal bellowed:

'EVERYONE OUT!'

The eight officer cadets scrambled out of the bus, tripping over one another in their eagerness not to be last. They formed some semblance of a straight line in front of their tormentor, who waited briefly for them to settle before he spoke again.

'Now, gentlemen,' growled the colour sergeant, '*this* side of that barrier you belong to your mothers. But once you cross that line there, you will belong to *Her Majesty's Forces*.'

McGarrigal stared at them all in turn, his eyes practically boring into their skulls it seemed. He allowed himself a hint of a grin, adding, 'It might have crossed your minds as to why such a charming chap as myself has been given the privilege of baby-sitting you little orphans this morning. Well, it's because I'm considered to be a *pussycat* that won't upset you little darlings too much before you meet the other instructors who work here. They make *me* seem like an ANGEL!' overemphasising the end of the sentence for maximum effect. Sergeant McGarrigal stuck out his vast barrel of a chest as if, rather than being an angel, he was the prize specimen at an award-winning turkey-farm.

'So, I suggest that if any of you think that perhaps you've made a MISTAKE and want to go home to your MUMMIES, now's the time to do so! Because once you cross that line, your feet shall not touch the ground for the next forty-four weeks!'

McGarrigal clasped his hands behind his back and rocked from the heel to the toe of his immaculately polished boots, staring above their heads enjoying the moment. No one said a word.

'I deduce from your silence, gentlemen that you've all decided to allow me and my colleagues to nurse you for the rest of your time here at Sandhurst Holiday Camp. Right, now I require you all to form up in a straight line on the other side of that barrier.'

These last words were said in an almost fatherly tone. *I think his bark's worse than his bite,* Nick thought, or at least he did for the two or three seconds of comparative silence before the air exploded as the colour sergeant's dulcet tones assaulted the sound barrier.

'Gentlemen, my regiment is the Scots Guards! I warn you now not to put so much as one little pinkie out of line. Now, stand at ease if you know what that is, and wait there.'

McGarrigal strode heavily back to the minibus, took off his forage cap and got in. He lovingly placed the prized cap on the engine cover, started the engine and drove the bus past the now open barrier, pulling up alongside the bewildered recruits. Thinking that it was expected, they all broke formation and moved forward as one to climb back into the bus. The sound barrier ripped open again.

'WHERE THE HELL DO YOU THINK YOU'RE GOING?'

The cadets turned from one to another, hoping someone would say something that would appease this madman, but none dared to speak.

'YOU DON'T ACTUALLY THINK THAT YOU ARE GOING TO RIDE IN HERE WITH ME, DO YOU, GENTLEMEN?' yelled McGarrigal. 'FALL IN BEHIND THE BUS. NOW! And God help anyone whom I spot in the mirror dropping behind!'

It had begun to rain. The distance from the barrier to the main induction block was all of a mile, and by the time they arrived, everyone was pretty much soaked, partly from the rain and partly from the sweat pouring from even the fittest.

Nick and the aristo were determined to beat each other. It was obvious to Nick that the aristo had quickly decided he disliked him intensely, and Nick wholeheartedly returned the feeling. Both began to tire towards the end and fell back from leading the other men to finish neck and neck in the middle of the pack.

McGarrigal put on his forage cap with all the pomp of the Pope donning his papal mitre.

'NOW ALL OF YOU LINE UP! When I give you the order, run at the double to that brown stone building you see over there, where you'll be met by people who, unlike me, don't have a kind disposition. So, don't give them any backchat! NOW MOVE!'

McGarrigal's final command proved remarkably effective in making everyone disappear at lightning speed.

At the brown building, after a cursory introduction to his platoon colour sergeant, an angular Welshman called Evans, Nick devoted himself to rushing from one appointed destination to the next as swiftly, and with as little fuss, as he could manage.

He received his army number and plastic name tag, then hurried to his classroom where he made sure that he blended into the background while his new platoon commander made clear to everyone exactly what was expected of them. After the briefing, Nick returned to his room to contemplate the impending reality of the harsh regime he'd volunteered for and was about to embark on. Like so many before him his initiation into military life had been harsh, he could hardly help wondering if he'd made the right decision.

As he had a pretty good idea of what the first, notoriously tough, five weeks of the Commissioning Course would be like, Nick was keen to make the most of the only decent night's sleep he thought he was likely to get for the best part of the next five weeks.

As things turned out, he was right.

2
Getting Stuck In

A grey drizzle greeted them the next morning.

The day started at 05.00 with a road run, followed by a rushed breakfast in the cookhouse, after which everyone lined up outside the entrance to the torture chamber where the Sandhurst barber plied his dreaded trade. After taking their turn in the barber's chair, they ruefully rubbed their newly acquired haircuts.

Through what had now become persistent rain, they hurried to the quartermaster's stores where they gathered the mountains of kit and assorted uniforms that were to see them through their training. Nick then hurried back to his quarters to drop off his kit before he had to attend another briefing. His muscles ached as he held the huge pile of uniforms in his outstretched arms. He caught up with a small group of cadets ahead of him and was about to overtake them when his foot sank into a rut in the path, which had become disguised by the downpour and he tripped and lunged forward in an attempt to regain his footing.

Nick's clothes and equipment flew from his arms in an arc as he tripped. The heavy steel-heeled drill boots, no longer resting on top of the kit, spun through the air as if in a slow-motion film sequence. In front, in response to the scuffling behind and his muffled yell, a fellow recruit turned his head to see what was happening.

The heel of the heavy right-foot drill boot caught the recruit squarely on the cheekbone, before the boot somersaulted onto the muddy grass beside the path. Nick picked himself up from the ground where he'd landed. Surveying his scattered kit, he despondently started picking up the crumpled, muddy effects, unaware that his boot had hit a fellow recruit. As he reached out, an arm grabbed his shoulder and a voice snarled.

'If you've left a mark on me, you fumbling idiot, I'll make you pay.'

It was the aristocrat, who was the recruit that Nick had encountered in the minibus, who'd got the boot in his face. His fine-boned face, expressionless blue eyes and moody grimace were more than memorable. He glared at Nick, 'I've had enough of your amateur fumbling from the moment you arrived. Do you understand? You're not going to last five minutes here if you go on like this, and if you do, by some miracle, get any further, I'll see to it that life is as uncomfortable as possible for you! Your bloody sort are always trouble. And by the way, one of your contact lenses is a different colour from the other one.'

The aristocrat hurried away, blood seeping through the fingers that he held over the wound on his cheek as another recruit, with a weasel featured face, started picking up the kit of the injured man after placing his own in a neat pile on the path.

'You certainly know how to go out of your way to make fwiends, don't you?' smirked this new arrival at Nick.

'Thanks for the advice. Who are you?' Nick asked the unwelcome commentator whose ability to pronounce the 'r' sound was a tad questionable.

'Who am I? Hugo De Lisle, a good fwiend of Twistwam.'

'Who's Twistwam?'

'Twistwam Wrath-Bonham.'

'Oh, I see,' said Nick. 'You mean Tristram?'

'That's what I said: Twistwam. The Wath-Bonhams have been officers in the Bwitish army for more than three centuwies. Haven't you heard of General Sir Michael Wath-Bonham, Twistwam's father? Or the even more illustwious Field Marshal Anthony Wath-Bonham?'

'They both somehow escaped my notice,' said Nick.

'Well, they shouldn't have done. The Field Marshal was Twistwam's gwandfather. A wemarkable and glowious militawy man, and a quack polo player in his day.'

'So, he was a weally good horse-wider, was he?' another voice enquired, from behind Nick.

Nick glanced round and saw a man who he hadn't seen among the group of cadets in the bus. The fellow had asked De Lisle the question in a friendly Newcastle accent, as if he were genuinely interested in the answer, and now he looked at De Lisle in a good-humoured way, as if he regarded him as a purely comic character, which was fair enough really. The new arrival had short black hair following his compulsory visit to the barber. He also had broad shoulders and muscular arms. He was a couple of inches shorter than Nick, but Nick could tell at once that the Geordie would be more than capable of looking after himself.

De Lisle gave a loud sigh, looked hard at the new arrival and said, 'you widiculous pwoletawian, Heligan,' He then strode off, staggering under the burden of the two piles of kit.

Nick glanced at the Geordie. 'Thanks, mate.'

'You're welcome. Thought you could use some help. I'm Steve Heligan. I'm in your platoon. Want some more friendly advice?'

'Please.'

'Shift this stuff double quick and make tracks for Colour Sergeant Evans before your new buddy and his 'fwiend' gets in first and start telling tales.'

Nick and got Steve hurriedly got going. 'I don't seem to be starting off too well,' Nick had to admit.

'Seems like that's putting it mildly, mate. Listen, I've come up through the ranks so I pretty much know the score already. Wind your neck in and don't ruffle too many feathers in your first week.'

'I'll try not to,' Nick replied. 'You're right. I'd better go and do some serious grovelling. See you later – if I don't end up in solitary confinement.'

Nick trudged back to his quarters with the sodden equipment, then made his way to Colour Sergeant Evans's office, knocked on the door and entered at the bellowed command. As he stood to attention, he was painfully aware of the muddied picture he must be presenting, and by the look on the colour sergeant's face he could tell that Tristram Wrath-Bonham had already been in to report him.

'You're a sorry excuse for a cadet, Mr Trevelyan,' Evans said, in his singsong Welsh accent, though his tone seemed to Nick one of disappointment rather than anger. 'We've hardly got you in a uniform and you're being accused of assaulting a fellow recruit! Next time you decide to rearrange someone's features, try and make sure it's not someone as pretty as Mr Wrath-Bonham, will you? He'll need a fair number of stitches in that wound and we don't think he's very happy about his first battle scar!'

'I'm very sorry about what happened, but it was actually an accident, Colour,' said Nick.

'Yes, well whatever it was, just get out of here and make sure your kit there is clean and ready for inspection first thing tomorrow morning.'

'Yes, Colour,' said Nick, and left the office, feeling humiliated.

Nick hurried to change, and only just made it into the lecture on time. He could hardly fail to notice the platoon commander's withering look.

It was going to be a long day, Nick thought, his only comfort being the sight of Wrath-Bonham, as he entered the lecture room shortly afterwards, sporting a one-inch raised wound on his cheek, with stiff stitches bristling along its length.

Wrath-Bonham shot Nick a venomous glance.

Nick was a practical and pragmatic man and having an alcoholic father had given him plenty of practice at making the best of things. Nick immersed himself in the daily life of Sandhurst.

He knew plenty about the Royal Military Academy even before he joined it. Sandhurst was a world-renowned training ground for potential officers who would eventually lead a variety of armies spanning the globe. The institute stood in seven hundred acres of countryside, boasting playing fields, woods and lakes, which were the locations of the rigorous programme of training that had only just begun for the latest intake at the Academy.

The Old College building – the splendid wide, white, much-photographed main building – had been built back in 1812. The main accommodation buildings – New College and Victory College – were less impressive externally but Nick found them comfortable enough. He'd been expecting fairly Spartan accommodation so there was no shock factor.

It was the Old College building that was home for Nick and the other graduate recruits throughout the intensive training period, designed to transform each one into an officer and – potentially – a gentleman. Every waking hour was crammed with vigorous activities aimed at making a soldier out of a civilian. Fortunately, Wrath-Bonham was in a different training group for most activities, and Nick managed to push him to the back of his mind.

The five weeks of the initial training phase of the Commissioning Course were reckoned to be equivalent to the twenty-one weeks a private soldier takes to reach a similar standard of drill. These weeks passed with a relentless concoction of physical training, lectures, weapon training, drill and more drill. Life was one hectic rush from one session to another, changing into a different type of uniform for almost every lesson.

Nick's platoon consisted of twenty-two men and two women. Each recruit knew from the start that some of them wouldn't make it to the end; a percentage of their number would fall by the wayside due to inability, lack of talent, unpopularity or just because they realised that army life wasn't for them after all. Friendship-forming with the platoon was rapid and even frenetic, as knowing how tricky and stressful these early weeks could be, everyone wanted an ally, and ideally a few of them.

Steve Heligan and Nick very soon became firm buddies. They had quickly realised they had had much in common and shared similar aspirations. Nick was particularly grateful for the advice Steve offered based on his previous experiences in the ranks. As they were the two who came from more ordinary backgrounds, this created a bond between them.

Wrath-Bonham and De Lisle also appeared to have paired up although the relationship was very much De Lisle playing Wobin (no, Nick thought, correcting himself, *Robin*) to Wrath-Bonham's Batman. Nick thought that the weasel ways of De Lisle were the perfect complement to Wrath-Bonham's strutting air of supremacy.

The training was tough. The long established military regimes aim was to take men and women from all backgrounds, break them and – if they were made of the right stuff – rebuild them as efficient leaders of soldiers. Time in the classrooms and lecture hall was a welcome break from the hours spent on the parade ground, assault courses, firing ranges and on-road runs. Finally, once the ultra-gruelling first five weeks were over with their 05.00 starts, punishing road runs, murderous obstacle courses, rushed meals, lack of sleep and endless, endless brain work in the classrooms and after the platoon had been inspected on the drill square and had passed the assessment, they were given a long weekend leave. Most headed for London and hopefully some fun as they had been deprived of any form of off-camp distraction during the initial five weeks.

By the time those first five weeks were up, the cadets were beginning to show signs of specialist interests. Various army units started courting cadets whose talents they thought might serve them most usefully. Those showing a particular flair for engineering, especially those having attained an appropriate degree already as a prerequisite, were, for example, hunted down by the recruitment officers from units like the Royal Engineers, Royal Electrical and Mechanical Engineers and the Royal Signals.

Nick was starting to get seen as someone showing promise for modern tactical warfare in the infantry. The Argyle and Sutherland Highlanders noticed him and started to take an interest, sending one of their recruiters to meet Nick and ask him about his career plans. The moment that happened, all other contenders for his talents fell by the wayside as far as Nick was concerned; he was more than delighted to have the opportunity of making his career in this famous regiment.

Nick and Steve also demonstrated a healthy competitive spirit in the pursuit of women. Winning girlfriends was an important sport; it provided yet another way to prove themselves. They were both still young enough not to realise that love could hurt.

The endless cleaning of kit was a ritual played out every evening. Steve and Nick got into the habit of doing this together so that they could use the time to chat about the day's events.

'Steve, do you remember the first day when I cracked Tristram's face with my boot?'

'Bloody right, I do! It made my day; no, actually my week!' He laughed.

'So, I did what Timothy suggested and looked up the Wrath-Bonham family tree.'

'Don't tell me they are six generations of fish merchants from Billingsgate,' he quipped.

'No you daft prat. They are practically blue blooded.'

'Well, you would know all about that given that you spilled some of it for him!'

'Their family tree goes back centuries, always military, very impressive. There appears to have been a Wrath-Bonham commanding British troops since the time of Charles II.'

'So, where does that put you, Nicky-boy?' said Steve, a little more seriously.

'I would say in deep shit as Tristram's father is a serving General.'

'He might be a General but he can't actually do you any harm … I don't think,' he added a little unconvincingly.

'I don't know why, Nick, but you certainly do seem to ruffle Tristram's feathers without even trying,' he laughed. 'A day doesn't pass without him finding something to dig at you for and that toad, Timothy, is right behind him with his nose up his arse.' Steve was making an attempt to take the sting out of his discovery.

'Yep, I can't think why he has taken it upon himself to have this vendetta against me. It's almost an obsession with him,' Nick replied.

'It's a campaign that isn't helped by the encouragement of that little turd Timothy. It's a mystery to me as to how he ever passed the entrance examination with such a speech impediment,' pondered Steve. 'He will be the butt of a lorry load of piss taking when he gets to his unfortunate regiment,'

'You are forgetting the illustrious General Montgomery, my friend, who had a similar speech problem which didn't hold up his promotion prospects. added Nick with a snigger.

'It appears to me that Timothy's tongue is far too large for his mouth which is the cause of his unfortunate predicament.' Steve laughed with all the authority of an ear nose and throat specialist.

'Ah professor, that's where your prognosis falls down.' Nick stroked his chin with his left hand whilst pointing at Steve with his right.

'I am of the opinion that it is in fact quite the contrary. The unhappy cadet of whom you speak has a quite normal size tongue; the problem lies with the dimensions of his head, which is too small to accommodate the tongue.'

With the banter over, they carried on with their kit cleaning, both wondering what might happen next in the Trevelyan vs. Wrath Bonham saga.

The training was tough but exhilarating, and after their platoon passed off the Drill Square, they were given a long weekend leave. Everyone headed off hopefully to find some fun as they had been deprived of any form of off-camp distraction during this initial period.

The occasional skirmish with Wrath-Bonham had kept things interesting, but generally Nick did his best to keep out of Tristram's way. Despite Wrath-Bonham's initial blustering, he had family traditions to maintain and with a little help from his Colour Sergeant, certainly showed that he had ability in his quest for the elusive Officer's pips.

Time in the classrooms and lecture hall was a welcome break from the hours spent on the parade ground, assault courses and on-road runs. There were many academic as well as physical lessons and the academic side of the course was generally undertaken by civilian tutors. Everyone was required to give several lectures when the rest of the platoon would be the audience. Finally, when the debate was thrown open for discussion, an opportunity to criticize was entered into with enthusiasm. It was Tristram's turn to give his lecture, which he did with all his usual bluster. After all, talking to the troops was something that was in his genes. His talk on the spread of the British Empire was actually very well done. As the lecture drew to a close, knowing that it had gone well, he was unable to resist the opportunity to slip in a snipe at Nick.

'And so from this great legacy, institutions such as the one we are attending at this moment were born. Here an attempt is made to make an Officer and a gentleman from even the lowest material,' he said, smugly. A discernible groan went around the room and Steve and Nick looked at each other and smiled, knowing that the pointed remark was obviously aimed at them. Who would answer? Nick decided that it had to be him.

'Gold braid and fine uniforms don't necessarily make a good Officer', he said. Tristram's face was turning decidedly red as Nick stole his thunder. It had tripped off the tongue quite nicely. Nick decided. He could see that Tristram was taken aback so he added another analogy that seemed to fit the occasion rather well.

'And as our illustrious forefather, the Duke of Wellington stated, "If a dog sleeps in a stable it doesn't make it a horse!"' There was a cheer from the other Cadets none of whom, apart from Timothy, thought too highly of Tristram who by this time was fuming. Nick expected a barrage from the speaker but another voice intervened and he was grateful to be spared the conflict.

'Your remarks are nothing but sexist,' shouted Louisa Aldridge who was one of the females in the platoon and renowned for her feminist viewpoint.

'*An Officer and a Gentleman indeed*! How chauvinistic can you get? Have the two women in your platoon suddenly become invisible? You will need to choose your words more carefully when you speak to your soldiers when you get to your regiment, or suffer the consequences of a tribunal,' Sally fumed.

Nick was grateful for her intervention, which took Tristram's attention away from him as he squirmed to get out of a self-made tight spot. He was not a happy man and although it was Louisa who had really put the boot in, there was no denying that Nick was the real focal point of his anger.

Nick became intensely focused on the daily demands of the course, and the overall objectives of his training. If he could strip away the unhappy events caused by TW-B, then his time at Sandhurst could have been close to idyllic. His knowledge of Military History was something that stood him in good stead. His love of rugby was also very useful; soon he became an important presence on the rugby field and ended up captaining the Academy team. Elsewhere he proved himself during the demanding outdoor activities. Steve matched him stride for stride, and the hard edge of competition between the two spurred them on to an impressive catalogue of performances in the field as the Cadets were pushed from one punishing exercise to the next.

Wrath- Bonham's constant hounding had become an obsession with him and was a constant nagging thorn in his side which meant that any time spent away from his tormentor was indeed quality.

3
Stanford Manor

It was close to six o'clock on a Friday evening in late September, a little more than a month and a half after Nick had made his first journey to Sandhurst and the sun had already set. He and Steve Heligan, in Steve's ancient and battered blue Ford Fiesta, were within a few miles of the pillared entrance to the Stanford family's estate.

'So, expecting to see an improvement in your love life this weekend?' Steve enquired, as they sped through the dark Sussex countryside.

'Well, yes, I'm beginning to think it might be nice to see someone for more than a couple of evenings. I fancy trying to find a lady who's going to phone me most evenings, someone really lovely, who I can go away for weekends with.'

'You're going soft in your old age! What makes you think anyone with half a brain is going to want to hang out with you for longer than a couple of beers? You've got no money, no car and you're not even good-looking.' Steve smiled, 'Even your eyes don't match.'

'Hey, it didn't do David Bowie any harm and some girls find it charming. Besides, might I remind you that you're the one who's had so many 'Dear John' letters you could paper your ceiling with them?'

'Anyway,' said Steve, 'neither you or me are likely to score this weekend.'

'Why on earth not?'

'There aren't enough zeros in our bank balances.'

But Steve pushed his foot harder against the accelerator, all the same.

Jonathan Stanford, Nick's roommate, had joined Steve and Nick's circle less than a fortnight ago, but friendships developed fast at Sandhurst. Jonathan was a well-spoken, friendly, warm-hearted guy, and while his parents were obviously wealthy, Jonathan was oddly unaffected by their wealth. The family's money had resulted from Jonathan's father getting into mobile phones in the 1980s, a time when mobile phones weren't fantastically popular. Having endured, he was well positioned to triumph in the business when their popularity soared and reap huge benefits.

Passing through the outer black, elaborate wrought iron gates of the Stanfords' estate heralded the start of a drive, winding through dark fields and paddocks for half a mile. The house, Nick saw, in the bright lights that flooded the car park at the front of the house, was surrounded by a variety of topiary, which included a neatly sculptured mobile phone, a champagne bottle, a pheasant and a salmon. Nick noticed about half a dozen expensive cars – including a dark blue Bentley sports convertible, a bright red Porsche and a purple Jag – parked in front of the house as they drew up.

Steve parked his Fiesta inconspicuously close to an adjacent stable block. He and Nick walked towards the house, their banter obscuring their trepidation. As they approached, Jonathan bounded down the elaborate steps of his family home and warmly greeted them.

'I thought you'd got lost, you chaps! You were meant to be only five minutes behind me and I got here an hour ago! Anyway, grab your bags and come in and join the party.'

Nick contemplated explaining that Steve's knackered Fiesta wasn't capable of covering the ground as fast as Jonathan's Aston Martin but thought better of it. Jonathan hurried them through the entrance hall and showed them to their rooms, so that they could quickly freshen up and join the rest of the guests for pre-dinner drinks.

Nick, who – like Steve – had never visited the house before, was expecting something special but the house astonished Nick even more than he thought it might. The Stanfords' home was a huge, ancient but fully modernised manor with a wide, white facade that Nick actually thought bore some resemblance to the main classical building at Sandhurst. But the house turned out to be infinitely more relaxed and fun inside - a kind of Sandhurst in heaven. Each of the dozen guestrooms had an en-suite bathroom and every other possible comfort.

Inside, the house was light and cheerful. Nick showered, shaved and changed his clothes. He and Steve met as arranged on the landing and joined the party. It felt good to Nick to be in different surroundings where they could relax away from the ever present, regimented staff, the smell of boot polish and sweat; hallmarks of the academy. Dinner – a smoked salmon starter, then roast pheasant with all the trimmings followed by a delicious strawberry and raspberry mousse – was excellent. Slowly, Nick began to feel himself relaxing. There were more than twenty guests, but apart from Nick and Steve no other single men, only wealthy married couples and their teenage children. There was also an evidently single lady called Clarisse, a friend of Jonathan's mother Gillian Stanford.

Clarisse was about forty, greyish-blonde and had a lovely figure but hardly smiled once during the dinner. Jonathan, sitting with Nick and Steve and sensing their disappointment at what seemed like the lack of romantic opportunities, whispered that the weekend wasn't over yet.

The next day, the Stanford's offered their guests the choice of either horse-riding on the extensive estate or helping Jonathan's father, Bernard Stanford 'Europe's leading mobile communications magnate,' as he'd been described recently in *The Sun* in an article substantially supplied by his public relations firm – give some of his stunning collection of vintage cars a run around the private roads across the huge estate, or else entertain themselves as they pleased. Steve decided on horse-riding whilst Nick, who had a fair knowledge of what went on inside a car – both in its engine and in its passenger seats late at night in country lanes – chose to spend time with Bernard.

Later in the morning, Bernard Stanford and Nick were tinkering with a vintage Morgan at the front of the house when a white Rolls Royce drew up. Bernard carefully cleaned his hands and hurried across to greet the occupants.

One was a tall, young, exceptionally stunning blonde woman with large blue eyes, and an athletically elegant figure.

The other was a balding, thickset older man who, Nick guessed, was in his mid-fifties. What was left of the man's hair was short and silver. He had a gold filling in one of his front teeth and was wearing a sharp casual black tee-shirt, more appropriate for someone maybe a decade younger. He exuded an air of power and influence. Nick wondered who this lucky devil was to be accompanying such a stunning female.

The man shepherded the young woman in a protective fashion. It suddenly dawned on Nick that they were, in fact probably father and daughter rather than a Sugar Daddy and his delicious escort, which had been Nick's first assumption. He wandered over to the group and was introduced by Bernard to the man, whose name was Warren Fisher. Warren shook Nick's hand powerfully and greeted him with a penetrating stare. Nick made a mental note that this was a man whom you would do well not to mess with.

His daughter Marina seemed friendlier. She gave Nick the warmest of smiles and he allowed himself a glimpse of hope that this weekend might turn out to be more interesting than he had anticipated.

The Fishers disappeared to their rooms later that morning. Nick didn't see anything more of them until the early Saturday evening when everyone gathered for pre-dinner drinks. He caught sight of Steve and Clarisse a few times. Steve was taking her for a walk on the estate and he noticed that she was smiling quite a lot more now. The whole occasion for the weekend was to celebrate Gillian Stanford's birthday, and people arrived in dribs and drabs throughout the day. There were a dozen more people than there had been for dinner on the previous evening. The meal was a splendid affair with Champagne and fine wine in abundance. There were many toasts and congratulations to the hostess on her birthday.

After dinner Nick managed to corner Marina for coffee in the lounge. During the meal Marina had been sitting too many places away from Nick for him to have a chance of talking to her, though he had succeeded a couple of times in making eye contact and when he did he thought that she looked pleased that he had.

When they finally sat down together on one of the sumptuous Chesterfield sofas, he felt instantly overwhelmingly attracted to her. Marina didn't seem to feel any need to hide the fact that she liked Nick, too; her smiles, fluttering eyelashes and flashing white teeth said it all. Then, when she had finished her second brandy, she casually leaned over to say goodnight allowing a provocative glimpse at a glorious cleavage. 'See you in an hour, your room!' before swiftly turning away to say goodnight to the hosts and leave. Nick stared after her with a mixture of surprise, delight and unexpected anticipation. This really was turning out to be an interesting weekend. He spent another fifteen minutes talking to the Stanfords' and then left, buzzing with excitement at the implications behind Marina's whispered promise. He hurried to his room, threw off his jacket, tie and shoes, brushed his teeth nervously in the bathroom and sat in the comfortable chair in the corner of his room to wait. He woke with a start and felt cold. Nick glanced at his watch; it was four-thirty in the morning. His confused mind slowly woke up and he remembered why he was still sitting in the chair and not lying in bed.

'Oh, great,' he muttered to himself as he slowly undressed and crawled into bed. '*Trust me to pick the party tease.*' He fell asleep dreaming of what might have been, to be awoken by the alarm on his watch after what seemed to be far too short a time.

He saw Marina at breakfast on the Sunday morning but had no chance to talk to her, as she had Warren on her left and on her right, a rather posh-looking elderly woman who dripped with gold and jewellery like a pirate treasure horde. Nick cast a few discreet glances in Marina's direction. He caught her eye a couple of times, but she didn't respond other than to give him a brief smile before continuing her conversation. Nick cooled his frustration by walking twice round the estate's lake. Seeing a yard-long carp magnificently hurl itself out of the water in the centre of the lake in a mighty splash took Nick's mind off Marina for a few moments, but not for long. After a lavish, but frustrating, Sunday lunch (extremely tender roast Welsh lamb) when Marina was again far down the table, sandwiched between her father and a tall man who reminded Nick of Basil

Fawlty, Nick still hadn't managed to corner Marina and had almost given up hope of talking to her. However, after lunch, everyone gathered in the front hall to go for a walk and Nick disappeared into the cloakroom to borrow one of Jonathan's Barbour jackets. Suddenly, he found himself alone in the room with Marina, who had sneaked up behind him and slipped her arm around his waist.

'I'm sorry about last night, Nicholas, but Daddy insisted in stopping in my room for a nightcap and fell asleep in the chair. He's incredibly possessive so I let him doze and by the time he woke, I thought it was probably too late.

'Nick, it's hard for me to talk to you here because most of the people here know me and I like to keep my personal life secret from everyone: well, apart from my father anyway who always finds out about it. In case I don't get a chance to speak to you again, here's the address of my boutique in London; do give me a call in the week.'

And she pressed a business card into his hand, her long, cool, pink nailed exquisitely manicured fingers lightly brushing his hand, and then kissed him on the lips just once before hurrying off to re-join the throng.

She was gone before Nick had a chance to react properly other than to realise that the sudden unexpected kiss had left him dumbfounded with delight. He stared after her in amazement, and then glanced down at her card. Her boutique was called Serendipity and was on Sloane Street, Knightsbridge, London SW1.

As he drove back to Sandhurst with Steve that evening, Nick told him about his encounters with the mysterious Marina.

'Well, all I can say is, go for it, you lucky sod. She looks like a pretty hot proposition and I think you might well have some fun there. Just one word of warning though: I spoke to her old man for quite a while and he made a lot of none too discrete inquiries about you. He seems quite unnaturally obsessed by her. I think there's some kind of story behind that. In the meantime though, I think Mr Fisher is a bit of a tough cookie. If you're going to play around with his daughter, make sure you find out what his ground rules are as quickly as possible, or you might get yourself into trouble.'

'One day, you're going to make someone a wonderful wife, Steve,' laughed Nick. 'Don't worry; the situation is under control.'

4
The Offer

When Nick got back to Sandhurst, he decided to try to play things cool and give it a couple of days before phoning Marina. So he was very surprised indeed, on the Monday evening after his return, to receive a phone call on his mobile from none other than the infamous Warren Fisher.

'Nicholas, good to talk to you again. Our meeting at Stanford Manor was all too brief,' boomed Warren Fisher. 'I hope you had a good trip home? Oh, by the way, I spoke to your chum Steve Heligan at the weekend and he gave me your mobile number.'

'Fine, thank you, sir,' Nick replied guardedly, wondering what on earth Marina's father could be calling him for and why Warren Fisher would have wanted his number in the first place.

'I enjoyed meeting you over the weekend, Nicholas,' Fisher continued in his self-assured manner. 'No doubt you're wondering why I'm calling you. Well, I'll tell you, but not over the phone. I'd like you to join me for dinner on Wednesday evening at the Regency Hotel. It's one of the best hotels in Camberley.'

The invitation was issued in a way that felt friendly enough to Nick, but somehow he got the sense he was being given an order and non-attendance was not an option.

'That's very kind of you, sir. I'm free that evening as it happens. Will we be having the pleasure of Marina's company?'

'Naturally,' replied Warren, in a brief, punchy, but courteous enough tone. 'She hasn't stopped talking about you for the last twenty-four hours.' Nick's heart started to thump. 'I wouldn't be able to keep her away,' added Fisher. 'But you and I will meet for a drink before Marina arrives; she isn't the most punctual woman on the planet. There's something I want to discuss with you, Nicholas.'

Nick wanted to phone Marina and ask her what this was all about, but some instinct within him told him not to do so until he met Warren Fisher on Wednesday, an evening he awaited with great impatience. Finally, the evening arrived. Nick reached the rather exclusive destination in his smartest navy blue blazer and Cavalry twill trousers.

He was slightly early and went into the hotel lobby. He was shown to the nearby bar where he ordered a vodka and tonic. Shortly afterwards, the powerful figure of Warren Fisher strode in, precisely on time. He greeted Nick in a business-like fashion and led him to a table in a quiet corner. The suave hotel manager appeared at Warren Fisher's shoulder.

'Mr Fisher, a pleasure to see you here. We've missed you these last few months.' The man had an extremely smooth manner, with classic dark, French good looks, but unable to entirely hide the nervous edge in his voice as he spoke to the daunting figure before him.

Nick took note of this as the manager continued, warmly: 'Please accept a bottle of 1995 vintage Bollinger with my compliments. An especially good year. I trust you'll be joining us in the restaurant later? Pierre will be delighted to prepare your favourite dish for you.'

'You're very kind, André,' Warren Fisher said. 'Yes, we'll be dining here. Please have a table prepared for three for nine pm. This is a business associate of mine. Nicholas, this is my old friend, André Delacroix.'

Nick exchanged pleasantries with André for a few moments, then the hotel manager bid them an enjoyable evening and left, shortly to be replaced by the head wine waiter who, with a flourish, produced the bottle of champagne which he expertly opened, filled their champagne flutes and then retired, finally leaving them alone.

By this stage Nick's curiosity about Fisher had been well aroused. Cautiously, he tried to start some polite small talk but Fisher immediately interrupted:

'Nicholas, I don't believe in wasting time, so I'm going to come straight to the point.'

Warren Fisher paused, all the same. He looked hard at Nick, the small black eyes drilling deep into Nick's skull as if now seeing him for the first time he felt transfixed and severely uncomfortable by the sensation. Or – Nick thought – could it be that Fisher was perhaps noticing for the first time his mismatched coloured eyes. Nick, who deduced that the meeting was about Marina and assumed that Fisher was going to warn him off her, possibly by some roundabout route which boiled down to him, Nick, supposedly not being sophisticated enough for her. Nick just sat there attempting to look respectful, though not intimidated.

Nick wondered whether he should say anything but decided not to; it was evident that Warren Fisher would lead this conversation.

'Marina appears to like you, Nicholas. I rather think she likes you a lot. Yes, yes, I know you and Marina hardly know each other, but let's face it, you're hardly going to not want to see her again and I know she wants to see you again too.'

Nick just stared. *Marina likes me*, he thought. His heart beat faster.

Fisher, keeping his voice unusually low went on, 'I've made a few enquiries about you through my contacts at Sandhurst and other locations. It appears you're a man whom others respect highly and feel that you have demonstrated much promise. You can obviously move with ease in circles that ... well, let's just say circles which you perhaps would not have been privy to, had you not decided to go into the army as an officer.'

'Mr Fisher, I only know the Stanfords' because I'm friends with Jonathan, and I've only known him for a couple of weeks.'

'Yes, I know that,' Fisher said. 'But I gather you come from, really, quite modest origins and that your father ... let's say that he only had limited success in his career. The fact is, Nicholas, that ...'

'Please call me Nick, Mr Fisher.'

'Thank you, Nick. And please call me Warren. To come to the point, I admire your adaptability and the natural facility you seem to have for getting on with people. I believe you would be a most acceptable escort for my daughter.'

'You ... you do?' Nick murmured.

'Yes. As I hope you've realised, I'm not a snob, Nick. I care more about a man's mettle and character than about what is in his wallet. Besides, if a man does have mettle and character, what's in his wallet tends to increase. Marina has had some rough times with certain men, Nick. They've mistreated her; taken advantage of her; tried to use her to get to me. Well, I know you're not the type to do that. So ... keep seeing Marina. Indeed, it would please me greatly if you would.'

Now he fell silent, but just went on looking at Nick. Fisher suddenly gave a little nod, as if agreeing with something he himself was thinking. 'All I ask is this,' Fisher said. 'Nick, my daughter is the most important person in my life. My wife, whom I loved very much, died three years ago, long before her time. Marina is all I have. I make absolutely no bones about being determined that she will only experience the best that life has to offer. I don't want her to be hurt by anyone ever again. So, all I ask is, if you're interested in being with her, I want your assurance that you will be good to her and will take every step to make her happy. If I've misjudged the situation and in fact, you are not as keen on her as I think you are, I apologise and we can part company without rancour.'

Warren Fisher again fell silent. Now Nick knew that he had to answer.

It felt worrying and, frankly, alarming that someone could discover so much about him and in such a short time.

In the second or so before he knew he would have to say something as a reply, the lady herself swept into the bar, distracting them both, along with every other heterosexual male present.

The figure-hugging designer dress she wore showed off her fabulously proportioned body to the best advantage. Marina reached their table, leaned forward and planted a kiss on Warren Fisher's forehead, before sitting down and breathlessly announcing:

'Sorry I'm late, I had to stay at the shop for longer than I expected because Prince Fawaz of Bahrain came in and was there for more than half an hour looking at everything, and in the end he only bought *two scarves* for his favourite wife. Anyway, I'm here now. Nicholas, I'm so glad you came. Daddy's been dying to talk to you and I've been *longing* to see you again.'

Nick had already picked up that Marina had a habit of over-emphasizing certain words in her speech; he'd already discovered that he found this curiously mesmerising. Nick had to pull himself together to make the appropriate response as they moved off to go into the dining room. Nick was so excited at seeing Marina again, he wondered if he'd actually be able to eat anything. He hadn't expected for a moment that Marina would be dining with them too.

As he enjoyed the delicious experience of being only a couple of feet from Marina, and as he inhaled the lovely delicate orangey scent she wore, he realised that the shock and resistance which he had felt in an automatic response to Warren Fisher's request were slowly fading away to be replaced by a yearning that he knew he was not going to be able to ignore or control.

Nick suspected that very little escaped Warren Fisher's notice. Somehow, Nick felt that Fisher knew everything that he, Nick, was thinking at that moment.

The meal was traditional French cuisine at its best – a varied and exquisite seafood platter, then a delicious Bouillabaisse, followed by fillet steaks in a delicious red wine sauce. Fisher was talking about how he'd built up his first emerging markets hedge fund and why his had done so well, when other emerging market hedge funds had failed. Nick did his best to listen, but he was finding it seriously difficult to pay attention. His mind was focusing on one thing and one thing only and he was trying hard to think of a way to either get rid of Warren Fisher, or get away somehow to be alone with Marina.

Finally, when they'd all finished their main course but hadn't ordered any dessert, Warren signalled to Delacroix, who had been hovering subserviently in the vicinity ever since the start of the meal.

'André, please continue to look after my daughter and her friend.'

Warren glanced at Marina, then at Nick. 'I'll be going now. Thank you both for a most pleasant evening.' Warren made a deliberately slow and theatrical job of crumpling his napkin before standing up and holding out his hand to Nick.

'So, we have an agreement?' Fisher said to Nick.

Nick stood up. He nodded rather helplessly at Fisher. 'Yes, of course.'

'An agreement about what?' Marina asked.

Her father smiled at her. 'Oh, just business,' he murmured, and then glanced at Nick again. 'Thank you.'

'Thank you, sir,' said Nick.

'I'm glad we spoke,' said Fisher. But he said it in a way that made things pretty obvious that if the agreement ever got broken, Nick would regret it.

Warren Fisher kissed Marina briefly, fondly stroking her hair in a manner that seemed to Nick more proprietary than paternal, and then he hurriedly left the restaurant.

'Oh, *thank God,*' declared Marina, taking hold of Nick's hand. 'I do love daddy, but he doesn't always catch on too swiftly when he's not wanted. Okay. *Let's go upstairs.*' She smiled, and keeping her voice right down, added: 'You don't want any dessert, do you? I do, but I want it to be you.'

'Shouldn't ... shouldn't we at least pay first?'

'Don't be silly,' she laughed. 'Daddy's a senior partner in this place. Dinner's always on the house, Come on! Let's go. I've booked a lovely room for us upstairs and I don't want to waste another moment.'

Nick, temporarily stunned by this blatant admission of premeditation, felt a momentary impulse to be cautious wash over him. *After all*, he thought, *I hardly know her.* In the distance danger bells were faintly ringing but the impulse indeed lasted no longer than a moment. A much more resilient, primeval emotion took over and he followed Marina across the lobby to the lifts and up to the fourth floor. There, he discovered, she had reserved a sumptuous suite with bathroom, lounge and bar. Nick sat down on the softly inviting bed while Marina kissed him lingeringly on the lips, murmured, 'Make yourself comfortable, darling.' She then disappeared into the bathroom.

No more than a handful of minutes later Marina walked out of the bathroom, her tanned bare feet sinking into the thick pile of the deep white carpet, her hips swaying provocatively. She stopped a few feet in front of Nick, her legs slightly apart. She stroked her hips with the palms of her hands. She was wearing a gossamer-thin, pink, silk full-length negligée that was, Nick could see, almost completely transparent.

'Well, do you like me?' she asked in a low, husky and incredibly sexy voice. Having asked the ridiculously redundant question, she tossed her head in a Flamenco style, causing her blonde hair that was framing the exquisite features of her face to cascade over her elegant shoulders. The effect of this sudden movement caused her breasts to quiver and the robe to fall open revealing her pert nipples.

'You're beautiful,' Nick answered trying hard to control his voice.

'So are you,' Marina whispered. 'I love your eyes, the way they're different colours.' She smiled. 'It's like there are two Nicks inside you, and I'm simply *bats* about them both.'

Nick didn't know what to say.

He knew even less what to say a moment later, when Marina stepped out of her robe and let it fall onto the deep pile of the luxurious carpet. Every ounce of Nick's common sense told him to run, that something was seriously wrong. This was all too good to be true. But what the hell. There could be no man alive on the planet that could resist what was on offer. Marina slowly slid her hands from her hips and took hold of the negligee by her fingertips easing it back over her shoulders, letting it drop silently to the floor. She moved forward, opening her long, tanned legs – straddling his – and pushed her soft stomach towards his face. He gently kissed the perfectly formed navel.

Lowering herself onto his lap their faces were level. Their eyes were locked. Marina brought her right hand up across his arm, over his shoulder and caressed his neck. Slowly she drove her long sensuous fingers into the hair on the back of his head; then suddenly and without warning, she grabbed a handful of hair, violently jerking his head backwards. Nick was caught off guard and his mouth opened as if to let out an agonised scream but before he had drawn breath, Marina's mouth had covered his and was pressing lips to lips with a powerful force.

Her wild tongue sought every hidden corner of his mouth. As the passion rose within her she twisted and jerked in ecstasy never letting the pressure between their lips relax. The violence of the jerking caused her teeth to cut into his lips and he could taste the salty blood. Initially, the shock had hit him like a baseball bat between the shoulder blades. Marina had taken the initiative entirely up to that point. But now he was aroused and fighting back with equal passion.

Slowly he brought his right hand up across her arm over her shoulder and caressed her neck. Then he drove his fingers into the hair on the back of her head and suddenly, without warning, grabbed a handful of hair, violently jerking Marina's head backwards. Now he really had the bit between his teeth and gave as good as he had received plus a little extra.

They held onto each other's hair as they writhed and kissed in a crazed embrace. Nick allowed himself to be pushed back onto the bed. At the same time he slowly turned and levered himself so that he was now on top. He raised himself up onto his knees and with a violent tug wrenched their mouths apart. He retained his hold on Marina's hair; her grip was lost in the sudden violence of his movement. He pulled Marina's head backward with his eyes fixed on hers. There were smears of blood on her cheeks and at the corner of her mouth. Her expression was of feigned pain although Nick knew that he must have been hurting her. He released his grip and stood up. He was still fully dressed. He took off his clothes whilst Marina squirmed on the bed with delight, occasionally whimpering with anticipation.

When his feet left the deep pile white carpet to climb into the bed, it was more than four hours before they touched the carpet again. This was the opening to a night of sex that he would never forget. It was also the prelude to an erotic and tempestuous relationship.

Just three days after that night, Nick received a surprise gift delivered to him at Sandhurst.

It was a gleaming black Porsche 911, and it arrived with a little handwritten note in an envelope.

Enjoy her, Nick.
Best regards, Warren.

Nick wasn't sure whether Warren Fisher was referring to the car or to Marina.

Nick didn't care too much, though.

He intended to enjoy them both.

5

Wrath-Bonham Sets a Trap

Marina and Nick fell head over hips in love, delighting in each other's company, minds and bodies.

The tough routine at Sandhurst didn't make it easy for Nick and Marina to meet much more than once or twice a week. But he was free on Saturday nights and the occasional Sunday night. Nick got into the habit of catching the train from Camberley station to Waterloo on Saturday mornings and then taking a cab to Knightsbridge, where he spent the day helping Marina out in her boutique Serendipity.

The handsome, tall, trainee military officer with the strong, sturdy build, kind face and unusual eyes proved unsurprisingly attractive to ladies for whom a weekly shop at Serendipity was one of their regular pleasures. Several discreetly asked Marina for Nick's phone number, only for an always-courteous Marina to murmur to them that the charming shop assistant was spoken for, 'and by me', she would add with the faint but distinct smile that comes with the confidence of romantic ownership.

As for Nick, he spent his snatched nights in Knightsbridge in passionate excess with the lady who had already come to mean a lot more to him than he'd ever imagined she would. She was just so beautiful, and all of her was his, all her beauty and wit and laughter and perfume and style and her splendid body that he grew to know so well at night when they kissed and loved each other in the king-sized double bed in her apartment.

With Marina mesmerising him, Nick's life at Sandhurst seemed to him to have wonderfully changed for the better, but he had plenty of other things to think about.

His friendship with Steve Heligan soon became a friendly rivalry that brought out the best in both men and intensified their devotion to their work.

The months passed for Nick in a hectic whirl of training, studying and such delicious snatched moments with Marina as he could enjoy. He believed himself in love with her, and while they didn't speak of love or the future, they were as close mentally as they were physically.

Autumn became winter, winter turned into spring, and spring into summer. As the final weeks of the Commissioning Course approached, the instructors started compiling a shortlist of those cadets regarded as the most likely candidates in the running for the prestigious prizes to be handed out at the Sovereign's Parade.

This parade, held at the end of each term, marked the passing out from Sandhurst of officer cadets who had completed the Commissioning Course. It was the grandest day in the Sandhurst calendar as friends, family and VIPs gathered in Old College Square to watch the cadets take part in their final challenge. During the ceremony, the Sword of Honour, the Overseas Sword and the Queen's Medal were awarded by the Sovereign or more usually her representative to the top officer cadets.

The parade traditionally ended with the adjutant riding his horse up the steps of the Old College as he followed the graduating officer cadets through the Grand Entrance. After a formal lunch with friends, family and Regimental officers, the day concluded in spectacular and celebratory fashion at the exclusive Commissioning Ball, where, at the stroke of midnight, the newly commissioned Second Lieutenants proudly displayed their rank and insignia for the first time.

Nick and Steve were each in friendly contention for the coveted title of Cane of Honour, while Nick had also been earmarked for the Modern History prize.

Tristram Wrath-Bonham, despite everything, had managed to knuckle down to some hard work and had shown that, contrary to appearances, he had a keen political brain, possibly deriving from his and his forebears' love of applying power over supposedly lesser mortals. In any event, Wrath-Bonham looked likely to walk away with the award for Politics and Economics.

Wrath-Bonham and the cadets, including the lucky one who had won the heart of Marina Fisher, looked forward with plenty of apprehension to the programme of rehearsals for the Sovereign's Parade and the prize that they had all been striving for: their commission and officer's pips.

There came a moment, during the rehearsal, when Wrath-Bonham caught Nick alone in a corridor he stopped to talk.

'You know, Trevelyan, I really don't know what that beautiful girl sees in you.'

'Well, obviously she does see something, or she wouldn't be with me,' said Nick, determined to keep calm.

'I suppose she just feels sorry for you,' Wrath-Bonham said.

Nick's fists were clenched, but he kept them in his pocket. He made a move to walk past, but Wrath-Bonham angled himself to block the corridor.

'You'll be following in the footsteps of your illustrious father, Trevelyan. I imagine Marina will come to her senses at some point and will have the sense to dump you, whereupon you'll doubtless take refuge in the bottle. Your career shall no doubt be like your father's; a waste of taxpayer's money.' Wrath-Bonham gave a haughty, horsey laugh, accompanied with a Hooray Henry-ish display of finger prodding. 'The only people to benefit from your father's career have been the pubs and breweries!'

Somehow, with a gargantuan effort, Nick kept his cool.

'As for your mother, Trevelyan, more fool her I say for putting up with an alcoholic like your father and ...' but the conceited aristocrat never got to finish the sentence. Lunging forward, Nick grabbed Wrath-Bonham by the throat, slammed him against the wall, pinned him with his left arm and drew back his right fist, ready to land the blow, which Nick had looked forward to ever since encountering this obnoxious man. Nick knew that he'd descended to the law of the jungle but, boy, it felt good!

'WHAT THE HELL ARE YOU DOING, TREVELYAN?'

Nick heard the far from dulcet tones of Colour Sergeant McGarrigal barking through the mist of his own anger. Nick released his grip on the dishevelled Wrath-Bonham who slid down the wall like a wounded cockroach, collapsing in a pathetic heap of aristocracy and self-pity.

Wrath-Bonham gathered himself looking up sullenly at the colour sergeant. 'I want this incident reported to the adjutant immediately.' Wrath-Bonham's voice was that of a petulant schoolboy.

'Mr Wrath-Bonham, this is something that you two should resolve privately,' McGarrigal said.

'Colour,' Wrath-Bonham retorted, 'I don't think you heard me. I said that I want this incident reported to the adjutant now!'

'Very well, then, Mr Wrath-Bonham, if you insist you leave me no alternative. Mr Trevelyan, I'm afraid I will have to report what has happened here.'

'Do your job, Colour. It's not your fault.' Nick had recovered his calm and was watching Wrath-Bonham who, having made a rapid recovery, had a broad smile on his noble features. He was looking supremely pleased with himself. He'd achieved exactly what he had set out to do and Nick had been an unsuspecting idiot who had jumped into his trap with both feet.

Nick knew what to expect. He would be hauled before one of the top brass at Sandhurst.

Hearing what Wrath-Bonham had said was all the more painful because Nick knew that what the aristo had said about his, Nick's, father had more than a little ring of truth about it. Nick could only assume that Wrath-Bonham had got to know something of the reality of the Trevelyan's domestic circumstances.

Home for Nick when he'd been growing up was a series of army houses in countries spanning the world from Hong Kong to Germany, with stints at the Household Cavalry's home barracks in Windsor. His father had often been away either on exercises or on overseas duty. What little time George Trevelyan did spend at home tended to be divided between his family, the mess, the Freemasons and an excessive enjoyment of the products of the Scottish whisky industry.

Indeed, George loved Scotland, especially Glenfiddich, Glenmorangie and Laphroaig. Thankfully, Nick's mother Annabelle had made up for the frequent absence of dad to Nick and his sister Sophie. Meanwhile, as the years passed, George Trevelyan had sunk deeper into alcoholism.

But Nick wasn't like his father. Nick had worked hard at Windsor Boys' School. He'd won a military grant that had seen him through university, where he read Modern History. His favourite period was World War Two. He had an encyclopaedic knowledge of the leaders, battles, strategies and tactics, and he considered the Allied Powers' great global coalition that defeated Nazi Germany and militaristic Japan to be the best of all morality tales.

6
Discipline ... and Consolation

Discipline at Sandhurst was mostly meted out by Academy Sergeant Major John 'Dusty' Miller, Grenadier Guards. A holder of the British Empire Medal, awarded by the Crown for especially meritorious military or civil service, 'Dusty' was indeed a formidable chap.

Nick had seen and heard Miller often enough in the drill square, or seen him walking rapidly down the corridors of Sandhurst engaged on some pressing business. Miller was not someone you tended to forget once you'd set eyes on him once. He stood six feet four inches tall and weighed eighteen stone, all of which – Nick could tell from the man's bollard-like arms and the body that looked as robust as beef – was hard muscle.

Miller's close-cropped, greying hair topped a face more square in shape than rounded. His relatively small broken nose was hardly noticeable above the wide black moustache, and the piercing blue eyes were barely visible below the Guards-style slashed peak of his forage cap. Nick had seen that one of the many noticeable features of this massive man was that he appeared to have no neck. It was as if his head had sprouted straight out of his shoulders.

Rumour had it in the college that most of Miller's spare time was dedicated to his awesome body. He worked out, pumped iron, and whenever he could find time from his busy schedule, threw his tremendous frame over the various assault courses scattered around the academy's vast grounds.

Nick found it hard to decide just which of Miller's many fabled attributes was the most striking. Eventually he settled the matter in a discussion with Steve when they agreed that it had to be the voice. 'Dusty' was, Nick felt certain, the owner of the loudest voice in the world. When Miller was operating at top volume, he made Colour Sergeant McGarrigal seem by comparison like a whisperer. Even Miller's speaking voice was a dozen or so decibels above the norm, although there were few enough occasions when he actually just talked.

But his drill square voice was something to hear. Everyone, bar none, stood in terror when the huge lungs expelled the air that carried forth the word. Miller's eagle eyes were capable of detecting the minutest flaw in a recruit's turnout. But it wasn't only the cadets who needed to be faultless in their appearance: anyone – even a colour sergeant – who put a foot onto 'His Square' was subjected to meticulous scrutiny, and should anyone be found to be less than one hundred per cent perfect, Miller gave the impression of taking it as a personal affront, and responding to it accordingly.

The tongue-lashing Nick knew he could expect to receive from the adjutant would be severe but in order to get to the adjutant, he would have to pass through the office of the academy sergeant-major (ASM) and that was a fate every recruit dreaded.

The ASM was Miller.

When, on a Monday morning, Nick got the summons to appear before the adjutant the following Friday afternoon, his heart sank deeper than the Mariana Trench. Nick had all that week to wonder what Friday afternoon was going to be like. Nick was sure that, whatever did happen, Friday afternoon wasn't likely to be a red-letter day for him.

The week seemed to Nick to last as long as a century. His evening phone calls with Marina, who reassured him that it was totally not his fault that Wrath-Bonham had targeted him, offered him some consolation, but unfortunately not even Marina could alter the unpleasant fact that Friday afternoon was looming.

Finally, the day arrived. When Nick walked nervously into the room he'd been told to report to, the company clerk told him to wait in the lobby for the ASM. It was here that Nick now found himself, sitting on a wooden bench, feeling like a schoolboy waiting for the headmaster from hell. He told himself to get a grip. *After all, it's only words,* Nick reassured himself.

The door was suddenly flung open and ASM Miller walked in. Nick sprang to his feet, determined not to allow his terror to get the better of him. Miller strode across the room and stood toe to toe with him, their faces only inches apart.

Being a tall man himself, Nick had never suffered from any feeling of inadequate height. But now, with the ASM seemingly towering above him, Nick felt like a midget. His immediate reaction was to take a step backwards, but he knew only too well this would have been a serious mistake, so he denied himself the luxury, fixing his gaze on Miller's knotted tie.

He was amazed to observe that Miller actually had breath that smelt of peppermint, as if he'd considerately chewed a Polo or even an Extra-Strong Mint before they'd met.

'Mr Trevelyan,' Miller began, in a surprisingly conversational tone, which threw Nick a little as he had been prepared for an ear-splitting yell. 'It may come as a surprise to you, but I've been taking a particular interest in your progress through this Academy.'

'You ... you have?' spluttered Nick.

'Yes, Mr Trevelyan, I have. You come from an army family, after all. You're one of us. After a shaky start you've settled down and shaped up. Your instructors speak highly of you and you have acquitted yourself well on the sports field. In fact, Mr Trevelyan, you are as near as can be considered to being a model cadet.

'Thank ... thank you,' said Nick, not sure whether to be fearful or to allowed himself to feel a little pride and delight.

'You don't have the same advantages as the majority of your peers in terms of family ancestry and finances. Now, Mr Trevelyan, I'm going to do something I don't do very often: offer some advice. It's this: *be very careful*. The old money, which you will have seen is very well represented here at Sandhurst, will always look after its own. You can't infiltrate the ranks of the old money, and they make bad adversaries. Not a single one of them will lose a moment's sleep if they trample you into the ground.'

Dusty Miller stepped backward one pace.

'Mark my words, Mr Trevelyan; they could spare you unhappiness in the future. Now, I'm going to march you into the adjutant's office and you'd better move fast.'

Only now did Dusty Miller raise his voice into something not a thousand miles from his familiar drill square bark. 'Orders, orders, 'shun! By the front, double quick march! Left, right, left right, left right, left! Right turn! Mark time! Halt. Salute. Officer Cadet Trevelyan, sir.'

And with that final bark, ASM Miller left the adjutant's office, leaving Nick completely stunned at how astonishingly nice Dusty Miller had unpredictably been.

The adjutant was sitting at his desk. Nick had seen him several times, but never had the displeasure of meeting him.

The adjutant was shorter than Nick, fair-haired, stocky, with a look of superiority in his eyes that, Nick had heard, was the product of an education at Eton. Nick also felt sure that if the adjutant had been a dog he would have been a pit bull.

The adjutant looked directly into Nick's eyes from the moment he marched in, scrutinizing him as if he was an alien who had been brought in by Luke Skywalker from another planet.

'Officer Cadet Trevelyan reporting, sir!' shouted Nick, standing rigidly to attention. Nick stared intently at a spot on the wall about six inches above the adjutant's head and braced himself for the impending ordeal, fully aware that his indiscretion was about to invoke a fearful response.

The adjutant stood up and walked around his desk. He slowly approached Nick. So far the adjutant hadn't uttered a word and the muscles in Nick's neck were aching with tension as he steeled himself for the roar of verbal abuse that was sure to burst at any second.

The adjutant seemed determined to enjoy his discomfort for as long as possible, but as he relaxed his muscles the merest fraction, the adjutant suddenly screamed into his left ear.

'MR TREVELYAN! I do not want to hear your excuses; I do not want to hear you so much as breathe. You will listen to what I have to say, and then you will give me your best reason as to why you think you deserve to make an appearance at the

Sovereign's Parade in three days' time, and not be dismissed from this academy or at the very least back squadded.'

Nick's body went rigid with tension. Dismissal was, of course the ultimate disaster for anyone aspiring to a career as an officer, but being 'back squadded' – forced to join another cadet squad that had begun its training more recently – was also seriously grim. It slowed your career by at least a couple of months and sometimes longer, depending just how long ago the squad you were forced to join had got back squadded and it carried an indelible stigma.

'Sir, I …'

'SHUT UP!' the adjutant roared, 'I've not finished with you yet, Mr Trevelyan. One more word from you and I'll have you shovelling manure in the stables for the next forty-eight hours. Mr Trevelyan, you will shortly be graduating from this Academy. But you can be sure that, apart from your usual drill rehearsals, your feet will not touch the ground from now until the Sovereign's Parade. Don't say a word, Mr Trevelyan! Get out of my sight. I will see you first thing in the morning and make sure your appearance is quite resplendent. Because Mr Trevelyan, if I see as much as a crease or speck of dust I'll … just get out of my sight until I have the misfortune to have to lay eyes on you again.' Nick trudged back to his quarters in a daze.

His spirits were too low for him to have any appetite. Even when he switched his Blackberry back on and saw he had an email from Marina, he felt too ashamed and demoralised to open the email for twenty minutes or so.

But finally he did take a look at it.

His spirits were so low he half-expected Marina to be dumping him.

Darling, I don't know what happened when you met the adjutant but I don't care, you're the handsomest officer cadet in the world as far as I'm concerned and I love you to bits and I am so proud of you. I know this is an evening off for you so pack a few things and come as soon as you can to the Churchill

Suite at the Regency Hotel in Camberley, where you'll find the following:

- *a lovely supper for two which we'll order from the menu when you arrive;*
- *two bottles of vintage champagne;*
- *a large, firm, and beautiful bed;*
- *the night ahead;*

and last but not least ...

- *me!*

Love you lots, Marina xxx

Nick drove into Camberley in barely ten minutes.

When Nick knocked on the beautiful ornate white and gilt front door of the Churchill suite, the voice of the Adjutant was still ringing in his ears, though somehow the voice no longer had the acid effect on Nick's morale that it had had two hours.

The door opened a fraction to reveal a tantalising narrow image of Marina. Her long blonde hair was falling down over her ample breasts, whose outline was suggested, rather than revealed, by the heavy, thick, white Regency Hotel bathrobe she was wearing.

Marina smiled. The narrow image of her became a full screen image as she opened the door and murmured, 'Darling!' and kissed Nick with a passion and abandon that made him instantly forgot the adjutant, Dusty Miller, Tristram Wrath-Bonham, Hugo De Lisle, and everything else but Marina.

Marina was naked under her bathrobe.

Supper – lobster salad, Beluga caviar, smoked salmon and Beef Wellington, one of Nick's favourite main courses – was already there on the table. The two bottles of champagne were waiting like gifts from heaven.

Nick had assumed that he and Marina would make love after supper, and they did, for several hours.

But they made love before supper, too, and indeed were in bed within five minutes of Nick's arrival. With Marina's long arms and legs around him, their questing tongues playing together, and Nick bathed in her perfume and in the infinitely sexual and endlessly intoxicating scent of her sweat, Nick found that forgetting the adjutant really very easy indeed.

7

The Sovereign's Parade

A little more than a fortnight after Nick had been greeted so lavishly and affectionately by his lady at the Regency Hotel, the morning of the Sovereign's Parade arrived.

It took place on a splendid day in early July. The only imperfections in the sky were wispy cirrus clouds high up in the jet stream. Otherwise the sky was as blue as Marina's eyes.

Nick greeted his mother Annabelle, his father George and his auburn-haired, fresh-faced seventeen-year-old sister Sophie, now a sixth-former at a girls' grammar school in Windsor.

The Trevelyan family were accompanied by Marina, who looked fabulous as usual. Marina's mauve designer suit was the height of sophistication but nevertheless the slit at the back of the superbly tailored skirt was cut high giving tantalizing glimpses of Marina's gorgeous legs.

The first event of the day, at 10 am, was a service at the academy chapel. Parents, family and friends could attend and stirring hymns, sung beautifully by the choir and with great gusto by the congregation started the day's proceedings.

After the service Nick, like all the cadets, hurried to pick up their rifles and belts. Then the platoon formed up for the final time in front of the adjutant on New College Square.

Nick knew that he had long been earmarked as a strong contender for the Cane of Honour but after the events of the last few days he had become increasingly anxious that he might have ruined his chances.

As the parade reached its conclusion, everyone lined up in front of the royal visitor in anticipation of the award ceremony. Nick stood rigidly to attention. As the winner's name for the Cane of Honour was announced, Nick didn't flinch when the award went to Steve Heligan. He was genuinely pleased that, if it wasn't going to him, the honour should go to Steve.

Nick was more worried about his parents' reaction; having mistakenly talked to them about the possibility of his receiving the award, he knew he could rely on his mother; but his father was likely to make his disappointment known in no uncertain terms. As further prizes were announced, his disappointment was muted by his being announced as recipient of the Military History prize, which was some recognition at least for his hard work.

With all the relevant ceremonial duties performed, the climax to the day approached. The ranks of cadets who had passed out marched up the steps of the Old College in slow time to the accompaniment of *Auld Lang Syne*, to be followed by the traditional mounting of the steps by the Adjutant on horseback. Once beyond the entrance, the elated Cadets handed over their rifles and belts, and then hurried to meet their guests and dignitaries for the Sovereign Parade's Luncheon.

Nick approached the gathering and now spotted his parents to one side of the throng. He smiled for what felt like the first time that day. His mother turned and caught his eye. She wordlessly conveyed to him across the room her feelings of pride in his achievements, giving his severely bruised confidence a well-deserved boost.

The look on his father's face was an altogether different picture. George Trevelyan's face was marred by a grimace that seemed to ward off the possibility of social advances from any of the other circulating guests. Nick walked up to them and greeted his mother and Marina with a hug, then stood stiffly and held out his hand to his father.

'I hope you enjoyed the parade, father,' he said politely.

'Splendid affair,' said his father, too loudly, and with what sounded to Nick like genuine gusto, and which made Nick wonder for a moment whether his father was talking about his, Nick's relationship with Marina than about the Sovereign's Parade. 'But tell me Nicholas,' George Trevelyan went on, still speaking with excessive volume, 'what happened with the awards? I thought you'd been hoping to win the Cane of Honour?'

Nick smiled nervously, aware of the proximity of the other guests and of the fact that his father had obviously already indulged in a couple of large whiskies.

'If you don't mind, I'd rather talk about that later, father, this is meant to be a celebration lunch. I've got to take you and introduce you to some of my friends.' Nick, keeping his voice down now so that it was only audible to his father, added, *'Do you think you can manage that without embarrassing me?'*

'Huh!' retorted his father. 'You seem to manage to embarrass yourself quite well enough. What am I meant to tell our friends when we get home?'

'We'll tell them that our son's passed out from Sandhurst Academy as an officer and a gentleman,' Annabelle Trevelyan said, cutting in with firmness and pride. 'We'll tell them that we're terribly proud of our wonderful boy and that we look forward to hearing of his successes in his new regiment. Now, please can you two stop for just one day so that we can enjoy ourselves as a family, for once?'

George Trevelyan and Nick looked shamefaced, reprimanded by the composure and dignity of the woman beside them whose serenity and understanding was a constant source of amazement to Nick. He discreetly smiled his appreciation of her intervention. His father coughed nervously.

'Certainly, my dear. Just as you wish. I think I'll just pop out and get another drink while we're waiting.'

'No, dear. No more drink until lunchtime. We've a busy day ahead of us and we're going to meet lots of different people. You'll never remember their names if you drink too much, and you know how much that irritates you.'

'Quite right, dear … very well. Come along then, Nicholas. Lead the way. The sooner we can sit down to lunch the better, as far as I'm concerned.' Nick allowed himself a silent sigh of relief. Once more, thanks to his mother, this might not turn out to be as much of an ordeal as anticipated. After lunch, his parents, Marina, and all the other guests, went home or to hotels to change for the dinner that evening.

This was scarcely the first time George Trevelyan had embarrassed his son. George was one of the last of the 'old school' soldiers; he had spent twenty-two years in the Army during which time he had only managed four promotions.

George's contemporaries had risen steadily upwards through the ranks, but his father had hardly moved up the promotional ladder at all. This was largely due to the bitter memories he retained of his own father's catastrophic demise and the effect this had had on his attitude to life: a huge chip which George carried that was sadly less positive than was expected of a potential Army officer.

Nick's grandfather, William Trevelyan, came from a well-heeled family that had made its money from Indian jute – owning plantations in India and a factory in Dundee that turned raw jute into a sturdy thread used mainly to give a robust underside backing for carpets. The Trevelyan family, back in the early twentieth century had been cautious with its money, investing it in ultra-reliable British Government Consolidated Stock, or 'Consols' as it was called. William inherited a reasonable fortune. Slowly, with the all too convenient collusion of alcohol, he squandered all of it away and died from sclerosis of the liver in his late forties, leaving his wife and son George to fend for themselves during the austerity years after WWII.

George always felt, not entirely unreasonably, cheated of the lifestyle he thought he had been born to. Too introspective to be a team player and too pessimistic to be an inspirational leader, he stuck with the Army life because it was an institutionalised existence which, if it was the path you wanted, required little independence of thought. George made the best of a bad job and ended up spending as much time in the Regimental mess and various local watering holes, as possible.

George's greatest regret was that he had never received a commission. So, it was left to Nick, his only son, to fulfil his father's dreams and join the army as an officer cadet. Nick however, had his own agenda, and was not joining the army just to please his father whose alcoholic antics left him cold. Nick had already made a pledge to himself that he would never allow himself to stay in the army if he were not an efficient soldier.

It appeared at this point in Nick's life that the world was his own particular, khaki, oyster.

And then there was the Sandhurst Commissioning Ball that evening!

The evening boasted an array of entertainments that exceeded even the Army's renowned organisational ability. A string of linked marquees housed all kinds of attractions, whilst the main buildings resounded with loud music from a variety of discos and bars.

Steve and Nick were standing together opposite the doorway of the Academy gymnasium. It was a long-standing tradition at Sandhurst that the insignia of each cadet's chosen regiment or corps was covered and not revealed until midnight.

Nick and Steve were dressed in their individual Regimental mess Dress, worn for the first time that night, proudly sporting one pip on each shoulder to show that they were no longer merely cadets, but had achieved the infinitely greater status of Second Lieutenant.

Marina was happy as only a truly beautiful woman, dressed stunningly and loved and attending an elegant event can be. She had the natural charm of a lily, garnering admiring glances from every man she passed. She seemed to benefit from the glances like a lily benefits from sunshine. Nick was ecstatic at having such a fabulous woman on his arm. He was thoroughly aware that he was the envy of just about every male present. Even Nick's now sworn adversary, Tristram Wrath-Bonham looked, Nick, was delighted to see, profoundly envious of the delicious Marina. The aristocrat's own escort was tall, black-haired, arrogant-looking, and had the face and teeth of a Grand National winner.

Marina flitted about between Nick and his parents, who seemed to be the people that she felt most comfortable with. Nick felt really happy about that. This was a one-off occasion and she wanted to make the most of it.

As usual, Nick left his mother to deal with his father's excesses of behaviour and imbuement. Annabelle and Marina were getting on extremely well; Nick suspected that Marina would be an additional gently encouraging voice helping to induce George not to get too drunk. In the meantime he took the opportunity to have a quiet chat with Steve before they went their separate ways.

Nick had been accepted as a second lieutenant with the Argyle and Sutherland Highlanders whilst Steve had the company of the men of the Parachute Regiment to look forward to.

'Nick, about this Cane of Honour,' Steve began.

'Steve, it's no big deal. I'm just glad it went to you. I just messed up with one of the big guys and there were bound to be repercussions. I can't honestly say it was unexpected. It's water under the bridge.'

'Really?'

'Really,' said Nick. 'I got what I wanted from the course and I'm proud of that. Now it's up to us to make the most of our careers. I'm looking forward to moving on; particularly to moving away from that specimen, Wrath-Bonham and his toady henchman, De Lisle. They'd better not cross my path for a while or I won't be answerable.'

'Yes, let's hope they're now only a historical item in our lives,' agreed Steve.

'Come on,' said Nick. 'I'm going to find my parents and put them in a taxi. I've also left Marina alone for too long. The vultures are circling.'

Nick extended his right hand to Steve. 'You've been a great friend, mate. Good luck and I know we'll meet again.'

'You bet we will,' said Steve returning the handshake with muscular energy. 'You've been a good mate to me, too. Good luck with all you do in the Argyles, and remember, stay true to yourself and the people you care about.'

'Will do,' said Nick. 'See you around, chum.'

Steve smiled back. 'See you.'

Nick found Annabelle and George at their table in the cocktail bar. They looked tired but contented as they engaged in an animated conversation with another couple at the table. Steve had introduced his parents to Nick's and the four appeared to have hit it off rather well. Marina herself was looking a little bored with the older company by now and was happy to see Nick return. She gave him a smile. He wondered if she was thinking along the line that he was.

Nick could see that his father had certainly had enough to drink. Nick had seen the signs plenty of times before, but in fact George was far from behaving in his usual belligerent fashion. Nick thought his dad must have mellowed in the engaging company.

After arranging his parents' taxi and saying goodbye, Nick took Marina by the hand. He'd wondered if she knew what he was thinking and now he was sure she did.

Like two naughty schoolchildren they sneaked away to his 'bunk': not the two-storey bed so beloved of children, but army-speak for the room where you slept.

Even before Nick had finished carefully locking the door, Marina practically tore his clothes off, and hers too.

For Nick the whole experience felt all the more exciting as while all the luggage of the man who shared the room was nowhere to be seen, meaning that almost certainly he'd left the room for ever, there was always the possibility that he might come back for some reason. Still, that was fairly unlikely, Nick thought with relief, as Marina began to divest herself at top speed from all clothes, obviously regarding them as a ridiculous hindrance to her plans.

'Hurry up, darling, I just want you so much,' she breathed, then eagerly assisted him to undress and they fell onto the bed locked into a steamy session of unrestrained lust. The regulation army pattern bed was never designed for the gymnastics that were taking place on it at that moment and as they had been used to the luxury of Marina's king-sized bed at her flat just off Sloane Street, they came close to falling out of it several times.

Another problem – at least at that particular moment – was that Marina had a tendency to be extremely vocal during sex. She always entered into the fun and delight of lovemaking affair with her heart and soul, utterly without inhibitions. Nick knew that this could be a problem and put his right hand gently but firmly over her mouth in an attempt to control the noise. This only had the effect of making her squirm and giggle even louder. It also made Nick feel he was dominating her and possessing her even more completely than usual. The thought made him especially potent, and he had a very good time; indeed so did Marina.

That was the first time in his life that Nick fully experienced the thrill of having sex in an out of bounds location. That frantic and frenetic and glorious lovemaking with Marina in his bunk seemed to Nick the best conclusion he could possibly imagine to the forty-four week course that had transformed him from a novice cadet into a second lieutenant.

8
Active Duty

Nick joined his regiment in Iraq as a rookie second lieutenant. He worked hard, and found himself in life threatening situations on several occasions.

When the tour ended his report said that he had served with distinction. Upon the return of the regiment to the Canterbury Regimental HQ they quickly found themselves dispatched back to the Arabian Gulf, one of the few infantry units to be involved in the Gulf War part 2 known as *Desert Storm*.

A pleasant reunion took place in the Gulf when he met up with Steve, who having spent a couple of years with 1 Para had applied to join the Special Air Service (SAS). After the usual tough initiation course, Steve had become a member of that elite regiment. He'd emailed Nick to say that he'd expected the training to be horrendous, but that it was 'fun'. *Just like Steve to find it that*, Nick had thought.

Soon after the SAS accepted Steve, he was sent to the Gulf as part of a unit assigned to free five military hostages, taken prisoner by the Iraqis. After the successful completion of the mission with the five hostages freed unharmed and their kidnappers all dead, Steve and Nick managed to spend a few evenings together, renewing their acquaintance with the ease of old friends who had been through much together. They vowed to keep in more regular contact when they returned to England.

When Nick returned from the Gulf it was as a captain and it was generally acknowledged amongst his fellow officers that Nick was destined for a fine career in the army. His ability to command men in a modern manner, by leading from the front and by example, coupled with his aptitude as a military historian and tactician, were qualities much sought after in the modern British Army. He loved every minute of every day that he spent in the army.

Nick had been worried that when he went away to see active duty his relationship with Marina would founder. After all, she could have pretty well any man she wanted. But it turned out that when Nick was away on active duty or unable to get back to London, Marina seemed to be quite content to spend the time alone or with her father, running her boutique and shopping. The time that they spent apart only served to enhance the intensity of the reunions, which could only be described as a clash of the sexual titans.

Within a year of returning from the Gulf, Nick won promotion to Major. He was aware there was a strong possibility that, in time, he would be offered a position at the Staff College – the headquarters of the British Army where the army's operations and policies were planned and set into motion – and the rapid rise in rank that went with the post.

When Nick was in the UK, his regiment, in common with most of the British Forces, was occasionally called upon to undertake certain ceremonial duties. They were required to furnish a drill display team that would accompany the regimental band of the pipes and drums at the Edinburgh Tattoo.

Nick was called into the colonel's office. During the meeting the colonel imparted the information that he, Nick, looked 'darn good in uniform, though don't let it go to your head, Trevelyan,' and that as a result of this observation, and also because of Nick's 'bearing and proven communication skills', the Colonel had chosen Nick to lead the Argyle detachment which was to attend the annual military display in Scotland. *Wonderful*,' thought Nick, '*so if I'd been a scruffy git I would have been spared the privilege!*

The Tattoo stretched over a period of four consecutive days. The Argyles were required to mount a display of marching and rifle drill accompanied by their Pipes and drums; once in the afternoon and once in the evening.

By now Nick had developed a relationship with his men based on mutual respect. The men of the Argyles were a hard and uncompromising bunch but if accepted, you were rewarded with their loyalty, and you knew that their allegiance would be unquestioning, no matter what the circumstance.

The whole Tattoo took place in the imposing setting of Edinburgh Castle, that magnificent building that looked even more magnificent at night when it was floodlit. Inside the castle, there were the inevitable Messes, the most elaborate being for the officers.

Traditionally, the Edinburgh Tattoo brought together a variety of armed units from all over the Commonwealth. This year there were contingents from New Zealand and Canada, a detachment of Ghurkhas and other military organisations. There were also British units from the RAF, Royal Marines and Royal Navy, with a musical ride performed by The Household Cavalry. All this made for very mixed and interesting bouts of serious drinking in all of the Messes.

Nick had not long arrived at his quarters in Edinburgh when he received an anonymous message to be in the bar of the George Hotel at 8 pm.

Intrigued, he washed and changed and arrived at the appointed destination shortly at about ten to eight. He sat down at the bar to await his mystery 'date' and it wasn't long before in through the door walked the welcome figure of Steve, grinning hugely as always.

'I don't believe it!' Nick shouted. 'What're you doing round here? I haven't heard from you for a couple of months so I thought you were off on some top secret mission somewhere.'

'Maybe I am,' replied Steve, tapping the side of his nose. Nick knew better than to ask any more of his SAS buddy and guessed that he was probably in Edinburgh to give close protection to some bigwig.

'How're you doing?' Steve asked.

'Things have been a bit tough since I returned from the Gulf. You've so much to sort out in your mind when you come back from something like that. It takes a lot to keep you occupied enough not to find yourself thinking about it all the time. I guess I'm still a bit hyped up.'

'Yes,' said Steve, 'you sound it. How are things with Marina?'

'I'm still seeing her but she couldn't come to the Tattoo due to pressures of work. Her boutique in Knightsbridge's been doing really well; she's opened two more over the past year – one on New Bond Street and the other in Hampstead village. She's a born businesswoman.'

'What's her boutique in Knightsbridge called?'

'Serendipity. The new one will have the same name.'

'Does Serendipity mean anything?'

'I've looked it up. It basically means finding something by accident, something really amazing.'

'Or being in the right place at the right time? Like you finding Marina?'

Nick smiled. 'I suppose so, yes.'

'Have you still got that Porsche her old man donated to you in a moment of madness?'

'Yep. Maybe I'll get an upgrade soon!'

'You mercenary sod!'

'Seriously, Steve, I don't care about the Porsche. I'd be happy driving a second-hand Hillman Imp if she was in it with me.'

'Any marriage plans?'

'We haven't talked about it. So, how about you? A girl in every port I suppose? What about Clarisse?'

'God no, she's ancient history. She became a Buddhist. Actually, after I joined the SAS there really hasn't been much time for gadding about so I was most definitely without for a while. Then I went for a two-week series of lectures all about something very top secret. The lecturer was this fantastic woman. She's forty and amazingly intelligent, and the rest. Made me feel like a schoolboy in a minute. I couldn't keep my eyes off her! The more she brushed me off, the more I went after her. I chased her for two weeks and she finally let me take her out. I really like her. The most incredible thing has happened. I've stopped looking at other women! Can you believe it?'

'I guess even a leopard can change his spots eventually,' Nick laughed.

'I guess so. Oh, and there's one other bit of news that I don't know whether you're aware of yet; guess who else is in town? I bumped into him not half an hour ago and exchanged a few un-pleasantries.'

'Won't be a very pleasant surprise, mate: it's His Honourable Righteousness, Captain Wrath-Bonham no less,' said Steve, raising his eyebrows.

Nick nodded slowly. 'No doubt he'll be in charge of the mounted detachment. I should have guessed. That's just the kind of cushy number he'd go for, with plenty of opportunity to show off.'

'Oh well, I guess you've got to just hope he's grown up and become a human being, but don't hold your breath, there's bound to be trouble if you two meet – so steer clear,' replied Steve.

The next evening after dinner, Nick found steering clear of Wrath-Bonham an impossible task. Immediately he showed up in the mess, made straight for Nick as soon as he realised he was there.

'Trevelyan! How marvellous to see you!' he drawled. Nick felt an immediate flash of *déjà-vu* as he stretched out his hand to renew his acquaintance with his old adversary.

'Pleasure's all mine,' Nick replied insincerely, allowing his eyes to linger on the thin scar on Wrath-Bonham's cheekbone which became a livid red as he saw the direction of Nick's eyes.

'Are you well?' The smile that Wrath-Bonham returned was as false as a Cheshire cat's, completely lacking in warmth, and as their eyes locked, Nick couldn't help but sigh inwardly. *So much for steering clear of trouble.* 'Yes, fine thanks. What about you?'

'I am in excellent shape, Trevelyan. I look forward to seeing you on the parade ground.' He abruptly turned away to return to his entourage and spent the rest of the evening ignoring Nick completely.

Which suited Nick just fine.

9
Disaster

Anyone who's ever marched to the sound of the pipes and drums will tell you they arouse something magical that stirs pride deep within the soul.

So far, the Tattoo had been a massive success for Nick and his men of the Argyles, and the other members of various units from the armed forces they were performing with at the event. The spectators had applauded their performances until the palms of many in the audience were practically glowing.

Thousands of miles away, connected with the event by satellite technology shown on ancient black and white TVs, new LCD and plasma screens, iPads and a host of other high-tech equipment, families lapped up the superb display of military precision and stirring martial music. Small boys from around the world felt their own ambition for a military life burst into their hearts at that moment, and many of them would pursue that ambition like Nick, who had once himself been inspired to join the army by seeing soldiers parading at Windsor Castle.

At first the assembled units spent time rehearsing the drills for the Tattoo. Finally, the full dress rehearsal reached the point of the finale and all of the participating service personnel were ranked up in the close confines of the castle parade ground. Nick's detachment was standing alongside two mounted troops from the Household Cavalry fronted by the upright figure of Captain Tristram Wrath-Bonham. There had been a Wrath-Bonham in The Household Cavalry since before the time of Wellington. Tristram's father, General Sir Michael Wrath-Bonham, had only recently retired after a distinguished career in the army.

As Nick watched Tristram Wrath-Bonham, he couldn't help yet again feeling that the fellow epitomized all that was the very worst of British aristocracy. Nick was acutely aware that most of his men were distinctly unhappy about having to stand so close to the huge cavalry horses, which was not surprising given that most of the men came from the tenements and council estates of Glasgow or Edinburgh and had never been closer to a horse than watching the racing on TV or at the bookmaker's.

The Jocks had no alternative but to remain at attention while the black mounts of the troopers were only three feet distant. The horses were impeccably well-trained and stood obediently still while the ceremony continued, but one or two of the horses became fidgety and threatened to trample on the feet of the motionless Argyles. Nick could feel the anger rising within his men, but the rehearsal passed without incident, much to his relief.

He knew that the pranks played out in everyday Army life could sometimes border on the excessive, but he didn't seriously believe that even Wrath-Bonham would jeopardize the continuity of such an important ceremonial occasion. He had a few encouraging words with his men at the end of the rehearsal and thought nothing more of the moments of friction that had marred the rehearsal for them.

At dinners and other mess functions Nick had miraculously managed to pretend to consume the required quantities of whisky and had escaped being labelled a wimp. At times it appeared that one of the hardest tasks he had been asked to perform since joining the Army was not to lose face as a non-whisky drinking Argyle. Although he was not a hard-drinking man himself, he loved the atmosphere within the mess, with officers from all of the participating sections resplendent in their individual mess dress.

It was expected that an officer in a regiment such as the Argyles, or indeed any Scottish regiment, should participate in taking the national drink. Nick knew better than most the power that the amber fluid could have over men who drank it. He had witnessed too many times his father's arrival home, creating hell in what was otherwise a happy home.

The first day that the Tattoo was open to the public was Monday and within reason, all went well. Nick made two more visits to the local Police station to retrieve another four of his flock who had gone astray and Tuesday passed without incident, although the close proximity of the Jocks and their equine neighbours was a potentially volatile situation that he kept a close eye on.

Wrath-Bonham continued to be an irksome presence. Nick tried to keep his distance from this old foe to ensure that there was as little opportunity as possible to renew previous conflicts.

Tuesday evening in the mess was as enjoyable an evening as the others had been, but spoiled by Wrath-Bonham and his entourage, who had taken up residence in the most prominent position in the room; in front of the massive fireplace.

This position gave him the vantage point that he clearly enjoyed as from there he was well placed to poke fun at whoever was unfortunate enough to cross his line of sight. Nick watched with suppressed annoyance as he witnessed Tristram pick on some of the overseas officers who were not quite up to the banter that was aimed at them. He had been a pompous idiot when Nick first met him but he had now taken it to a much higher level. Inevitably, Tristram's eyes settled on Nick.

'Hey there, you in the plaid skirt! It appears as if your fellows are about to wet themselves with fright when my horses are around. I do hope that the rumour about you types not wearing anything under those skirts is only a myth. Otherwise, there's bound to be a lot of splashing going on tomorrow.'

This outburst was directed at Nick but meant for all in the mess to hear. Nick smiled politely and nodded. Inwardly, he was seething and wished that he had used the opportunity to let Bonham know exactly what he thought of him, but tradition and etiquette prevented this, along with the indoctrinated service ethics that he was proud to uphold. Nick watched Tristram gather his crowd of cronies and leave. The incident was over in seconds but he felt disgust, not only for the posturing Wrath-Bonham, but also for himself for not returning his fire and giving as good as he got.

The Wednesday afternoon display proved to be a trial for Nick. It was obvious to all of the Jocks that the cavalry had been primed to push their horses even closer to the Argyles in order to give them a hard time. It was very easy for a trooper to irritate his mount with one of the huge swan neck spurs, which was out of sight on the inside flank of the horse. Nick felt sure that Wrath-Bonham was behind this prank.

A deputation led by Lance Corporal McTaggart asked to see Captain Trevelyan.

'We're not gonna take it, sur!' argued McTaggart. 'Those bastards Donkey Wollopers on their black horses cannee treat us like this. We're gunna gie over te their barracks and gie 'em a kicking, sur.'

Nick sympathized, but it would have been unthinkable for him to allow such a thing to happen, although inwardly he wished that he could let the Jocks deal with this affair in their own inimitable, age-old way. Instead, he had to lay down the law and threaten to place under arrest any Argyle who was seen within one hundred yards of the Cavalry Barracks.

That evening in the mess, Bonham was occupied with other matters and only occasionally did Nick catch a glimpse of him looking in his direction with a smug grin on his face. Thursday afternoon brought the longest two hours of his life.

The cavalry were having a great time making their horses do a tap dance right up to the highly polished toecaps of the Argyles' boots. Nick expected that at any minute, one of his Jocks would leap up and drag a gleaming cavalryman down onto the cobbles, but if it did happen, how would he deal with the incident? God only knew. Miraculously, the afternoon passed without any major disaster.

Nick knew that by the time the evening display took place, the Jocks would have had a few drams and that would be the dangerous time. He took the unusual decision to go to the mess bar after lunch, and there he made the even more unusual decision of having a couple of scotches to help him through the afternoon.

By the time that the evening display had arrived the tension in the air was electric. Nick had tried to reduce his own personal pressure by having a couple more swift drams before marching out to lead his men.

They'd now performed the sequences a dozen times and could carry out the required drill with their eyes closed. They had become used to the crowds of spectators and even the TV cameras held little interest for them. All went well to begin with.

Any man or woman who has ever marched to the sound of the pipes and drums will tell you that there is something magical that stirs latent feelings of pride from deep within.

The Argyles were certainly big on pride and for good reason: their forbears had bequeathed them a magnificent legacy that every member of the regiment held in great respect.

Eventually, the massed troops were again ranked up for the finale. Wrath-Bonham walked his charger into position at the head of the two troops of Cavalry.

At first, Wrath-Bonham centred himself upon the leading section of cavalry, but upon giving a sideways glance and recognising Nick standing rigidly at his side, he edged his mount over until he was directly alongside.

Even Nick would have had to admit that Wrath-Bonham looked good astride his magnificent horse. The aristocrat wore the officer's ceremonial scarlet State Uniform and exuded total confidence, and obvious contempt for any people he regarded as inferior to him – which, as far as Wrath-Bonham was concerned, meant just about anyone on the planet who *wasn't* Tristram Wrath-Bonham.

Nick had often seen that quality in aristocrats; he supposed it had come across with their forebears during the Norman Conquest, when William the Conqueror, having won the prize of Britain with only maybe five thousand hardened and tough Norman soldiers, began populating his new kingdom with effete and supercilious French nobles who were, Nick imagined, contemptuous even then of less privileged folk.

'Chilly evening, Trevelyan. Cold enough to freeze the balls off a brass monkey, or the bollocks off a Jock.'

Nick made no effort to reply. He continued to stare forward, quelling his feelings of anger. The policy of not being drawn into dialogue with Wrath-Bonham paid off as he soon became bored and returned his gaze to the crowd.

He obviously considered all had paid their entrance fee in order to catch a glimpse of him, resplendent in his magnificent uniform astride his splendid steed.

The mounts of the Household Cavalry were big horses, mares or geldings, and underwent long and extensive training before they were considered fit enough to take part in ceremonial occasions. Captain Wrath-Bonham's charger was aptly named Hercules. The huge gelding stood eighteen hands high and had a neck like a carved chess piece. Hercules was a massive horse and he possessed an equally enormous bladder.

Yes, the training of a military horse is extensive; but there are some things that can't be controlled. You cannot train a horse not to relieve itself in one of the two ways, and often in both. Horses can be trained to do many remarkable things, but not to be continent. Television usually avoided showing the consequences of that inevitable flaw in their training, but there was no concealing it in the actual show.

The Household Cavalry had a procedure when a horse decided to pee. The rider leant forward in the saddle in order to relieve the pressure on the animal's kidneys and bladder. But as it was not always evident to the rider that his mount had decided to take a leak, the rider directly behind would pass on the order, 'lean forward'. The rider behind could detect the impending emission, though, as the horse would arch its hindquarters, something not usually visible to the horse's rider.

And so it was on that eventful evening that at that time, in that place, Hercules decided to pee. The trooper directly behind Captain Wrath-Bonham shouted:

'Lean forward, sir.'

Wrath-Bonham's immediate reaction was one of annoyance at being given an instruction of any description by a trooper – a mere private soldier in the Cavalry – even though the uttering of such an instruction from a trooper to an officer was a standard procedure in these situations. But as the possibilities of the situation dawned upon him, Wrath-Bonham was delighted to ease himself forward in the saddle, give his mount some relief and await the outcome.

The horses themselves don't actually like to pee under these circumstances, as it is unnatural for them to have their legs and feet splashed by their own urine. The hard surface of the road or in this case a parade ground is not their natural environment in the wild they would always be on soft grass. In an attempt to keep their feet dry the horses spread their legs as much as possible. All of this looked less than attractive but given the predictable outcome of the incident Wrath-Bonham was prepared to put up with the slight indignity.

Glancing to the side, he could see Nick marching towards him. Barely half a minute later and Nick had almost reached the left side of Wrath-Bonham and Hercules. Now, as the formation marching required, Nick, the Captain of the Argyles, came and stood at attention next to the officer leading the Cavalry display. That; was Wrath-Bonham, he smirked inwardly, delighted that the present situation was better than anything that he could have hoped to contrive. The distance between the end of Hercules's member and the ground was about three feet. Six pints or so of warm yellow urine splashed everywhere. Nick couldn't do a thing to avoid the tidal wave. His legs deflected most of the deluge, but his feet, boots and socks were soaked almost up to the knee, and there was absolutely nothing that he could do other than continue to stand rigidly to attention facing forward.

The steam rose upwards into his nose, carrying a pungent stench that scorched the membranes of his nostrils. The warm liquid ran down Nick's legs. Then, to make matters even worse, Hercules noisily deposited a large pile of steaming dung neatly in front of him. Wrath-Bonham leaned back in his saddle, glanced at Nick and gave a barely audible snigger of pleasure. He then slowly turned his head and looked down at the unfortunate infantryman at his side.

'Warmer now?' he enquired.

There was no need to add anything more. The actions had spoken far louder than any words could. Nick's ultimate indignity was complete, and in front of more than 100 million people enjoying the event on TV and on the Internet.

When the Tattoo was over, Nick marched his men back to their start point and dismissed them. He was so soiled, and felt so disgusted and humiliated by what Wrath-Bonham had done to him that he was struggling to face his men and to shout out the words of command staring above their heads where before he had always made a point of looking directly at them. He gave the command to dismiss without feeling, wishing them to disappear as soon as possible.

In the privacy of his bunk he tore off his filthy uniform and threw it into a corner. He sat on his bed and took a long swig from a bottle of J&B fifteen-year-old whisky, a present from his father from his time of graduation from Sandhurst that he kept in the top drawer of his dressing table.

For some reason as a last-minute thought he had thrown the bottle into his holdall before leaving for Scotland. Nick sat for maybe half an hour, gazing at the wall, and wondering how such a thing could happen without there being any possibility for recourse on his part. Once again, Nick thought, Wrath-Bonham had had the upper hand. The old resentment and memories welled up as he remembered their earlier encounters. It appeared that little had changed since the time of Wellington. Wealth and parentage obviously still ruled.

ASM 'Dusty' Miller's advice rang through Nick's mind. *The old money, which you will have seen is very well represented here at Sandhurst, will always look after its own. You can't infiltrate their ranks of the old money, and they make bad adversaries. Not a single of them will lose a moment's sleep if they trample you into the ground.*

Nick eventually snapped back into some semblance of his usual self and took a hot shower. He'd arranged to meet Steve Heligan for a final quick drink, although Nick didn't particularly feel like facing the throng in the mess, which was bound to be in a loud party mode after the stressful few days of ceremonial duties.

Nick slowly dressed in his mess uniform. At ten o'clock, he walked into the officers' mess, feeling as if all eyes had turned towards him; that all were aware of the humiliation he had suffered on the parade ground that evening.

Nick felt that every drop of blood in his body was boiling with his hatred of Wrath-Bonham.

He walked up to the bar and ordered a double whisky. He caught sight of Steve chatting to a group of people. Steve was probably busy so rather than try to attract his attention, Nick sat down in a corner by himself to nurse his whisky and wait for Steve to finish his conversation and come over. At some time after ten o'clock that evening, there was a general increase in noise volume, and – as if preceded by his very own state trumpeters – in strode Wrath-Bonham. At first he took up his usual position at the fireplace, but on sighting Nick, he walked out into the centre of the room and pointed straight at him.

'Hey, you, Argyle chappie!' he called. He meant Nick, of course. 'We've locked up two of your unruly roughneck Jock privates,' Wrath-Bonham went on. 'They were at our stable trying to cause trouble not half an hour ago, or maybe they wanted to bugger our horses. Be a good chap and come and take the peasants away, would you? They're making the place look terribly untidy.'

Nick could hardly believe how Wrath-Bonham appeared to have completely eliminated from his aristocratic mind the events of less than a couple of hours before. Nick looked up, slowly focusing on the posturing figure. He was alert enough to realise that he was dangerously close to snapping. He tried to quell the waves of anger that were starting to cloud his vision and reasoning. He felt that he'd just about got himself under control, then Wrath-Bonham said:

'Maybe if you didn't wear a skirt, your men would have more respect for you. By the way, I'd keep your back to the wall, if I were you. Your Jocks fancy you, I'm sure, given a chance, and they'd be more likely to bugger you than our horses! Not that you'd complain, I don't imagine!'

Wrath-Bonham slowly turned back to his group of attendants, laughing in his unique, lazily nasal way.

Nick rose to his feet as if in slow motion. Out of the corner of his eye Nick saw Steve turn and shout something that he couldn't hear. It felt to Nick covering the ground between himself and Wrath-Bonham took a lot of time, but in reality, the look of amazement on Bonham's face betrayed how swiftly Nick actually moved.

Nick grabbed Wrath-Bonham by the shoulder and turned him to face him. The punch, when it connected, was directly to the point of his aristocratic chin. The sound of Wrath-Bonham's jaw breaking sounded as loud as the report from a small pistol.

The punch lifted Wrath-Bonham several inches off his feet and sent him back across the room to fall in a heap at the feet of his startled fellow officers.

There then followed total silence. Nick stared in disbelief at the crumpled mass that seconds before had been an elegant Cavalry officer.

Wrath-Bonham was out cold.

A major from the Medical Corps ran across the room to offer First Aid to the broken bundle on the floor. The pounding of the major's boots on the wooden floor of the mess eventually broke the silence. A Grenadier Guards colonel glanced around the room, and realising that he was the senior officer present, walked over to Nick.

'Go back to your quarters, Major, and remain there, please.'

The rest, for Nick, was just a blur. There was not even time to have a quick exchange with the startled looking Steve. Nick went back to his room and lay on the bed. At midnight, an orderly knocked on the door and told him to return immediately to his unit in Canterbury, Kent, and to be there for Colonel's orders at ten o'clock the next morning.

From Edinburgh to Canterbury was a drive of about 500 miles. Nick drove south throughout the night, expecting that at any moment, he would wake up from the nightmare that had unfolded in such a short time.

There was a dull ache in his right hand, which was quite swollen. There was also a pounding headache right behind his eyes. Slowly, it was dawning on him that he was suffering from a hangover. The realisation that he had consumed a lot of whisky during the day was slowly making him aware that his actions of the previous night might have been those of a man whose judgment was clouded by alcohol. He was confident he was not over the breathalyser limit, and he was sure he was driving well and safely. But all the same, he felt overwhelmed by a sense of unreality. The whole drive from Edinburgh to Kent felt to Nick like being a very, very bad dream.

Colonel Angus Dumfries was a father-like figure; his red hair and enormous eyebrows gave him a faintly eccentric appearance, but he had proved himself time and time again to be a fine leader.

At the same time, he was known to be a harsh judge if crossed. His punishments could be excessive, but the worst punishment was the tongue lashing that he could unleash on the unfortunate soldiers whose bad luck caused them to be brought before him.

As Nick waited outside the Colonel's office, he contemplated what his chastisement might be. Transfer to a loathsome desk job somewhere in the middle of nowhere? A month's punishment of being confined to barracks as permanent orderly officer? A harsh fine to accompany the punishment and, of course, a good bawling out by the Colonel whose voice was often to be heard all over the barracks as he castigated some poor unfortunate sole.

The sense of unreality, coupled with the hangover, was still paramount in Nick's mind at ten o'clock the following morning as he stood before his Colonel.

'Major Trevelyan, you stand before me on a grave charge. You have brought the name of the Argyles into disrepute by striking a fellow officer and you have behaved in a manner unbecoming an officer holding a Royal Commission.'

Colonel Dumfries hadn't lifted his eyes from the charge sheet when Nick entered the room, nor had he lifted his eyes as he read the charge. But now, when he looked up, his eyes were sympathetic and this made Nick feel suddenly very, very uneasy.

'And worst of all you hit the son – and grandson – of a very powerful man. Nick, in all my time as an officer, I've rarely seen a man with such capabilities as you, but now you've thrown everything away in a minute's indiscretion.

Major Trevelyan, I must ask that you formally resign your Commission forthwith.'

The words hit Nick like an exploding ten-ton bomb and he feared that his knees would start to shake as he struggled to take in the words he had just heard.

It was now almost two weeks since the night that he had broken the jaw of Wrath-Bonham at Edinburgh Castle and the aftermath had been harsh and swift. Within four days of the incident, he found himself driving through the barrack gate of his ex-regiment as an ex-soldier.

All Nick's dreams and aspirations seemed to him to have collapsed into foul-smelling dust. Yes, he'd considered appealing against the verdict. The whole affair seemed to him to be totally unjust, but the Colonel advised him to face up to his lot and move on, as there would never be a future for him now in Her Majesty's Forces.

And so it was, that Saturday afternoon following a brief lunch of toast and peanut butter, which was pretty well all he had been able to digest ever since the dreadful verdict, Nick turned his car away from Canterbury towards the M25 to head for London.

He hadn't yet told Marina what had happened. He hadn't felt able to tell her. She knew about him breaking Wrath-Bonham's jaw, of course, but so far no news about Nick's punishment had appeared in the general press. They'd spoken on the phone several times, but he'd told her that the Colonel was still considering whether to impose a fine or a confinement to barracks.

Nick simply hadn't been able to bring himself to tell the woman he loved that he'd been fired from the army and now, at the age of twenty-eight, was unemployed and would have to find some way of start in a completely new career, with no financial benefit at all, or seniority whatsoever, to show for his seven years as an officer.

But now he was heading to London. He knew he had to tell her the truth. And he knew he wanted to tell her in person.

10
Ex-Serviceman

'What d'you mean, you've been fired from the army?'

A few minutes earlier, the day's trading at Serendipity in Notting Hill, the fourth branch of Marina's growing empire, had come to an end.

Nowadays, as well as the original Serendipity in Knightsbridge, Marina had branches on New Bond Street and in Hampstead, not far from the tube station.

Marina's expansion technique had been brutally simple but effective; borrow the capital needed to fund the expansion from her father Warren at a zero interest rate, and pay him back a year later from the profits of the new store. And, because the outfits Serendipity sold were, ironically, so expensive that they were recession-proof, as only ladies working in recession-proof industries (or who had husbands or partners who did) could afford them, Warren Fisher had always been paid back and frankly, wasn't unduly worried if he wasn't.

The growth of Serendipity had made Marina's boutique increasingly well known. In the world of fashion, the maxim 'nothing succeeds like success' is even more true than usual. The illusion becomes the reality, and the more real it appears to be, the more badly people crave it. Basically, if you worried about the price of a Serendipity garment, you quite simply couldn't afford it. By now, about two years after she'd met Nick, Marina was already a millionaire in her own right from the success of her boutiques, quite apart from the multi-million pound family trust that Warren had vested in her name.

Marina's doting female friends, themselves all from rich families, or wealthy from pursuing lucrative careers, or both, had frequently asked her, in the delicate tones of doting female friends, why she stayed with Nick when she could have her pick of any number of investment bankers, hedge fund managers, night club owners and plenty of other eligible young men.

'I stay with Nick because I love him,' Marina had always told them.

And anyone who knew her well would have had little choice but to have agreed that her loyalty to Nick had been wonderful, especially when he'd so often been away on military business.

True, those who knew her *very* well would have been aware that there'd been some lapses in her loyalty, with elegant male friends whom she had afterwards sternly commanded to complete silence. But what's a girl to do, if her man is away, often for several months? All the same, in her own way, Marina loved Nick; everyone knew that.

Still, comments made by one's doting female friends do have a habit of lingering in one's mind.

'What d'you mean, you've been fired from the army?'

Nick had arrived at the Notting Hill branch of Marina's empire at just after four o'clock that afternoon. She was spending a lot of her time in this, her newest branch, which she'd opened only a month before. The Notting Hill branch, like all her shops, stayed open until seven o'clock on Saturdays.

Nick spent almost two hours in the boutique that afternoon, helping Marina out in the shop in the suave way he'd always managed to purvey successfully in the past and somehow also managed to summon today.

Now, a few minutes after the shop's assistant Helen had left for the day, Marina had locked the front door of the boutique and had started counting the day's takings. Marina looked up at him and asked the question.

'It's true,' Nick said.

'Because you hit Wrath-Bonham?'

'Because I broke his jaw, yes.'

'I thought you soldiers were always having fights? Why would they sack you for that?'

'I give up,' said Nick. 'Maybe because his grandfather was Field Marshal Anthony Wrath-Bonham.'

Marina stopped counting the cash. She put down the wad of crimson £50 banknotes that was in her hand, and took a few steps towards Nick. He was expecting, or rather he was hoping, that she'd kiss him and hug him and say she loved him. He had vague ideas that he might even be able to help her run her growing business empire; until he found something else he really wanted to do.

But she didn't kiss him or hug him. She just walked up to him until she was maybe a yard away, then said:

'What are you going to do?'

Nick shrugged. 'I haven't quite worked that out, yet.'

'Well, shouldn't you give it some thought? I mean, basically you're unemployed, aren't you?'

'Yes, for the time being.'

Marina frowned. She frowned just at the moment when he wanted her, needed her, to smile and kiss him and tell him she'd love him through thick and thin, whatever happened to him.

But to his surprise and disappointment what she actually said was:

'Nick, I've made lots of sacrifices for you, you know. You've been away a lot, after all. I've ... well, I've always been loyal to you.'

'I know you have. And I've been loyal to you.'

That was true. He had been. He'd no idea if she'd really been loyal to him though.

'Nick, I need you to have a career.'

'I thought maybe I could help you to start with, and then.'

There followed a long pause. ..'

The instant the words had left his mouth, he knew he'd said the wrong thing. Marina wrinkled her nose as if she'd just noticed a bad smell. Her blue eyes turned opaque and expressionless, and as he saw that, he realised whose eyes hers reminded him of at that moment: Tristram Wrath-Bonham's.

'Don't be ridiculous,' she said. 'You're not working for me.'

The abruptness of her tone dug into his heart like an icicle.

'You're not being very nice about this,' he said.

'How can I be nice about it? *You've been sacked by the army!* You don't even have a job anymore.'

He looked at her calmly, impassively. He felt her manner at that terrible time in his life eroding his love for her even as he stood there, looking at her.

'Did you want me or just any army officer?' he demanded.

'What's that supposed to mean?'

'I think you heard me.'

Marina folded her arms in front of herself, always a reliable sign of her being 'really serious.'

'Nick, things between us haven't been too great recently, you know. I've just been so busy with my business that I haven't had time to ...'

'Are you dumping me? Are you dumping me after two years?'

'Feelings can change, Nick.'

'And have yours?'

She was still folding her arms. 'They might have done. Especially now.'

'Oh, I see, because I'm not an army officer now you don't care for me anymore? Well, you'd better ask daddy to find you a replacement.'

'Don't you say a word about daddy.'

'God forbid,' said Nick. 'So, is this goodbye?'

Marina nodded slowly. There were no tears in her eyes. At that moment, he had the strange and painful feeling of being one of her employees, who was being 'let go' because his work wasn't up to scratch.

'Yes,' she said. 'I think it is.'

Nick stared at her for a few moments longer, then turned and left the shop by the back door.

A few minutes later he was in his Porsche, heading for Windsor.

The London streets were busy on Saturday evening, full of couples enjoying themselves. Nick needed close to an hour to get out of London and on the M4.

All throughout the drive to his parents' home he hoped Marina would send him a text, saying she loved him and of course they were still together.

Not long after he'd turned off the M4 onto the road that led into Windsor, his Blackberry buzzed. Nick smiled, though he didn't glance at the Blackberry at that moment. *She's my girl; she's still my girl. Of course she is.*

Keeping his right hand on the steering wheel, he picked up his Blackberry with his left to see who the sender was.

But the text wasn't from Marina. It was from her father Warren Fisher, whose gift of a Porsche had been a sort of interim dowry for Nick, a reward for him squiring Marina.

The text said: *I've just heard the news from Marina. Whatever can you have been thinking of, to punch Wrath-Bonham?*

That was all. No, 'so sorry about what happened.' No expression of sympathy at all, just that curt text.

With complete certainty, Nick knew at that moment that his ejection from Marina's life was total, and permanent.

He wondered whether he'd soon get another text from Warren Fisher, to ask for the Porsche back.

Sometime around ten o'clock that evening, Nick parked outside the terraced house on the Windsor council estate where he'd grown up. The car seemed to him at that moment so irredeemably contaminated by the failure of his relationship with Marina that he actually hoped a text *would* come before not too long from Warren Fisher asking him to return the Porsche.

Nick felt, not unreasonably, that he had no alternative but to go back to his parents' home and lick his wounds while he considered what to do next. His parents had always kept his room ready so that whenever he decided to come home on leave it was there waiting for him.

Their pride in their son, 'the officer', had been total and he knew with horrible certainty just how devastated they'd be by what had happened.

Using the car's hands-free, he'd phoned his mother to say he was on his way. After he rang the doorbell, Annabelle Trevelyan came to the door at once. She greeted him in such a comforting way that Nick experienced an instant calmness he hadn't felt for the past two weeks, and certainly hadn't experienced at Serendipity Notting Hill a couple of hours earlier.

Annabelle quietly fussed over him and told him not to worry, that everything would be sure to turn out for the best. Nick's sister was away at University and her absence in the family home was obvious – her cheery disposition had always been a calming influence throughout the house.

His father's reaction, as Nick had feared, was very different.

When Nick came into the room, his father had been sitting on the sofa, looking as lost and ineffectual as ever in his tatty grey cardigan, grey school boyish trousers and the regimental tie which his father wore even at home. The moment Nick managed to tell his father the terrible news that he had already stammered out to Annabelle, his father seemed to shrink on the sofa into an even more disconsolate, pitiful and hopeless state than he usually presented. It was as if George Trevelyan's desperate and dreadful awareness of the appalling disaster that had afflicted the family had permeated his entire being, yet another thunderbolt of pain at the disappointment that life can inflict.

For Nick, his father's reaction seemed far worse than his, Nick's, own feelings at being ejected from the army. For Nick, his father's reaction seemed much worse, too, than Marina's. His father seemed, to Nick, quietly obliterated by what had happened, strangely reduced to nothing, and perfectly pathetic in his horror at hearing the news.

Nick suddenly realised, in a dreadful moment of complete understanding, that his father incubated a permanent, and in fact perfectly reasonable, deep shame at his own failure and descent into alcoholism. It broke Nick's heart to understand, in that terrible moment, just how much his father had relied on Nick, his only son, to bring the family salvation by achieving the proud, glittering and successful military career that George's own fecklessness, laziness and love of the bottle had forever barred him from. And now here was Nick, his son, no longer a soldier at all because in a moment of madness he'd lost his temper with one of the numerous toffs that everyone knew you simply couldn't lose your temper with!

George Trevelyan's obvious utter misery at hearing what had happened came very close indeed to breaking Nick's heart completely. Nick felt tears spring into his eyes, and he sat down next to his dad and, doing something he had not done for years, hugged the old man and kissed him on his forehead.

'Don't worry, dad,' Nick murmured. 'I'm not finished. Far from it. I'm going to make something great out of my life, I really am.'

Annabelle bought them all tea and chocolate digestive biscuits.

Nick knew that he absolutely could not tell his parents, at that moment, or perhaps at any time, that – as if being sacked by the army wasn't enough – Marina had, that very evening, dumped him. He didn't think that any parents should have to put up with that much bad news on one evening.

He resolved not to say a word about Marina until such time as his life was back on course, and he'd found a woman who appreciated him for what he was, not what she'd imagined he might be. *A woman who stands by me when I have trouble*, he thought.

Nick had been at his parents' home for a few days when Steve rang to bring him up to speed with events.

Steve had left the Tattoo shortly after Nick, he had been in touch with members of the Argyles with whom he'd become friendly, to see if he could get the full picture of what had happened after Nick had been dismissed.

'Nicko, I heard that Wrath-Bonham was whisked away in a private ambulance, got his jaw set and was then flown to London by private jet where he was admitted to a highly reputed private clinic. I heard he lorded it over everybody, sending messages of progress on his injury back to his squadron leader, indicating his need for a lengthy convalescence and threatening all kinds of grievous action against 'that Grammar School thug, Trevelyan.''

'The bastard,' said Nick.

'Yes,' said Steve. 'But he's a bastard who's still got his Commission. I wish you hadn't let that aristo ponce get to you so badly.'

'You don't think I feel the same way?'

Steve went on to say that Wrath-Bonham duly turned up for desk duties in London within forty-eight hours, sporting an attractively wired jaw, grumbling incoherently, about injustice, revenge and other such matters that few of his colleagues were interested in. Steve reassured Nick that the men of the Argyles he, Steve, had spoken too were universally of the opinion that Wrath-Bonham, 'Hadn't got haff as gud a kicking as he deserved.'

The men of the Argyles, Steve reported, all thought that Major Nick had suffered a grave injustice and were devastated that he would no longer be serving with them. Nick was much encouraged and touched by this show of support and on this positive note said goodbye to Steve, promising to keep him in touch with his plans for the future.

Two days after getting this phone call, Nick received a small package through the post. Opening it, he found it to be a chunky, silver plated cigarette lighter embossed with the Argyle and Sutherland's coat of arms and engraved with the words 'Set the world alight'.

It was from his men in the regiment.

Nick, who was feeling that his life had collapsed all round him, was so moved by this token of regard from the bunch of Highlanders a lump sprang into his throat. He was also much amused by the incongruity of the gift as he didn't smoke. This would always serve as a reminder of their sense of humour and staunch loyalty. He again felt a sting of regret at what could never again be.

Nick certainly had plenty of thinking to do, to try to redirect his life after the bitter disappointments of recent events. During the day his parents were at work and this gave him the space he needed. He was able to consolidate his thoughts and get on with planning his future, although he felt that he had made little or no progress.

He summarised his position to himself. He was twenty-eight; he had an Honours degree in Modern History. Additionally, as it was he who had resigned from the Army, in consequence, his military record still looked okay, at least if you didn't probe too deeply, which he hoped prospective new employers wouldn't.

In more practical terms, he was fit, intelligent and had a bank account in which he had managed to save several thousand pounds from his army salary. Plus of course, the Porsche. But what to do next? He still felt that he was a soldier and a good one at that, but where could he make use of his skills?

He made enquiries about becoming a mercenary but there wasn't much going on that looked interesting enough, or sufficiently well-paid, to be worth the serious risks. The days passed and the feeling of no longer belonging in the family home washed over him once again as it always did after the first week of leave.

He continued very much to miss the regiment and, in particular, the men of his platoon. 'Crazy Jocks' they may have been, but he had learned to understand them and respect their way of looking at the world. He missed the mess and his fellow officers, the horseplay and the camaraderie.

He'd never realised just how much he'd come to rely emotionally on his mates and all the upsides of army life. Nick had often heard people say that you don't really know what you've really got until you lost it. For him, that had just been something people said. Now, in those terrible weeks when his army career was snatched from him, Nick came to know the dreadful truth of those words.

He realised that he missed the army very much indeed; far more than he'd ever imagined he would. But he missed Marina even more, though after their last conversation, he had far too much pride to get back in touch with her.

11
A Plan of Escape

George Trevelyan, ineffectual and pitiful as he was, had made more contacts during his time in the army than might have been expected. There was often someone dropping by to take his father down to the pub for a pint and a jaw about old times.

While Nick was staying at his parent's home, one such friend of his father's, Chris Kelly, arrived at the house one evening. Chris, a handsome, somewhat craggy-looking fellow with white hair, a short white beard and intense dark-blue eyes, was one of George's few friends who discouraged him from drinking more than a pint or two with a single shot of whisky. Chris treated George with a firm, kind hand and George respected him all the more for it.

Nick had always liked Chris, who would turn up once or twice a year at the Trevelyan's when he was back in the UK. Chris now lived in the Algarve, where Nick remembered hearing his parents saying he was involved in the tourist industry. He was not as loud as the majority of his father's friends, and there was something relaxed and reassuring about Chris, despite the intensity of his gaze. Annabelle profoundly approved of Chris, but she left the men in the living room to talk among themselves.

'Your father tells me that you have had some trouble, young Nick,' said Chris, while George Trevelyan was paying one of his all too frequent visits to the bathroom. 'Let me tell you my story Nick, I joined the army at the same time as your father but after three years walked away from the life I loved and it's something that you may understand. I had quite a few run-ins and near-misses with officers.'

'You did?' said Nick.

'You bet I did. I was young and could never quite come to grips with the inequality that existed between the enlisted men and the commissioned officers. The divide in all of the Guards' regiments is no less enormous as you've experienced yourself, first hand, and there's a lot of unfair privilege that I just could not agree with. So I decided that it would be better for all concerned if I left the army.'

Chris shrugged. 'After all, who was I to think that I could change something that had existed for centuries? I have to say that although I agree with you, I do feel that it's all changing now and much of the class-consciousness is diminishing. Having said that, there are some places where the aristocracy still holds the reins.'

His father's visit upstairs had ended and he walked at his dithering pace into the room.

'Are you ready, George?' Chris asked.

'Yep,' said Nick's father.

'We'll be at the pub, Nick, in case you fancy a pint later on 'Come and join us.' Chris offered.

The two older men left and Nick turned on the TV. He looked at the screen but his mind was miles away. Sometime after nine he pulled on a sweater and headed off to the pub to join his father and Chris.

The pub was full. His father and Chris were part of a large group. They were being entertained by a local wag who was in great form, keeping his audience in hysterics with jokes that were mediocre and fairly unfunny if you heard them while sober, but which improved greatly when the listener was drunk or close to it. Nick joined the edge of the group and managed to attract Chris' attention and draw him away so that they could continue their earlier conversation.

'If you ever want to get away for a while, come down to the Algarve and pay me a visit. You'll be very welcome, and it's a great place to relax and decide what your next step will be. I'll be flying back home tomorrow but you only have to pick up a phone and you will get me.'

'I might well take you up on that,' Nick replied.

He knew that the sooner he left his parents' home the better. By leaving home and joining the army he had flown the nest. But now by returning he had made a negative move, which was acting upon his subconscious. He slept badly and dreamed a lot. His personal demons were haunting him.

Two more days passed. He looked up some old friends from school and pre-army times. They arranged to meet up and have a drink. Although it was nice to see them again, they now shared nothing in common – the topic of conversation lingering around children and mortgages.

Early the next morning, Nick was busy making phone calls. He called a local travel agency in Windsor and inquired about car ferries to Portugal. There were several options including crossing the channel by the shortest route and driving through France, Spain and then into Portugal itself.

The option which required the least driving was, Nick discovered, to board a ferry in Plymouth, sail up the Channel around the Brest Peninsula, and from there across the Bay of Biscay. Thirty-six hours later the ferry would disembark its passengers and vehicles at the port of Santander in Northern Spain, from where he could drive due south down to the Algarve.

Nick decided that the option of travelling via Plymouth sounded the more interesting. He phoned his insurance company and arranged cover for the journey.

Eventually, when he felt happy that everything was in place, he made a long-distance call down to the Algarve to Chris Kelly. He was delighted to hear from Nick, of course, his offer still stood.

A few days later, Nick kissed his mother goodbye and hugged her and then his father. Over the past few weeks after the ignominy of being sacked from the army and then being dumped by Marina (his parents still didn't know about that, and if they'd guessed they hadn't commented or said anything) Nick had got closer to his father than he'd ever been since his childhood.

Annabelle had baked Nick a rich fruitcake stuffed with sultanas, raisins, almonds, cranberries and dates. George had gone into town and used some of his monthly pension to buy the book *Teach Yourself Portuguese* for his son.

Nick was so moved by the gift from his dad that he was careful not to mention he'd bought a copy already and had it at the bottom of his red Samsonite suitcase. *Well, I might lose one*, Nick thought, *and then I'll be glad I had two.*

After final hugs with his parents and promises on his part to email his mum, who had recently opened her first Hotmail account, Nick slipped the Porsche into first, revved the engine, waved his parents and his home goodbye and set off for Portugal.

As he reached the end of the obscure little street where his parents lived, a lump came to Nick's throat.

The lump stayed there all the time during the three-hour drive from Windsor to Plymouth.

12

A New Life

The Algarve, a strip of land at the southern end of Portugal approximately one hundred miles long by about twenty miles wide, gains its name from the Arabic *Al-Gharb* meaning 'the West'. This was what the region was first called in the days, centuries ago, when the Arabs were the masters of the Iberian Peninsula.

At the eastern extremity is the border with Spain, the frontier being the Guadiana River, which divides the two countries at this point. At the Western extreme lies the windswept Cape St Vincent, the most south-westerly point in Europe. To the north, the Monchique Mountains divide the province from the rest of the country and to the South; the Atlantic Ocean washes the entire coastline. The capital of the Algarve is Lagos, a walled city whose history is long and varied, dating back to before its occupation by the Romans.

In its time, the Algarve has known and survived many invasions. The Phoenicians, Romans and Moors are some of the better-known ancient civilizations that have conquered and occupied the region.

Yet perhaps the greatest and most widespread invasion ever to take place is the twentieth century invasion of tourism. The invading army is multinational with the largest contingent by far being British. This intrusion has certainly not had an adverse effect on the province; in fact, quite the opposite. There has been huge investment which has brought with it prosperity and employment into an area which was, in its not so distant past otherwise pitifully poor.

Many people, wherever in the world they come from, who visit the Algarve just once often find themselves hooked on the enchanting province many wanting to return and spend as much of the rest of their lives there as they can which makes it a popular retirement location. The Algarve was especially popular with British people, for whom the climate was a welcome relief from the cold and wet of England. If they lived here for more than a year or so, they soon start to think of the Algarve as home.

Chris Kelly was one Englishman who fell into this category. For more than a decade, since his retirement from the military, he'd lived in the village of Praia da Luz, three miles west of Lagos.

Luz, as it's affectionately known by its local native and expatriate inhabitants alike, is a pretty fishing village where fishermen have been catching fish since before Roman times. The village has a large sandy beach protected at one end by a magnificent rugged cliff and at the other end by a picturesque church and a handsome fort. The Atlantic Ocean embraces the beach which is for the most part placid, but occasionally when the winter storms buffet the beach the spectacle can be quite dramatic.

There are hundreds of attractive beaches in the Algarve, but what is undoubtedly the most appealing feature for this region of the Iberian Peninsula is the fabulous weather, which gives close to wall-to-wall sunshine for most of the year. Due to its geographic location the area enjoys a sub climate which is the envy of Europe. The fantastic economic growth rate which has taken place in the region over the past ten decades earned it the title of 'The California of Europe'. There is no doubt that Portugal has also benefited greatly as a whole from its membership of the European Common Market. As one of the poorer and smaller member countries there was nothing for it to lose by becoming part of a larger economic community, and everything to gain.

Because of the Algarve's remote location, it has in the past felt almost cut off from the rest of Europe until the late fifties, giving the region the feel of the land that was left behind. But now the region is being dragged into the twentieth century, not kicking and screaming, as is the popular terminology, but rather shrugging and yawning, reflecting the attitude and character of the Algarvians themselves. The region stayed in the medieval period until the twentieth century.

Nick finally pulled up in front of a Praia da Luz restaurant called The Mirage at about a quarter to eight on a Monday evening. This, Nick knew, was the property owned by his host, Chris Kelly. Nick had driven the best part of ten hours since leaving Salamanca in central Spain that morning.

The journey had been most pleasant and the Porsche made it all the more enjoyable, this kind of motoring was what the car had been built to do. Nick had coasted along at a comfortable speed, enjoying the scenery as much as he could while keeping his eyes on the road, and finding himself able to relax for the first time in more than three weeks, ever since his career progression in the army had been summarily ended.

Crossing the Spanish and Portuguese border at Badajoz, he noticed at once that there was a marked difference both in the quality of the roads, which were not as good on the Portuguese, side of the border, but more dramatically, in the standard of driving. It had been reasonably good in Spain.

Now that Nick had entered Portugal, it appeared that every driver was filled with an uncontrollable death wish. The desire to overtake seemed overwhelming, no matter what the prevailing situation. Quite often he would find himself being overtaken on a narrow road where the overtaking driver had absolutely no view of the oncoming traffic. By the time he arrived at The Mirage, he was stressed and tired. The place was far bigger than Nick had imagined from Chris's description. He knew that Chris had built the property some years before and ran it himself.

Nick loved The Mirage from the moment he walked in. The beautiful, white-painted, architect designed, single story building radiated character and charm from the high domed striking circular entrance which led on one side to the large friendly bar with its alcove seating and doors leading out to the terrace and garden. There is a wood burning stove in the bar and the wide-open fireplace in the restaurant for those occasional colder winter nights secluded lighting and good music. The elegant restaurant where the fine dining element was to treat him to many superb and memorable meals. The garden with its palms and myriad Mediterranean colours, only short walk to the glittering sun-drenched sea, all added up to a world about as far from army life as Nick could imagine.

He wasn't sure what to make of being in Portugal at all. He was aware that his life had changed forever. Barely a month ago he had been wedded to his career path as an army officer. His life had a structure to it and a clear meaning. A regime that he could rely on, one which was always there even on days when he wasn't at his best.

He had had his relationship with Marina, too.

And now he had neither the army nor Marina. His life felt solitary, without structure, without consolation, but more worryingly, without a future.

But nature had imbued a strong and sturdy heart in him, and in a strange way, he was convinced that life meant well by him. He had no idea what would happen to him in Portugal, but he knew, beyond any doubt, that what was happening now was a step into the unknown in way that his life in the army had never been.

A step into the unknown, a journey without maps.

But weren't those the best journeys?

Nick walked into the bar and ordered a beer which, when it arrived, was thankfully chilled. The first beer went down quickly and felt wonderful. His thirst was great, so he called the barman over and ordered a second beer, preparing himself to attempt to communicate with the man using the smattering of Portuguese words learnt from the particular *Teach Yourself Portuguese* book that his father had given to him, and which Nick had studied, feeling much sadness because of his father's pathetic failed life, on the long ferry crossing.

The barman smiled at his pitiful attempt to speak his language.

'I believe what you are asking from me, sir, is to call Mr Kelly?' enquired the barman in perfect English.

'Er, yes,' Nick replied, feeling more than a little inadequate. The barman turned around and picked up the telephone. He spoke a few words in Portuguese, and then turned again to face Nick.

'Mr Kelly sends his apologies, and will be here in twenty minutes.

He has also told me that you are to be given whatever you need. My name is Tony, I am your service. Mr Kelly has told me to give you whatever you want.'

The bar was beginning to fill up with holidaymakers, all looking extremely healthy, sporting their newly acquired suntans. Nick felt decidedly washed out and drab in comparison, but the beer gave him a pleasant glow within and he began to relax. Chris Kelly arrived as promised twenty minutes later, by which time Nick had started to calm down from his tiring ten-hour drive.

'Hey, Nick great to see you. Welcome to the Algarve.' Chris strode across the bar and pumped his hand warmly.

'I hope Tony's been looking after you?' The barman smiled genially. Nick nodded his appreciation for the most welcome glasses of cold beer and polite conversation that he had been supplied with while waiting for Chris.

'You must be starving. Have you eaten?' Chris enquired.

'Actually, I am a tad on the hungry side,' Nick confessed.

'Then you've come to the right place,' said Chris. 'Go and check out your apartment, get yourself showered and relaxed, and then come back here and enjoy some of the excellent local cuisine and some of the best wine you'll ever taste.'

Tony left his bar to and showed Nick his accommodation: a ground-floor studio apartment with a French window that gave out onto a small private patio furnished with black rattan table and two rattan outdoor chairs on the patio's white marble paving stones. From there a little gate led onto the street.

The apartment was furnished in a simple Portuguese style; pleasant brown wooden furniture, cream-coloured floor tiles with a couple of soft blue woollen rugs, a desk and chair, and some English-language books on a wooden shelf above it. Beyond noticing that the books were all in English, Nick didn't pay any attention to them. They were more than likely to be a holiday read purchased at the airport and left behind when the tourists had gone home.

He threw down his suitcases and took a shower, unpacked a few clean clothes, dressed and wandered back into the Mirage Bar. It was crowded with a mixture of Portuguese locals and holidaymakers. The atmosphere was terrific. The doors to a tropical garden were open and many of the customers were sitting outside, enjoying their drinks in the warm evening air. Chris buzzed backwards and forwards dealing with the inevitable problems that constantly arise in a catering business. Nick found a comfortable stool at the end of the bar and ordered another drink. In between organising the staff, Chris still managed to find time to sit with him.

'Everything okay in the apartment?' he asked.

'Couldn't be better Chris, I'm really obliged to you,' Nick replied.

'You're welcome, Nick. You've had a tough time back in Blighty. I want you just to relax here and rest, get some serious R&R.'

'That's really kind of you, Chris, but you've got to let me pay for my accommodation and food.'

'Nick, I'll charge you a tiny rent for your accommodation and not much more for your food, though of course what you spend in the local hostelries is up to you! You're George's lad, and he's my friend. I know what upper-class toffs like that Wrath-Bonham characters are like; they'd drive a saint to punch them on the jaw! Trouble is, old habits die hard in the army, and the fact is that at the heart toffs run the place. When one of their numbers gets a well-earned punch, they tend to close ranks. I know you'll want to start planning your future sooner or later, but for the meantime, relax and enjoy yourself. At some point I'll start introducing you to some of the residents who live around here; then you'll know you've really arrived. But I warn you, be prepared for a culture shock, there are a lot of unconventional characters about. Now, time for supper.'

Chris glanced at a nearby waiter and said something to him in Portuguese. The waiter nodded. *'Certeza, Senhor Chris!'*

Chris glanced at Nick. 'You're in for a treat!'

'What treat, Chris?'

'You'll see.'

About ten minutes later, after chatting with Chris about Britain, discussing how bad the climate was and how uptight most of the people seemed to be these days, the food arrived. The waiter bought to the table a large, elliptical copper-coloured pot with four small coppery-coloured legs at the bottom of its base and a lid the same shape and size as the base. The waiter placed the container on the table, and then lifted the lid using a handle at the front.

The moment the lid was raised, just about the most delicious aroma Nick had experienced in his life came out of it: a mixture of fried fish, seafood, chillies, onions and tomatoes, and yet somehow even more delicious than any of those aromas could have been individually.

Nick glanced at Chris. 'What is it?'

'*Cataplana.* One of our local specialities. I've ordered it for you to celebrate your first day here in paradise. There's squid in there, king prawns, clams, scallops, black mussels, haddock, rockfish, monkfish, and whatever other fresh fish the chef has in the kitchen today. I hope you like it. As a matter of fact, the *cataplana*'s the name of the pot it's cooked in and served in, just like the Spanish call *paella* after the pot they cook it in. I suppose *cataplana* is a kind of Portuguese version of *paella*. But do get on with your supper. It tastes best hot.'

Nick tucked in. The *cataplana* tasted absolutely wonderful. To accompany it, Chris fetched a bottle of a Portuguese wine that had a curious green tint behind the clear white glass of the bottle.

'The green comes from it being a very young wine,' Chris explained, as he expertly extracted the cork. 'I think you'll like it. But maybe best to settle for just one bottle, Nick. It's pretty potent stuff.'

Chris compromised, though, and after Nick had enjoyed the first bottle, joined Nick in sharing a second one. The two men talked late into the evening about the army, England, Portugal, George, Annabelle, Wrath-Bonham, Marina, women, the sea and much else besides. By the time Nick went to bed it was two in the morning, and he was so tired he could hardly think clearly.

The sheets of his bed had a faint scent of lavender and the bed was almost unbelievably comfortable. *Quite a change from army life*, Nick thought. He took out the fruitcake his mum had baked for him, broke off a piece and chewed it even though, after the *cataplana* and a lovely strawberry flan that had followed it, he wasn't really hungry.

As he finished chewing and swallowing the piece of his mum's cake, Nick's heart, so elevated by his arrival at The Mirage, sank at the thought of how disappointed his parents must be with him.

He showered, brushed his teeth and went to bed. He could only hope that, somewhere in Portugal, he'd find some way ahead, some new direction that would wind up making his parents feel much better about him. That was the last thing he thought before he fell asleep to the chirping sound, so familiar in the warm climes of the world, of cicadas trying to summon a mate or whatever it is that cicadas do at night.

In the morning, the cicadas weren't chirping any more. Nick checked the time on his mobile; it was just past six o'clock. He'd slept well, but had a dream of Marina naked in bed and making love with Steve Heligan.

Nick got up, splashed cold water on his face and went outside. The Mirage was silent. Nick found the wrought iron garden gate and headed into the soft morning sunshine, which seemed to him already to contain some warnings of the much less gentle heat it would be generating within a few hours.

The sea was already close to blinding from the sun; he walked along the shore that was deserted apart from a few people out walking their dogs.

After a while, Nick felt hungry and headed back to The Mirage. The building was still and quiet, but there seemed to be some kind of promising sounds in the kitchen, so Nick returned to his room in an optimistic frame of mind. Not sure how to kill the time between now and breakfast, he sat down at his desk and looked along at the row of books on the shelf.

From where the row ended on the right to where the shelf met the wall on the left, there were five books.

From right to left, Nick took them each down off the shelf and glanced at them before replacing them on the shelf. The books were: a *Reader's Digest* edition, bound in dark green, of four condensed novels; the *Wisden Cricket Almanac* for 1994, and a copy of some novel called *Fiesta* by Ernest Hemingway, a writer Nick had obviously heard of but none of whose books he had ever read. There was also an extremely old, musty-smelling edition of a guidebook entitled *The Region of the Algarve,* bound in dark brown and basically falling to pieces, and an edition of Winston Churchill's *My Early Life.*

Nick, keen student of World War Two as he was, had read Churchill's enormous history of that war while still at university. But though he'd heard of *My Early Life,* he'd never seen it before.

An hour later he stopped reading. His eyes were sore, they needed a rest. He'd got more than a third of the way through the book in that hour, and he only broke off from reading because, as well as his eyes being tired, his stomach was growling with hunger.

Nick put the book down, quickly showered, went down into the restaurant where he had a first-rate English breakfast with Chris of fried eggs, ham, black pudding and fried tomatoes.

'I love Portuguese food,' said Chris, '*cataplana* among the rest, but you can't beat a proper English breakfast.'

Nick had no problem agreeing with that.

As that first week passed, Nick finished *My Early Life*, and then he picked up *Fiesta*, a book he'd never heard of. He went down to the nearest beach and started reading.

What certain books mean to us is massively intensified by where we are when we first encounter them and what might be happening in our lives, During those first few weeks in Portugal, Nick – as well as having some great time at the Mirage and by the sea – became an earnest devotee of *My Early Life* and *Fiesta*. He resolved to read more Hemingway whenever he got the chance.

For the first time in his life, he delved into himself to try to find who he really might be. He began to wonder if he had ever known how to unwind in his previous lifestyle. His hair grew longer than it had ever been in his entire life and he obtained a deep healthy tan. Some days, he didn't bother to shave, missing the daily ritual that he had carried out religiously, every morning of his life, since he was fifteen.

Of the two suitcases full of clothes that he had brought with him from England, all but a tiny percentage were folded or hung neatly in his studio wardrobe, having never been worn. His everyday attire was a pair of shorts, occasionally a T-shirt and flip-flops. Only at night did he 'dress up' but this only required a pair of casual slacks and shirt. Each day was his to spend as he chose. Chris seemed positively determined for Nick to rest and recover from everything that had happened to him in England, and the only times Chris got cross were when Nick asked him if it was all right 'just to hang out here and take it easy.'

'That's exactly what I want you to do, Nick,' Chris explained.

None of Nick's days there at the Mirage were structured as they had always previously been in his life, particularly in the army. Sometimes Nick felt that the whole experience at the Mirage was rather like a mirage itself. But was it really that life there seemed less real than normal life? Nick actually didn't think so. By contrast with his life in the army, so full of potential danger and competition and pressure, life at The Mirage slowly seemed to Nick to be more like reality, more human, the kind of life we were put on this earth to enjoy.

He decided to read more Hemingway. Chris told him that the local library, like the bookshops in nearby Lagos had an English-language section to cater for the large expatriate British population. Nick borrowed *A Farewell to Arms* and *The Old Man and the Sea* from the library. He adored them, too, though *Fiesta*, which seemed to Nick to have become part of his DNA the moment he'd finished reading it, remained his favourite.

When Nick wasn't reading or talking to Chris he spent his days swimming, playing tennis and golf against other guests, or horse-riding, followed in the evenings by the slightly less healthy pursuits that were offered by the nightlife of the Algarve.

The numerous bars and restaurants were waiting to lure the ever-willing band of tourists and locals alike. As promised, Chris introduced him to a very mixed bunch of residents. Nick was frequently invited to drinks parties and dinners. For the most part, the company was fine, but as in any society there were the inevitable bores and idiots. Chris steered him through the minefield of personalities with the expertise of a U-boat captain.

One of the holidaymakers whom he spent some time with, was a man called Tom Holland, who Chris knew well because Tom, and his wife Beverley and been coming to The Mirage for several years and were thinking of buying property nearby. Tom came regularly into The Mirage bar and struck up a good friendship with Nick. Tom and his wife were on a two-week holiday but by the evening his wife was tired and went early to bed leaving Tom to pop out for a couple of beers before turning in himself.

He and Nick had plenty in common. Tom explained that he had been in the Army for twenty-two years and had achieved the rank of Warrant officer. He left the Army aged forty-two which gave him plenty of time to have another career and a second pension. His new job was in security. He was now the manager in charge of some high security vaults, which were located in Chancery Lane, London. Tom was proud of his position and chatted openly about the unusual circumstances of his employment. During the two weeks Tom was in Portugal he and Nick spent many enjoyable hours chewing the fat.

'I have to go to a place called Cama Da Vaca today,' explained Chris one morning a few weeks after Nick had arrived. 'It means 'The Cow's Bed'. It's just along the coast about two miles west of here. A friend of mine has a home there. If you fancy a drive out, you'll find it interesting, I promise,' Chris added. Nick said he'd love to come. Later that morning Chris picked Nick up and they drove west towards the village of Burgau.

It was a typically hot Algarve day, and it felt good to Nick to be driving through the countryside with all the windows of Chris' jeep open, allowing a strong, warm, Atlantic breeze to blow through the vehicle. The air was rather salty from the sea, and scented with various wonderful aromas from the exotic plants, shrubs and Atlantic herbs that grew in abundance along the roadside.

'We're going to visit a friend of mine. His name's Felix Bartholomew, an ex-actor who owns and runs a boarding house and restaurant in a wonderful old manor house called Quinta Da Felicidade. He trod the boards of a few repertory theatres in the Midlands about thirty years ago – Agatha Christie, J.B. Priestley, that kind of stuff – then he got a lucky break and was cast as one of the main characters in the movie *Over The Top*.'

'He was in *Over The Top*?' Nick exclaimed. 'I love that film! I've got it on DVD. I don't remember his name from the cast, though.'

'His stage name was Bill Kitchener. A modest chap, our Felix. If you love the film I'm sure Felix will intrigue you even more, I am confident that he will. By the way, 'over the top' is a pretty good description of Felix himself. Still, I'm, sure you'll cope.' Chris smiled. 'The Quinta Da Felicidade's rather like a Portuguese version of *Fawlty Towers*, with no fewer oddballs than its TV counterpart. People who stay there tend to be either very hard up, very adventurous or seriously eccentric, and often all three. It's one of those places you either love or hate. Many of the guests have been coming back year after year because they enjoy the atmosphere so much.'

Chris slowed the jeep as they approached a large colonial estate house. As he explained: 'The main house boasts six suites that Felix rents out. In order to avoid confusion the rooms are colour-coded. There's a yellow suite, a blue suite, a mauve suite and so on. At the back of the main house is a cottage. This was a barn, which had been converted into a renting unit. Through necessity, everything has been done with minimum expenditure.'

'Why's that?' Nick asked.

'Between you and me, Felix has struggled to pay the bills for most of the years he's lived in the Algarve.'

'But *Over the Top* was a big success.'

'Yes, and he told me he gets repeat fees even now when it's on TV anywhere in the world. But you can't live in the Algarve on repeat fees from a supporting role in just one movie, no matter how successful it was. After all, it's the director and producer who make the big money from a movie, not the actors unless they're Julia Roberts or Harrison Ford etc. So, our Felix has had to become an expert in the art of living on a shoestring. He could teach the SAS a thing or two about survival.'

Chris gave a shrug. 'I've never met anybody who's better than Felix at robbing Peter to pay Paul. Behind Felix's house there's a large plot of land, which supports the odd caravan that's drifted in, plus a donkey or two. As Felix has a substantial amount of accommodation, has been around for some time and is well known, it quite often happens that people will turn up and ask for a cheap room, because they can't afford to stay anywhere else. To tell you the truth, Felix just hates turning people away.'

'That sounds like good business, if they can pay.'

'Yes, but often they can't, then Felix ends up losing out and not receiving the rent when his guests do a moonlight flit. There are people staying at the Quinta Da Felicidade who can't find the rent and who come to an agreement with Felix to work their ticket. These are people from all backgrounds. Some will wait at table in the Quinta Da Felicidade bodega style restaurant, a treat you really must experience; while others do a little gardening or maintenance in return for free board and lodging. Felix calls the people who fall into this category, his servants. They seldom last for more than a month and almost never honour the agreement that they have made with him.'

Chris shrugged. 'The only thing about the Quinta Da Felicidade that can be relied on is that there is always something new and outrageous occurring on a day-to-day basis. Oh, by the way, Felix is gay.'

'Kitchener gay? Who would have thought it?'

'No-one, least of all Kitchener himself, I imagine! Yes, Felix is very camp, though totally harmless. But no need to worry!'

Nick couldn't help thinking that experience had taught him that when someone says '*don't worry*' that's exactly the time to start worrying.

'When he meets you, he'll expect you to kiss him,' Chris explained.

'What! You have got to be joking.' Nick was doing a quick calculation of the distance they had come and how long it would take him to walk back.

'No … no, don't worry! Think of it like a Russian thing. We're not talking tongues here.' Chris was laughing out loud, unable to suppress his reaction to Nick's sudden panic.

'Are you sure?' Nick asked gingerly.

'Trust me.'

As they drove into the car park, on the right hand side of the road, set back fifty metres stood a beautiful old period building. There had been a devastating earthquake that had flattened most of the old buildings in southern Portugal two hundred years before and therefore it was unusual to come across anything so exotic in a rural setting such as this.

As the jeep pulled into the car park, it became very evident to Nick that the Quinta Da Felicidade was in a seriously bad state of repair. Paint was flaking off of the walls that were themselves missing rendering in many places. The wooden window frames were dry, split and completely bereft of paint. The garden, which had at some time in the past been formally laid out, was overgrown and unkempt except for a few patches where lawn must have at some time existed and had recently been cleared to allow some broken items of tatty garden furniture to stand.

Growing up over the front of the house were several brightly coloured Bougainvillaea that extended to the eaves and over the roof. They looked as if they had not been pruned for years and had virtually taken over the front of house. Weeds grew through the cobbled pathway and there were pieces of furniture, broken toys and other discarded items lying around.

Quinta Da Felicidade must have once been an elegant building but was now sadly much neglected. It was crying out for help; but, even though all the apparent neglect, the old house retained a certain degree of elegance. Perhaps there was still time for it to be restored to its former glory.

Chris and Nick got out of the car and together walked over to the main entrance. Two overweight, scruffy dogs stirred themselves as the strangers approached. They made a lazy attempt to bark, thought better of it and resumed dozing in the shade of a magnificent dragon tree – a surreal-looking grey trunk composed of more than two dozen intertwining stems surmounted by a canopy that was a crown of thick, spiky green leaves and wouldn't have looked out of place in a Tolkien movie, which dominated the driveway.

Inside, the house was remarkably cool and had the friendly, relaxed silence that large southern European houses have on a hot day. The walls had been decorated with a marbling effect, which Nick thought must have looked spectacular in its prime, particularly around the central wrought iron staircase that was illuminated from above by a pyramid shaped glass apex.

'Felix, are you at home?' called Chris as the two men walked into the entrance corridor.

'In the dining room, darling,' came the reply and they walked towards the source of the voice.

Felix Bartholomew was sitting at a dining table that was strewn with plates, cups and the remains of breakfast. He was a large man in, Nick thought, his mid-sixties; his grey hair was cut very short and his face was still handsome. Nick recognised Kitchener immediately. Indeed, Nick thought Felix looked like an older and slightly seedier Kitchener from an alternative universe where Kitchener had survived the First World War and had moved to the Algarve.

Felix wore a large Fedora hat that accentuated his theatrical appearance. Nick couldn't be quite sure, but would have hazarded a guess that Felix was wearing some kind of eyeliner. But by far the most striking feature about him was his voice. Nick placed the accent as being somewhere between mid-

Atlantic and well educated English, to which was added a wonderful gravelly quality.

'Hello, Chris,' said Felix warmly as they entered the room.

'Good morning,' replied Chris, walking towards him.

'Kiss, please,' demanded Felix and Chris dutifully bent over and kissed him on both cheeks.

'And who's this handsome young man whom you've brought with you?'

'Felix, meet Nicholas Trevelyan.' replied Chris. 'Nick loves *Over The Top*, by the way. And I've told him that you certainly are.'

'Chris darling, how right that is! So ...' Felix got up from his chair, took a couple of steps towards Nick and looked at him intently, '... you like my film, dear boy?'

'Very much,' said Nick, honestly enough.

'Felix calls it 'my film', you notice, Nick,' Chris explained, with a smile, 'as if the other stars had nothing to do with it.'

'They were mere extras, mere *extras*, darling,' said Felix. He glanced at Nick. 'There was only one real star in that film, dear boy, and you're looking at him *right now*. Chris darling,' Felix said this without taking his eyes off Nick, 'he may kiss me too.'

Nick, seeing little alternative, kissed Felix on the left cheek. Nick kept his eyes closed, trying to dredge up images in his mind of Russian leaders congratulating meritorious soldiers.

'Both sides!'

Nick smiled, bent again, braced himself to kiss the other cheek.

'And now, Nicholas, what brings you here to my Quinta Da Felicidade? Do you want to use my beautiful house to make a film or as a location for a fashion shoot? Or are you an emissary from a horrible bank who wants me to pay them some money?'

'None of these things, Felix, this is purely a social visit,' Nick replied politely.

'Well,' said Felix, 'if you're not here to make me some money, that's bad; but on the other hand, if you're also not here to take my money, well then that is good. So, Mr Nicholas Trevelyan, you are welcome at the Quinta Da Felicidade.'

'Thanks, Felix,' Nick said.

Nick was sure Hemingway would have enjoyed meeting Felix and would probably have put him somewhere in the pages of *Fiesta*. Nick and Chris and Felix spent a pleasant half hour being talked to by Felix about his acting years *'oh, darlings, how I loved the theatre, the greasepaint, the lights, the dusty back-stage, the tingle of stage-fright, the endless applause at the end, and the buzz, the buzz afterwards in the bar, my darlings, and the talking until the small hours!'* over cups of strong coffee and a local treat, small custard tarts called – as Nick discovered; he was eating them for the first time – Pasteis de Nata, before Chris and Felix said their goodbyes and left to return to The Mirage.

'Well, Nick, what did you think?' Chris asked as they drove out through the gates of Quinta Da Felicidade.

'Great fun, that man can certainly tell a tale,' Nick replied, laughing.

Slowly and lazily the hazy days rolled into weeks. Nick found that as he awoke each morning, it became increasingly difficult to remember which day of the week it was – so indistinguishable was one sunny morning from the next. He also noted that while he had once been only too happy, willing and able to jump out of bed reasonably early in the morning, breakfast on the terrace, often with Chris, and then disappear eagerly to pursue some energetic activity, he was now starting to spend more time in bed in the morning, often lying in until midday. He wasn't unduly worried by this development as he knew that he was fit and he felt that it was perfectly reasonable to be making the most of the local entertainment as he was after all, meant to be relaxing.

Nick did however notice with more than a little concern that his bank balance was, predictably enough, starting to look less healthy. He realised that this downswing seemed to correlate quite distinctly with the increase in the amount of time he was spending in the local hostelries. In reality, he was living very cheaply as his needs were few and his living costs minimal, most of his outgoing appeared to be purchasing alcohol.

Chris had been as good as his word about the rent, charging Nick the euro equivalent of less than a hundred pounds a month for his studio apartment and another hundred a month for all his meals. But Nick often went out to eat, even though with his meals provided at The Mirage he didn't need to, and his stints in bars within a thirty-mile radius also ate into his savings at a time when his income was non-existent. But he dismissed this slight slide in his fortunes as an inconsequential blip; after all, he told himself, he'd soon have figured out what to do with his life, and money wouldn't be a problem. Meanwhile, he was there to take advantage of the opportunity to relax and enjoy himself.

As the financial warning bell rang unheeded in the distance, Nick continued his pursuit of the Algarve pleasures. His recent problems were all but forgotten, and Chris found moments between running The Mirage to pass some time with Nick.

They spent many hours sitting in the gardens of The Mirage, people-watching and discussing life. Chris had lived in Portugal for fifteen years, during which time he'd had plenty of opportunity to observe the odd assortment of folk that had passed that way. Some stayed and set up home there; others were only passing through, like ships in the night. There were some who would have loved to have been able to stay but were not made of the right stuff and lost everything they had. A smattering found it necessary to get out quickly, usually leaving a trail of unpaid bills in their wake.

It was late in the afternoon, the sun was scorching as usual and the incandescent blue sky was as cloudless, as it had been on just about every day since Nick arrived.

'It all looks idyllic but don't be deceived by the obvious charm,' said Chris. 'This place takes no prisoners, I can promise you that. There have been many times I thought that I'd be making a one-way journey to Faro airport.'

Nick had started to feel a little uneasy about the way Chris seemed regularly to be emphasising the pitfalls of the place, rather than the more obvious attributes. Nick himself felt he was still riding on the crest of an Algarvian wave. Whilst naturally concerned about his future, he wasn't yet ready to come down from his perch to confront the reality of his existence as well as that of those around him.

He found it particularly easy to make friends with the holidaymakers who passed though the resort. They were there to have a good time, as was Nick, and Nick slightly resented the more cynical outlook of the local ex-pats who appeared to increasingly be trying to spoil his fun with their tales of woe. It was with some reluctance that he patiently prepared to listen to Chris as he came to the end of his sermon for the day.

'We all tend to live our lives these days thinking that TV, films and the books we read are a true reflection of real life. No matter how much life piles on the problems, in the movies there always seems to be a wise person who takes the time to explain where the unfortunate victim has been going wrong and from there on the victim becomes the hero and life becomes worth living. In real life there are no wise men.'

Nick nodded sympathetically and made his excuses, leaving Chris to his thoughts. Nick showered, changed and then headed for the bar and some welcome early evening refreshment.

After almost three months on the Algarve, Nick's lifestyle had slipped into a pattern of relaxed directionless repetition, a pattern familiar to many visitors to the Algarve, doubtless including the Visigoths who had invaded it fifteen hundred years ago, and the Moors who had taken over a couple of centuries later.

Nick made some preliminary efforts to get to grips with the Portuguese language that was, he discovered, universally proclaimed by all non-Portuguese he encountered there to present a considerable challenge to any newcomer. But eventually he gave up on both of the copies of *Teach Yourself Portuguese* he'd brought from England. He therefore tended to hang out with English speaking people whether they were holidaymakers, ex-pats or locals, so many of whom spoke English very well.

Apart from Chris, Nick didn't find himself making any really good new friends on the Algarve, though Nick soon had sufficient acquaintances to be assured that he could walk into almost any bar in the area and be assured of an entertaining evening's worth of conversation. He also had some flings with women he met, but the flings never seemed to last more than a few nights. And then there was always the Mirage Bar to finish up at, where a welcome 'one for the road' and Chris's ears to bend were always awaiting him.

Nick read lots. He found that Amazon delivered just as efficiently to Portugal as to England, and as browsing bookshops wasn't really his style, he completed his reading of Hemingway's books by ordering on-line. So while Nick's daily life was laid-back, largely indolent and relaxed, his imagination during those weeks in Portugal that soon became three months, was full of fire and dreams of heroism, courage, war, suffering, triumph and the winning of the hearts of a beautiful, fickle, intelligent and remarkable woman.

But he had started drinking too much, and regularly going to bed in the small hours and getting up too late. He was still enjoying being in Portugal, but he was aware that his life was starting to unravel, and what most concerned him was his awareness that he was starting not even to care very much that it was.

13
The Mad Hatter's Tea Party

One morning, a few days after the three-month anniversary of his stay on the Algarve, Nick found himself woken in his apartment in the way he often was woken up there nowadays: the bright midday sun had crept around and up into the sky, high enough to find the familiar crack in the curtain through which a penetrating ray of glaring sunshine annoyingly pierced his state of semi-consciousness.

As he struggled to raise himself slightly to turn and escape the painful wakeup call, his head seemed irredeemably glued to the pillow. He gave up trying and became aware of distant scuffling and rustlings in the far corners of the apartment.

He attempted to open his eyes to try and detect the source of the puzzling and unwelcome noises, but continued to be thwarted by the ever-present blast of white-hot light from through the curtains.

As he finally managed to prise his eyes open a fraction, he witnessed an alluring flash of tanned back as someone pulled on a T-shirt over a pair of cut-off denims. He heard the French window that led to the patio open and a whispered voice:

'Thanks Nicky, it was lovely.' And then she was gone.

With some difficulty, Nick managed to pull himself up onto his elbows. He furrowed his brow painfully, mumbling incoherently to no one in particular:

'Who was she?' The events of the night before, as was often the case, remained a fuzzy blur. He was damned sure he'd had a good time, but where and with whom, of this he couldn't be sure. It would undoubtedly come to him later. In the meantime, maybe a little nap might help him remember.

It was mid-afternoon before he managed to find his way to the shower and it was not until a comforting snake of soapy water was cascading down his back that he blurted, *'Martina? Martine? And was she from Barking or was it Basildon?'*

He comforted himself with the knowledge that she'd probably just been another of the many holidaymakers who passed through, looking for nothing more than a fleeting contact, a holiday romance or memory to be able to boast about when returning home.

All the same, Nick couldn't help feeling that Ernest Hemingway – and the young Winston Churchill too, for that matter – would have managed things with rather more decorum.

Nick's black Porsche 911, while of course no longer new, was an even greater rarity in the Algarve than it was in Britain. Chris had warned him to be careful as the local police would have certainly taken a keen interest in it.

He was soon to realise exactly what Chris meant. The car was fast, expensive and had British number plates. Driving in the countryside with the hood down was a delight and a pleasure that Nick treated himself to when boredom surfaced, which it did fairly often.

It was just one of these excursions that he had been enjoying late one evening when he approached the traffic lights at the junction of the Lagos-Luz road.

The lights were about to change as he got to within fifty metres. It was one of those split second decisions and as he had a fast car, he floored the accelerator and roared over.

At once there was the unmistakable sound of a police siren. Nick pulled over, stopped the car and rolled down his window. A smartly attired *Guarda Nacional Republicana* officer, or GNR for short, arrogantly strolled towards him, smoothing the creases in his own immaculate uniform as he approached. He wore full length black riding boots which looked pointedly out of place on a tarmac road and would have never stepped into a stable. Nick winced at the thought of an eight-hour shift driving a car in the heat of the Algarve with your feet encased in leather to below the knee.

The GNR officer leaned down to speak through the open window, touching the peak of his cap, and enunciated, in almost perfect English,

'My name is officer Braga. Can I see your driving licence, sir?'

Nick groaned inwardly.

'Certainly, Officer.' Nick fumbled in the glove compartment and produced the necessary documentation.

'Thank you, sir.'

'That's very good English that you speak, Officer Braga. Where did you learn it?'

But Braga completely ignored Nick's query. The policeman's stern mouth, framed by a well trimmed but luxuriant black moustache stayed firmly closed. The officer turned back to his jeep and had a seemingly casual ten-minute conversation with his colleague, punctuated by laughs of amusement and much gesticulating and finally lighting a cigarette.

At last, Braga came back, leaned down to the window again and politely asked:

'Please could you step out of the car, Mr Trevelyan?'

Nick sighed deeply and did what was asked. The officer took a final nonchalant drag from his cigarette and threw the butt onto the road grinding it out with the heel of his riding boot. He stood with his hands clasped behind his back, a politely inquiring yet disquietingly smug expression on his face.

Nick smiled nervously at Braga, shrugging his shoulders. He raised his palms in a show of bewilderment. Braga was obviously unimpressed by Nick's display and removed a notebook from his breast pocket. After having written slowly and deliberately in it for several minutes he turned to Nick and announced.

'Mr Trevelyan, you must appear at the Lagos GNR post indicated on this paper within the next twenty-four hours with full documentation and suitable reasons for having taken up valuable police time. There is also a fine of two hundred Euros for your having crossed a set of red lights, payable as indicated.'

Braga tore off the sheet he had been writing on and handed it to Nick, then turned to go.

'But you can't do that,' Nick stammered lamely.

'Yes, I can,' replied Officer Braga smugly but firmly, with a look of satisfaction on his face, 'and unless you would like to come down to the police station with me now, I suggest you leave right away.'

Nick turned quickly, got into his car and drove away slowly, to return to The Mirage.

After he'd parked at The Mirage car park, Chris cornered him. Nick didn't feel like chatting at that moment but was obliged to feign interest.

'Nick, we've had an invitation this morning from Felix, asking us to join him for dinner tomorrow night at his place. I won't be able to make it but I strongly suggest that you go along.'

'Why, Chris?'

'Oh, it's bound to be good fun if nothing else; and it'll fill another page or two in your memoirs.'

Chris smiled. Nick knew he had to smile back, so he did. Nick agreed that it was an opportunity not to be missed. After all, Chris was his host and Nick knew that he could only continue to be there in Portugal at all because of the tiny, well below market rate, cost of accommodation and food that Chris so generously allowed him to pay.

After a light supper in the restaurant and a few more drinks with Chris, Nick returned to the apartment, weary and demoralised in advance at the prospect of having to go to Felix's. Nick had been to a couple of Felix's soirées. If you were in the right mood, they'd offer an interesting feast of eccentricity; if you weren't in the right mood, it was like being caught up in a bad dream. Such was the disarray that could be caused by the eccentric bunches of people who often gathered together at Felix's home.

Nick knew there was no escape. Chris had said yes to the request and Nick knew that Chris would by now have told Felix that Nick had accepted his invitation.

Nick fell into a troubled sleep. He awoke the next day at about midday, aware, as he usually was when he woke late, what a difference this was from early morning reveille in the

Army. He felt rested but in low spirits so he busied himself with minor domestic duties such as shopping and a little mild tidying up to distract himself.

As the evening approached Nick found that he was feeling a certain curious anticipation of the impending events and hoped this meant that he was in the right mood for the party. He went along to the local *adega* and bought a bottle of acceptable Dão red and a Casal Garcia, an especially popular brand of the ever-popular Portuguese young green wine.

Nick returned to the studio and showered. He dressed, spending some time deciding what to wear. The clothes he was most comfortable in were dirty or inappropriate for dinner at Felix's because they were too smart.

With reluctance, he opened the wardrobe door to reveal a selection of clothing he had barely set eyes on since he had arrived in Portugal. Nick had quickly discovered that, by and large, the casual look was the only look out there. He contemplated a jacket and regimental tie, thought better of it and plumped for a pair of dark trousers and a white collarless shirt. The final touch was a pair of socks under the smart black brogues that he hadn't worn once since his arrival.

This all felt decidedly odd as it had been months since he had worn socks but he was happy about the end result. He walked to his car feeling happier than he had for many weeks and found to his relief that he was actually starting to look forward to the evening ahead. His biggest problem of late, which was the motoring fine, had been paid and although it hurt to part with the money, he was able to consign the incident to history and hopefully erase the sting of it from his memory.

At close to eight that evening, he drove through the open gateway of the Quinta Da Felicidade. There were several other cars in the car park. As he walked towards the house, the usual two overweight, scruffy dogs beneath the dragon tree waddled over to greet him. They were obviously feeling quite sprightly in the cool of the evening as each managed to bark twice before returning to their bed at the base of the dragon tree. The front door to the house was open as it always was.

Nick walked into the entrance hall, waited a few minutes then called Felix's name. There was no reply so he continued on through the downstairs hallway towards the dining room, where he could hear laughter and voices. He knocked on the door, pushing it open at the same time.

'Nicholas, *darling,* I'm delighted that you have been able to make it,' boomed Felix who was wearing another huge mauve fedora that was even more extravagant than the others that Nick had seen and which made Felix look even wackier than he normally did. Felix was famous for his hat collection.

'Do come in and meet my friends, Nicky, but first, please, a kiss,' the flamboyant actor pleaded.

Nick dutifully kissed the host on both cheeks and allowed himself to be dragged around the room as Felix, with all of the panache of the owner of the Supreme Champion at Crufts showing off his prize-winning pooch, introduced Nick one by one to the assembled guests,

The dining room's walls were half panelled and the high ceiling was decorated with a very elaborate moulding effect which on closer inspection turned out to be plaster, cleverly made to imitate wood.

There were two French windows that looked out onto a raised patio, commanding a view over the land to the rear of the house. The patio had been originally designed by the architect to take advantage of the view from the back of the house. But now, alas, the patio was home to a collection of dead refrigerators and rusting washing machines.

The furniture that adorned the room was probably best described as 'elegantly aged', having been new back in about 1965 in its time, but now well used. The flooring was made of bare boards worn fashionably smooth with age. There were about fifteen guests.

Nick found the most noticeable to be a couple who Felix introduced as 'my very rich friends.' They were from Surrey but now lived in America; he was 'in computers' and she, interior design. They were both in their early thirties with an eighteen-month-old baby boy who was accompanied by a young English nanny.

Another interesting duo consisted of two young women – Debbie and Sharee – obviously in their late twenties, and, Felix explained, from Los Angeles. Debbie had short black hair, was somewhat overweight though very pretty, while Sharee was blonde, slim and, Nick thought, simply ravishing, with the face of an angel. She reminded him of Marina, though Marina was taller. As always when he thought of Marina, a pulse of longing swept through him. He tried hard to think of the two Californian women and not Marina.

Debbie and Sharee wore elegant Portuguese clothes with lots of reds and yellows in them, and they both had teeth so dazzlingly white Nick half-regretted he wasn't wearing sunglasses.

Felix explained that Debbie and Sharee were in the film business and extremely important in that field. Nick could see for himself that the two women were obviously very much in love with each other and made no effort to hide the fact, holding hands at the table and embarrassingly, sometimes spontaneously kissing each other on the cheeks. Nick had no difficulty imagining Debbie and Sharee naked in bed together, kissing and entwining themselves round each other, both of them sighing with pleasure. Nick was quite sure he wouldn't have been averse to joining them.

'Debbie and Sharee got married last week,' Felix explained. 'They're on their honeymoon.'

'I *so* love my wife,' said Debbie, in her pleasant Californian intonation, and smiling affectionately at Sharee.

'I so love my wife, too,' said Sharee, smiling lovingly at Debbie.

'Debbie and Sharee are truly wonderful people,' Felix commented, approvingly.

Nick had already noticed that there were no descriptive words in Felix's vocabulary that were less momentous than *brilliant* or *wonderful*. The word *lovely* was about as negative as Felix ever got. Nobody in his world was ever allowed to be ordinary or average, at least not linguistically. Mediocrity had no place in Felix Bartholomew's life, not as least as far as Felix was concerned.

Felix referred to those who were working for their keep as 'his servants'. The incumbent servant appeared to be a man named Paul. Nick was somewhat begrudgingly introduced to him, which caused him to deduce that Paul was perhaps coming to the end of his stay at the Quinta Da Felicidade. Felix explained that Paul had been a producer at the BBC, but a messy divorce had caused him to lose his job, his money, and by Nick's estimation, most part of his dignity. Paul moped about, serving drinks and offering around the *hors d'oeuvres*.

There was a German husband and wife who were on a walking holiday and had wandered, by chance, into the Quinta Da Felicidade; they had not yet decided whether their stumbling across the place was a stroke of good fortune or very bad luck. So, they stood in the corner, resplendent in their leather shorts, braces and sturdy boots looking bemused, as well they might have done.

There was also a fair-haired Norwegian with a short grey goatee beard, who introduced himself as Carl (the Norwegian, not the beard) and who explained to Nick that he ran an alternative health clinic in the nearby hills and should Nick ever require his services, he had only to give him a call.

'Thanks,' said Nick, thinking *I'm about as likely to phone and go to see him as I am to cut off my manhood with a pair of rusty scissors.*

The last people to be introduced were a couple from Wales. Geraldine was a flamboyant lady of about forty-five; everything about her was outrageous from her blonde hair to the tip of her six-inch stiletto heeled shoes. Her dress, which had a complicated design of red, pink and light blue flowers, fitted like a second skin and she was adorned like an Indian bride with the most extravagant jewellery.

But by far her most conspicuous features were her ample bosoms, which were like a mantelpiece in front of her. Her vast cleavage, which looked to Nick as if in its heyday it could have nourished a whole regiment of babies, strained the confines of her dress, threatening at any moment to burst from this unwelcome restriction, as she wobbled from one place to another. Her husband, by contrast, wore a very sober tie and jacket and appeared the sort of man that might be an accountant or bank clerk. To all other men present, her husband simply appeared to be a very lucky man. Nick noticed his shoes were built up to give him extra height. The husband had a rather exhausted look about him, and as Nick could easily imagine that his wife's sexual demands were far from trivial, Nick felt sure he knew why.

A late arrival appeared at the doorway causing a flurry of attention from Felix, who dutifully made a block introduction to all those assembled, of Rosemary who was a forty-year old 'counsellor' (as she described herself) from Essex. She sported bright red hair and wore a skimpy black dress that showed off a cleavage which, while not competing with Geraldine's (but then few cleavages could have done) was itself far from negligible.

Rosemary was, as she was only too keen to explain, a great believer in something she called 'transcendental inner visualisation' which she spoke about with the conviction and energy, Nick thought, that only a true expert in gibberish could achieve. After less than five minutes of listening to her, Nick concluded that she was barking mad.

'Sit down everyone! We're going to eat now,' Felix mercifully cut in, at which Rosemary shut up more promptly than Nick would have expected, perhaps – he thought – because she was now far more interested in her transcendental inner visualisation of Felix's supper into her stomach.

Felix ushered his guests to the table like an experienced shepherd at a sheep dog trial.

'Nick, you'll sit at my right hand,' said Felix. *Like Jesus at the last supper,* he thought to himself. The long table looked as if it hadn't enjoyed the luxury of polish for many years, the chairs were of varying pedigree and very few pieces of crockery matched, but the food was delicious, all served by Felix from the head of the table and passed along from guest to guest.

Felix stood, an imposing if demented figure, dishing out food whilst engaging all of his guests in conversation. He was a remarkable host. He was also extremely clumsy. He constantly knocked things over in his exuberance to feed everyone, so food was splattered about all over the place, but Felix appeared not to notice. As is normal at such dinner parties, the conversation to begin with was pleasantly polite, punctuated on occasions by the Germans in the leather hose who, every now and again offered totally irrelevant interjections, in very broken English.

'In Deutschland we have many fine bridges made from vood and *Stein*,' said the husband.

'Ach, *stone* is vot you are meaning, husband dearest,' said his wife.

'Ach ja,' the husband conceded.

'And the *Wurst* – I mean the sausages – from Hamburg are delicious,' added his wife, with equal irrelevance, especially since sausages weren't actually on the dinner menu.

The Wurst is yet to come, thought Nick, anticipating the remainder of the evening.

'Marzipan is most popular in Deutschland,' the husband put in, obviously anxious not be outdone by his wife in the irrelevance stakes.

The various conversations or bizarre soliloquies continued, and the wine took its welcome effect on Nick, who could at least use his mild tipsiness to become increasingly oblivious to the absurdity of the dialogue around him. But at least the barriers started to fall away and Felix's dinner guests relaxed.

During a quieter moment, while Felix was engaged in the kitchen resolving some inexplicable crisis, Nick took the time to sit back and collect his thoughts; something had been in the back of his mind since he had sat down to dine. What was it that this party reminded him of?

In a flash it came to him, the *'Mad Hatter's Tea Party'* of course!

On cue, the Mad Hatter himself returned with a selection of desserts. The young nanny, who up to that point hadn't uttered a single word, proceeded to knock back a couple of glasses of wine. Then suddenly, to the amazement of Nick and probably of everyone else, she let rip with a torrent of conversation about her parents, severely boring everyone until as suddenly as she had started, she stopped, sat still for five minutes and then proceeded to burst into tears. Felix made the necessary excuses and packed her off to bed, explaining that this was the first time she had been away from home and she was a little homesick.

The evening continued much as before, with much of the conversation revolving around spiritualism, astrology and faith healing. Nick recalled that Chris had told him about the local popularity of these subjects. In his current, troubled frame of mind, he wasn't really in the mood to be discussing the nature of the universe and the whys and wherefores of existence at weird dinner party at Felix's, but he gamely humoured his fellow guests and participated in the proceedings as enthusiastically as he could. Then Felix, completely unexpectedly, produced a collection of children's colouring crayons and some paper and then proceeded to scribble like a demented chimpanzee on the paper, selecting different crayons at will.

'This is your wonderful colour chart, Nicholas,' announced Felix proudly, and proceeded to read Nick's fortune with the help of the colourful mess that lay before him. Nick found the experience more than a little incomprehensible as the chart had become adorned with unexpected supplements, to help or hinder the reading – such as gravy, sauce, cream and a healthy dollop of caramel pudding.

'You will be surprised by love,' Felix concluded, having completed his examination of the mess.

'I can't wait,' said Nick, with a smile, though he stopped smiling a moment later, when he started to wonder whether Felix himself planned to be doing the surprising.

At the far end of the table, Rosemary was doing her own prediction with her Tarot cards, her subject being Geraldine's future. Nick, without the help of Tarot cards, was sure he could also predict the future for Geraldine. Given the intake of wine and the excitement of having her fortune outlined by the mad woman with the bright red hair, Nick felt that in the very near future Geraldine's barely contained vast bosom was going to take a giant step forward for mankind and burst onto the dining room table, possibly injuring someone in the process.

Geraldine squealed with delight as Rosemary related yet another revelation in her future.

'Wunderbar!' shouted the German hiking husband and was smartly kicked in the shins by his wife's size nine crag-hopping boots. Carl in the meantime watched the proceedings with distaste, leaving the party tricks to the amateurs; after all he was a professional. Debbie and Sharee gazed into each other's eyes.

The time finally came for coffee. Felix was organising this event, standing in his usual position at the end of the table, dishing out cups, saucers and orders. The seating arrangement had altered slightly, guests had moved around as conversations were struck up with other diners.

Nick noted how most of the men had managed to position themselves at an advantageous point from which they could better observe Geraldine's extensive heaving cleavage. None wished to miss the magical moment of release that could surely now not be too far away.

Suddenly, from upstairs, there came an ear-splitting scream, shocking the group into silence. Nobody moved except Felix, who continued to serve coffee, completely unfazed.

'Perhaps you would like a little more milk, Nicholas?' he asked politely. Such was the shrillness of the scream that the bosom-watching fraternity momentarily lost their concentration, but they quickly regained their composure and settled back down to observe the matter at hand.

After a time, the interior-decorating mother left the room to investigate. She came back five minutes later, sat down and informed the assembled guests that the ornate plaster ceiling in the green room had collapsed onto the bed where the nanny was sleeping. Nanny was not injured and was now asleep in the blue room. There was then a wonderful exhibition of telepathy as Felix, without a word, fixated his servant, Paul, with a steely stare for ten seconds.

Paul threw down his serviette and sloped off to clear up the debris and after a period of fifteen minutes he reappeared dragging several black bin liners full of plaster through the dining room and deposited them in the refrigerator graveyard out on the patio looking most disgruntled about the whole episode. Felix, in the meantime continued as if the event had never happened. The port was passed around and gradually the guests made their excuses and left.

Geraldine's fan club, bitterly disappointed that they were not to be treated to a grand exposure, slowly melted away. The German hiker went off to the yellow room to bathe his badly bruised shins and suffer the wrath of his wife. Geraldine's husband left with her and with a wry smile on his face, perhaps – Nick thought – because hubby knew that he alone would savour the delights that the other men could only dream of.

'Well Felix, I have to go, too,' Nick said. 'I must thank you for a most enjoyable evening,' he added, and in a perverse way he meant it. Nick had enjoyed himself, but only in the way Alice had enjoyed herself at the Mad Hatter's tea party. Indeed, Nick couldn't help thinking that compared with the evening he'd just had, the experience of taking tea with the Mad Hatter, the March Hare and the Dormouse would have been a model of conventional normality.

As Nick headed towards Felix's front door, he contemplated the past three hours and the eccentric charm of Felix's home. Now, though, he was looking forward to getting back to the Mirage Bar where he could have a quiet drink with Chris.

'Thank you for coming. We enjoyed your wonderful company, Nicholas,' Felix said, as they walked towards the open front door, then reached the reception area, Felix stopped, put his hands on Nick's shoulders and looked into his eyes.

Oh no, Nick thought, *what's this?*

'Nicholas, I knew I was right; you do have different coloured eyes.' Felix was holding Nick's shoulders and peering straight into his eyes, looking very excited.

'Er … yes, it's something not everyone notices. You're very observant, Felix,' Nick replied, wondering where this would go next.

'Nicholas, that's so wonderful, I'm sure that this must mean that you have mystic powers.'

Nick knew that Felix and his group of wacky friends were looking for the occult and esoteric in whatever they could. Nick needed to make good his escape quickly before Felix decided he was a Druid chieftain.

In the reception area of the entrance to Felix's house there was a tall bookcase full of old dog-eared paperbacks. Nick had noticed the bookcase before, of course, but had never paid much attention to it. Now, though, he saw his chance to swerve the conversation onto another tack.

'Would you mind if I borrowed a book, Felix? I've been reading lots recently but I've almost finished reading all the books I've bought recently or borrowed from the library.'

'Yes, of course. Please help yourself. I do have some wonderful books,' Felix said, enthusiastically.

As soon as Nick began to read the titles, he realised that this move had been a mistake, somewhat out of the frying pan and into the fire. For all the books were on the subjects of spiritualism, astronomy and other allied supernatural matters.

'That's very kind of you, Felix, I'll have this one.' Nick decided, grabbing any book so as to be able to make good his escape.

'Oh! That's one's fantastic; you'll absolutely adore it,' Felix said encouragingly. Nick briefly glanced at the title for the first time; *Master Hypnotism in Just 30 Days.*

'Keep it, keep it, dear boy,' said Felix. 'A gift from the wonderful Felix Bartholemue.'

'Thanks very, Felix and to him too,' Nick said. He kissed Felix on the cheeks in the prescribed Russian manner, thanked him again for a marvellous dinner and headed off to the car park. As Nick passed the two sleeping dogs under the dragon tree, he called out to them.

'Master bloody hypnotism in just thirty days!' and laughed wryly.

The two dogs lounging under the dragon tree made no comment.

14
A New-Found Skill

Nick could never have imagined that the crazy book from the Quinta da Felicidade could possibly have such a profound and instantaneous effect on the rest of his life.

He'd thrown the book into the back of his car on the night that he drove home from Felix's dinner party and there it had stayed for over a week.

Then one day he picked it up and took it into his studio where it remained untouched for a further ten days. Then suddenly, and for no apparent reason other than boredom and a lack of reading material (he'd just finished *A Moveable Feast,* Hemingway's memoir of Paris) Nick picked it up and casually browsed through the pages.

The print date was 1932 and the pages were yellowing. But no matter what the age of the book, Nick had dismissed from the outset the idea that a book could possibly teach anyone to be a hypnotist. He assumed that the book was something of a literary joke: mumbo jumbo aimed at those who sought the answers to life in the exotic and absurd.

Inside the flyleaf was a smudged, cheap rubber stamp that proclaimed that the book belonged to the Algarvian Book Club. Nick assumed it had been donated to the club along with a pile of others by somebody who had cleaned out their garage, and from there presumably the book had made its way to the Quinta Da Felicidade. Nick settled back on his bed, ready for a doze, but instead picked up the book again and started nonchalantly flicking through it.

He was amused as he read with unexpected interest how to hypnotise whoever he wished and he laughed at his own stupidity for continuing to read such rubbish. It seemed to Nick that the book was about as credible as a 'do-it-yourself' manual on brain surgery.

Eventually, he slammed the book closed and was surprised to note that he had spent over four hours with his nose in the nonsense that lay on the table before him. He was actually annoyed with himself for having delved into the book as much as he had. *This kind of crap is only going to addle my mind even more than it already is by my being here.* All the same, Nick would have had to admit that there were some sections that he found interesting and thought provoking.

Reading the book about hypnosis had made his mind more active than he wanted it to be at this time of the evening, so he decided to return to the bar for a nightcap. He realised with a sense of hopelessness that he was starting to find it difficult to get to sleep unless anaesthetised with alcohol, but despite this sobering acceptance of reality, he left his room in search of a large tumbler of whisky. It would have been simple to have sunk into a depression, if a group of holidaymakers whom he'd befriended a week ago hadn't dropped in and swept him up into a bar crawling evening which ended with a party on the beach.

He still often dipped into *Fiesta* and *My Early Life,* and generally he had the impression that it was only his reading that was keeping him sane. But he knew well enough that one can hardly spend one's life doing nothing but reading great books written by other people.

The next morning Nick found himself sitting in the garden of The Mirage. He was feeling decidedly fragile and was starting his second coffee by the time that Chris arrived to sit with him.

'Well, you certainly look as if you've had a good night,' smiled Chris as he sat down to join Nick for coffee and read his mail. This was something that had become a ritual over the preceding weeks.

'I guess it was all worth it,' Nick replied, somewhat dreamily. Chris carried on working his way through the pile of letters. He occasionally grunted and tutted. Then with a huge grin on his face he looked up and exclaimed,

'How about this! It's from my accountant in England; the Inland Revenue has given me a rebate of six thousand pounds. Bloody hell! I can't believe it.' He was thrilled and promised to take Nick out for a meal to celebrate. Nick was delighted that

Chris had received some good news at last but his thoughts were miles away.

'Chris,' he said in a low voice.

'Um.' Chris's mind was still with the Inland Revenue.

'Chris, look at me,' Nick repeated again in the same low voice.

'What's the problem, Nick?' enquired Chris, still having trouble dragging himself away from the good news and the attached cheque that he held in his hand as if it might suddenly disappear.

'Look into my eyes,' this was said half as an order and half as a request.

'Do what?' asked Chris, a little confused but complying with the request before he had time to think of what he was doing.

'Look deep into my eyes Chris, very deeply into my eyes.'

'Bloody hell, Nick! I never noticed that before – you've got different coloured eyes.'

'Yes, Chris, and your own eyes are becoming tired now; you're sinking deeper into a hypnotic trance deeper, deeper, your eyes are becoming more and more tired.'

Chris blinked lazily; he was going along with the charade.

'Your eyelids are becoming so heavy that you can't keep them open.' Nick directed. Immediately Chris's eyes banged shut like the doors of a double garage.

'You are now totally at my command,' Nick announced triumphantly.

'Yes,' came the faint reply. 'I am at your command.'

Nick leaned back lazily in his chair stretching his legs out in front of him. He stared at an aircraft that was cutting a silver swathe across the pale blue morning sky.

It was, Nick assumed, probably taking suntanned tourists back to the greener shores of England, sporting a suntan and clutching their bottles of port and green wine. Chris sat motionless, eyes still closed, calm and breathing deeply. Nick sat opposite, waiting for Chris to become bored with the game and break the silence. Then he decided to carry on with the charade.

'Chris, you are now at my command and whatever I ask you to do, you will obey because you know that no harm will come to you. Do you understand?' Nick asked.

'Yes, I understand,' replied Chris obediently.

'Chris, open your eyes, walk out into the car park, turn around three times and then come back here and sit down,' Nick further instructed.

Chris's eyes sprang open. He was sitting directly opposite Nick, no more than a metre away across a garden table, but his eyes looked straight through him. He stood up and walked out through the garden gate and into the car park.

There he slowly turned around three times then walked back over to where he had previously been sitting and sat down. And there he sat, his gaze fixed rigidly forward with an expressionless look on his face. By this time, Nick was becoming more than a little apprehensive. Chris was making a great job of going along with the joke. Or could it be possible? Could he have actually hypnotized his friend?

'Touch your nose, Chris,' Nick said in a calm voice, although he was now starting to become a little unnerved by what was happening. Chris obeyed and touched his nose as ordered. Nick studied the man sitting in front of him. His eyes gazed forward and he really looked quite normal apart from his general overall quietness, noticeably reduced movement and the slightly glazed look in his eyes.

'Surely not,' Nick murmured. Chris's eyelids fluttered almost undetectably, instantly giving Nick cause to think that he was going to jump up, claiming a victory at playing Nick along at his own game. But still there was nothing. He continued to stare ahead.

'*Oh Hell.*' Nick's mind was moving towards panic. Chris remained virtually statuesque. In Nick's estimation, ten minutes must have passed since the incident had started. Surely it would be impossible for anyone to keep up the pretence this long. Chris must be hypnotized. The thought at first made him want to laugh. After all, it was so ludicrous.

He continued his observation of the man sitting across the table, who Nick was now convinced must surely be in some sort of a trance that he had induced. Now he began to worry about his friend. Could there be any lasting effects?

Could there be a possibility of some deeper psychological damage? Would this incident have any long-term effect on Chris? He looked around the garden, slightly in desperation and partly in search of some inspiration. The curtain in his nearby apartment fluttered momentarily in the breeze.

'That bloody book!' Nick whispered angrily to himself. He slowly got up from the table, not knowing what effect this might have upon his subject. He half expected Chris to get up and follow him but Chris continued to stare into space.

Once Nick had walked slowly out through the garden gate, occasionally looking over his shoulder to reassure himself that Chris hadn't moved, he sprinted the twenty metres around the building to the studio door. Fumbling with the keys in his haste to get the book, he burst into the room like a deranged maniac. He grabbed the book and started to scan the pages for the section that he remembered seeing about bringing the subject out of a trance. It was then that he heard the voice, just outside the studio window, which looked out onto the garden.

'Senhor Chris?' enquired a female Portuguese voice. 'Oh, Senhor Chris?'

'Hell, Hell, Hell,' Nick could barely contain himself. He ducked down and moved over to the window carefully so as not to be seen, pulling back the bottom corner of the curtain. He peered out into the garden. A middle-aged Portuguese cleaning lady with a dustpan and brush in her hand was addressing Chris, presumably inquiring of her boss his opinion on yet another of the continuous stream of minor problems that arose. Chris stared forward, totally oblivious of the woman who was becoming increasingly impatient.

'Oh, Senhor Chris!' There was obvious irritation in the cleaning lady's voice. She inquired for the third time. Nick was tempted to show himself and attempt to make some sort of lame excuse for Senhor Chris's lack of attention, but he knew little or no Portuguese and was equally convinced that the cleaning lady knew no English.

There was nothing that he could think of doing that would help the situation so he had to be content to observe the bizarre scene that was being enacted in the tranquillity of the garden and hope for the best.

His prayers were answered. After two more attempts to attract the attention of her 'patron', the cleaning lady stormed off in a huff to resolve the problem herself. Nick tore around the building like a demented greyhound and reached the garden gate.

He stopped before entering the garden in an attempt to get his breath back. He was sure that now he was armed with the book it should be a relatively easy matter to restore Chris to normality before anyone else came into the garden.

'I'm going to count backwards from ten to one,' Nick explained. 'By the time I've reached 'one' you'll be wide awake and feeling great. You'll remember nothing of what has happened to you, just a good feeling all over, a feeling of well-being.'

If this didn't work what the hell would he do?

'Ten ... nine ... eight, you're feeling happy and slowly waking up. Seven ... six ... five, you're more awake. Four ... three, you're even more awake and feeling good. Two ... one, you're wide awake and feeling great.'

Chris sat in his chair with a puzzled look and a faint smile on his face. He was still holding the letter from his accountant in his hand. He looked down at the letter and then across at Nick.

'What was I saying Nick?' He asked.

'You were telling me about your tax rebate,' Nick reminded him.

'Oh, yes. Great news ... and it came at a good time too,' Chris's composure was returning rapidly. 'That's the best bit of news that I've had for ages,' he enthused. 'Made me feel bloody marvellous.'

By this time Chris was beaming all over his face, while Nick looked on bewildered. He was the complete opposite, covered in perspiration, his T-shirt was soaking from the exertion and worry and his hair was stuck to his forehead and neck. His heart was still pumping wildly. The panic was over and he slumped down into the chair. Chris looked across at him and remarked in a fatherly fashion.

'Nick, you look bloody awful! I don't think these late nights are doing you much good.'

'I think you could be right,' Nick admitted.

'How about a drink to celebrate your good luck? I'm gasping,' Nick said, sorely in need of some refreshment.

'But Nick, it's only ten in the morning,' Chris replied. 'Go to the bar and help yourself,' he offered. 'I have to go too and sort out some problems with the cleaners.'

And with that Chris bounced off, obviously a happy man in a very good mood.

Nick staggered to the bar and poured himself a large beer, hardly able to believe what had taken place in little more than twenty minutes.

He felt so relieved he downed the beer in one gulp.

There really was no doubt in his mind that he'd stumbled in the most absurd and accidental way on something he could do really well, and for which he, amazingly, had a natural talent, partly by inclination, partly by temperament but perhaps most of all because his eyes were different colours and people tended to find them a tad hypnotising even before he's started doing anything.

15
The Rock

The Mad Hatter's Tea Party had brought Nick some light relief, but when it was over so was the respite, at least as far as Nick was concerned, and he quickly slipped back into the mood of despondency.

He'd felt that now for quite a while. The despondency stayed with Nick like a particularly obstinate dark cloud overhead that was determined to stay with Nick despite the wonderfully (as Felix might have put it) hot balmy weather and abundant sun that blessed the Algarve, that beautiful southerly outpost of Europe.

The sunshine didn't cheer Nick up; indeed, on the contrary, it tended to emphasise to Nick how unhappy he was, because he felt that there in the sun he ought logically to be much happier. After all, didn't exhausted northern Europeans jet down to places like the Algarve to relax and unwind? Well, yes, that was undeniable; they did. But Nick felt anything but unwound. He felt purposeless and lonely and life felt strangely futile.

Along the shore to the easterly end of the beach at Luz there stands a pinnacle of volcanic rock at the base of an unusual and unique geological feature. A magnificent towering black volcanic cliff whose base is washed twice daily by the sea. Nick had got into the habit of walking to the foot of this rock and looking out at the sparkling sea, diamond-studded and dazzling where the sun struck it, rich shades of blue from the beach to the horizon. He found himself vaguely hoping that, somehow, the mighty ocean might in provide him with an answer to his problems.

Nowadays, looking out to sea from the magnificent setting of the rock was, Nick would often ruefully reflect, just about the most constructive thing he did. Not even his reading of Hemingway brought him much consolation nowadays, or at least not for the time being. He found it difficult to find anything to do that either interested him or managed to lift his mood, or anyone to talk to who really engaged him. He was even starting to find Chris's company trying, as he felt unable to communicate his dejection, which left him feeling even more inadequate and isolated. He took to spending much of his afternoon walking on the beach or wandering across the rocks, sitting for long periods, pondering his situation in an aimless and futile fashion.

Late one afternoon when Nick was sitting on the rock before dusk had fallen, he noticed a woman with blonde hair standing at the top of a cliff, maybe half a mile away and a couple of hundred feet above sea-level. He couldn't see her face at that distance, of course, but she reminded him of Marina. He smiled at the stupidity of the idea that it might be her.

But, thinking of Marina, his heart gave a jolt as he again realised how successfully he'd managed not to think about her; partly because her dumping him had of course been a direct consequence of his being kicked out of the army, and so much of his life since then had involved him being in Portugal and doing his best not to think of the past, and of his life in England. Also, she'd hurt him deeply in the completely unexpected manner she'd shown towards him the last time they spoke (and he assumed it *would* be the last time they spoke) and Nick did not have an especially forgiving nature when someone hurt him.

'Besides, why should I forgive the stupid woman anyway?' he thought, except that the moment he finished thinking this, he realised he'd said it aloud.

He watched the blonde woman as she took a couple of steps back from the top of the cliff, and as she vanished from his line of sight, he forced out of his mind.

He did he best to think of other things. He couldn't devise any answers to his current predicaments and didn't know where else to look. The only method of escape was his evenings in the bar. He'd even stopped going to other places and making friends with the passing players. He just wanted to sit alone and drink until he could no longer remember. This was a trick he had now most successfully mastered. The Mirage also extended him a line of credit that was most welcome, as his funds had continued to dwindle seemingly in proportion to his inability to deal with his situation.

The day after the tea party was Sunday. Once again he got up and squinted out through the curtains at the burning mid-afternoon sun. The warmth of the sunshine and the brilliance of the blue sky no longer gave him any pleasure; it might as well be a grey, grim drizzly February weekend in Windsor.

Nick left his ground-floor room by the gate in the patio. He walked around to the car park. He hoped he wouldn't meet anyone, for he certainly wasn't in the mood for conversation. He climbed into his car and slowly pulled out of Praia da Luz. He passed through Lagos, casting a disdainful glance at the determinedly cheery holidaymakers as they swarmed around the walled resort town like scavenger ants, desperately seeking a good time.

Thankfully, he headed away from the scene and put his foot down as he moved out onto the Route National 125. He hadn't been on the road for more than five minutes when, looking in the rear view mirror, he caught sight of a GNR Police jeep three or four cars behind. Nick smiled smugly, glancing at the speedometer, knowing that he had been keeping well within the speed limit and they had no reason to approach him.

Not me today, mate! You can pick on some other poor sod, Nick thought with satisfaction. There was no denying that the Porsche did stand out rather boldly, even though it was now less than pristine. The police jeep hung back in the traffic for some minutes. Then, when the flow allowed, it gradually caught up with him. Slowly pulling out beside Nick's car, the driver motioned for him to pull over.

Nick couldn't believe it.

'*What the hell is it now?*' he said to himself, angrily, as he coasted to a halt on the hard shoulder. This really was all he needed! He sat for a minute, rigidly holding the steering wheel, staring ahead trying to compose himself.

Then he turned and rolled down the window as the approaching officer took off his cap and lowered his face to the window. Nick could not help but close his eyes in dismay. Unfortunately, the bristling moustache and dark piercing eyes of Officer Manuel Braga were firmly imprinted on the inside of his eyelids.

'Any problems, Officer?' Nick asked calmly, refraining from using Braga's name as this might indicate a familiarity he was not desperate to remind him of.

He noticed with regret that, by the glint in the Officer's eye, he was fully aware of who Nick was. *Maybe it's time to try a different tack,* he thought.

'Nice to see you again, Officer Braga. I trust you're well? If there's anything I can do to help?' Nick left the question hanging, remembering too late that from previous experience, his antagonist didn't respond too encouragingly to the niceties of such occasions.

'Papers, if you please, Mr Trevelyan and step out of the car,' said the unsmiling officer. Nick decided to adopt the line of least resistance and say nothing more unless requested. He complied with Braga's wishes and waited silently to find out which particular game they were playing today.

'How long have you been in Portugal, Mr Trevelyan?' Officer Braga inquired, looking down at the registration documents that Nick had given him.

Too long, Nick felt like saying, but didn't. 'Five or six months,' he replied, trying to be as helpful as he could.

'Perhaps you could be more precise, Mr Trevelyan?' Braga intoned, coldly. Nick silently cursed his stupidity in allowing the man this obvious opening. He didn't like the way this conversation was going at all.

'Sorry, Officer, I came in the third week of April and it's now the end of September that would make it either five months and one week or,' he paused to calculate, 'twenty-two weeks.' *Half the length of the Sandhurst Commissioning Course*, Nick couldn't help thinking.

Officer Braga surprisingly smiled, seemingly satisfied with the response.

'I see, Mr Trevelyan, that you have a British MOT certificate.'

'Yeeess,' Nick replied, cautiously, as his mind started working furiously, and a cold feeling of anticipation started prickling his stomach.

'Which means, please correct me if I'm wrong, Mr Trevelyan, that this certificate became invalid, according to my calculations, precisely eight days ago,' Braga could now barely suppress the smile of satisfaction that twitched at the corners of his moustache curtained mouth. To assert his authority even more he stopped the proceedings to light a cigarette.

'Well, okay,' Nick replied curtly, 'I suppose you're right.' He couldn't think of any other way to reply. He'd been so demoralised recently that he could barely remember what month it was, let alone what date. All he knew was that he'd committed the ultimate stupidity of letting something as simple as getting a new MOT certificate pass him by.

Here, in the Algarve, there was no tolerant British bobby to tell him off for his misdemeanour and send him packing to get the discrepancy rectified as soon as possible at the local garage. No, there was only this mini Nazi, who Nick thought, probably slept in his highly polished black boots and chewed carpet tacks for breakfast.

Nick felt numb with resignation and succumbed to the remainder of his ordeal with a weary lack of resistance. Braga lectured him on the severity of the oversight, cited the laws that he had broken and invited Nick down to the station to further discuss this serious offence. He duly stepped into the police car with the smirking Manuel Braga, as the other officer had already radioed for a tow truck to come and fetch the Porsche, and he braced himself for the impending ordeal.

Braga, however, was determined to have his day, and took great pleasure in reading him the riot act. He impounded Nick's car until further notice, and imposed a fine on him that he wasn't going to be able to pay in three months of Sundays, let alone within the fourteen days that Braga gave him by law. Apparently the alternative was a possible custodial sentence as the car's insurance was now also invalid. Nick was not contesting the charge, there was no point. Impounding his beloved car seemed to be the unavoidable outcome.

Braga had strutted and preened before Nick, gloating at his little victory. He obviously felt annoyed at Nick's total lack of acknowledgement of his position. Apart from the perfunctory answers to any questions required to fill in paperwork, he stared unmovingly ahead. This was scant compensation for the anger and frustration that he felt. Two hours later, Nick returned to The Mirage by taxi. It was late afternoon and thankfully, no one seemed to be around to witness his humiliation. He sat on the bed staring blankly, registering nothing. He felt totally desensitized, bereft of any emotion.

As Nick, back in his studio apartment, reached out to smooth down some imaginary creases in the covers on the bed, he noticed that his right hand was trembling with anger and frustration.

At that moment, Nick felt his life was at its very lowest ebb.

Later that evening, sitting alone on the rock, the brilliant low rays of the early evening sun caused him to squint and create a shade for his eyes with his hand. He looked out towards the horizon.

He saw the tiny fleet of wooden fishing boats moving westwards from their cosy berths in Lagos harbour across the calm surface of the Atlantic Ocean to the fishing grounds of Cape St. Vincent thirty kilometres distant. The boats slid across the smooth surface of the water like a collection of snails across a pane of hammered glass.

As his eyes grew accustomed to the powerful light, he slowly realised that there were several flocks of seagulls lazily soaring on the invisible thermals, way, way out to sea, spiralling upwards as if they were on some unseen moving staircase. He left the rock and wandered along the beach, allowing the soft Atlantic waves to wash over his feet. Looking up at the huge dramatic wedge of volcanic rock, he made an estimate of its height as being two hundred and fifty, three hundred feet perhaps.

He picked up a small black pebble. He reflected that thousands of years ago it would have fallen from the black rocks that dominate the eastern end of the beach and for centuries it had rolled and tumbled in the surf. *A reminder of how insignificant our time here on this planet really is.* He wondered if other folk had such a place where they could go and contemplate their deepest, innermost feelings. He decided that most people seemed immune to depression or, in some cases oblivious to any feelings at all.

Nick had tried hard to lose himself and search for oblivion in the bottom of a bottle, as so many visitors to the Algarve had done before him. But drinking had not been the answer. 'Algarve Fever', Chris had called it.

No matter how much alcohol Nick consumed, he always retained a certain sense of awareness. He could never get so smashed that he lost touch with the reality of the world around him. He almost envied those hardened drunks who were at least able to push their minds beyond sensibility and sink into another world where personal pride had no meaning.

There appeared to be no way forward, no reason to continue. How could an end be brought to the mess that his existence had become? If only he could close this chapter of his life, wake up and start again with a clean sheet. When would the nightmare end? How do you give up? He churned the question over in his confused mind. To whom do you shout? *'Okay I give up! Stop the fight.'* Who is the referee in this unfair contest of life? Supposedly you could lie on the floor and admit defeat, but to whom? Sooner or later the floor would become cold, hard and uncomfortable and you would be forced to get up. What nonsense. *What crap's going through my mind,* he thought.

He knew it was time to make some tough decisions. Nick was till there on his seat on the sandstone rock that overlooked the mighty Atlantic Ocean, which spread before him.

He picked up a length of bamboo that had been left by the receding tide and returned to his seat on the rock. He drew a vertical line in the sand to list the pros and cons of his present forlorn state. Left of the line he set down the negatives; right of the line he listed the positives.

The problem was, he couldn't think of many positives.

The biggest negative was obvious, and he wrote the word in the sand: *money.* Or lack of it in his case. To go back to England and start again in some new career – assuming he could even find something he wanted to do and which wanted him – would, he knew, be a huge and in many respects, horrible challenge. Besides, this option posed its own problems, as apart from having a drained bank account, Nick felt certain his credit at The Mirage was slowly but surely turning toxic.

Chris couldn't have been more understanding, but Nick knew that the apartment where he was staying was supposed to earn money for the business and not act as a refuge for a waster, which was certainly how he now saw himself. The credit that enjoyed in the bar was a luxury that Nick did not intend to abuse.

On the positive side (he wrote *being here* in the sand), there was no denying that out here in the Algarve he was in a wonderful location. Endless days of sunshine, beaches, women and cheap wine but it just wasn't working for him.

What could he actually do if he decided to stay? Maybe work in a bar or restaurant but everyone knew that the wages were pitiful and the season only lasted for, at the most five months max.

Yes, there was a smattering of estate agents that catered for the British retirement element, that might be quite nice if he could persuade someone to take him on but there was a Portuguese estate agents' licence to be gained and for that you needed fluent Portuguese and Nick, like so many of the British residents, had learned no more than about six words in the local language.

Nick drew a big cross through the words *money* and *being here,* then stood up and headed back. He knew that he'd made his decision; he'd have to go back to England and attempt to create a new life for himself and the time that he had spent in the Algarve would be consigned to a chapter in his memoirs.

Assuming, that is, I ever get a life, which I'd want to write about, he thought.

16
Sport at the Airport

'Chris, I have to go back to England.'

Nick and Chris were starting a hearty English breakfast together one morning a few days later. They had three fried rashers of bacon each, three fried eggs, fried mushrooms and slices of a Portuguese blood sausage called *morcella* that Chris said was the closest he'd managed to find in Portugal to black pudding. They also had Heinz baked beans: a popular shop in Lagos sold these and many other brands that made expatriate Brits feel more at home there, 900 miles south of Land's End.

Chris nodded slowly. 'I got the feeling you might be wanting to go home before too long. The only surprise for me is how long it's taken you to decide.'

'Well, there've been lots of things about being out here on the Algarve I love.'

'And lots you don't,' put in Chris, with a wry smile.

'That too,' Nick agreed.

Chris shrugged. 'This is basically a retirement place, at least for the Brits. No British expat can easily live out here without first having had some career success and made some real money or a decent pension.'

'What about Felix?'

'I suppose he's a rare exception. But, you know, Nick, it's not so much that you need the money to enjoy living out here as that you can only really enjoy an Algarve retirement if you first have the feeling you've achieved something with your life in Blighty. Otherwise, one can have a sense here in the sun, and living the rather luxurious leisured life, which we do, that life has passed us by. I don't feel that myself, but I can understand why a young chap like you would.'

Nick nodded. 'Yes, you're right; I just don't feel I've done enough with my life yet. Listen, thanks for being the best host here I could ever have hoped for. You're a really great guy and

I know we'll meet again, but right now I do need to find some direction in my life, and I need to go away.'

'I understand. So, when will you be going?'

'In about a week, I thought.'

'Let's make it a good one then.'

It was. The week went by so fast, and so pleasurably (helped by Raffaela, a young Portuguese lady friend of Chris who was taking a few days off at The Mirage from her high-stress advertising industry job in Lisbon and found Nick delightful), that Nick was almost tempted to stay longer. But no, he'd made his decision, and when he made decisions he stuck by them.

But he enjoyed that week very much, just like a holidaymaker might, and he enjoyed his holiday romance, too.

At last the morning came when Nick finished his packing, including the dozen or so books he'd bought from Amazon while out there. He'd bought his own copies of *Fiesta* and *My Early Life*: those two books had meant so much to him in Portugal for him not to want to take them with him. Of course, he left the room's copies on their place on the bookshelf, and he hoped they might provide comfort and inspiration to some other British expat who found himself or herself in the room.

The Porsche now, due to Officer Braga, no longer being in Nick's possession, Chris drove Nick to Lagos station in his own car, a Japanese Jeep that ran on diesel.

'I'll miss you, Nick.'

'I'll miss you, Chris, and everything else out here. The sun, the women, the food, even Felix! And Raffaela, of course.'

'Yep, pity she had to go back to Lisbon yesterday.'

'Yes, yes it was.'

The two men shook hands in the car park at Lagos station.

'Send me a postcard, Nick.'

'A postcard?'

'Yes, please. Of England. Blighty. Home. I love it out here, but I miss her.'

Nick could tell from Chris's tone that he meant it.

Nick wondered whether every British expat in the Algarve secretly missed Britain, but didn't want to speak about that yearning.

He was pleased he hadn't told Chris how little money he had. Nick realised that one reason why he hadn't told Chris about his meagre finances was that he didn't want Chris to offer him a loan.

The ticket office at Lagos railway station is housed in a beautiful Portuguese colonial-style listed building that had a green tiled façade and intricate roof supported by skilfully designed slim cast iron pillars. Nick paid four euros for a ticket to take him on the hour-long journey by train from Lagos to Faro. Nick knew that, at Faro, he could get a taxi for the ten-minute drive to Faro international airport. His financial situation was desperate. He was down to his last euros and even getting back to England wasn't going to be easy.

Sitting on the platform waiting for the train to arrive, he had time to contemplate his future. The station was busy, for the most part with young back-packers who had made it this far having achieved the last stop off point for budget travel before continuing to make the requisite pilgrimage to Sagres and Cape St. Vincent, the most south westerly point of Europe. The majority of the backpackers based themselves in the ancient walled town of Lagos, which had, over the years, developed a vigorous nightlife.

The atmosphere in the station was animated and helped to lift Nick's flagging spirits. He didn't, after all, have much sense of playing the role of the returning hero. He had no idea what he was going home to or how he was going to achieve getting there; but he was glad to be going making the return journey.

Yet, waiting there at the station, he had a strange awareness that his sojourn on the Algarve had perhaps had a more positive impact on him than he'd thought. He'd read some great books (he somehow felt that the zest for life of Hemingway and the young Churchill were now forever part of his DNA) and he thought maybe he'd come to some accommodation with his inner demons. At any rate, he knew he was determined to put the past behind him and carve out a new life for himself. The time for self-pity had passed. Also, there was a new weapon in his armoury.

He could hypnotise people now pretty well at will and he was getting better at it every day.

He hadn't felt any need to hypnotise Raffaela, though. She'd been extremely enthusiastic about him of her own accord.

Lagos is as far west as what the Portuguese call the *Caminho de Ferro* ('Track of Iron') goes. Lagos railway-station is the last stop on the line. The Faro diesel train backed lazily into the station announcing its arrival with a deafening blast from its horn. An almost identical mix of back packers exited the carriages as those who got in to take their places.

Nick found a seat facing forward. The carriages were pretty basic, but this didn't worry him as the view from the window more than occupied his attention.

The train pulled slowly out of the station with rapidly increasing momentum to a slow rambling pace. It ran along the southern Algarve coast passing through quaint villages, golf courses and orange groves laden with fruit, their bright orange crop contrasting with the lush green of the leaves. The warm afternoon wind blowing in through the open windows smelled of fennel and other aromatic Atlantic herbs. Nick smiled as the train clanked along never exceeding fifty kilometres per hour. With every kilometre that passed he felt as if scraps of his own negativity were being shed and left behind in the colourful Algarve countryside.

As the train reached Faro station, Nick felt himself jolt back to reality. Soon he was jostling to grab a taxi to the airport. Finally, he joined forces with two young student nurses who agreed to share the fare with him. When they arrived, the airport was in pandemonium with package-holiday crowds milling around the concourse.

Time to come up with a plan. He just wanted to return to England – anywhere in England – and, from wherever he landed, on to London. Given the small amount of money he had left, he needed a miracle. He was carrying just a holdall so at least he was mobile, which was more than could be said for the hundreds of holidaymakers who were lugging huge suitcases, surf boards and enormous sets of golf clubs.

His attention was taken by a group of around twenty golfers all dressed in the same fire engine red polo shirts and black slacks. They were congregating around a bar, which was doing a brisk trade serving them local beer at an astounding rate. These middle-aged men were making the most of their final hours of freedom, using up the remains of their 'foreign' money and generally acting in the boisterous way of a group of Englishmen abroad.

The use of various versions of 'air golf clubs' – a direct relative of the 'air guitar' beloved of enthusiastic would-be rock stars the world over – was being demonstrated by members of the group, all connoisseurs of the invisible swing. The noise increased as more beer was poured down gullets. Nick chose a seat in the bar at a convenient distance and observed them.

The most noticeable member of the group was a man who, Nick guessed, must be the tour leader, judging from the way he was busying himself, checking that every member had got their passport and had tied on their baggage labels. The tour leader was clucking around his charges. Check-in was going to take longer than usual given that the golfers would need to take their bags of clubs to the oversize item counter once they had booked in.

The organiser moved away from the group and sat alone at a table away from the noise and gyrations of his club mates. This was Nick's opportunity; a plan was beginning to develop in his mind. Casually, he wandered over to the man who was now busy tying labels onto his own luggage. This was going to be the first real opportunity to put his hypnotic ability to the test.

'Looks as if your club mates have had a great time,' Nick said.

'Yes, played six of the best courses on the Algarve we 'ave,' he replied. 'Eight competitions and won 'em all.'

Nick went along with the conversation which was predominately a list of the club's achievements and specific members' merits. He and Nick were sitting a reasonable distance from any other people; conditions were good enough Nick judged to get this man under his influence.

'Right bunch of pros my lads are,' the organiser boasted.

'Yes, they sound it,' Nick said, with bogus enthusiasm. 'It's been great talking to you.' He pumped the man's hand enthusiastically. 'I wonder if there would be any chance of one of your team shirts. They look great and my friends would be hugely impressed.'

'Well, I shouldn't really,' the team organiser said, as if his naff club shirts were Picassos, 'but I suppose it wouldn't matter this once. I always carry a couple of spares just in case one of the lads has an accident. Can't give it to you out here though, one of them might see me and complain, but go into the men's room and I'll be there in a couple of minutes.'

Nick thanked the organiser once more and walked across to the nearby WC. Sure enough after three minutes the man came in and proudly presented Nick with a neatly wrapped bright red polo shirt before returning hurriedly back to his flock.

When Nick was alone, he tore open the wrapper and changed from his own shirt into the gaudy new one and then put on his lightweight jacket. Leaving the men's room, he circled around the loud golfers like a hungry hyena and found a good observation position. The 'lads' were herded to the check-in by the shepherd Nick had been talking to. The golfers all checked in and made their way to the oversize article desk where they guardedly handed over their beloved clubs to the care of the two airline employees, who unceremoniously dumped them onto a conveyor belt, leaving the owners bereft, like mothers leaving their children on their first day at school.

The organiser took charge again and corralled the group towards the departure lounge. Nick knew this was to be the first real hurdle to overcome. Taking off his jacket, and still carrying his walk-on cabin luggage, he tacked himself onto the end of the golf group, acting as if he was one of them. The organiser waved a bundle of boarding cards at the gate official and the red shirted group was ushered through en mass and from there on to the security check. Once inside Nick distanced himself from the crowd and watched. He was now in the departure lounge.

There was no way back and (Nick would have had to admit) no actual plan for going forward; it would just have to unfold. Now less like a hyena and more like a lion stalking a herd of wildebeest, Nick surveyed the group for a weakling. Sure enough one gradually appeared. A little potbellied man with huge ears was beginning to show serious signs of alcoholic wear and tear: a glazed look in his eyes, a white face, queasiness in his expression and general demeanour that betokened serious imminent chundering. The combined pace of the golf holiday with its continual drinking was, Nick could see, taking its inevitable effect on the little pot-bellied fellow.

The man drifted to the edge of the group and then headed off swiftly to the nearest gents. Nick followed; it didn't need a Sherlock Holmes to locate the little fellow in the WC as he was making a fine job of throwing up the contents of his potbelly. The door of the cubicle where he was doing this was wide open. It was obvious that the man in the cubicle, clinging to the porcelain toilet like a survivor from a shipwreck hanging onto a piece of wreckage, was going nowhere.

Nick hurried out of the men's room. The main group moved off through passport control still playing on their air golf clubs and fortified with Super Bock beer, totally oblivious of their missing comrade. Nick knew that his next move was crucially all about timing.

The airport tannoy system was calling for the last remaining passenger 'Mr Canton' on the flight to Luton to go to the departure gates. Nick ran towards the departure desk waving his passport, the courtesy bus was about to close its doors and the desk staff waved him through, confident that the red-shirted golf team were all accounted for.

Nick scrambled onto the bus which would take them to the aircraft much to the annoyance of the other passengers who had been kept waiting in the crowded bus.

Once on board the plane, Nick settled himself into a seat at the back of the partially full plane, quickly changing back into his own shirt. He was on his way to Luton and from there, to a new life. He relaxed, wondering if Mr Canton had surfaced yet, but not really caring much either way.

17
Vaulting Ambition

Back in London, within a week Nick had rented a pretty minimal bed-sit in North Kensington, a somewhat less than slick part of the capital, but that didn't matter to Nick. He was just glad to be back in Britain. He'd discovered a few hundred pounds in a building society account he'd forgotten about, but he didn't need to pay his deposit and rent, for he successfully managed to hypnotise his already somewhat vague landlady into believing that he'd paid the deposit, and six months' rent, already. This was a mercenary action, which he wasn't happy about but was borne out of near financial desperation and he had every intention of rectifying the matter as soon as his financial situation improved.

Nick felt just very much back in action and full of energy, life and motivation. He realised that he'd stayed too long in the Algarve. He felt it wasn't only that Chris was right about the Algarve being a place for people who'd already made their fortune, but also that ultimately living for too long in a region devoted to retirement and leisure, was not the best place for a young man itching to make his way in the world.

Nick welcome the feeling of again being in control of his own destiny as a man dying of thirst welcomes a glass of ice-cold lemonade.

His chance meeting with Chris's friend Tom Holland, while languishing in the Algarve had given Nick the inspiration for an idea. Armed with his newly acquired hypnosis skill, which he had now put to the test many times and thought he had pretty much perfected, he telephoned Tom and arranged for a conducted tour of the London Silver Vaults in Chancery Lane that Tom had promised in The Mirage.

Tom was surprised and delighted to hear from Nick and, true to his word, arranged a date to meet. Nick's financial situation was far from healthy but making use of his hypnotic skills did allow him to negotiate his financial affairs with a definite advantage without actually stealing from anybody. Outgoings such as his rent were delayed and his tab at the local convenience store became extended well past the point that would have been the norm.

He'd managed to accost the store manager at the back of the shop, near the shelves containing inspiring consumer products such as Brillo pads, J-cloths and Domestos and convince the store manager, using hypnosis, that he had deposited five hundred pounds with the store manager, to be spent as Nick chose.

Nick knew, though, that to the outside world he needed to create the impression of being a successful young man. He had a respectable wardrobe of civilian clothes left over from his days as an army officer. He'd left these clothes at his parents' house in Windsor, and had picked the clothes up when he went to see his parents not long after returning to England. Annabelle and George were delighted to see their tanned son, who assured them that his stay in the Algarve had given him 'lots of new contacts' and that he soon intended to start working in the 'precious metals business'. *Truer words were never spoken*, thought Nick. His parents still assumed he was going out with Marina.

'How is she?' his mum asked.

'Oh, she's fine,' said Nick.

He assumed that was true, so he didn't feel he was telling a complete lie to his mother.

Now, in his North Kensington bedsit, Nick had suits, tweeds, regimental ties, and even (a gift from Marina) a good-quality Crombie overcoat, which sported a moleskin collar. To complement the ensemble he added a silk scarf as a finishing touch.

As Nick left his bed-sit, he checked his appearance in the full-length mirror. He liked what he saw; he would easily pass as acceptable in the higher echelons of London society. At any rate, he was very aware of being a far cry from the miserable wreck that he had descended to at the end of his months in the Algarve.

The meeting with Tom Holland went well; first he took Nick to lunch at a rather pleasant little bistro in a side street off Holborn where they reminisced about their time in southern Portugal.

Tom remarked that Nick's appearance had altered radically from the laid back look that he knew from the Algarve. Nick explained that he had been enjoying a well-earned rest from the pressures of military life when they had first met which Tom said he completely understood.

Tom then proudly gave Nick a full tour of the impressive subterranean vaults, which were on Chancery Lane, not far from where that famous London street met Holborn.

Nick was fascinated by the vaults, which were buried deep under London in a section of the London Underground that had been built but never used for trains. Tom proudly gave Nick a conducted tour of the world famous Silver Vaults introducing him to some of the dealers who traded there. Tom gave Nick a pamphlet which gave a brief history of the Vaults and which he read in detail.

The Chancery Lane Safe Deposit Company opened in 1885 utilising London Underground tube tunnels, which were built but never used for trains. The tunnels were converted into a safety deposit vaults, renting security boxes at that time, mainly to London's wealthy elite in order to safeguard their household silver, jewellery and personal documents.

Entrance to the building was gained by special arrangement and the strong rooms were guarded day and night. In fact, it remains the proud boast of the Safe Deposit that there had never been a robbery within its precincts. The business remained the same for several years, but with many of the original clientele being replaced by silver dealers who required secure premises for their burgeoning stocks. This need was made more pressing by the outbreak of the Second World War.

As knowledge of the Vaults began to spread, they became a 'must' for visitors from overseas seeking quality silver at dealers' prices. The rapid expansion of this business led to many more dealers renting strong rooms within the, by now renowned London Silver Vaults, and it had been in its present format since 1953 when it was extended after the completion of rebuilding necessary to repair bomb damage sustained in the London blitz.

Behind the huge safe doors and within its vaulted walls, it was possible, Nick soon realised, to find anything from a champagne swizzle stick to a full size silver armchair. Although English silver predominated, there were specialists who deal in silver from every corner of the world. In fact, every period and every style was catered for, in this unique setting.

The London Silver Vaults, Nick gathered from the pamphlet, was 'an unusual, interesting and exciting place to explore and many regular visitors make it their first stop when arriving in the city.' It was the finest centre for silver in the world today and to quote a famous collector mentioned in the pamphlet 'If you can't find it in the Chancery Lane Vaults, you can't find it anywhere.'

Tom Holland had made sure that Nick was given the full five-star treatments. The tour was detailed and thorough; this was a man who was extremely proud of the establishment that he was in charge of.

Nick gathered from his visit that the London Silver Vault was, in fact, only part of the overall safety deposit vault. Tom showed Nick the biggest stronghold door that he had ever seen which they walked through and into the second part of the underground building. Fifty per cent of the subterranean edifice was designed as a huge ultra-high security safe where private articles could be stored.

During the tour he'd noticed that there were private, secure booths where clients could spend time with the contents of their boxes, unhindered by cameras or company. Each booth was furnished with a leather-topped table and two chairs. These areas were completely private, away from the CCTV cameras, which bristled at every corner although they were still within the high security protection of the vault.

Obviously, security was at the highest level but the client's privacy was also vital. The contents of the safety deposit boxes were of no particular importance to the organisation that ran the vaults, whereas their overall security was paramount.

Nick couldn't, of course, see the actual clients poring over the contents of their boxes; it was a calculated guess that gemstones were the main treasure secreted away down here. The majority of other clients that he glimpsed seemed, from their distinctive attire of black coats and black hats that they wore even now, in the height of summer, Jewish diamond merchants. Hatton Garden, where so many shops that sold diamonds were clustered, was only a short walk away, on the opposite side of Holborn.

Nick could tell that, while the vaults were around 130 years old, technology was the key word in this establishment. The application of the latest equipment had reduced the need for employees, an observation that Nick fielded to Tom.

'Just the six of us, Nick. That's all we require to keep this place safe and sound,' Tom expounded. 'Amazing, isn't it?'

The London Silver Vaults, Nick gathered, were open to the general public in contrast to London Safety Deposit Vaults, which were under strict security. The building was split into two underground sections. There was a staircase going down, at the foot of which, through a door on the left, were the London Silver Vaults, which was open to the public. A door on the right led to the London Safety Deposit Vaults, another ultra-secure vault, which did not allow public access.

There were two guards in reception, both male and ex-police or military service personnel.

Nick realised that the only other employee that he needed to consider was the cleaner. Due to the sensitivity of the safety deposit vaults, cleaning was not something that could be undertaken by just anyone. The vaults cleaner was a retired Warrant Officer from the Scots Guards but again there was little chance that he could compromise Nick's plans as his working hours were outside business hours.

Nick was certain he would need to devise an infallible strategy, which was slowly taking shape in his mind as the meeting progressed. The three key players in his plan were

Tom and the two inner guards, whom he was about to meet. Nick made his opening gambit.

'Tom, I've been searching for a building with facilities similar to those you have here,' Nick enthused. 'It's actually really lucky for me that we met. I need just such a place as this to keep my stamp collection.'

Nick explained that he had inherited an extraordinary collection of rare stamps from his late grandfather. 'It even includes one of the beautiful, red, world-famous Post Office Mauritius stamps, with a one-penny face value but a value in the stamp world estimated at more than a million pounds in the current market. Only five hundred were printed, you see, and hardly any survive.'

Nick knew that a fiction is all the more believable the more detailed you make it.

Tom, who just nodded blankly, was Nick guessed, obviously not a frequent visitor to globally renowned stamp dealer Stanley Gibbons on the Strand. 'At the moment my stamp collection's in my bank, Coutts,' Nick went on. 'Getting access is a tiresome affair. There's a lot of work necessary to categorise and catalogue the collection before I can ever think of selling it – if indeed I ever do. It's going to take months. My grandfather was an exceedingly keen collector from the time he was a small boy until his death at the age of eighty-two. I need somewhere to store the collection safely and where I can come and go and catalogue it.'

Tom smiled. 'Nick, I'm delighted that we can offer you the conditions that you are looking for. And as an additional bonus we will be able to go for a pint occasionally and continue our chats from the old days in The Mirage.' Tom sounded truly happy at the prospect of having Nick around; Nick guessed that being head of the vaults was a fairly lonely life, with nothing but safety deposit boxed and occasional secretive wealthy clients for company.

At the end of the tour Tom took him to his office and made coffee for them both.

'Take a look at these,' offered Tom, proudly opening one of a dozen leather bound ledgers, which were housed in a cast-iron Victorian bookcase. Nick could see that they were all meticulously hand written.

'Of course it's all computerised now,' said Tom, 'but these ledgers go back to 1885.'

The detail in the ledgers was interesting with a large percentage of the names obviously those of wealthy European families. The names Rothschild, Lazard and Salomon cropped up several times.

Nick's brain, always pretty active anyway, started working overtime. Tom continued his explanation enthusiastically.

'When a box hasn't been opened for sixty-five years and the key holder can't be traced, I have the legal authority to break into the box. We call this 'Drilling.' Of course apart from the locksmith there's an official presence from the City of London Police and an official from the court when the box is officially opened. You wouldn't believe what we find in some of them.'

To say that this remark whetted Nick's appetite was to put things very mildly.

'What happens to the contents after that?' queried Nick.

'They all become property of the court.'

As the information of the previous hour percolated into Nick's brain, the possibilities of infiltrating the security system and gradually removing items began to formulate into a more detailed plan. His methodical mind noted every detail with keen interest.

Why would someone keep items locked away in a high security vault? In the case of the everyday movement of the diamond dealers it was easily explained, high security in close proximity to Hatton Garden. Yet, as Tom explained, this only accounted for about twenty-five per cent of the clients. The majority of the boxes contained objects, which were valuable but needed to be hidden for a variety of reasons.

Tom had admitted that there were probably all sorts of clandestine reasons for using the Vaults but the client's anonymity was always protected. The conversation continued in a relaxed manner and he began to confide in Nick a little.

'The visually most impressive item is the actual vault door. It's a seven and half ton circular giant made by John Taylor Company who built the doors for the Bank of England and many more.'

Nick had become chillingly proficient in hypnosis, honing the skill by reading and researching everything on the subject that he could get his hands on. The fact that his eyes were of different colours had never been something that Nick had paid much attention to; he had in the past tended to forget about the non-matching colours unless someone pointed them out to him. But he'd already realised that it gave him the great advantage of concentrating the subject's attention directly on his eyes.

Using hypnosis had become a tool necessary for his survival over the past months and he could now put someone under quickly and with relative confidence. Sitting alone in Tom's office gave him the perfect opportunity to get to work on Tom.

In addition to reading the book on hypnosis, which he had discovered at Quinta Da Felicidade some months before, Nick had refined his knowledge by practising at every suitable opportunity. A favourite book of Nick's by Lisa Selvidge had a particularly good explanation of how the mind works:

"The subconscious is by far the larger part of the mind. Our subconscious controls much more than just our organs, it controls our entire being. It is thought that our minds are five per cent conscious and 95 per cent subconscious. Consider what we do automatically every day without thinking. Walking, breathing, seeing, hearing, smelling, we don't have to think about these things because our subconscious is dealing with it all. It just happens subconsciously. We are uncontrollably in control of our subconscious. Psychologists and others have performed numerous experiments on people who are in a hypnotic trance. This research shows clearly that the subconscious mind does not make the selections and comparisons that are necessary for the reasoning process. Our subconscious mind will accept any suggestion, no matter how false. Having once accepted the suggestion, it responds according to the nature of the suggestion given. "

An interesting and useful tool, which Nick had perfected, was the use of a 'trigger' word. This is a word that is embedded into the subconscious of the person being hypnotised.

The mention of the trigger word would immediately put the subject into a trance from where auto-suggestive orders could be implanted. This he used on Tom. As soon as the two of them were comfortable in his office and Nick was sure that there would be no sudden interruptions, he began to hypnotise him.

The trigger word for Tom was, Nick decided, to be 'Excalibur.' It might have been heard by the subject in all manner of situations but only from his mouth would the word 'Excalibur' evoke the required effect. He embedded the trigger word and in addition gave the orders to which Tom was to react. Fortunately, he was very receptive to hypnosis. Nick then brought him out of the trance and continued with the normal conversation.

'Okay, Nick,' Tom focussed on the moment as if he had just shaken himself out of a deep daydream, of which he was entirely unaware, 'let's get on with filling in the application.'

This went well until they got to the question of Nick's bank account. He hadn't planned for that, '*Hell*'. The details of his bank account would never stand up to scrutiny given the way the past year had evolved. There was a pregnant pause and a feeling of panic began to form in his mind. Tom's pen was poised to add the banking details to the application form; Nick had to do some fast thinking. 'Excalibur!' Tom's head dropped onto his chest. Although Nick had become proficient in his newly acquired skill, nevertheless he was still wary of using it as it was all so new to him.

'Tom, I'm going to give you my bank details.' Nick inserted the required fictitious details into Tom's subconscious and brought him out of the trance. There was a pause as Tom collected his thoughts.

'So, that's that, Nick. Everything appears to be in order.' He closed the completed folder. The application was accepted.

The account number and contract passed to Nick. He explained to Tom that he would be bringing his treasured stamp collection for safekeeping in one week's time. Tom said that the timing was perfect and a box and key would be waiting. The first phase of Nick's plan was successfully in place.

On the way home on the underground, Nick had time to contemplate what he was getting into. He figured that he had nothing to lose. It felt as if he was getting back at the Establishment, who in Nick's mind were responsible for his being in the situation he now found himself.

Nick had always been aware of this, but his reading of Hemingway and – ironically – Churchill, had absolutely convinced him that, if you don't strive successfully to make your own way in the world, the world will have no hesitation at all in treading down on you. *You have to make your own way in the world that's true to you,* Nick thought, *and you need to transform resentment into focused action.*

Nick was quite sure now that he was transforming his resentment of Wrath-Bonham and all that the aristocratic meathead stood for, into focused action.

His plan was only to open boxes which had been unattended for sixty-five years or more, meaning that its owners, unless they'd been given ownership of the contents when they were single-digit children, were either dead or so ancient they would be fairly soon.

Either way, he didn't imagine anyone would miss what he was planning to take. After all, he reasoned, if you have title to something valuable but haven't been to inspect it for more than sixty-five years, the chances are that, even if you are still alive, you've forgotten about your possessions and aren't likely to miss them.

Nick also recalled a robbery some years earlier in London when thieves had broken into a security vault. They spent the weekend working their way through half of the safety deposit boxes before they ran out of time. Later when the robbery was discovered and the clients had been contacted, no complaints were made as everything in there was clandestine and there was also never an official list compiled of what had gone missing.

The only doubt, which was nagging at him was about Tom. He was a decent man and a friend. How would this affect him? Nick had no intention of dragging him down or causing him any harm. Nick decided, as an officer and gentleman, that should he ever be caught he would confess and explain how he'd pulled off the robbery. That way, Tom could not be implicated.

After much thought, Nick decided to go ahead with his plan.

18
The Plan

The next day was a Saturday. Nick got up early and headed out of London until he reached Langley, a few miles west of Heathrow. From living in Windsor, he remembered that there was a car boot sale every Saturday on the outskirts of Langley village. He soon found what he was looking for, and a delighted stallholder willingly took his tenner in exchange for six tattered leather-bound photo albums. The albums looked at least fifty years old. Any photos inside had long been taken out and quite a few pages still had hinges on them which Nick carefully removed after he left the boot fair. Once the hinges were gone, Nick had what looked not unlike six old stamp albums, or at least would once he'd put his cheap stamps into them.

He navigated his way via public transport to the centre of London then on to the Strand and the famous stamp dealer shop of Stanley Gibbons. There, he bought twenty cheap starter packs of mixed world stamps containing used and mint ones, a large magnifying glass with a stand, a carton of stamp hinges for the used stamps and little cellophane pockets called Hawid strips for the mint ones. He also bought three stamp tweezers, two A4 note pads and an illustrated colour booklet entitled *Great Stamps of the World,* which contained some colour illustrations of the famous, indeed fabled, Mauritius one-penny red and two-penny blue stamps. He paid in cash for everything and returned to his apartment in north London.

Once he'd put his stamps into the albums the collection looked strangely credible. He was careful to devote an entire page to 'his' Mauritius stamp, an illustration of which he carefully cut out from the booklet and mounted in a Hawid strip that he cut to size. It was an illustration of a used stamp, but this was hardly a stamp which, if it were real, anybody would stick in with a hinge and risk getting glue on the back of it.

He inspected his handiwork; the one-penny red Mauritius stamp looked eerily convincing in its elegant mount. As for the albums, they had the appearance of a collection assembled over many decades. It would require scrutiny by a keen collector to discover that the stamps were virtually worthless. He had done a good job but it was for his own benefit, rather a stage prop than a collector's piece. After all who was going to examine them?

Precisely one week later, as arranged, Nick returned to Chancery Lane. He was greeted by Tom, who'd finalised all of the required paperwork and ceremoniously handed Nick the key to his own personal security box.

Together they went through the security measures and entered one of the private booths. Over his shoulder Nick carried a finely tooled leather Victorian gentleman's holdall which was about the size of a large traditional doctor's instrument bag. He had bought the holdall in a high quality leather goods shop in Windsor. It wasn't cheap and he worried about the cost but felt that it was a necessary prop to complete his portrayal of a well-to-do young man. The bag contained the stamp collection plus some other items he had purchased from W.H. Smith's. In addition he had two pairs of white cotton gloves bought from a small shop in Windsor dedicated to the masonic community. Nick knew from his army days, from fellow officers who were masons that masonic white gloves were a masonic requirement and they added the final touch to an elaborate fraud.

Tom accompanied Nick to the client's quiet area assisting him to settle in. He personally fussed around ensuring that he had everything that he needed.

Tom's assistant at the vault was a lady called Veronica, whose official title was Custodian.

Veronica was, Nick supposed, in her late forties. She was blonde, though Nick suspected that her blondeness was the result of Boots rather than birth. She was a little overweight. She told him she commuted to work each day from Basildon. Indeed, the problems of commuting were one of her major conversational themes, as was the awfulness of the English weather. Even when the sun had shone all day like a furnace fire, if there'd been a little light drizzle for about three minutes in the afternoon, Veronica would still give her opinion that the weather was 'bloody awful.'

Nick thought Veronica's intolerant attitude towards the weather somewhat inexplicable anyway, as she spent most of her working day inside the windowless reception of the Vaults.

Veronica brought out Nick's safety deposit box on a trolley. Nick was especially polite, courteous and friendly to her. He needed her on his side.

In the privacy of one of the private booths, Nick opened his safety deposit box and carefully arranged his spurious stamp collection inside. Once he'd done so, he pressed the buzzer to indicate that he was ready.

He explained to Tom and Veronica that he'd be coming in about three times a week to work on his collection. Tom appeared duly impressed and content that he had settled Nick in nicely.

On each subsequent visit Veronica brought him his box on her trolley. Nick soon formed a friendly rapport with her. Veronica was, beyond any doubt at all, a rather disillusioned person. She was married to a man who, according to her, was interested in cricket, snooker, beer and Indian take-always, in that order. If Veronica featured on his list of priorities at all, which judging from what she said about him Nick doubted, it must have been very low down the list. But Veronica, for all her grievances about her life, became relaxed in Nick's company and even tried a little light flirting.

'Ooh, Nicholas you do have lovely eyes, differently coloured just like that David Bowie. And I love your tan, too.'

Nick knew that Veronica was right about this, at least. David Bowie's eyes were renowned for being different colours. As for the tan Nick had inevitably acquired in the Algarve, he'd grown so used to it that he hardly thought of it any more but it was rapidly fading.

But he did know that his plan would only work if he proceeded slowly and became established and accepted at the Vaults, and that meant gallantly flirting with Veronica in turn.

'Your eyes are pretty cute too, V.'

'Ooh, Nicholas, you do say all the right things.'

Nick noticed over the following week quite a few of the Vaults' clients made use of the private booth facility. Though each cubicle was completely independent, he knew that he would have to proceed carefully. In the second week he decided that the time was right for him to try his powers of hypnosis on Veronica. He needed to put her under and embed a trigger word into her subconscious.

Veronica turned out to be the person most susceptible to hypnotism that Nick had encountered so far. Her major vice was that she was a heavy smoker. To brighten up his visits, Nick decided to attempt a standard hypnotic procedure on Veronica. He implanted the desire to give up smoking into her subconscious. This paved the way to a new dialogue between the two of them. At every meeting he would politely ask if all was well and added a remark to see if the smoking habit had disappeared. Sure enough she kicked the habit much to her own amazement. Her trigger word was installed and ready to be called upon when needed.

Veronica had a desk at the entrance to the Vault. It was her duty to coordinate and log everything that happened at reception. When given the client's number she could electronically open the rack in the zone where the box was located. The client could then take their box from the rack and open it in the private room in complete seclusion.

Sitting – literally – above Veronica was Stanley, the third member of the Vaults inner security team. He was positioned on a raised podium, which backed onto the end wall of the vault and was surrounded by glass at the front. From this vantage point he could observe everything that happened on the floor of the vault. The job that he did must have been boring in the extreme. His brief was to watch all of the comings and goings within the vault.

Nick could see the logic in the method. Stanley represented the human element and was not susceptible to the foibles that computers and electrical gizmos are prone to. It was a clever, if antiquated additional human system, but it was efficient and

Nick knew he would need to think deeply about how to get around it. The observation cubicle bristled with gadgetry enabling Stanley to shut down the complex in a nanosecond if something was out of the ordinary.

Were all the equipment to fail, there was Stanley, to take over the situation manually. Anything suspicious and he could automatically set off the alarms and close down the system. Tom had said that as the Vaults posed a high security risk there were pre-determined procedures and codes in place with the police. Stanley, naturally enough, had direct lines to the City of London Police with codes that could start an automatic course of action in seconds. As far as Nick was concerned, Stanley was the next hurdle for him to deal with.

Week three and Nick decided that Veronica was well and truly prepared – the time was right to concentrate his attention on Stanley. Nick worked late on his collection until the Vault was about to close and, as they were leaving the building together, he invited Stanley to have a drink at a local pub.

The closest pub to the London Silver Vaults is the Knights Templar, also in Chancery Lane. Their conversation covered several subjects but usually returned to football, Stanley's favourite subject.

It took little time for Nick to have Stanley under his influence and get the trigger word embedded, although he was far more difficult than Veronica and was the type of man whose eyes were always darting about the room, never settling, which was probably why he was the right man for the job that he did.

Nick and Stanley were sitting in a quiet corner of the pub; nobody was paying them any attention until Nick noticed Veronica arrive at the saloon bar. He knew he needed to work quickly to bring Stanley out of his trance before Veronica spotted them, came over and noticed something unusual. By the time she had arrived and sat down, Nick had completed the reverse countdown and Stanley was back with them again.

'What's up, Stanley? You look a bit put out – Fulham lost again?' asked Veronica as she joined them at their table.

'No … no, I'm just contemplating another pint,' Stanley replied looking a little confused, but – Nick was gratified to see – obviously completely unaware that he'd been under a different kind of influence.

Two weeks passed. One sunny and pleasant Monday afternoon with the sort of weather that not even Veronica would have been likely to complain about, Nick arrived at the Vaults. He felt nervous. He had thought about filling a hip flask with Famous Grouse (one part of Scotland his father had never explored, at least not so far) to help his nerves but knew that this wasn't the answer. There was still time to walk away and nobody would know what he had been planning to do. *Keep going!* He told himself, *it'll be ok. Just keep moving forward.* Having passed through reception, Nick stopped by for his regular chat with Tom in his office down a short corridor in the opposite direction to where the private inspection rooms were. Tom was chipper after having a glorious weekend pottering around in the garden and washing the car. The coffee was brewed in what was now becoming something of a ritual.

Tom was always eager to chat and reduce the boredom of his day. When Nick thought that the time was right and Tom was sufficiently relaxed, he gave him the trigger word and he was again at his command. Tom sat silently in his chair. Nick took the office phones off their cradles and picked up Tom's mobile, which was on the desk. Luck was with him. It was a model that he knew, so he quickly turned the ring tone to silent.

Nick took the opportunity to study the ledgers. He discovered that the oldest boxes had not been opened for a long time and were approaching their overdue period. Finding his way through the ledgers for the first time took longer than expected, next time he would be able to do it more quickly. Making a list of the numbers of the ten oldest boxes, Nick placed the paper in his pocket.

A final check of the room to be sure that everything was in place and then he put the phones back as they had been. Now he could gently wake Tom from his trance. As Nick reached the end of his reversed countdown the office phone sprang into life. From the peaceful ambience that had existed in the room the phone sounded much louder than usual, causing Nick to jump slightly and Tom to look startled. Tom answered the phone falteringly, looking around the room in bewilderment. Slowly he regained his composure. He made some obscure reference to daydreaming and finished his coffee.

Fortunately, Tom was completely unaware of what had happened and continued to be oblivious. They talked some more and then Tom telephoned Veronica on the internal system to tell her that Nick was on his way. Nick thanked him for the coffee and went down into the private cubicle he used, the second on the left. There were eight private rooms altogether.

When Veronica brought his box to the privacy of the booth she stopped to chat as usual, discussing the events that were making the news, and of course the weather. Once he felt comfortable that the time was right, Nick gave her the trigger word and was relieved when she fell directly into the pre-ordained trance. Slowly and concisely he instructed Veronica to bring the first of the boxes from the list that he had in his pocket. Without hesitation she did as requested then returned to her desk, leaving him alone. To Stanley everything seemed to appear quite normal.

Box 178 – Nick chose it because it was the first on the list that Nick had taken from Tom's office – was a little smaller than the box in which Nick had stowed away his fabulously non-valuable stamp collection. Nick already knew that there was a range of sizes of the boxes, with correspondingly different prices.

Much of the black paint from Box 178 had been worn away so that where the steel was exposed there was a light coating of rust. It looked as if it had been well used at some point in its existence but now with a liberal coating of dust it had a neglected look about it.

Nick sat looking at the metal box in front of him for some time, waiting for the alarms to sound and the closedown procedure to be initiated, trapping him inside the vault – a culprit, caught red handed. Three minutes passed. He decided that he had to continue – there was no going back now.

One problem he needed to overcome was the removal of the owner's padlock. They were only standard, low-priced affairs and some could be picked quite easily but the locks were old and he needed a more reliable method of removing them.

To this end he had purchased a pair of short-handled bolt cutters, which just fitted into his Victorian holdall. On one of his earlier visits he had taken the bolt croppers and packed them into his security box. On a following visit he took six new padlocks of the same size as those used in the Vaults. His preparations were complete.

A disadvantage of encouraging Veronica to be so friendly was that she was occasionally prone to peeking in to see how he was faring, and often asked if she could come in. But Nick had his back towards the security camera while he did what he was doing, and he knew that if Veronica did knock, he could ask her to wait for a few moments before entering, and in those few moments he knew he could easily use the holdall to conceal what he was doing.

Apart from this Nick was quite at liberty to take his time removing the padlock, Nick did know that any sudden unexplained noise would be noticeable and might alert Stanley.

Nick placed the jaws of the bolt cutters over the padlock's steel hasp and draped his overcoat over the cutters hoping to deaden any sudden noise. Long-handled cutters, Nick knew, would have cut through the steel more easily, but in order to fit into his holdall and then the box, he had to compromise with a more compact model. It took a lot of pressure to sever the lock. His arms were shaking with the effort. The padlock finally gave way with a sharp metallic snap. The box was open! He quickly returned the bolt croppers to his box and covered them with papers and albums. The now useless padlock he threw into his holdall. The time had come to look into the box and reveal its secrets.

Disappointment!

The box was full of old comics lovingly wrapped in tissue paper. All the preparation and planning – for this! He sat back in the chair and thought hard, and then an idea came to him. He knew that this box had remained unopened for almost seven decades, making the comics in fact of some value.

He transferred the contents of the box to his holdall. Upon uncovering the bottom of the box his eye fell upon two large manila envelopes. Opening the first envelope, he scattered the contents onto the table. There was a pile of stamps, which he estimated must have numbered about one hundred. The second envelope contained what looked to Nick's fairly unpractised eye like a complete set of Third Reich bank notes from the period spanning the Second World War.

These were stuffed into the holdall with the comics, while the stamps were added to the albums. Now he really did have a valuable collection. Nick tidied up the table and snapped one of his new padlocks on the plundered box. Making a final check to see that everything looked good, he called for Veronica using the call button, which was located at the entrance to the booth. While she wasn't needed, Veronica sat at her desk close to the vault entrance, just inside the huge steel door. She arrived at his booth.

'All done for today, Nick?'

'Yes, that's enough for one day. Come and sit down for a minute.'

Veronica, never guilty of missing an opportunity to while some time away from her boring job and flirt a little, she sat down on the seat opposite. Nick let her settle down and then uttered the embedded trigger word. Veronica's head dropped onto her chest.

'Veronica, you'll take Box 178 back to its place in the racking, lock the rack and return here.' His orders were calm and precise. Veronica placed the now slightly lighter box onto her trolley and did as she was instructed. When she came back Nick told her to sit down and she obediently obeyed.

'Veronica, when I wake you up, all your memory of taking box 178 will have disappeared. You will remember nothing of bringing the box to me or of returning it to its location.' Counting backwards from six, Nick returned Veronica to her normal state of consciousness.

'What was I saying, Nick?' queried Veronica with a vacant look on her face, 'I've forgotten what we were talking about.'

'You were telling me about giving up the vile weed,' he smiled.

'Ah yes, now I remember. I can't understand it, just don't fancy a fag anymore! Bit of a pity really – don't know what to do with me 'ands these days.' Nick slung the strap of his holdall over his shoulder and said his goodbyes. He waved to Stanley in his goldfish aquarium. He had seen nothing that looked remotely suspicious and waved back.

'See you on Wednesday!' Nick called back as he left the Vaults.

He walked out of the front door of the building expecting to be stopped by a security guard or policeman at any moment, but nothing happened. He walked on into Chancery Lane and was swept along with the stampede of commuters returning home. It was a cool evening and he was aware that he must have been sweating due to being worried whilst inside the Vaults and the contrasting chill air made him shiver.

He needed a drink but was careful not to choose a pub where Stanley or Veronica might wander in. He turned right into Rolls Passage and slipped into the Blue Anchor pub. Sitting at the busy bar he was able to reflect upon the events of the afternoon. His first reaction had been severe disappointment at discovering the comics but the real triumph was that he had successfully pulled off what was to be the first of many such sorties to the London Safety Deposit Vaults.

The beauty of his plan was that the owners of the boxes that he intended systematically to plunder were indeed almost certainly dead, so nobody was going to complain and even when the time came for the boxes to be officially opened, if they were found to be empty, who cared.

If this isn't the perfect crime, Nick thought, *what is?*

19
Payday

The next day Nick set to work converting the spoils of the previous day's work into hard cash.

He found dozens of websites dedicated to collectors of comics and plenty of dealers scouring the net for bargains.

Three hours of checking out these sites revealed that the comics had, conservatively, a value of about £4,000, and there were still the bank notes and the stamps.

By now Nick knew a great deal about security at the Vaults.

He'd learned, partly from Tom, partly from Veronica, partly from doing his own research and snooping about, that in order to access the contents of a security deposit box there were three stages to be passed. The vault itself was below ground, the only entrance being a huge circular door with all the latest high-tech devices fitted. This represented ninety-five per cent of the security protection and was, Nick knew, virtually impregnable. The boxes themselves were housed in aisles according to size. The most popular and more numerous were the smaller boxes. All the boxes were numbered. Each one was constructed from light gauge mild steel painted black with a hasp and clasp, secured with a standard padlock which the box owner supplies. The keys to this padlock were held only by the client.

Each of the boxes slid into a wall-mounted rack, which was, in turn, locked. It was Veronica's job to unlock the particular rack section electronically and allow the clients to carry the box to a booth where they could add, remove or work on the contents, as they desired.

The larger boxes were placed on a trolley, which Veronica steered around the vault with the dexterity of a ballroom dancer. With prior arrangement, when a client who wished to spend time working with the contents of their box arrived at the office to sign in, the box could be taken to one of the private security rooms.

Nick went to the local Internet café and placed a selection of the comics on the Internet after lunch. Then he visited all of the comic book dealers that he could find within a reasonable radius of his flat and managed to sell seven comics, netting £534 in cash. Building his personal fortune was turning out to be harder work than he had had expected but he was now at least able to pay off some of his debts starting with his landlady.

Gradually, Nick began to get back on his feet financially. After six months of visiting the Vaults, his fortune had grown substantially with all outstanding bills paid he moved from his one bedroom flat in North Kensington to a two-bedroom apartment in the infinitely more fashionable Windsor. He also upgraded his second-hand Ford Granada to a Jaguar sports. He was dealing a lot in cash.

Nick thought life was looking a whole lot better. He began to realise that he was becoming strangely addicted to his latest activities. He knew that although nobody was actually being harmed by what he was doing, it was no way to live his life. He was accumulating all of the toys but apart from the concern that what he was doing might be discovered and the added excitement that disposing of his 'loot' created, life did seem to be very shallow. There was a huge vacuum in his existence.

His parents were oblivious of what was going on. They believed the story that he had fed to them explaining his new career as a commodities consultant, just as they continued to assume that he was still seeing Marina. Nick was vaguely aware that they'd have believed anything, so desperate were they to see him succeed after such a disastrous episode as his ejection from the army. He saw less of them these days; partly because the lies that he was living hurt him when he was in their company.

The 10.45 from Datchet rolled into Waterloo Station and disgorged its human cargo. Nick joined the last of the stampeding commuters heading into the underground. He squeezed into a tube train, which took him the short journey to Chancery Lane, where he thankfully re-emerged into the winter sunlight and walked to the Vaults. He considered himself lucky that he didn't have to make this journey on a regular basis with a time limit and the constraints of a boring job to contend with.

This morning was slightly different from his regular routine. He needed to get a new list of numbers of all the boxes that hadn't been opened for a long period. By now, with Tom and Veronica still under his hypnotic command, he'd worked his way through the original set that he had obtained from Tom Holland.

To get the new numbers he would have to get Tom into his office and under his control so that he could get the information. The task should be easier this time as the trigger word had already been implanted. Putting someone under the influence is always a little daunting as there must be no interruptions such as someone walking in or a phone ringing at the wrong moment.

Tom Holland was in the foyer when Nick arrived. He always enjoyed Nick's visits since they gave him a chance to break the repetitiveness and monotony of his day.

'I'll tell Veronica you're here,' said Tom, shaking his hand in a warm welcome.

'No hurry! Still got loads to do on the stamp collection – probably a couple of months or more. It's turned out to be a much bigger project than I envisaged at first.'

'Fancy a cup of coffee?' suggested Tom, eager for the opportunity to chat.

'Just what I need,' Nick agreed. The two of them walked down the steps, which led to the underground tunnels, then into the office where Tom switched on the electric kettle in the tiny executive kitchen.

'Problem with this job,' said Tom, 'is that we have state-of-the-art security that's so sophisticated it's practically eliminated the need for personnel. This can make life a little boring. I'm always glad of an excuse to break the monotony.'

The coffee made, Tom he sat down at his desk while Nick wandered around the office pretending to admire the various framed prints.

'I can see why you need to get out of here sometimes,' Nick said. 'Having no windows does make the place pretty claustrophobic.'

Nick wandered over to the desk, coffee cup in hand, and sat down opposite Tom. He waited for Tom to drink his first mouthful of coffee and put his cup down.

'Tom, listen to me carefully. *Excalibur.*' The embedded trigger word worked immediately and Tom was under.

Nick had become adept at hypnotising people by now but was still surprised at the ease and speed with which the trigger word worked. He went over to the desk and took the telephone receiver off the hook.

One wall of the office was made over completely to shelving which housed a series of impressive old leather bound ledgers. He walked across to the ledgers and took down one marked 1941. Tom made no movement; he stared unblinkingly at the coffee cup on the blotter in front of him.

Nick took a pencil and paper and worked his way through the ledger looking for likely possibilities. He had watched carefully on his first visit when Tom explained the system, which had been adopted by the company.

It was a mixture of the old and the new, the old ledgers were still relevant as safety deposit boxes were generally taken in perpetuity, and the cut-off age was set at one hundred and ten years to alleviate the chances of error. The period of time that a box was, he knew, considered abandoned was sixty-five years. He made a list of twelve likely boxes and then went to the computer where he checked out the last time that they had been opened. Six boxes fitted the criteria that he had set.

Nick knew this was good news. There would be plenty to be getting on with over the next week. The first number on his list was 1276 and the absent owner was a Mr Alfred Horn who hadn't bothered to pick up his booty for more than seventy years.

A remote distant bell rang in the back of Nick's mind for this was a name that he had come across before, but it was insignificant enough to be pushed back to where it had come from.

Well, Mr Horn, whoever and wherever you are, let me give you a helping hand. Nick thought. He tidied up everything that he had touched, reset the phones and returned to his seat. Time to bring Tom back to the land of the living.

Tom Holland blinked and picked up his coffee cup wondering how he had managed to go off into such a deep daydream while someone was with him in his office. Daydreaming and reminiscing was something that he did fairly frequently these days, but always when he was alone; and why was his coffee nearly cold – surely he'd only just made it?

'Never mind,' he heard himself say aloud. 'So, Nick, you were saying that your stamp collection will need some time yet to knock into shape.' He picked up the conversation where he thought it had left off.

'Probably at least two months at the pace that I'm going, there's so much that has to be researched,' Nick replied, allowing himself the merest hint of a smile. 'Better get on with it I suppose,' he said, 'got a lot to do.'

'I'll call Veronica and get your box taken to your usual booth,' Tom suggested picking up the phone.

Nick thanked him for the coffee and went down to the vault where his box was waiting. There was the usual polite exchange of pleasantries with Veronica and Stanley and then he got on with the pretence of working on his precious stamp collection. He allowed ten minutes to pass before calling Veronica into the booth. It was easy to put her under using the pre-set trigger word and then to give the instructions for the box that he wanted her to bring to him.

'I want you to bring me Box 1276,' Nick instructed and Veronica went off pushing her trolley to return five minutes later with the box. It was, he knew from the Vault's website, 40cm x 25cm x 15 cm.

Nick always found opening a new box intensely exciting. Every box contained items that were there for some clandestine or devious reason. Opening them was like checking a winning lottery ticket.

At first glance the contents of Box 1276 were notably uninteresting, just a brown envelope and six photographs. At first glance the envelope appeared to hold very little of interest, hardly worth bothering with.

There was no way of knowing exactly how long it had been since this box had been opened but guessing from the ledgers in Tom's office it was likely to have been around six decades. The box was covered with a mixture of dust and rust.

The envelope inside had become stuck to the bottom of the metal box. Taking it out without damaging the contents in any way was practically impossible even though Nick did his best to preserve the documents inside. The bottom of the brown envelope and the lower three drawings became torn as they were prised from their resting place.

Perhaps, as it was still early, Nick had time to return this box and try another one.

The envelope was marked 'War Office'.

It had originally been sealed but had subsequently been roughly torn open. The contents consisted of six old sheets of paper, a little smaller than A4 with rudimentary diagrams and strange illegible writing. It was obvious that they were very old but he could understand nothing of their meaning. He examined the outside of the envelope again.

The 'War Office' mark had been made with a rubber-stamp but underneath there was something written in pencil. Age had caused the writing to deteriorate making it barely legible. In his bag of stamp collector's equipment there was a magnifying glass. Nick adjusted the focal length and the faint writing came into focus.

The writing consisted of two words. Nick assumed that it must be a name but the lines were blurred and the rubber stamp was exactly on top, which added to the difficulty. Finally, he deciphered what was indeed a name and sat back in the leather chair bewildered.

Rudolf Hess! What the hell is all this about?

Nick's degree in modern history had given him a major knowledge of, among things, World War II and he immediately recognised the name of Hitler's deputy, Hess, who had made a mad flight to Britain in 1941 to try to meet with Churchill and discuss peace terms between Britain and Nazi Germany. Hess parachuted from his plane, which crashed in a remote part of Scotland.

Hess was not allowed to see Churchill, but had been imprisoned in Britain for the rest of the war and then, at Nuremberg in 1946, had been sentenced to life imprisonment in Spandau Prison in Berlin. The West would have been happy for him to have been released, but the Soviets were steadfastly against it, and Hess had died in 1987, still in prison.

Suddenly everything clicked into place in Nick's mind. Alfred Horn. *Yes, that was the name Hess gave when he was captured by the two Home Guards who had first discovered him when he parachuted into Scotland in 1941!*

Nick had already discovered items in the Vaults, which while valuable, couldn't easily be sold without arousing suspicion and had to be returned to their original boxes. He knew he now had to decide whether to take the papers with him or to lock them away again.

Finally, the temptation proved too great and he decided to take them with him and attempt to unravel the history at his leisure. Placing the envelope into his leather bag, he called Veronica who replaced the now empty box back in the rack where it had spent the last six decades. Nick then brought her out of trance and she returned to her desk at the entrance to the Vaults. He packed up his equipment and called Veronica back again to lock away his own box.

'That's enough stamp collecting for one day,' he joked. He bid her and Stanley a cheery good afternoon and did the same to Tom Holland as he passed his office.

'See you in a couple of days, Tom,' he called as he left the building and headed back to Chancery Lane tube station.

Nick found plenty of references on the Internet to Rudolf Hess and many theories as to why he made that dramatic flight in 1941, but it was all conjecture. Hess's flight to Britain was an historical enigma, which had attracted more conspiracy theories than most.

Had Hess been simply mad? Had he been on a secret mission under Hitler's orders? Hitler had certainly disowned Hess the moment the Fuhrer heard about the flight to Scotland, but disowning people he had supported but who had then fallen out of favour with him had been one of Hitler's trademarks. Or had Hess simply been a naïve idealist, absurdly believing that after all Nazi Germany's treachery, gangsterism, rapacity and murder, Winston Churchill would have paid little heed to Hess's wish for any kind of peace that left Hitler in power?

It seemed obvious to Nick that the story of Rudolf Hess held far more secrets than were common knowledge. So where then did the strange papers that Nick had recently liberated from their hiding place in the centre of London fit into the equation?

He focused his attention on the sketches. There was something about them, which had a familiar look, but what was it? There was a distinct medieval feel to the drawings but what was the link to the Second World War?

Why would Rudolf Hess hide something so old in London?

The mystery deepened. If Nick had acquired the sketches in an honest manner, it would have been easy to take them to a museum or a reputable dealer in antique manuscripts for valuation but that would be too dangerous given the circumstances.

The papers stayed in his flat hidden in the bottom of a wardrobe. From time to time he would take them out and attempt to unravel their origins. But it was obvious that the mystery could not be solved by him alone. He was going to need outside help

Afterwards, he went into the nearest Starbucks to the Vaults for coffee. The shop was busy; he queued, got a latte and looked around for a seat.

He settled himself into one of the larger armchairs, close by a booth containing a group of male and female students who were, Nick thought, in their early twenties. They were pretty noisy but he paid the students little attention; after all they were causing him no problems.

As the raucous chatter continued it was impossible for anyone it the vicinity not to hear. The butt of their joking was a pimply-faced youth who was trying to defend himself, but his stutter was so distinct that he stood little chance. The more agitated he became the more he stuttered and the more he stuttered the more his contemporaries piled on the pressure.

Nick tried to block out the barracking that the young man was suffering but it was difficult. Eventually, bored with the sport, the group left and Nick relaxed. His latte finished, he stood up and prepared to leave. Glancing over his shoulder to where the rowdy group had been sitting he was surprised to see the youth was still at the table staring into his empty coffee cup. Nick walked over and sat down in the booth opposite the young man.

It was plain to see that he had been crying and he looked uncomfortable and embarrassed to have a stranger sitting in front of him, perhaps to add insult to injury. He made a move as if to leave but Nick reached across the table putting his hand on his shoulder gently pushing him back onto the chair.

'Look at me please.' It was a request not an order. The lad looked at Nick with eyes like a startled fawn.

'What's your name?' Nick asked gently but firmly.

'Robert,' he mouthed not quite knowing how to deal with this tall stranger who had suddenly entered into his space. He looked confused, probably more scared to run away than to stay.

'Okay, Robert, look into my eyes just for a second.'

Nick could see the puzzled expression on his face as he noticed his unmatched eyes. Robert's forehead wrinkled into a frown as his focus darted from his left eye to his right.

Nick knew what he was doing now. 'Robert, I want you to remember a time when you felt really good about yourself.'

'Yes.'

'Perhaps you'd accomplished something you were proud of, or maybe you were being complimented for your effort,' said Nick, then added, in a murmur, 'the actual incident isn't so important. What is important now is the feeling that this memory generates within you. When you have that memory; focus on your feelings and your emotions. I want you to remember how it felt inside enjoying those emotions.'

'Yes, I do,' said Robert faintly.

Nick smiled. 'Good. Now, allow those feelings to grow stronger and more positive while you take in a long, deep breath through your nose and press the thumb and the middle finger of your left hand together. Robert did as he was instructed. In future Robert, whenever you do this those confident feelings will be there for you. You can feel them anytime, anywhere, in any situation; these feelings are now becoming more and more a part of you. You are growing into a stronger, more confident person. Remember, any time you want to feel confident, take a deep breath through your nose and press together the thumb and the middle finger of your left hand. You will never stutter again because you are in control. Robert, I am going to count back from six to one and when I have finished you will be wide awake feeling more confident than you have ever done before in your life.'

The counting over, Robert was sitting with a huge grin spread across his face. Nick eased back into the chair.

'Hey Robert you were just telling me about the course you are taking and your mind must have wandered,' Nick broke the silence.

'I'm sorry ... er ... I don't know what happened there,' Robert replied in a bewildered tone.

'So what are you studying?' Nick asked him.

'A four-year media studies course. This is my second year.' There was no trace of a stutter.

'I'm sorry to run but I have to meet some friends,' Robert added. 'Good talking to you.'

'See you again sometime,' Nick replied with a goodbye wave.

With that Robert rushed out through Starbuck's door and into the street looking happy but dazed. The last thing that Nick saw him do as he walked away was to press his thumb to the middle finger of his left hand. He held the hand in front of his face, looking at it as if it belonged to someone else. Nick let out a sigh of relief and sank back even deeper into the chair.

'That was just about the kindest thing I've ever seen,' a woman's voice said from the next table. The voice was rather husky, soft and definitely forceful. Her accent was American; gentle but definitely noticeable. *East Coast*, he thought, though he wasn't certain.

Her back must have been almost against Nick's but he had been so focused on the event with Robert that he hadn't noticed.

She was a lovely woman, about his own age, he thought. Her long dark hair framed a face with strong, very feminine features, and a slightly large mouth with fine, even white teeth. Her eyes were green, and complemented perfectly by the soft glow of her flawless, tanned skin. Her mouth was full and sensuous, her neck elegant and long. She was tall and slim with an athletic figure. The clothes she was wearing were sophisticated, a sober suit with a crisp white blouse, which he assumed must be her working attire.

Nick smiled one of his most handsome smiles.

'Would you mind if I came round and sat with you?' the woman enquired. A hundred thoughts flashed through Nick's mind.

Have I compromised myself? Is she maybe a plain-clothes detective or an agent of some description?

He felt a rising sense of dismay. He'd decided that his ability to hypnotize would be his secret and his alone. More than that, if his plans were to work no other person must know that he had the ability. Now he had blown the whole deal to some nosey woman in Starbucks. Did she want to speak to him so he could hypnotise her and stop her from eating four pounds of chocolate a day?

Nick groaned inwardly and didn't answer hoping that she would disappear. He glanced at her, and their eyes met – she was truly, truly lovely – but he didn't reply to her.

She wasn't to be so easily put off and moved around to sit in the seat so recently occupied by the youth.

Nick blinked, struggling to retain his composure. There was a long pause, whilst they each composed themselves. Neither had been expecting this; finally:

'I really am sorry to barge in like this,' the woman said, in the same husky, soft, forceful voice. 'But I genuinely wanted to say well done for the way that you helped that poor boy. My name's Tamsin Richards, by the way.'

She put out her right hand towards him and he shook it. Her hand felt soft, cool, yet also curiously firm and her handshake was decisive: the handshake. Nick thought, of a woman who knew what she wanted from life.

'Hi, I'm Nick Trevelyan. You're really kind, but I wasn't doing anything special. I just wanted to help him.'

'Don't be so modest, that was a wonderful thing to have done. Now, won't you let me get you another latte? I should apologise for listening to your conversation with that young man. But I was sitting so close by, you see; well, frankly it was impossible not to hear.'

Nick smiled. He could tell that she was anything but a plain-clothes police officer.

He loved the sound of her voice. There was a distinctive air of confidence about her, which was tinged with modesty.

They had coffee and they talked. Nick was pretty reticent about himself, though he did tell her that he'd studied history at university and had just started working 'in the City' after spending some time in southern Portugal. *Well, that's true enough*, he thought.

'Tell me more about yourself, please,' he said.

So she did. She explained that she'd spent a lot of time in the States. Her father was from Washington DC, which was where she had spent the first twelve years of her life.

Her mother was English and after her parents became divorced she came to live in England where she continued her education, going on to university. She'd studied for five years and was now a practising solicitor. Tamsin's mother had wanted her to become a doctor, but as her education progressed it became apparent to all that her real love and interest lay with the law. She had found the studying and training fascinating and after successfully acquiring her degree had moved to London to share an apartment with her oldest and dearest friend who had graduated with her. Tamsin had been accepted by Digby and Short, Solicitors, in Battersea in London, as a junior and had recently been made a partner. She loved her work and was encouraged all the way by her employers who could see her potential.

'But that's just me, what about you, Nick?'

'Perhaps we could discuss me over dinner tonight?'

He'd thought she might be taken aback by the boldness of his offer. She gave no signs of that but agreed. She smiled.

'That would be lovely, thank you.'

'Can I have your mobile number? I could call you around seven thirty and we'll arrange something. Oh, and any preferences for food?'

Tamsin smiled. 'I'll eat pretty well anything that won't eat me first,' she said.

There was a twinkle in her eyes as she said this. Nick wondered very much what the twinkle meant.

He smiled at her. 'That's just great,' he said.

After giving Nick her mobile number Tamsin explained – not very believably, Nick thought – that she hadn't been too successful with the men she had met in the past, mainly because her studying had taken so much of her time and energy.

That first date they had was quiet and friendly rather than explosively passionate. Nick took her to a charming little Italian bistro just off the Strand where the waiters wore smart black jackets, white shirts, black trousers and black bow ties and sang snatches of *Rigoletto, Cavelleria Rusticana* and *Turandot* while serving hearty, tasty portions of good, solid, reliable Italian cuisine.

The romance/affair with Marina had been full on and steamy in the extreme if not a little intermittent due to Nick's military commitment. It had certainly worked for him and he, perhaps somewhat mistakenly until that final fatal day had thought that Marina felt the same.

The many glancing blows of romantic liaisons, if romantic was the correct description for the series of one night stands and holiday romances that he enjoyed whilst in the Algarve, had been fun but shallow in the extreme. None of the women had seemed to him a patch on Marina; though of course he regarded them as having a big advantage over her in that they wanted him, for a night, anyway.

Now back in England, Nick's full attention had been focused upon getting his life into some semblance of routine and the on-going episode, which was developing at the safety deposit vaults, took up practically all of his time leaving little space for perusing the opposite sex.

By the time Nick met Tamsin the spade work at the vaults was complete and Nick was on an even keel financially with exciting prospects ahead. The timing couldn't have been better; a new woman in his life was an ideal addition.

The difference between Marina and Tamsin was immediately obvious. Sex was certainly the driving force in the Marina liaison whilst a much gentler approach was required with Tamsin and it was a month before she finally submitted to Nick's more amorous advances and she agreed to go to his bed.

Surprisingly, he was happy to wait for the prize, which made it all the more sensuous when the time arrived. Making love to Tamsin turned out to be more like savouring a fine wine whilst Marina had tended to detonate like a bottle of champagne. Tamsin's kisses were lingering, passionate in a sultry, silky kind of way whereas Marina's kisses were simply an overture to a resounding Wagner opera.

Tamsin introduced Nick to cultural delights as well as amorous ones. They spent weekends visiting museums and stately homes; an introduction to classical music was a surprising delight he had never thought would have tempted his more macho interest but all of these things savoured in the delightful company of Tamsin he found genuinely interesting and enjoyable.

As the romance progressed they seemed to settle into a relationship that Nick was aware was, beyond any doubt at all, the most meaningful relationship of his life so far. Nick was utterly delighted to have become involved with his new lady. He'd never managed to get Marina completely out of his mind, and deep down he knew he missed her company, and making love with her, very much indeed, but as he didn't ever expect to see her again, he'd decided some months ago now to make the best of a bad job and to look for affection – and sex – elsewhere.

Meanwhile, his systematic plundering of the London Silver Vaults continued. The items he liberated (this was how he preferred to view what he was doing) varied considerably, but by far the largest percentage was made up of diamonds, due to the proximity of Hatton Garden, which had been the centre of London's jewellery trade for centuries.

This posed something of a problem that he needed to deal with quickly and efficiently. He studied the diamond trade in detail and learned all he could about the intricacies of the business.

As the months progressed his haul from the Vaults grew. Bizarrely, the actual liberating of his loot was the easy part. Disposing of it was another matter and required careful thought. Again the Internet proved to be invaluable in discovering information. Nick *googled* the diamond trade and found masses on the subject and printed off the following:

In the past, the South African mining and marketing company DeBeers had controlled about sixty per cent of the rough-diamond market; they would sell diamonds to a chosen two hundred dealers, who would in turn redistribute to cutters. The cutters sent them to wholesalers, who would then sell them to retailers. In the year 2000 the DeBeers diamond cartel ended as the group made its biggest change in focus for more than sixty-five years. From then on, it ceased to support world diamond prices by buying up and stockpiling diamonds and gems, concentrating instead on enhancing the demand for gems by persuading the jewellery industry to spend much more on advertising.

This change was in some degree encouraged by the continuing wars raging in Africa, and in particular the twenty-seven-year Angolan civil war which had caused a flood of diamonds onto the market; these were called 'Blood' or 'Conflict' diamonds. A Conflict diamond was one mined in a war zone and sold, usually clandestinely, in order to finance an insurgent or invading Army's war efforts. Contemporary examples may be found in Angola or Sierra Leone, where the sale of diamonds had funded rebel groups in both countries' brutal civil wars. This had led to the Diamond Registry's policy on 'Conflict Diamonds' in February 2003. All members of the World Federation of Diamond Bourses were required to subscribe to the 'Kimberley Process', which required that all rough diamonds purchased complied with United Nations resolutions and came with the following statement:

The diamonds herein invoiced had been purchased from legitimate sources not involved in the funding of conflict and in compliance with United Nations resolutions. The seller hereby guarantee that these diamonds were conflict free, based on personal knowledge and/or written guarantees provided by the supplier of these diamonds.

All of this added to his difficulties. His diamonds had been out of circulation for at least sixty years. Some were quite large and could be traced back to the original cutting company.

On the positive side, this was a business where some dealers would ask few questions as long as the price was right. Through a careful process of elimination he had whittled his buyers down to two in London, three in New York and three in Amsterdam.

Nick knew that if he was going to smuggle and eventually sell anything, then precious stones had to be the chosen items, the smallest objects with the highest value.

He gathered from the Internet that the hardest substance known to man showed up beautifully on X-ray machines.

Nick ventured to make one short (three day) exploratory trip to New York with a few diamonds he hid in his cabin luggage in a plastic bag containing broken almonds that Nick had first scorched under in the grill in his kitchen. According to a website that discussed the question of how to hide things from airport scanner, diamonds were carbon (of course Nick knew that) and scorched almonds were basically just carbon and oxygen, so were efficient concealers of diamonds.

The plan worked well. Neither the airport scanner at London's Heathrow or New York's JFK airport detected the diamonds. He sold the diamonds in New York and they more than covered the cost of his trip and the cheap hotel on the Upper West Side. Nick decided that when he made a longer and more ambitious trip to New York he'd need more storage space than the bag of scorched almonds in his carry-on luggage could provide so he devised another plan hiding diamonds. He made his way over to Slough on a shopping trip to get an unusual array of items. His first stop was a toy shop where he purchased three ten-inch porcelain figures: Fireman Sam, Postman Pat and Bob the Builder; all nicely packaged in sturdy display boxes with cellophane fronts.

Next, he visited an arts and craft shop for silicone mould-making equipment, plaster of Paris, an acrylic paint set, brushes and craft knives. In the town centre he dropped into Boots and made his most unusual purchase - a box of condoms. His next destination was the local builder's merchant where he bought a roll of roofing lead and a soldering iron.

Once home, Nick smiled to himself as he unloaded the shopping. It was an eclectic assortment. That evening he got to work. Carefully opening the three cartoon character boxes so that they could be re-used, he set them aside. Then he made a two-section mould from the silicone for each of the porcelain figures. As the moulds were setting he selected the diamonds to be taken to New York and divided them into three groups.

He slipped each group inside one of the condoms. Using the craft knife, he fashioned the lead sheet into envelopes and placed the diamond-loaded condom inside, then sealed each package with the soldering iron. This would make them indiscernible as separate items and appear as just a blob on the scanners. The silicone moulds were now set and ready for pouring. As the plaster was setting he placed the lead envelopes into the moulds so that their flat bottoms were level with the figurines' bases. This was as much as he could do that evening; it would take several hours for the moulds to dry completely.

Nick stretched his legs; on the desk beside him was a small black pebble about the size of a blackbird's egg. He had picked it up on the beach at Praia da Luz. He took the pebble and weighed it in his hand. It was a convenient reminder of the depths to which he had sunk, not so long ago. His determination to never again return to those depths was strong. He was filled with a new resolve.

He checked his watch; it was 1am. *Time to go to bed and allow my evening's work to dry*, he thought.

Next morning, he opened the moulds with some trepidation. All three figures were a good reproduction of the original. Trimming off the casting flash, he prepared them for painting. Using the original figurines for reference he painstakingly painted the copies and by mid-afternoon his work was complete. He figured that what with the scorched almonds, his planned concealment in a personal part of his person, and the use of the three figures, there was a pretty good chance that he could transport his diamonds to New York without them being detected.

He made his excuses to Tamsin saying that he needed to go to New York on business but leaving out the real reason for his visit. She accepted this and wished him a safe journey.

20
New York

Trying to look as calm as he could, Nick walked out of passport control and through the security check at Heathrow Airport's Terminal Four. This was always a nerve-racking time. In his baggage, already checked-in at the British Airways desk, he had carefully concealed a considerable fortune in diamonds in their toy town containers. This was the point of no return; if he were to be stopped, from now on the game would be up.

Suddenly the alarm sounded.

Hell, Nick thought.

'Hands to your sides and spread your feet, please sir,' said a security guard who appeared to have arrived from nowhere.

Nick co-operated. The security guard ran his hands professionally over Nick's body. 'It's the metal buckle on your belt, Sir. Best take it off next time, to save any further inconvenience,' suggested the guard.

'Thanks very much,' Nick replied, now trying to sound just as calm and collected as he could.

The flight to New York passed without too much distress and the British Airways jet touched down at Newark Liberty Airport on time. Getting through US customs was a long, drawn-out procedure post 9/11 but he passed through without difficulty. Nick pushed his loaded baggage trolley over to the bank of telephones dedicated to local hotels and located the phone for the Phoenix, a Best Western Hotel on the Upper East Side, where he was staying.

After twenty minutes the courtesy bus arrived and, in the company of other travellers he settled down for the ride across the Hudson Tunnel under the Hudson River and up into Manhattan.

His hotel could only boast a three-star rating but it gave him everything he needed. He checked in during the early evening and settled into his single room. After unpacking, he took a shower and, feeling a lot more refreshed, dressed and went down to the lobby where he bought a copy of the New York Times and a magazine.

'I wonder if you would mind putting that into a plastic sack for me? Newsprint is so dirty, it ruins clothing,' he politely asked the young girl who was serving.

'Why certainly, sir,' came the equally polite reply.

Nick wandered into the restaurant and asked for a table for one in a dimly lit corner. The meal was pretty good, and by British standards enormous. Delicious ravioli to start with – he chose this as it reminded him of his first meal with Tamsin – then a ten-inch T-bone steak, fries, French beans, salad, and to finish, a large helping of cherry pie with an abundance of whipped cream that topped the pie like a snowdrift.

Nick slipped the butter knife into his pocket.

After dinner, shattered from the flight and the jet-lag, he took the lift to his room on the eighth floor.

He spread the newspaper on the bed and placed the three plaster figurines in the centre. By knocking one against the other he broke off the legs of the plaster cartoon characters and prised out the lead envelopes with the butter knife. The whole operation took just five minutes but made a mess, which he wrapped in the newspaper and placed in the plastic sack.

It took another five minutes to open the envelopes and extract the condoms protecting the diamonds. He would dispose of the rubbish himself since he imagined that the chambermaid would quite rightly become suspicious if she discovered three broken figurines and three used condoms after only one night in the hotel. Before finally getting into bed he took his cell phone and sent a text to Tamsin, telling her that he'd arrived safely. Then he changed the UK SIM card to a US 'pay-as-you-go' SIM that he had bought on a previous visit.

Next morning, carrying the plastic sack with its unusual contents, Nick stepped out into the bright Broadway sunlight and walked two blocks down the street.

Off to the right was an alleyway with several dumpsters. He threw the sack into one, then walked briskly back to the hotel for breakfast. The waiter showed him to the same table as the previous evening. While waiting for the food he made four phone calls from his mobile.

The first was to Bert Bergheart, a diamond dealer with whom Nick had made contact with on his very first, short visit to New York. Bert was greedy but dependable. He haggled all the way but it invariably culminated in a deal.

Nick arranged a meeting for eleven o'clock that morning. The second phone call was to Moses Litherman, a middle-aged Orthodox Jew whom Nick had met also briefly on his previous visit to New York.

The meeting was arranged for 3.30 that afternoon. Nick's third call was to the Chase Manhattan Bank, where he said he needed to talk about his investments. This appointment was scheduled for the day before he was to leave New York, three days hence.

Breakfast arrived. Nick tucked into another enormous meal of three fried eggs sunny side up, mushrooms, tomatoes, pork sausages, and the streaky bacon; a start to the day that New Yorkers love and which Nick always asked to be served well-cooked, as this tended mostly to evaporate the otherwise excessive fat. Nick complemented this morning's feast with bagels dripping with butter and honey, and washed it down with a large glass of delicious orange juice and two cups of milky coffee.

Returning to his room, he took two of the three packets of diamonds and carefully poured each into a Plaza Hotel envelope, which he then placed inside a leather wallet that he had brought with him. The third package he placed in a secret pocket that he had carefully sewn into the front of his trousers, only accessible from the inside. When he went out later that morning, he asked the concierge to put the wallet in the hotel safe. He wished the desk clerk good morning and walked out onto the bustling Broadway sidewalk.

He hailed a yellow cab to take him to West 47th Street. Yellow cab drivers usually having about as much knowledge of New York's geography as a xenophobe trapper from the depths of Siberia does of the London Underground system, thankfully the cab driver actually knew where West 47th Street was.

Nick had learned from the Internet that the United States was the world's largest consumer market for diamonds and more than ninety per cent of those sold went through New York City. More than 2,600 independent jewellery businesses are located on New York's diamond district, which was centred on West 47th Street between Fifth Avenue and Avenue of the Americas, also known as Sixth Avenue.

Nick took a cab from his hotel to the diamond district. It was a long walk on a hot and humid day – it was one of those days when New York's humidity was so high that you start to think the city was doing it on purpose – but more to the point, it was also much safer to take a cab, considering that Nick was carrying a healthy hoard of precious gemstones. The swarthy cab driver grunted and pulled out into the Broadway traffic to the usual accompaniment of disgruntled drivers' horns.

Within ten minutes they had arrived at Bert Bergheart's offices. When the office suite had been last decorated in 1970 it may have looked fashionably acceptable for that decade but now it seemed decidedly jaded. If the style-police had raided the place, Nick thought, they'd have had a field day. Nevertheless, it served its purpose as every visitor who entered the dreary office was from the jewellery trade and was more interested in making money than in Bert's interior decorating.

Bert didn't deal with the general public. The receptionist was the same vintage as the décor, her hair piled high into an apparently powdered Beehive hairdo that Nick mused would not have looked out of place in the Court of the French Sun-King at Versailles.

'Is Mr Bergheart expecting you?' demanded the receptionist in a far from friendly interrogative drawl, when Nick went into the office at 10.55 that morning. Nick smiled inwardly. Was that accent for real or was this lady doing an exaggerated impersonation of Barbra Streisand?

Restraining an impulse to reply, *No, I'm just here to see your hairdo*, Nick replied, briskly:

'Yes. I'm Nick Trevelyan. My meeting's booked for eleven o'clock. Could I use your lavatory, please?'

'The washroom is back into the corridor, first door on your right.'

Nick noted that *washroom*. The Americans loved euphemisms, didn't they? It was a country when tens of millions of people kept loaded guns in their houses and where in many States, if you knocked on someone's door late at night to ask directions you were very likely to be shot dead through the door. But all the same, they couldn't bring themselves to call a toilet a toilet.

'Thanks.' Nick did an about turn and headed off to the men's room. In order to get to the hidden pocket where the diamonds were he actually had to take off his trousers.

An hour later Nick was in a taxi heading back to his hotel. The bulge in his trousers had disappeared but now he had a new one in his inside breast pocket made up of American dollar bills. He stopped off at the reception desk to pick up his key and the leather wallet. Back in his room he took the second parcel of diamonds from the wallet and replaced them with the dollar bills from Bert Bergheart.

It was time for lunch.

In the afternoon Nick set off for the second of his meetings. Moses Litherman's office was in the same block as Bert's but about a hundred metres west. The procedure was the same. Arrive five minutes early, retrieve the diamonds from where they nestled in his secret trouser pocket and enter the fray with Moses. It was like a well-rehearsed script.

Moses had a pale face, long forelocks and a habit of staring at Nick with a piercing, perplexed look, as if he thought Nick might recently have arrived from Mars.

Nick liked Moses. The opening gambit Moses played that day, just like he had before, was to berate his esteemed British customer for having bothered to cross the Atlantic with gems that were 'zuch vubbish'.

But after an hour of bartering Nick walked out of Moses's office with a smile on his face and a bulging bundle of dollar bills in his pocket. Moses would, as usual, start by going to great lengths to tell Nick that he'd wasted his time buying an air ticket. *Anyone would have thought I was offering Moses pieces of sheep dung I gathered from some field near Heathrow Airport before setting off.*

His meetings over, he decided to go and buy a gift for Tamsin from a jewellery shop in the district. He headed instinctively down a side street, sure he would get better value from some small obscure shop than one that paid hefty rent for one of the large, in-your-face kind of shops that abounded on one of the main roads of the diamond district. He wandered along the street looking for a likely shop, his concentration focused on Tamsin and the gift.

'Hey man, could you spare a couple of dimes for a coffee?' A huge, scruffy white American was blocking his way. With scruffy clothes, the smell of his rancid breath and body odour was immediately sickening. Before Nick could think, another, smaller, man hemmed him in from the other side and pushed a gun under his chin. The big man pushed another gun into his ribs.

'Move or we'll shoot you right here!' The smaller man was doing all the talking.

They bundled him into an alley, the sort of locale he had seen hundreds of times in American movies, the kind of alleyway that you should never, never go into. He was roughly jostled along, falling over dustbins and tripping over rotting garbage until they finally stopped. Thoughts pounded through Nick's mind. How the hell could he have allowed this to happen? He just wasn't streetwise to the level necessary in New York. The street was only a hundred feet away but it might as well have been a mile. He could see at the entrance to the alley people and cars passing by in the bright winter sunlight but this dank-smelling hellhole never saw the sun. This was their territory. Nick prepared to fight his way out and make a run for it but the look in his attackers' eyes was frightening. They were both obviously high on drugs and very dangerous.

'Okay, give us all you've got,' the shorter man demanded. Nick measured the distance to the street. He was fit and felt sure that he could outrun these two, but the guns! With two guns in a closed environment like this, he was sure to be shot in the back. What a place to die! Play for time, get them closer. Nick had never attempted to hypnotize two people at the same time but he knew that it could be done. The three of them now formed a triangle. His back was against a crumbling, damp, brick wall and his attackers were standing back with their arms raised, guns pointing at his head. He spoke quietly.

'What did he say?' the big guy asked. Nick whispered again.

'What are we playing about at?' said the shorter man.

'Waste him now and get it the hell over with.' They moved in closer, perhaps to hear what Nick was saying or maybe just to get a better shot. They were now about three metres away. His heart was pounding as he started to talk to the men and attempt to influence them. Any second they could have decided they had heard enough, pull the trigger then rob his dying body of more than they could ever have dreamed of.

But luck was on his side. He was gaining control. Cautiously he began the procedure, which would put his attackers under his influence. When certain that they were both hypnotized, he gave himself a few seconds to regain his composure. Now, how best to conclude this affair?

'Tell me your name.' He concentrated his attention on the shorter man.

'Winston.' With a feeling of relief, Nick could see the aggression had disappeared from the man's eyes. He was standing like a partially deflated doll.

'Move over there, Winston,' he ordered. Moving Winston further down the alley away from his partner, Nick then walked back to the bigger man.

'What's your name?' He felt confident now but anger still bubbled in his mind.

'Joshua,' said the bigger man.

'Okay, Joshua, I have something important to tell you, something that you have to act upon as soon as I give you the signal. Do you understand me?' Joshua nodded his large head like a naughty child.

'Joshua, Winston is going to kill you. He wants everything for himself. As soon as you hear three blasts from a car horn you must shoot him before he shoots you. Do you understand Joshua? You must shoot Winston before he shoots you. The signal is three blasts from a car horn.' Nick walked over to Winston and repeated the message.

'Winston, Joshua is not your friend. He will shoot you as soon as he hears three blasts from a car's horn. You must shoot him first. Remember, three blasts on a car's horn. On the last blast, you must kill him.' Then Nick led Winston over to Joshua so that they were two metres apart.

'Winston, point your gun at Joshua's head!' he ordered. The response was slow.

'Joshua, point your gun at Winston's head!' Another slow but deliberate response.

The two men's wrists were almost touching, their arms rock steady but their eyes were glazed, bereft of the anger that had burned there previously. Nick surveyed the scene. For the first time since he had entered the ugly alleyway, he looked up to check if there was anyone witnessing the bizarre scene that was being played out below. The walls, which flanked the alley were solid with no openings or windows. At the far end there was a chain-link fence piled high with rubbish. Nobody could pass or see through. Time to leave. He walked towards the street, stopping at the end of the alley to check out his two attackers, almost expecting them to have walked away. But no, they were still standing like two statues, guns pointing at each other's heads. Walking out onto 47th Street, there was a battered yellow cab sitting at the kerb with its window open. Nick leaned in and pumped the horn three times.

'Hey what the hell are you doing, man?' The taxi driver was irate but his words were drowned by two simultaneous gunshots from the nearby alley.

Nick calmly walked a block then took a taxi back to his hotel. He fell onto his bed, exhausted. It had been a busy day; he felt shattered. The spectre of the two men in the alley flashed through his mind and played with his conscience, although in his heart, he knew they would not have hesitated to end his life. Relieving the planet of two undesirables did not unduly worry him; nevertheless he was conscious of snuffing out two lives, no matter how objectionable they may have been. It was simply a case of kill or be killed.

But then, wasn't that what life in New York was all about?

21
Mercedes

The lift reached the ground floor. Nick stepped out, walked across the foyer and into the hotel restaurant. After the events of the day he was relieved to swap the solitude of his single room for the bustle of the restaurant.

The hotel was a small to medium-sized affair; the restaurant could only boast fifty to sixty covers and he had never seen it more than a quarter full. The serving staff had become familiar with his dining habits; as soon as he entered, the headwaiter swooped and showed Nick to his favourite table. Danny had quickly acknowledged that this Englishman was a client who wasn't afraid to tip well.

'How was your day, Mr Trevelyan?' inquired the head waiter.

'Fine thanks, Danny, just a couple of annoying interruptions but nothing that couldn't be sorted out,' Nick replied genially. He ordered a vodka and tonic and studied the menu. Having made his opening gesture, Danny allowed the other waiters to look after the 'Englishman in New York' while he busied himself elsewhere.

Nick ordered a steak, but only an eight ounce one, which he was aware, was hardly a steak at all by New York standards. Indeed, the waiter looked puzzled at Nick, as if he thought his British customer must have made a mistake, but Nick explained that he didn't want half a steer. As if to cheer the waiter up, Nick added a bottle of good Beaujolais to the order before he settled back to enjoy his vodka and tonic and indulge himself in a mixture of daydreaming and people watching.

He allowed his thoughts to drift towards the following day's agenda when he would cross swords with Mario Burlace.

Nick had only dealt with Burlace once before and although the meeting had gone to plan; his sixth sense told him that this was a man not to be trusted. When the dealing was completed he had paid up but he wanted to know more, far too much

Where was Nick getting these high-class diamonds from? If he could find out and cut Nick out of the loop, then he could make an even bigger profit; the driving force in his life.

After about fifteen minutes the steak arrived and Nick realized that he was quite hungry. He almost, but not quite, regretted his minimalist order. He ate his steak, fries, and mayonnaise-drenched salad quickly, washing it down with, so far, about half of the bottle of Beaujolais. He'd not long finished eating when his attention was attracted by a flurry of movement at the restaurant entrance. Danny had suddenly become highly animated and was gesticulating in a plausible impression of Basil Fawlty. Nick was curious as to why this usually urbane man should have undergone such a rapid transformation. The answer was soon clear.

Danny was moving in reverse, traversing the tables with a high degree of dexterity while ushering a tall, elegant woman to her table. There was obviously not a shortage of options where she could sit but eventually the decision was reached and she chose a table not too far from his.

All heads in the restaurant turned furtively to observe the arrival of this stunning woman. Once her seating arrangements had been resolved, Danny turned his attention to making an unnecessary fuss over the table layout. Most of these events Nick viewed with a certain disinterest concentrating his thoughts between the wine and the forthcoming meeting.

The woman was tall, slender and elegant. Nick could see at once she was something exceptional, rather special. Nick, in common with most heterosexual red-blooded men, considered himself a connoisseur of the female form and the woman standing so tantalizingly close was as fine an example as he ever had the good fortune to observe.

She wore an immaculately tailored charcoal grey business suit. The front was low cut allowing her lace bra to be seen. The cleavage visible between her tantalising breasts which, while not huge, were certainly adequate. The tight fitting skirt was cut slightly above the knee with a side slit which allowed alluring glimpses of shapely legs. Her body looked toned to the extent of being hard. Nick decided that she must be an athlete of some description.

Her skin had a Mediterranean olive tone and her long black hair was tied back in a severe, classical style. Her features were elegantly sophisticated and she exuded self-confidence.

He guessed her to be in her late-twenties.

Two observations puzzled him vaguely. First, her eye makeup was dramatically theatrical: dark and somewhat heavy. Secondly; she wore far too much expensive jewellery. The flurry of the mystery woman's initial entrance was over and the restaurant returned to normality. Nick continued to savour his wine acutely aware of the beauty sitting and facing him no more than two tables away. Danny enquired if the lady would like a drink while she studied the menu.

The reply was for a Caipiroska, which confused Danny. She politely explained that this was a Caipirinha with a shot of vodka, a new trendy drink, which Danny hadn't yet encountered. He accepted the information enjoying any opportunity of engaging her in conversation and taking advantage of peering down into the delicious cleavage. When the drink arrived she sipped it delicately.

Holding the glass in front of her, she gazed across the room in Nick's direction. He decided not to make eye contact and continued with his wine. A mobile phone ended the standoff, causing the woman to retrieve the telephone from her Gucci handbag. The distance between them was no more than twelve feet and she made no effort to be discreet when answering the call.

'Yes, I understand completely Mr … Simmonds. If your daughter's ill then of course I understand you can't make the meeting. Please call me tomorrow and we'll arrange another date.' Her accent, as far as Nick could make out, was cultured Middle American, though Nick was aware of hardly being an expert in North American accents. But something seriously important must have occurred to the mysterious Mr Simmonds for him to cancel an appointment with a woman like this, Nick mused.

Conversation over, the mystery woman returned to her Caipiroska and continued to look in Nick's direction, obviously deep in thought. Danny hovered attentively close by like a hungry bird of prey.

'Is everything okay with your meal, Mr Trevelyan?' he asked, hardly taking his eyes off the woman.

'Fine thanks, Danny, just fine,' Nick replied.

The moment he said this, the woman turned sharply to him, so sharply that in fact he half-expected a rebuke, though what she said, in a quiet, sultry voice that was clearly only for him, was:

'So sorry to bother you, but that accent ... it's just lovely. I just *adore* the English accent. I wonder if I might ask you, do you perhaps know Hugh Grant?'

'Not personally, I'm afraid, no,' Nick said, with one of his friendliest smiles.

'That's a shame. I just adored *Three Weddings and a Funeral.*'

'Actually,' said Nick, clearing his throat politely, 'There were four weddings.'

'Four? Oh yes, of course.' The woman smiled the brightest of smiles.

'So you have a lovely accent and you're a movie buff!' she added, in the most winning of voices. Making an obvious attempt to open a conversation.

She just kept on smiling, so naturally causing a pause which he ended by asking her to join him, which she did immediately, bringing her drink to his table. He was glad he'd finished eating; it was never too easy to be romantic with a mouth full of food. Nick caught Danny's eye and smiled at him; he cleared away Nick's plate, his eyes flickering at Nick that universally-understood glance of one man being impressed with the slick potential sexual success of another.

'Hi,' Nick said to the woman, once Danny had left their table, 'I'm Nick Trevelyan. Delighted to meet you.'

She smiled back. 'I'm Mercedes. The pleasure's mine, Nick. What about *Notting Hill*? Have you seen that?

Fortunately, Nick had. Their evening progressed most successfully. Mercedes loved British movies. Her favourite was one called *Kind Hearts and Coronets*, which Nick hadn't seen, but even this turned out to be a positive advantage, as it allowed Mercedes to tell him the plot, though only after he reassured her that he didn't mind her telling him what happened. In any event, he was content to pay more attention to her lovely face and beautifully sensuous mouth than to her account of the storyline from an old black and white movie.

Mercedes had a light supper of scallops in ginger sauce and a small Caesar salad, and together they worked their way through two bottles of Beaujolais, followed by brandies.

The conversation flowed easily, moving on to Mercedes's often amusingly ironic accounts of her life in the New York cultural scene. She also told him she loved dancing. Meanwhile, Nick expounded his life as a global commodities dealer making it sound as exciting as he could make it at such short notice. She appeared genuinely fascinated. Nick decided to pitch his Britishness somewhere between David Niven and Hugh Grant and entered into the charade with enthusiasm. Finally, after a delightful evening, Danny brought the bill, which Nick paid, giving a generous tip, and then Danny brought Mercedes coat; and together he and his new lady friend walked out into the foyer. He didn't exactly, not think of Tamsin at that point. She had certainly been in the forefront of his mind whilst he had been in New York, but he had to admit to himself, not right at that precise moment. He consoled himself with the thought that he needed to further research the immediate set of unusual circumstances in which he found himself.

'D'you like jazz, Nick?' asked Mercedes. 'I'm having such a great time and it's too early to go home yet. On the next block there's a great blues bar that I'd love to show you.'

'Sounds fine to me.' He was having a pretty good time himself. In the blues bar the drinks changed to Jack Daniels and the music was all that you would expect from a New York basement blues club. It was one thirty in the morning when they left the smoky atmosphere and walked out into the invigorating night air. As they walked along the sidewalk towards his hotel, Mercedes slipped her arm through his.

'Wow, you Englishmen certainly do have charm,' Mercedes whispered. There was a mixture of emotions running through his brain: flattery at such a high level and from someone as delightfully sensuous was slightly intimidating although thoroughly agreeable.

'Nick, I can see that you are a perfect gentleman who wouldn't dream of asking a lady up to his hotel room at this hour so I'll spare you the embarrassment and invite myself. How does that sit with you?'

Nick smiled. 'How can I resist such an offer? It could irrevocably damage Anglo/American relationships,' at which Mercedes smiled very warmly and kissed him on the cheek.

Arm in arm they walked up into the hotel, across the foyer and into the lift. They were the only passengers. Nick hit the button for the eighth floor. As soon as the lift started to move, Mercedes pushed him roughly against the back wall of the lift. Taking his face in her hands she kissed him passionately, her tongue exploring every region of his mouth. Her right leg curled around his left thigh, demonstrating her athletic prowess. She pulled him onto her, ardently.

The embrace lasted until the lift bell announced their arrival on the eighth floor. Along the corridor and then, while Nick fumbled with the door lock, Mercedes continued fondling, kissing his neck and pushing her warm, moist tongue into his ear. They fell into the room.

Nick needed a little time to catch his breath; so sudden had been Mercedes' passionate advance. He flopped into the only single armchair where he felt safe for the moment. He kicked off his shoes and took in the scene. She sat opposite on the two-seater couch. For a minute or two she sat, simply looking at him and then she slowly stood up.

Taking a stance with her legs slightly apart, she slowly unbuttoned the front of her immaculately tailored suit, pushed the jacket back over her shoulders and let it fall to the floor. Her hands went behind her back and undid the bra clip. She took the bra by a shoulder strap and flung it teasingly into his face. Her breasts were delightful, certainly not large but of prefect dimensions; in contrast the nipples were large, dark and extremely pert.

Mercedes's hand disappeared behind her back again; there was a sound of a zip being opened. The skirt fell to the floor revealing that she was wearing nothing beneath the skirt apart from black hold-up stockings, the tops of which were made of delicate lace which gripped the well-muscled, sleek thighs. Her stomach was perfectly flat; below, the pubic mound shaved and inviting. She stepped out of the skirt and with her toes flicked it towards him, the movement causing her breasts to quiver exotically. This was a woman who knew how to tease a man. Balancing on one leg she removed one shoe and then the other. Apart from the stockings and jewellery she was completely naked.

Again her hand disappeared behind her head and her beautiful hair cascaded down onto her elegant shoulders. She shook her head to allow the hair to fall naturally and again her breasts quivered pleasingly.

'Like what you see, Nick?'

'Rather a superfluous question,' Nick replied, continuing to play the English gentleman.

Mercedes walked over to the hotel radio selector, scanned through a couple of channels and found one dedicated to classical music. The volume was turned up high. Nick was convinced that the whole seventh, eighth and ninth floor could hear but he couldn't have cared less. Mercedes began to dance. He was aware that, apart from what he'd told her about movies, his conversation so far had been something of a farce as far as he was concerned.

He had been lying from the start, making up his background as he went along, and he assumed that Mercedes might have been playing a similar game. If she was, though, what she had told him about her love of dancing was certainly true. She was quite obviously a trained dancer. She performed as if he wasn't in the room, her beautiful naked body conveying the beauty of ballet with the subtlety of a concert pianist playing a classical masterpiece.

She had the poise of a ballerina combined with the savage grace of a lioness. Nick looked on, mesmerized. Finally the music ended. Mercedes stood in front of him, her chest heaving from the exertion, her wonderful body glistening with a thin covering of sweat. Standing in front of him was one of the most beautiful women that he had ever seen. She was offering herself and it was a temptation that few heterosexual men would be able to refuse. But ... Nick's intuition told him that all this really was just too easy. He couldn't help it, he felt intensely suspicious. A moment later, he'd convinced himself that he needed to discover the reason why she'd come on to him so readily, there must be more to it. Up to this point the conditions hadn't been convenient for him to attempt to hypnotise her, or perhaps that was the excuse that he was making to himself to cover his guilt at allowing this to progress the way it had. Her company was pure golden honey.

Mercedes walked across the room and stood face to face with Nick. Her breathing was heavy, her chest rose and fell from the exertion of the dance. As she had done earlier in the lift Mercedes cupped his face in her hands pulling it onto hers kissing him passionately. Quickly and with nimble fingers she unbuttoned his shirt and before he had realised what had happened his belt was unfastened and the zip at the front of his trousers was opened. Mercedes pulled his shirt off of his back and tossed it aside. Nick's trousers had fallen to his ankles and he had no option but to step out of them. Mercedes squealed with delight at the sight of Nick's toned body. Her voice descended into a low sensuous growl as she theatrically dug her long black painted finger nails of her right hand into Nick's shoulder; from there she dragged them down his body, across his chest down to his stomach finally sliding her hand into his boxer shorts where she grabbed the hard root of his masculinity. Nick took a sudden intake of breath through clenched teeth. She smiled, almost wickedly tossing her head backwards in delight. Without taking her eyes from his her left hand now slid down Nick's chest and stomach past his waist, her hand gently cupped his testicles with well-practised skill. They looked deeply into each other's eyes.

'Nicky you can do anything that you like with me as long as you don't hurt me.' There was a slight moment of hesitation whilst they each contemplated what that offer might mean. Mercedes was a tall, willowy woman and had complemented Nick height wise but now that she was minus her four-inch high stiletto heels she needed to look up into his eyes.

'Wow, Nicky you really are something! Two different coloured eyes; now that has to be special. What other surprises do you have?' Mercedes lent against Nick and slowly began to slide down his body. There were no prizes for guessing what was about to happen next.

The spectre of Tamsin loomed hugely in his mind and he was tormented by that thought which motivated him to make his next move. They had both had a large quantity of alcohol and Nick wondered if this could reduce his ability to hypnotise someone. Likewise Mercedes had consumed a lot of drink and could this render her unreachable to hypnosis? In addition, they were each highly sexually aroused, which also could affect both his ability to deliver the hypnosis and her ability to be receptive to his entrancing technique.

'Mercedes, look into my eyes.' Nick started the procedure for hypnosis and within ten seconds she was under. Her lovely head sank onto her chest. An amusing thought flashed through his mind. This was the first time he had hypnotized someone who was simultaneously holding his wedding tackle. *Oh Lord, forgive me for what I am about to do! This is as close to heaven as a man can be.* Allowing himself time to adjust to the situation, he continued.

'Mercedes, what are you really doing here?'

She nodded a couple of times, and then obediently murmured:

'I was sent by Mario Burlace.'

Suddenly it all made sense.

'What did Burlace want you to do?'

'I am to find out where you get your diamonds.'

'And what else?'

'Nothing else. Just give you a good time and learn where your diamonds come from.' Nick needed to think about this.

'Mercedes, why are you working for Burlace?' Their time together had been brief but he had actually developed affection for this obviously talented woman. Whatever she was, she was not a hooker.

'I have two addictions which Burlace knows about and uses to manipulate me.'

'What are the addictions?' Nick expected the answer to be drug related but was astounded by the reply.

'I have an insatiable addiction to expensive jewellery. I just have to buy the things that I see. Burlace has a beautiful store and allows me to run up a heavy account there as long as I help him on occasions.' This answered a lot of questions that had been milling around in Nick's brain.

'And what's the other addiction, Mercedes?'

'I have a limitless appetite for sex.'

Quite a revelation, Nick thought. His next move was crucial in ensuring his safety while in New York and maintaining a useful business contact for the future.

'Mercedes, when you report to Mr Burlace you'll tell him that we had an enjoyable evening together. We spoke of many things and I explained I was in New York to sell diamonds. These were from my father's business in London. Occasionally, there is a surplus of diamonds which the company do not want sold on the European market and so I am sent to the U.S. to dispose of them.'

Nick thought that the explanation was simple and plausible and he decided to leave it at that.

'Now Mercedes, I want you to think about jewellery.' He knew it was more than probable that he would never again meet Mercedes but the memory of her dancing and their night together in New York would be burned forever on his memory. He couldn't help but like her and he wanted to help. He implanted thoughts deep into Mercedes's mind that would rid her of the craving for expensive jewellery. He considered giving the same treatment for her sex problem but decided to leave well alone. It was something she would have to deal with herself.

'I'm going to wake you up now. When you're awake you'll feel content but tired. Then you'll make your excuses and leave.' He took her through the reverse countdown and soon Mercedes was awake, sitting naked on the couch.

'Wow Nick, did the booze catch up with me? I must have dozed off.' Her nakedness now appeared to be a concern and she quickly gathered up her clothes, made polite goodbyes and was gone. Nick couldn't stop himself from regretting that they hadn't thoroughly indulged her second addiction, but while he had little compunction about taking gems from long neglected and effectively abandoned safety deposit boxes, making love with a woman whom he had just hypnotised went far beyond his ethical principles, Mercedes left. Nick checked the time. It was 4.26 am.

Time to crawl alone into bed. It had been a memorable night.

22
Burlace Goes Under

Bert and Moses had been relatively uncomplicated to deal with, but Mario Burlace was a very different matter. Bert and Moses hadn't needed to be hypnotised; Nick's charm and negotiating tactics were enough to seal the deal.

Burlace was Italian, and quite possibly of Sicilian extraction, which in this city could under some circumstances herald sinister overtones. Mario Burlace had attempted to infiltrate Nick's operation without success so far, but he would need all of his guile to keep ahead of the game and he knew it.

The Burlace offices, whilst located in the same district as his previous appointments, were a million miles away in style. The offices were above a lavish jewellery store, which wouldn't have looked out of place on Fifth Avenue. There was a separate entrance to the offices immediately adjacent to the side of the shop front. Five minutes before his appointed time, Nick entered the building; he took the lift to the fourth floor where Burlace's offices were located. The reception area was modern and expensively decorated. The receptionist looked efficient and business-like. He introduced himself to the receptionist and asked for the gents' (washroom). Once safely inside a cubicle, he removed the diamonds from their snug hiding place, returned to the reception area and took a seat. After about ten minutes the receptionist announced.

'Mr Burlace will see you now, Mr Trevelyan.' The door to an office was opened by a heavy-set man in a well-tailored suit, Nick walked in.

'Hi, Nicholas, how are you?' Mario's office was lavish. It boasted hardwood-panelled walls, expensive 'repro' furniture and deep pile carpet, probably not the height of good taste but nevertheless, lavish. Burlace sat behind a huge walnut desk with tooled leather facings. He was overweight, in a shiny designer suit, over-the-top expensive jewellery shone from his chubby hands and around his bull neck. His thinning hair was slicked down with gel, he sported a large, black moustache his cheeks and neck were severely pockmarked. Nick estimated his age to be about ten years older than his own. On either side stood two men who did not look very much like diamond dealers.

'Good to see you again, Nick.' Burlace stood up and offered his gold ring bedecked hand across the large expanse of desk. Nick reached across and shook hands with him. He made no effort to introduce the two men. Nick wondered how the debrief with Mercedes had gone. There was nothing of any significance to report he had seen to that and he imagined that Burlace would have been less than pleased with the limited information that Mercedes would have told him. Nick sat down in the seat adjacent to Mario's.

'So – are we going to do business again? I hope so.' There was a distinct air of insincerity about everything that Burlace said, making Nick feel increasingly ill at ease.

'Yes Mario, I think that we can perhaps achieve something this morning but I'd rather that we talked in private.'

'Don't you just love the way that these Limeys talk? Hey Tommy, Chuck, go take a coffee break!' The two men did as their boss demanded, slightly reluctantly. Nick felt more comfortable when they had left the room.

'Mario, you're looking a little tired,' he observed, sympathetically.

'Lot of work lately, Nick, Yeah, I suppose I am a little tired if the truth be known.'

It turned out to be easier than he'd expected. Within less than a minute Burlace was under. Nick couched his first question.

'Mario are there any CCTV cameras or microphones in this room?' Mario's head had slumped onto his chest. It bumped up and down as he spoke.

'Yes, but they're not working – waiting to be upgraded.'

'Mario, what are your plans for me?'

'Tommy and Chuck are going to follow you to see if we can find out where you are getting the stones from. If they discover nothing then they will jump you and get back the money I pay you.' Nick gave the situation time to sink in. He needed to think fast.

'Okay, Mario, I'm going to tell you something that is very important. Listen to every word that I say.' Nick began his preposterous story.

'Mario, how many brothers did your father have?'

'Five.'

'What was the middle brother's name?'

'Antonio.'

'Did you know that Antonio was a World War Two hero?'

'No, my uncle Antonio spent most of his life in Alcatraz. You must mean Uncle Frank. He died on the beaches in the D-Day landings.'

Mario's voice was slow and laborious.

'Yes, Uncle Frank, Burlace. Well, your uncle Frank was in England before the D-Day landings and he fell in love with an English girl. He promised to come back after the war and marry her but sadly he was killed. That girl was pregnant with his child. That child grew up and became my father. So you see Mario, we are cousins. I came to America not only to sell my father's surplus diamonds but to try to discover a missing part of my family. It appears that diamonds are in our genes.'

Nick knew the story was slightly preposterous but with an element of credibility, but he also knew that, planted deeply into Mario's subconscious, it would have total believability. Nick had passed the guardian at the gateway and was now dealing directly with Mario's subconscious mind.

'We're cousins, Mario, that's why I came to New York to find you.'

A smile spread across Mario's face.

'Cousins.' Burlace whispered the word like a six-year-old boy.

'So Mario, you see that you have to look after me and make sure that I have everything that I want because I'm family. Give me a good deal on my diamonds and tell Tommy and Chuck to look after me while I'm in the city.'

'Yes, cousins … family,' said Burlace, as his head bobbed on his chest.

'All of this is our secret, Mario, only you and I know the truth. It must be our secret and ours alone, do you understand? Our secret.'

'I'm going to wake you up now and when you're awake you'll remember all that I have told you but it will remain something that only you and I know. Ten ... nine ... eight ... waking slowly and feeling relaxed, seven ... six ... five ... more and more awake and ready to do a good deal on the diamonds, four ... three ... two, feeling good and contented, one ... wide awake.'

Mario Burlace sat back in his walnut and leather armchair; a childlike grin cracked his swarthy pitted face and a tear began to well at the corner of his eye. He looked around the room with a mixture of bewilderment and contentment like a four-year-old boy on Christmas morning.

'Nick, I always look forward to seeing you. Why don't you come over more often and hey, bring your mom and dad next time?' Nick relished the thought of his father meeting Burlace.

'I might just do that, next trip. By the way they send their love. Now listen, Mario, I have a lot to get done while I'm in town, so can we get on with the deal?'

Nick made a mental note. *Send Burlace a Christmas card and a boxed copy of 'Saving Private Ryan'.* The dealing over, Burlace called the two heavies back into the room. The third wad of US bank notes was safely tucked into Nick's inside breast pocket.

'Now, is there anything else that I can help you with?' Burlace asked eagerly.

'Well there is one thing. I'd like to buy a present for my girlfriend,' Nick replied.

'Got a girl, Nick? Great. I'll bet she's a stunner. Love to meet her some time.'

'You will, you will. I'll make sure of that, I know that she would be delighted to meet you and your family. We must keep in touch more in the future, there's so much for us to catch up with.' Nick was quite enjoying the charade, feeling that he had done his work capably. Any pressure that had existed disappeared from the meeting, turning it into something of a family reunion. All of this was much to the confusion of Tommy and Chuck.

'Tommy, take Nicky down into the showroom and let him pick out a present for his girl. Tell Abe not to write a bill. It's on the house.'

'Okay, boss.' If Tommy's weak brain was confused before, it was doubly confused now. Burlace jumped up from his chair and walked enthusiastically around the desk. First he pumped Nick's hand and then almost uncontrollably he converted the handshake into a hug. Nick went along with the scene. Tommy and Chuck looked on in bewilderment. As he left the room, Nick saw Burlace wiping away a tear with the cuff of his Armani suit. In the lift Tommy muttered that the boss was a little emotional today, as if he was hoping for an answer to the conundrum. Nick gave none. In the glittering showroom, Nick browsed the display cases, followed by the over-attentive manager who he assumed must be Abe. His thoughts were tinged by the vision of Mercedes, browsing these same showcases. Tommy hadn't spoken to Abe yet and the manager was anticipating a good sale and a fat commission from the well-dressed and well-spoken Englishman.

Nick finally decided upon an unpretentious gold and platinum bracelet. Abe fussed about packaging the gift but was noticeably deflated when Tommy walked over and explained that Mr Burlace had sent orders not to charge this client. Abe was transformed, almost off-handed in his approach from then on, but Nick put the package into his overcoat pocket and walked out onto Forty Seventh Street. This time he was well aware of who walked near to him.

He didn't want a repeat of yesterday's fiasco. The alley where the mugging incident had taken place was across the street and crime scene tape fluttered in the afternoon breeze. He hailed a cab and headed back to the hotel. Nick picked up his room key and wallet from reception asked for his bill to be made up and went straight up to his room. He tucked the bundle of notes from Mario Burlace into his ever more bulging wallet, then changed his clothes to something more casual and went to lunch. This was to be the last lunch of this trip; he would be booking out the next day at noon. He paid the hotel bill in advance and in cash. That afternoon he took a sightseeing tour of the Big Apple to justify his visit should questions ever be asked.

Returning to his room, he completed the last of his packing and then divided the money from the wallet into two piles, leaving some notes for casual spending money. He put on a suit, placing half of the money into his inside pocket. The rest he put back into the wallet, which he returned to the reception desk for locking into the hotel safe for the final time. He reached the Chase Manhattan Bank five minutes before his appointment but this time he didn't need the excuse of finding the washroom. Nick found it quite refreshing to have a meeting where there was no hidden agenda, just banking and investment options. The meeting was over in forty minutes.

Nick took a cab back to the Phoenix Hotel. Back in his room, he changed into comfortable clothes for the return flight to the UK, retrieved his wallet and checked out. The courtesy coach headed back beneath the Hudson River, this time via the Lincoln Tunnel to Newark airport. Nick allowed himself to relax. He had achieved all he had come New York to do. Later, settled into his seat on the British Airways 747 heading east back across the Atlantic Ocean and home, he reflected on the events of the past four days. Life was certainly unpredictable. His thoughts meandered through the previous months and his time in the Algarve He was just so pleased he'd had picked up the crazy book *Master Hypnotism in Just 30 Days* at Felix's Quinta Da Felicidade four months before. The contrast between New York and the Algarve felt to Nick impossible to measure.

23
Old Friends Revisited

Second Lieutenant Hugo De Lisle walked across the drill square at the regimental headquarters of the Shropshire Regiment.

He couldn't help feeling a serious amount of trepidation.

This was hallowed ground and although he actually outranked the regimental sergeant major, Hugo was well aware that he, Hugo, was considered nothing but a nonentity, a Rupert playing at being a soldier who was openly despised by the entire senior non-commissioned staff. The RSM had an annoying knack of belittling him when he was in his presence and the drill ground was his territory and his alone. Anyone who walked across the square did so at their peril. Should there be one small item of uniform that was incorrect or even minutely scruffy it would be seen from the Regimental's Office, which perched like an eagle's eyrie at the head of the square next to that of the colonel.

These offices were adorned with colourful, neat gardens edged with white painted stones, flanked by two flag poles, all of which looked strangely out of place in this testosterone-rich environment. Hugo's demons (and sometimes his speech impediment) tormented him; the other junior Officers appeared capable of taking the situation in their stride but Hugo was always on the back foot where the 'Regimental' – soldiers slang for the Regimental Sergeant Major – was concerned. And so it was with some relief that Hugo finally reached the verge that marked the boundary of the drill square and the neatly edged pathway, which led to the Colonel's office.

One ordeal over, he now faced his second of the morning. Colonel Mike Evans had summoned him to his office for what he supposed was to be a statutory periodical interview for he had now completed almost three years in the Army and his promotion to captain was a possibility which lurked fondly in the back of his mind.

Colonel Mike, as he was popularly and affectionately known, was a grammar school boy, born to be a soldier and a leader of men. From the day that Hugo had arrived at the regiment, it was blatantly obvious that Colonel Mike had taken a dislike to him.

Hugo had made numerous attempts to win the Colonel's approval but whatever he did only resulted in a disaster, which aggravated the situation even more. In the outer office, which doubled as the regimental clerk's domain, the adjutant and the Regimental Sergeant Major stood talking in a corner.

'Good morning, Hugo,' came a polite greeting from the adjutant before he returned to his conversation with the RSM who was a bull of a man, prone to explode into seemingly uncontrollable rage at the most trivial incident. Thankfully, the Regimental made no comment.

'Go straight in, Hugo,' the adjutant said in a friendly tone, 'The Colonel's waiting for you'.

The RSM and the adjutant glanced over their shoulders as Hugo made his way to the door of the Colonel's office. The clerk, a certain Lance Corporal Doyle peered over his counter like an expectant meerkat waiting to see its cousins swept up in the talons of a swooping eagle. Hugo was receiving negative vibrations that he didn't much like. Colonel Mike was sitting behind his desk, legs stretched out before him and hands clasped behind his neck.

He fixed Hugo with his iron gaze, got up from his chair and walked around the desk. His eyes never left Hugo's as he sat down on the corner of the desk. It had always been a mystery to Hugo why rugby players allowed themselves to be disfigured in such a gruesome way. Cauliflower ears and broken noses did not figure highly in the scheme of things in his world and Colonel Mike had both. It had to be something akin to German Officers and their love of sporting duelling scars. He was brought abruptly out of his thoughts.

'Hugo, your time with the regiment has hardly been a happy one,' the colonel began. 'Neither for you, I suspect, nor for your platoon. Perhaps your choice of regiment could be at fault as I feel that you would have been better suited to a regiment that was rooted more in the past than we are. You've almost completed your first three years of service with the colours and now you must decide what you are going to do next. One option would be to sign on for a further nine years and make a career of the Army. The other would be to leave when your three years are up and return to Civvie Street with a clean record from the Army and take up a new career.' There followed a long pause. 'I recommend that you choose the second option.'

Colonel Mike had a reputation for being forthright, but this was brutal. It was a bombshell but not an altogether unexpected one.

'I'm going to give you twenty-four hours to consider what I have said, after which time I expect an answer.'

A stunned De Lisle marched out of the Colonel's office. No need to think about getting that third pip sewn onto his uniforms now, he reflected.

And so it was that Lieutenant De Lisle left the Shropshire Regiment with the minimum amount of ceremony and returned to London to pursue a civilian profession. He had a clean Army record even if he hadn't scaled too many dizzy heights; nevertheless there was his qualification in accountancy to fall back upon. Hugo was many things but it must be said that he was never one to let the grass grow under his feet.

Within a month De Lisle was starting a new career with The National Criminal Intelligence Service as a fast track officer. He had maintained his friendship with Tristram Wrath-Bonham whose own career in the Army was moving at a spanking pace, helped somewhat by the patronage of his father. Wrath-Bonham tolerated him as a useful lackey but never allowed him to get too close, occasionally inviting him to parties where he was useful to make up the numbers.

Britain's National Criminal Intelligence Service (NCIS) was launched in April 1992 to provide leadership and excellence in criminal intelligence. The organization aimed to combat the top echelons of crime and sought the ultimate arrest or disruption of major criminals in the UK. NCIS was one of the first services to be set up in Europe to deal with the development of criminal intelligence on a national scale with approximately 500 staff drawn from the Police, Customs and Excise and the Home Office and of course the armed forces.

The NCIS aim was to help law enforcement and other agencies, at home and abroad, by processing and disseminating information, giving guidance and direction, and analysing major criminal activity.

Apart from a resources division, NCIS comprised the Headquarters (HQ), United Kingdom (UK) and International divisions. HQ Division included an operational support unit, an intelligence co-ordination unit, policy, research unit and a strategic and specialist intelligence branch. The latter's responsibilities varied from organised crime to football hooliganism.

Five regional offices in London, Birmingham, Bristol, Manchester and Wakefield are overseen by the UK Division, which also included a Scottish/Irish Liaison Unit, currently based in London.

The International division managed a network of European Drugs Liaison Officers (DLOs) and was linked up with the worldwide DLO network managed by Customs and Excise. The UK Bureau of Interpol was also based within this division enabling NCIS to have direct access to Interpol's 176 member countries. Information processed by NCIS played a vital part in tackling serious crime in Britain, and was used to assist Police forces in other countries. The service gathered intelligence on offenders ranging from drug traffickers, money launderers and organized criminal groups to paedophiles and football hooligans. 9/11 had brought about many changes. Money laundering by drug barons had become a high profile target that affected anyone with a bank account. Any money moved around the world, which might be used to finance terrorist activities received high priority scrutiny. Everything that passed through banks and building societies had to be accounted for.

Hugo's new job kept him on his toes and so his delight was hard to disguise when one day a file landed on his desk, which was to make not only his day, but his whole year.

The file was not unlike others that had ended up on his desk in recent months now that the authorities had decided to clamp down on unexplained large amounts of money finding their way into British bank accounts. This was just such a file – a man whom the banks had flagged up as amassing a fortune with no obvious source of income. Nothing outstanding in that, until Hugo read the name of the suspect – Nicholas Trevelyan!

Oh thank you, God, thank you, this is a weally exciting wevelation, thought Hugo. Delight surged through him as he scrutinised the report in every detail. Apparently, several banks had become suspicious of Nick Trevelyan and reported the matter to the authorities. There had been some investigative work carried out but the file was fresh and the suspect had no idea that he was the subject of an inquiry. Hugo wasted no time at all in contacting Wrath-Bonham. No point in explaining the details of his windfall over the phone when he could milk it to the limit.

'Hello Tristwam, it´s Hugo.' De Lisle made every effort to remain cool and collected although he could hardly contain himself. 'I have something I just know you will want to see! Can we meet, old fwiend?'

'Busy time of year, old boy, Trooping of the Colour coming up; it's the silly season, state visits etc. etc. Much to do, you know.'

Hugo played his ace.

'Pity weally as I have recently received a file on an old chum of yours and I thought that you might just be intewested.'

'Old friend, eh? Tell me more.'

Hugo was revelling in the charade. 'Someone from your past, Tristwam.'

'And who might that be, pray tell me?'

'Someone from both our pasts.'

Another pause to draw out the drama that was to follow. Hugo was well aware of Tristram's loathing of the man who had broken his jaw in Edinburgh and knew that he would go to any lengths to wreak his revenge.

'Nicholas Twevelyan!'

'Bloody hell!' Tristram's delight was complete as he considered the implications of a file being on De Lisle's desk knowing what he did for his living these days.

'Can you make it to the mess here in Knightsbridge this evening, Hugo?' he asked in an altogether more friendly tone.

'Yes, of course, Tristwam,' was the smugly confident response. Dinner in the Household Cavalry Officers mess was an opportunity not to be missed. Especially as he had never been invited before.

'Seven for seven thirty, and don't forget to bring the file. Nice to hear from you,' and as Wrath-Bonham had decided that was the end of the conversation, there it ended.

Dining at the officers' mess of the Household Cavalry in Knightsbridge was an undeniably privileged invitation. Hugo felt at home. This is where he should have been his entire army career, he thought, not slogging it out with a line regiment like the Shropshire's where mere grammar school boys ruled the roost. He felt that fate had dealt with him cruelly.

His daydreaming was brought to an end when the now Captain Tristram Wrath-Bonham took him by the elbow and led him to an ante-room. Tristram was resplendent in his immaculate mess dress. Scarlet bolero jacket bedecked with gold trimmings, right down to the gold accoutrements on his spurs. If ever Hugo had been guilty of jealousy this was the time.

'So tell me Hugo, what do you have on Trevelyan?' The next hour was taken up with the details of the file and further enquiries that Hugo had made.

'There's no wecord of where the deposits have come from and it looks evident to me that our mutual fwiend is acquiwing money from some suspect source. I have permission to carry out a full enquiwy into all aspects of his life, including phone taps.'

'Excellent Hugo, excellent, I couldn't be more delighted,' encouraged Tristram. 'Let's have a bwandy I mean brandy shall we?'

And so the events that were to lead to Nick Trevelyan's second downfall were set in motion and, by a strange twist of fate, the perpetrators were the same as on the previous occasion. The hounds were baying and they could smell blood. As they saw it, Nick was culpable, he had laid his head on the axe man's block and they could barely wait for the axe to fall.

Hugo De Lisle delighted in his visits to the Knightsbridge mess. He thrilled at experiencing the lavish, exaggerated lifestyle that he wanted so much to be part of and if it were to be only for brief interludes then he would take whatever he was given. He would love to be as close to Tristram, again, as he had been at Sandhurst.

Yes, Hugo indeed felt it wholly unfair that he'd been assigned only to the line regiment. He knew that Tristram only tolerated him for his intermittent usefulness but this didn't matter. In fact, he enjoyed being abused by him and in a perverse way he actually wanted Tristram to mistreat him.

Because the truth was that Hugo was, had (it seemed to Hugo) always been hopelessly in love with Wrath-Bonham but only in his private thoughts. This was something that he alone knew. Hugo's preference for men was a secret he'd kept well hidden. Very few knew of his liking for men and his obsession with sex-play based around domination.

There were professional people with whom he used to play out his own preferred scenarios. These were well paid not just for the service that they administered but for the anonymity that was a hallmark of their trade. Strange how the veiled abuse that he received whilst with the Shropshire's did nothing to excite his strange sexual eccentricity. It had to be an aristocratic male or even female to push all of his perverted buttons.

There were to be many visits to the Household Cavalry Officers' mess over the next months when Hugo reported to Tristram. They were both deriving great pleasure from the exercise.

And so the hunt progressed. Hugo focused his attention on pursuing Nick, keeping the file away from his colleagues in the intelligence service lest they became interested and moved the case out of his control. He wanted nobody else involved. Hugo thrived on the situation and squeezed it for the last drop of blood.

While his visits to the Cavalry mess had become more frequent, Tristram was becoming impatient, relishing the delicious thought of Nick Trevelyan being dragged through the courts and ruined. Hugo sensed that this current set of circumstances was to be only a temporary pleasure. He knew that when the case reached its finale, Tristram would cast him aside with contempt like a worn shoe from one of his magnificent cavalry horses.

The phone taps had revealed nothing. As far as Tristram and Hugo could find out, Nick was living a reasonably normal lifestyle. His relationship with Tamsin Richardson checked out. They found that she was whiter than white. Nothing unusual there.

Unknown to Nick, he was followed for ten days but his movements showed nothing spectacular apart from regular visits to the London safety deposit Vaults which were a mystery. Hugo finally decided that some positive action was needed; he visited the Vaults to interview the manager, a Mr Tom Holland, on the pretence of a regulation call. Hugo danced around the topic of general security, broaching the subject of money laundering but eventually he was forced to open up and asks questions about Nicholas Trevelyan. Tom Holland appeared a little surprised.

'Yes, I know Nicholas Trevelyan quite well as it happens, both as a client and socially. A most industrious young man, no doubt he'll go far,' enthused Tom as the interview progressed. 'As far as anybody tampering with the security,' Tom laughed aloud, 'No-no, never been the slightest hint of a problem in over one hundred and thirty years.'

Hugo ended the meeting and left the building feeling thoroughly confused. He felt sure there was something deeply suspicious about Nick's involvement with the London Silver Vaults, but with no crime having been committed, he had no case. But where was the money coming from? There were the occasional overseas visits but Hugo's remit didn't give him the resources to follow the suspect out of the British Isles unless he upgraded the case and that would mean that it could be taken out of his hands.

Hugo found himself in a 'Catch 22' situation. Soon he would have to make a move but his options for action were decreasing. There was one alternative, which was to arrest his suspect; search his house and take the chance that enough evidence could be discovered to make the charge stick. At a meeting in the Knightsbridge mess, Hugo explained the details of his dilemma to Tristram.

'Absolutely no argument, Old Boy, go in and bag the bastard,' Tristram advised.

'Yes, but if there's no evidence to support the case, then I'm in big twouble,' whimpered Hugo.

'Got to be done, just has to be done, old man.' Tristram sensed blood.

With that, Marina Fisher joined the two men and the subject was closed. Hugo had heard rumours that Tristram and Marina were now an item but not actually seen her since Sandhurst.

Marina had first been bedded by Tristram Wrath-Bonham just over three weeks earlier, but she didn't think of herself as his girlfriend. She found him moderate fun; he would do for the moment at this time of her life before she carried her long-maturing plan into action. Besides, she was actually quite intrigued by what it was about this man that had so rankled Nick.

However, after spending a few hours with Wrath-Bonham, she had a pretty good idea.

Marina didn't even *like* Wrath-Bonham very much. The aristocrat was also a seriously selfish lover. Also, foreplay really was not Wrath-Bonham's forte; he was very much a man who, when in bed with a woman, wanted things being done to *him*.

Only a few nights ago, while in bed with the aristocrat, she'd complained to him that he never gave her an orgasm, whereupon Wrath-Bonham had given one of his horsey laughs and said, 'You mean women can have them too?' Marina told him she assumed, and indeed hoped, that he was joking, and he said he was, but then he said a lot of things to her that she didn't believe: such as that he'd been to Oxford University, that he had a degree in Philosophy, that he was on first name terms with the Prime Minister, and that at Eton he'd won a prize for Good Character.

While Marina and Wrath-Bonham had recognised each other by sight almost as soon as they'd met, they hadn't got acquainted through military channels at all. Wrath-Bonham happened to be shopping alone in Knightsbridge about a month before and was buying a silk scarf for the latest horse-like Sloane Ranger to whom he was extending the dubious privilege of being his girlfriend, when he encountered Marina. She and Wrath-Bonham met again that very evening and he never saw the Sloane Ranger again.

He told Marina he'd been buying a scarf for his sister.

24
Betrayal

Tamsin spent most nights in the week in Nick's flat in Windsor. Nick wasn't entirely sure how he felt about her; he didn't think he was in love with her, but they got well and she was an excellent companion. Yes, he still often thought about Marina, but it was a little over four years now since they had split up and he had literally not heard a word from her since then.

One Friday evening, he got home first to his flat in Windsor and cooked a risotto for himself and Tamsin: they washed it down with a good bottle of red wine. They'd decided to have a lazy evening listening to a new classical CD that Tamsin had bought that day. Nick found that he was becoming increasingly passionate about the wonderful sounds that large classical orchestras created. After dinner they cleaned up the kitchen, loaded the dishwasher and flopped out on the sofa. Tamsin took advantage of the tranquil moment to ask a question, which had obviously been puzzling her from their first meeting.

'You've never told me anything more about your hypnotic skills Nick. I wish you would. And also, could you hypnotise me?' These were questions Nick had been anticipating for some time and his answer had been well pre-empted.

'That's just an old party trick I can do, nothing more,' he added blandly – an answer that Tamsin seemed to accept without question and he was relieved that she had accepted his explanation without digging deeper. After a busy week they were both tired and went to bed early. They made love but somehow it was shallow, different from the previous occasions. More automatic than loving. Nick felt that there was something wrong but he was unable to decide just what it could be. He was naturally a light sleeper; the wine had put him into a troubled, restless sleep.

He was rudely snapped out of his sleep towards dawn by a tremendous crash followed by all hell breaking loose in his flat. About half a dozen burly armed policemen broke into the building shouting like maniacs. As he leapt out of bed the door to the bedroom burst open and the room flooded with armed police. Nick was wrestled naked to the floor, unable initially to retaliate, overwhelmed by the number of his attackers. His face was rammed into the floor; two men sat on his shoulders.

He was still able to see that Tamsin had found time to cover herself with a bathrobe. She was standing by the bed talking to one of the police officer in such a reserved manner that she could have been chatting to her uncle. What the hell was happening? She should have been screaming her lungs out. Then even stranger, *what the hell is Hugo De Lisle doing in my bedroom?* Nick's world slipped into slow motion. It was like a scene from a low budget, badly directed B-movie.

Then the adrenalin kicked in and he regained his feet erupting from the floor like a one-man human volcano throwing off two of the attackers and his arms were free. Everything seemed a blur seen through a red mist. There was no past or future only the instant. As he glanced to the right, a man's face was at shoulder level and at a convenient distance so he gave the man the full ferocity of a back elbow jab which connected with the man's nose. He toppled backwards screaming and holding two hands over what was obviously a broken nose.

Another man was conveniently standing squarely in front of Nick so he gave that one a short arm jab to the throat, which put him out of the game. All of this new action brought a fresh face to the party. Standing in the doorway was a policeman in body armour; Nick noticed that he had two pips on his shoulders. He never had understood the police rank structure but this was obviously the man in charge. Heads turned towards him.

'Stand back! Taser!' He gave the order with authority and everyone obeyed, knowing what was coming. Now the craziness of the scene took a further twist. All the policemen scurried away as if Nick had suddenly contracted rabies. He was standing in the middle of his now destroyed bedroom, naked, and as if this wasn't bizarre enough, the 'two pipper' took something from his belt which resembled a child's toy gun.

All eyes were on the officer holding the bright yellow toy space Taser. The eye contact between Nick and 'two pips' was intense. He could feel an uncontrollable smile breaking out in the corners of his mouth, so surreal was the situation and so ridiculous was the yellow toy gun. 'Two pips' was smiling too.

When 40,000 volts hits your nervous system, all smiling stops. Nick felt as if all the Christmas lights in Oxford Street had been re-routed through his body. Every muscle went into spasm and that was before he had fallen to the floor. The fight was over and he lay on the floor, a twitching mess. The initial pain was excruciating and then slowly faded. He attempted to get back on his feet again and continue the fight. This was only a momentary situation as three more policemen pulled him down again. He was shouting with rage, indignation and total surprise. The thought flashed through his mind that this might actually be a terrible nightmare and he would soon wake to find Tamsin lying beside him. He heard one of his attackers shout.

'Just do it!'

Two pips was shouting orders again. Nick felt a sudden sharp pain in his right buttock and knew that he had been injected. His head began to arch backwards; there was a loud buzzing in his ears. It became louder and louder. His head continued to arch backwards, making him feel as if he were falling into a chasm. Backwards, backwards, more buzzing, louder and louder. Then the muscles in his calves went into spasm; the pain was agonizing, backwards, backwards and then darkness and silence.

He finally came out of the anaesthetic to find himself in a prison cell; he was still naked, lying on a minimal bed, covered with an itchy Army issue blanket. On the floor was a neat pile of prisoner style clothing. In a corner there was a stainless steel toilet and wash basin. *Not quite Four Star*, he thought. Nothing else for it but to get up, wash, dress and make myself respectable for visitors. Room service would undoubtedly be along soon. His head was banging and his mouth felt like the bottom of a magpie's cage.

He decided that the only way to deal with this was, keep it light, don't let them grind you down and say as little as possible. What could they possibly have on him? Nick almost relished the thought of the inevitable interrogation. After all, there was little incriminating evidence in the apartment and nobody was going to make a case against him.

But where did Tamsin fit into all of this? Oh yes, and that slimy little creep De Lisle – what was his role in this charade? Nick's head felt like a cement mixer full if bricks. The spy hole in the cell door scraped open and he could feel himself being watched. Ten minutes later the door opened and two Police Officers came in.

'You bastards drugged me!' he shouted as they entered his 'hotel suite'. They read Nick his rights and officially cautioned him.

'So where am I?' he asked. The reply was something of a shock.

'Paddington Green Maximum Security Police Station. Mr Trevelyan, you are being held under the proceeds of crime act.' This was serious stuff but Nick felt confident that this was an over-kill situation that would soon be resolved. He tried to remain upbeat.

'I'd like my one telephone call now,' he said.

'Ah-well Mr Trevelyan that's something that you might have seen on your TV but this is slightly different', said the policeman who had been standing in the doorway possibly anticipating Nick to go into explosive mode again.

Nick gave the name and phone number of Steve Heligan.

'He's in the SAS and a security adviser to the Cabinet,' Nick said.

Nick was allowed to make the call.

'Good morning, Nick. Good to hear from you. How are you?'

'Ah – you might well ask, mate. I'm currently being held at Her Majesty's pleasure in a cosy little abode in the charming location of Paddington Green and so far I haven't encountered and cuddly little bears in red wellie boots.'

'What? I'll be there in twenty minutes.' And he was. And because of who he was, Steve was allowed immediate access.

'Before we start talking, Steve, can you bring me a tea or coffee and perhaps a Panadol or two? And any chance of adding a bacon sandwich? I'm starving and appear to have inadvertently missed breakfast this morning; room service is shocking.'

Steve left Nick's cell and was away for thirty minutes. When he returned it was with a mug of coffee and a bacon sandwich.

'Okay,' Nick said, 'so what's happening?'

'Well, it appears that the CIA has been interested in you for some months. You're an ex-British Army Officer, highly trained and of some considerable experience, with a serious grudge against the establishment. In recent months, after arriving back from abroad, you have amassed a substantial, undisclosed fortune. They thought that you had gone rogue. You have all the traits of a 'broken arrow'.

'A broken what?'

'Broken arrow, that's CIA terminology for someone with clout who changes sides and is a security threat. You have to admit, Nick, your profile does tick all of the boxes and our American cousins were bound to pick up on you. I'm afraid to have to tell you that Tamsin, if that's her real name, was sent by the CIA to check you out.'

Nick's attitude was suddenly and viciously transformed. Anger stepped.in.

'You mean that the whole thing between Tamsin and me was a lie? I can't believe it.'

'Sorry, buddy, but you had better get used to it.'

'Are you telling me that she is just going to walk away?'

'Nick, at this moment she's on a jet headed for the US. Later today she will be getting a debrief from the CIA director of intelligence in Langley, Virginia.' Nick slumped back on the bed.

'If you think back you will remember that the days when you made your trips into London always coincided with Tamsin being in town for the day. The fact of the matter was that she and her colleagues were tracking your every move.'

Steve gave a helpless shrug.

'Everything that you said was being listened to. Everything that is, apart from the moment you entered the Chancery Lane Security Vaults. Their surveillance equipment was certainly sophisticated but not good enough to follow you down into the Vaults. Once you were inside the building they lost contact. This infuriated them and made them even more suspicious. Half of the legitimate diamond dealers in Hatton Garden have been scrutinised by the CIA over the past couple of months. In addition to all of this and in parallel, Hugo De Lisle was also leading an enquiry into your activities completely unbeknown to the CIA and vice-versa. Classic case of the right hand not knowing what the left hand is doing. The dawn raid was orchestrated by De Lisle. The CIA knew nothing of it but clearly it's blown Tamsin's cover and she's been withdrawn.'

'Withdrawn!'

'I'm afraid so,' said Steve.

'That's a nice technical term for being kicked in the balls when the woman you love and who you thought loved you turns out to have been a total fraud.'

The following day, Nick was charged with stealing from the London Safety Deposit Vaults, Chancery Lane. Steve immediately pulled the requisite strings and again visited Nick in his cell at Paddington Green.

'I don't know if I can get you out of this mess, Nick, I'll do all that I can to help but you have to tell me everything, in detail,' Steve advised. Nick then told him the whole story from beginning to end, missing nothing out, including his ability to hypnotize. 'Are you telling me, Nick, that you can hypnotise someone to order?'

'Pretty much, as long as the conditions are all okay, yes.'

'And are you prepared to demonstrate this ability to me?'

'What, do you want me to hypnotize you?'

'No, I can't have that, I'll send in a guard with some more coffee and tell him that you are cleared and will be released later without charges. You can work your magic on him, if you really can that is.'

'Deal! Just put another bacon sandwich on that order.'

Steve left the cell and after thirty minutes a guard came in armed with a steaming mug of coffee and a bacon sandwich. He was alone and had obviously been primed that Nick wasn't any sort of a threat. He was quite ready to enter into conversation.

When Steve returned fifteen minutes later, Nick was finishing the remains of his sandwich and coffee. Sitting opposite, in his underpants was the guard having a great time singing *Bohemian Rhapsody* in an extremely tuneless voice.

'Wow, I knew that you were a strange bird, but this takes the biscuit,' was Steve's amazed comment as he stood surveying the scene, 'but for God's sake, sort him out. He's one of my lads from Hereford and if anyone else sees this, he'll never live it down.'

Nick obligingly brought the guard out of his trance and made him forget what had just happened.

Three hours later, Nick was taken from the cell by four tough-looking guards in a closed van. He was driven for about twenty minutes across London. Then he was hurried through the back entrance of what looked like a government building and unexpectedly, after checking the view from a window, found himself in a musty ante-room at the War Office, surrounded by a new team of four guards who were evidently highly professional and had obviously been made aware of his hypnotic ability and refused to talk to him.

After half an hour the door opened and Steve Heligan walked in. He was dressed in his uniform and Nick noted with admiration that Steve was now a full Colonel.

'Come with me please, Nick,' said Steve, in a firm tone. Together they walked into the inner sanctum. The surprise on Nick's face was impossible to hide, for besides Steve and the other six high ranking Army Officers gathered in the room, sitting at an imposing desk, was the Home Secretary.

'Mr Trevelyan,' began the Home Secretary, 'before we start I must warn you that we are aware of your, shall I say, 'talents'. Should you make an attempt to influence me in any way during this interview the meeting will be terminated immediately, is that clear?' Nick nodded his acceptance.

'Mr Trevelyan, I'll be brief. You've been caught red handed. You could be facing an extremely long jail sentence. However, I'm prepared to offer you a deal. We realize the importance of your abilities. Together with your military training and experience, these abilities could have remarkable advantages for this country, particularly in the field of espionage. I am therefore offering you the possibility of exoneration from the serious charges that you're presently facing. In addition you will be given back your military commission with the rank of full colonel and assigned to the Army Intelligence Corp.'

Nick's jaw dropped.

'Mr Trevelyan, we all know that there is no such thing as a free lunch. We will require, in return for this arrangement, your services as a special agent. We feel that this is an area to which your ... er ... particular skills may be well utilized. All of this will be probationary and can be withdrawn if you fail to meet our expectations. Colonel Heligan, who is now involved with the Intelligence Corp as well as his duties with the SAS, will be your probationary officer.'

Nick shrugged. 'I agree.'

'Good chap, sensible decision. Now, I want to see for myself the extent of your ability to hypnotize people. Much hinges upon this. So we've devised a small test for you. Mr Hugo De Lisle has become something of a thorn in our side regarding this matter; therefore we have decided to allow you to deal with the problem in your own particular manner. At this time he believes that he has you cornered and is champing at the bit to bring charges against you. He's waiting in an interrogation room within this building as we speak. The room has a one-way mirror system which will enable myself and the other gentlemen here to see and hear how you will deal with Mr De Lisle.'

With that, the assembled group moved off to reconvene again in fifteen minutes at the interrogation room.

'Just time for a coffee and then you're on, Nick,' suggested Steve.

'Think I need more than a coffee,' Nick replied.

The two potential colonels walked into the staff canteen, Steve bought two coffees and they sat down. The canteen was almost deserted and they were able to talk freely.

'There's a lot riding on this, Nick, so for God's sake get it right, I've staked my reputation on the outcome of this travesty.'

'Don't worry, Steve. I want what you have created for me and I have no intention of screwing things up either for you or for me.'

'By the way, the coffee in Paddington nick was much better than here.'

As agreed, the group re-convened in a basement area where the bare concrete walled interrogation room was housed. Its most striking feature was a one-way window, which was about six feet wide but only two feet high; it looked onto a room with very little furniture.

In the centre of the room was a table about the size of a normal dining room table that was firmly bolted to the floor. There were two chairs at adjacent sides and sitting at one of the chairs was the unmistakable Hugo De Lisle. In front of him, strewn across the table, were piles of photocopied papers, which he was shuffling and arranging nervously. It had been some time since Nick had seen Hugo, apart from the rapid glimpse that he had caught of him when he and his buddies had so annoyingly disturbed his sleep yesterday morning. He had changed little over the years. His weasel ways were just as evident now as they had been years before at Sandhurst. He had simply exchanged his uniform for a city suite.

'Ready for it?' Steve whispered in his ear. 'Some of the brass here think I've lost my marbles, so for Christ's sake do a good job.'

'Let's get on with it shall we?' Nick walked to the door and entered the room.

The initial meeting between the two of them, watched with fascination by the onlookers enjoying the benefits of the one-way window, was tense. Hugo apologized profusely explaining that he had made several attempts to pass this unhappy affair on to a colleague, one who didn't have such a close history with the accused but his superiors had insisted that he must see the case through. And so, unhappily, it had fallen to him to interview Nick – much against his wishes.

Yeah, my heart bleeds for you. The last thing that I want to do is hurt you but you're still on my list, Nick thought as he sat down in the vacant chair.

'Nick, I had no option but to get on with this sad situation, odious as it may be,' squirmed De Lisle. Nick sat forward in his chair and focused his attention on Hugo.

He lent forward folding his arms on the table.

If I were to agree with you then we would both be wrong. Nick deleted the thought from his mind and started the work at hand.

'Before we start, Hugo, I was wondering if you were feeling all right you. You look a little tired to me,' Nick commenced his work.

'Yes, well actually I have wather been burning the midnight oil wecently.'

'Your eyes must be feeling heavy, you must be feeling sleepy,' Nick continued.

Steve told Nick later that the sceptical onlookers were all amazed at the speed with which Nick took control of the situation and quickly gained total manipulation of Hugo who was soon sitting quietly looking like a pensioner taking a nap on a park bench. Nick got up from his chair and walked out of the room leaving him to his siesta.

25
Legoland

'That's very good, Colonel Trevelyan. I'm impressed.' The Home Secretary was obviously happy with what he had seen; also, it was the first time Nick had been addressed as 'Colonel' and he enjoyed the feeling. The brass were all chatting amongst themselves. Nick felt as if he were heading the bill at the London Palladium.

'And how long will the subject remain in that hypnotic state?' the Home Secretary enquired.

'About twelve to fifteen minutes if I leave him alone,' Nick explained. 'He'll wake up automatically, feeling as if he'd just dozed off. Whilst he is under I can now implant suggestions into his subconscious which he will act upon so long as the suggestions are acceptable.'

The Home Secretary nodded. 'The gentlemen here will tell you what implanted suggestion they want you to put into agent De Lisle's mind. After all, he was really only doing his job. Colonel Trevelyan, I've enjoyed this afternoon's diversion and I have no doubt that you will be an impressive addition to Military Intelligence. Colonel Heligan will keep me informed of your progress; I expect to hear superlative results from you in the future.'

The whole meeting was over in less than an hour. The Home Secretary excused himself and left, taking with him his entourage, explaining that he had many other affairs to deal with but as a parting remark he added that he doubted that his next engagement would be as agreeable as the bizarre episode that he had just witnessed.

Hugo was given the information that had been concocted which rendered him inert as far as his case was concerned. He left feeling a little confused about the morning's business. Steve and Nick found themselves standing in the anteroom again once the guards had gone.

'Well, Colonel Trevelyan, I guess we had better get to work and sort out the De Lisle aftermath,' grinned Steve. 'Then, let's get on with the rest of your life,' mused Steve as they walked down the steps of the War Office and out into the sunlight of Whitehall.

'I think that dinner would be in order, and it's your shout.'

'You name it; I'll pay it,' Nick replied. 'I certainly owe you that, Steve.'

Over dinner, Steve explained to Nick all about the advanced training.

'To begin with, you'll be spending two weeks with the regiment in Hereford. This will bring you up to a very high level of proficiency in all aspects of weaponry. You aren't going to thank me for that too much as you need to get prepared to get your knees dirty down there with the lads. I have noticed that you aren't at the same levels of fitness that remember you were so proud of. And don't think that the rank of Colonel will give you any privileges; you will be wasting your time with those guys. It will also get you back into the machine; after all you have become a little soft recently.'

'Okay, well I won't argue about that,' Nick replied.

'It isn't just you, Nick. We all get soft when we're not on an operation, no matter how hard we keep on training. Okay, you'll make six HALO jumps.'

'Does that mean I end up as a saint?'

'No, it means High Altitude Low Opening.'

'Sounds scary.'

'It is, but you'll get used to it. You need to know how to HALO jump in case we have to slip you into a locale in secret. Another reason for bogeying you away in Brecon is to let the heat die down here in London. That little shit De Lisle, we'll have to have a keen eye kept on him but with what you have put into his mind, I'm convinced that you have sorted him out. Oh, yes, I've no doubt that the people in GCHQ will be able to dig up some dirt on the De Lisle that can be used to have him develop amnesia where you are concerned, should the need arise.

Steve took a swift swig of mineral water; neither of them was drinking alcohol. 'Then I have you booked on a week's advanced driving course with the Met Police. That'll be fun for you. Get you out of some of the bad habits you've doubtless picked up while driving that fancy bloody Porsche.'

'You're only jealous.'

'Of course. Then it'll be a month in Cheltenham at GCHQ learning the marvels of the technology that those fellows love so much. And finally three months in London getting to grips with the wondrous workings of MI6. They will be the people whom you will be immediately answerable to, apart from myself and my bosses. While all this is going on, the aftermath of your recent escapades will need to be tidied up.'

Steve paused, obviously thinking fast on his feet. 'We have people who will see to that. We have to establish an impeccable background for you that cannot be cracked. You are to become an independent financial advisor so you will need to mug-up on that subject whilst all the other stuff is going on.'

Steve drank some more mineral water. He seemed to Nick to be deep in thought as he came to the next subject on the agenda.

'Now, Nick, we come to something that's posed a major dilemma. The proceeds from your surreptitious visits to Chancery Lane have created something of a problem.' There was evidence of a smile at the corners of Steve's mouth.

'We know you've amassed quite a fortune over the past year or so. There is your property in Windsor, various bank accounts, works of art, diamonds and more, including a rather nice Jaguar. God only knows what you have stuck in the vaults that we haven't been able to get at – and to tell you the truth, we would rather not know.' Nick feigned a look of surprised hurt.

Steve stopped to reflect. 'Yes we know about most of it. The problem is that although we know that you stole these items, there is nobody to make a case against you. You have in fact, committed the perfect crime. It has been decided that to attempt to return the property would open up a large, unnecessarily difficult can of worms. Far better to leave things as they are, which has the advantage of giving you a strong cover from which to undertake your new role.'

Steve leaned back in his chair and stretched. 'Nick, you really are a lucky bastard. For millennia, military strategists around the globe in particular the Russians and Americans have been pumping countless millions into discovering the secrets of paranormal subjects such as remote viewing, hypnosis, ESP and parapsychology. There's not much doubt that, if these subjects could be mastered, their potential in warfare would be phenomenal. The remote viewing project in the US attempted to gather information about distant or unseen targets using paranormal means or extra-sensory perception and ran for years. It was eventually abandoned never having reached a satisfactory conclusion.'

'You're serious? The CIA has really been into this?'

'I'm deadly serious. The military hierarchy knew that if they could crack the understanding of these extraordinary subjects creating a network of Psychic Spies they would have added an immensely powerful weapon to their arsenal. The CIA and the US Army thought enough of remote viewing to spend millions of taxpayers' dollars on Stargate. The programme involved using psychics for such operations as trying to locate Gaddafi of Libya and the locating of a missing aeroplane in Africa. And now due to a catalogue of bizarre circumstances, Nick, you have perfected a technique that the CIA would pay a King's ransom for. Even more uncanny is the fact that you have landed in the lap of MI6, which explains why they were swift to recruit you into their ranks.'

And so it was that the hunted became the hunter. In order for Nick to be able to sustain a plausible cover story, it was decided that he ought to maintain the same level of lifestyle that he had become accustomed to from the proceeds of his exploits at the London Security Vaults.

He wasn't going to argue. He knew that MI6 desperately needed operatives who could infiltrate society at all levels.

Nick cleared his flat of anything that reminded him of Tamsin. Her treachery had cut deep. This was the first time that he had really been hurt by a woman. Steve, yet again had proved what a sincere friend he was; their friendship went back years and had proved irreplaceable.

Fate had thrown them together at Sandhurst and fate in its own unfathomable way had caused them to finally work together. Steve knew Nick better than he knew himself. The training that he threw him headlong into was so intense that Nick had little time to dwell on Tamsin, Marina and the past. The establishment scars were slowly healing. The military vacuum, which had existed in his life, was now filled.

So here he was, a new agent with a new life, part of a Military Intelligence team working out of Thames House, the MI5 headquarters by the river that was known as Legoland, due to its resemblance to a Lego building.

He spent hours in the basement of Thames House where the paper archives were housed, studying old cases and documents. He had to learn the location of safe houses, how to break into cars and buildings undetected and dozens of ways of killing someone quietly and without the use of obvious violence. There was a whole new language to be learnt: the banter that these people used to communicate. Surveillance gadgetry was constantly being updated and all operatives were regularly brought up to speed with the latest technology. Nick eagerly immersed himself into the training enjoying it all although there were some of the more personal aspects, which gave him cause for concern. His life and indeed his personality were required to undergo a fundamental sea change. Whoever he met, his training dictated that he automatically scrutinised them for any small chink in their personality that he might later be able to capitalise upon. He was taught that through the smallest of psychological personality flaws an emotional tyre lever could be inserted and pressure could be asserted which would give him an advantage. This was something that bothered Nick as it was undoubtedly one of the more ugly aspects of the profession in which he was now employed.

26

The New Agent

Walking along Millbank on his way to the office, Nick slowed his pace as he passed curious locals and tourists gathered along the Embankment parapet wall. His attention was drawn to an animated girl among the group, pointing excitedly towards the grey January river waters. Some people had cameras ready; others were videoing the spectacle or capturing it on their mobiles.

A TV news crew, newly arrived on the scene, were preparing themselves. The attractive presenter checked her notes, collecting herself for the live broadcast. Nick was close enough to hear her piece to camera.

"... Initial sightings of the Northern Bottle-nosed Whale were reported several days ago, although her wayward journey up the River Thames to visit the City of London may be this whale's last port of call. This is the second time that a whale has found its way up the Thames this decade. Rescuers have had little success redirecting her to the open seas...."

Nick watched the river. Across the water on the other bank he could see the MI6 building, known to those in the business as "Legoland". That's where he worked.

He couldn't believe what he was seeing. Dozens of the buildings' supposedly "top secret" employees were out on its balconies, in full view of the general public, all attempting to glimpse the spectacle of the lost creature's final hours. *Bloody idiots!* How the hell can they be so dumb? Nick knew that if he ran, he could be there in five minutes and get them back inside. Getting a man on the spot so quickly would have been difficult but not impossible. Once the opposition had seen the error they would have seized the opportunity and taken full advantage. Nick was edgy and the repercussions that could result from such a simple lack of thought could have severe consequences, particularly for the more junior staff, if they were recognised by any interested parties. His attention was now focused on getting to the balcony and clearing it of its spectators.

His cell-phone signalled a call. It was Steve. He sounded troubled.

'Nick, get yourself into the office as quick as you can. I need you back on the grid.'

'I'll be there in five.' With the Thames between him and his destination he set off at a run in the direction of Vauxhall Bridge. Maybe Nick should have told Steve about the whale watchers but he felt that he could better deal with it himself and prevent what might be a prickly scene from occurring.

The River Thames was the unlikely stage for the whale drama and it played to a captive audience. The four ton bottle-nosed whale surfaced, exhausted in bewilderment. It slapped the surface of the murky Thames with its sickle shaped tail and disconsolately blew a fountain of spray into the chill morning air. It was an extraordinary sight and a heartrending one, even in a city like London, where the curious is more often the rule these days. It was obvious to all watching that these were the final sad hours of a remarkable creature.

On the balcony of 85 Albert Embankment (Thames House or "Legoland") the assembled whale watchers watched with intent, oblivious of the danger that they were exposing themselves to. As he walked out onto the balcony a nerdy cipher clerk popped up next to him like a Meerkat on patrol. He shouted angrily, arguing that something should have been done sooner as if Nick had a direct line to "Whales in crisis". Nick nodded, but knew that the whale's survival was impossible; her battle was lost as soon as she had passed the Thames Barrier.

The vantage point on the embankment was the mysterious MI6 building. Nick had visited the office block many times in recent months but was amazed to see so many employees crowding the balconies. He had no idea that so many people worked here in Thames House as each section was a secretive business which tended to cause each department to keep themselves to themselves.

Nick looked back across the river to the embankment where he had been standing five minutes earlier. Crowds were gathering in the winter sunshine to watch the distressing spectacle. TV news stations were running minute-by-minute coverage, crowding out all other stories. This was cheap TV. His eyes were focused upon London's lost whale but his thoughts were temporarily elsewhere. It was sixteen months since he had been caught red-handed relieving the Chancery Lane Safety Deposit Vaults of their clandestine treasures and he had then been unceremoniously hauled before the Home Secretary. It had felt like the end of the line and most likely would have been but for the intervention of his old Sandhurst buddy, Steve Heligan. Steve was serving in the Special Air Service and was now Chief Security Advisor to the Cabinet. He had risen to the rank of Lieutenant Colonel. After hours of bizarre negotiations, which included some not too veiled threats and very few options on his part, Nick had been given what pretty much resembled an ultimatum and was recruited into a little known group operating out of MI6 – called the SIS. It was not just a case of walking in on his first day and saying.

'Hi! – I'm the new bloke!'

Oh no. Nothing so easy. He had been thrown straight into an intensive training regime, which lasted a year and involved working with several of the intelligence agencies and a lot of time spent at Hereford with the SAS. The course was rugged but he loved every minute of it. He was a soldier again, something that he felt born to be.

His daydreaming was suddenly interrupted when Steve appeared from an office and strode out onto the terrace. He was a well-known and highly respected individual at Legoland.

'What the fuck are you all doing out here?' Steve Heligan barked at the whale watchers.

'Don't you think half the Islamic underworld would love to know who works in this building? Idiots! Fucking idiots! Get inside! Your ugly mugs could be circulating around the world by tomorrow by the very people that you are supposed to be monitoring.'

Steve had positioned himself so that no happy snapper could get a mug shot of him. The whale watchers shuffled back inside dejectedly not quite knowing how to react.

'If I had wanted you to do this in slow motion I would have told you so. Now move!'

They all filed sheepishly back to their various hidey holes and within fifteen seconds the balcony was cleared leaving Steve and Nick alone. Nick knew only too well that inside this man beat a heart the size of a polar bear's, but when he reverted to anger mode he was a fearsome character.

'Not too sure those people are used to your way of putting over a point. They're civvies not squaddies, you know,' Nick grinned.

'And you, Nick, you should know better,' chastised Steve. There seemed little point in explaining to Steve that he had himself been about to get the people inside, having seen the danger himself but he didn't get a chance as the action moved swiftly forward.

'No time for this crap. We have business to attend to; get out of that suit and into a sweater, jeans and trainers! I'll get us a car and driver.' Steve's anger had suddenly abated as he switched seamlessly into a different high-efficiency mode.

'Where are we going?' Nick inquired to the back of Steve's head as he ran off along the corridor shouting over his shoulder.

'I'll brief you in the car.'

While Nick changed from his sober office suit into casual clothes, he was perceptively aware of all the pressures that would surface when the call eventually came for him to go into action for the first time in the new role that he had been groomed for. Military action was not new to him. He had seen combat many times as an infantry platoon leader in the Argyles with all of the support that went with modern warfare, but this was different. He was a Special Operations Agent now and couldn't help but wonder if, when the time came, he would be able to repay all of the trust that Steve had shown in him and measure up to the job.

Nick met Steve again in the underground car park where a driver was waiting. The car was a two year-old BMW 7 series; the man who drove it wore scruffy civilian clothes and looked as if he had just walked off a building site. Tomo was on secondment from Hereford, a complete non-conformist and exactly the guy that you would want by your side when the nasty stuff hit the fan and going got tough. Steve gave the order to move off. The unmarked vehicle emerged from a secret exit in another nearby building and slotted itself into the London traffic.

2 7
The Incident

'London Heliport, Tomo, normal speed,' Steve instructed. 'We don't want to attract attention.'

'Yes, boss.'

The car pulled out of the side entrance and slid into London traffic. There were three occupants Nick, Steve, and the driver Tomo, the SAS colour sergeant who was Steve's permanent driver and accomplice. He was a big, strong man – unconventional, nonconformist and thoroughly reliable; he accompanied Steve on all of his operations.

'Okay, Nick,' Steve said, 'here's the situation. A group of Islamic fundamentalists has taken over the Cheshire home of Sir Humphrey Taggart; he was the last British Ambassador to Iraq and subsequently Islamic advisor to the government during the second Gulf war. Fortunately for us it's an old manor house, totally concealed within its own grounds. We have had the place completely sealed off by the local constabulary, plus five SAS four-man teams bogeyed away at strategic positions ready to go at a seconds notice. The big plus in our favour is that the media haven't received wind of this yet; they are too busy watching your bottle-nosed friend.'

By the time Steve finished the briefing, they had reached the heliport. They walked briskly through the departure lounge and out to the waiting private helicopter. The flight to Cheshire took fifty-five minutes, during which time Steve outlined his plan and the specific part Nick was to play in it. Helicopters were noisy beasts and Steve shouted the information rather than spoke it.

'What are they demanding?' Nick asked.

'The release of eight detainees from Guantanamo, ten million sterling and an unhindered flight to Iran.'

'And what cards are they holding?'

'The hostages: Sir Humphrey and his wife, their two daughters, a cook and a manservant. There is also an unfortunate postman who just happened to be there when the attack took place.'

'How do we categorize their intentions?' Nick asked

'Deadly serious. They've stated a willingness to martyr themselves for their cause. We know they have Sir Humphrey and the eldest daughter strapped into suicide bomb waistcoats. We have top level Cabinet clearance to use whatever force is deemed necessary, so if we have to waste them all, then so be it.'

'And my part in this pantomime?'

'You, my friend, are to be the negotiator. We have telephone contact. Their leader is one Abdul Kharmi, a Pakistani, born in England, educated at Sheffield University and trained in Pakistan and Iran. He's a radical zealot, indoctrinated with a hatred of all Western culture.'

'Just my kind of guy.'

'They have agreed to a meeting between our negotiator and Abdul. Your brief is to go in and buy us some time. You can use the excuse that gathering ten million in sterling and getting flight clearance takes time, not to mention the deal in Guantanamo and the need to win over our American cousins. By the way, we have no intention of meeting any of their demands. It's government policy as you know. Never give in to terrorists' demands. While you are inside, assess the situation and report back every detail. And now the biggie … I want you to use that special hypnotic ability of yours to control this man. What do you think – are you up to it?'

'The first part I am trained for. I know I can do what you want, and I don't expect any problems there. Now for the hypnosis part, I'm certain that if I can get Abdul alone for just one minute, no more than three metres away from me without interruptions, I can get to him. There has to be nobody else within hearing distance for just one minute.'

Thinking fast and speaking fast, Nick went on: 'You must also understand that I can only plant suggestions which are subtle; direct orders won't work if they are against what the subject would normally believe. So, I'll need time to devise a viable story and get these suggestions, which must be restrained, embedded. I can activate these implants with a trigger word, but given the conditions, we have to accept that the outcome will be very sudden. I will only be able to make Abdul carry out one task. It has to be backed up by an all-out attack from your men. We are only going to get one go at this.' Nick stared at Steve as he delivered his options. It wasn't going to be easy. 'One more thing – there are no guarantees.'

The helicopter landed in a field a mile away from the Taggart house. They were transported to the target area in an unmarked police car, which was waiting for them. By the time they had reached the stable block, which acted as a forward base for Steve's men, the final details of a plan had been cobbled together.

'Something else that you need to know, Nick: you go in unarmed, un-wired and the targets are out of range of our marksmen.'

'Any other good news, mate?'

The stable block had been hastily furnished with field equipment, radios, and even a desk. All conversation ended abruptly when the red phone on the desk sprang into life.

'That'll be him! Are you ready to go in?' asked Steve. Nick nodded.

'Hello Abdul, Colonel Heligan. As you can see we have met your demands. There are no armed personnel within shooting distance,' Steve lied. The voice on the other end sounded agitated, which accentuated the Sheffield accent.

'Where's the money and the coach to take us to the airport?' Abdul was screaming his demands into the phone.

'Abdul,' Steve attempted to answer but was cut short.

'Listen to me, Western pig. These people will die if you don't do exactly what I say.'

'Okay, Abdul. Take it easy; we don't want any bloodshed. We can end this amicably but it will just take a little time. You know what bureaucracy is like. We have to get a lot of signatures in order to do what you are asking.' Steve sounded conspiratorial.

'Stop stalling and get on with it or you will have these people's blood on your hands. Allah is great!' Abdul ended the conversation abruptly.

'They're getting stressed in there; these are young arrogant men who are convinced they will be martyrs for the cause.' Steve picked up the red phone; it was answered immediately.

'Abdul, this is Colonel Heligan, I have news concerning your demands. This line cannot be guaranteed secure and we need to know that all of the hostages are okay with you?' Steve looked meaningfully at Nick. There was an uneasy pause.

'Send him in but if I suspect anything, he will be shot,' replied Abdul.

'You are calling the shots, Abdul. We'll do it your way.' The brief conversation ended.

'Ready to go, Nick?' asked Steve looking a little apprehensive.

'I guess I'm as ready as I will ever be.' Nick didn't want to appear nervous. He tried hard to look confident. The culmination of a lot of training and more importantly, his abilities, were about to be seriously put to the test.

Sir Humphrey Taggart's country home was an imposing Tudor manor house. On a summer's day and under happier circumstances a visit would have been a pleasurable affair; but today, in midwinter, and given the prevailing circumstances, it was anything but pleasant. Nick's trainers crunched the gravel on the path leading to the Elizabethan porch. He was six metres from the front door when a heavily accented northern voice ordered him to stop.

'Take everything off; I don't trust you, you bastard!' demanded a voice. Nick shrugged his shoulders and did as he was ordered.

January in Cheshire is not a good time to be standing in someone's front garden, naked. Nick decided that allowing them all their demands was a negative approach, so he made a demand of his own:

'All right, you can see I'm unarmed; would you mind if I put my clothes back on? It's bloody freezing!' Having attended several lectures at GCHQ on the art of hostage negotiating,

Nick knew that it was considered beneficial to keep the mood as light as was practical. He also realised that his body temperature was dropping dramatically and he would soon start to shiver – a bad position from which to negotiate.

Grudgingly, the voice agreed. He dressed, immediately feeling the benefit of his clothing. The door was pushed open.

'Keep to the middle of the hall!' ordered the voice. 'Any suspicious move and I'll shoot you.' So they definitely did have a gun – or perhaps guns – in addition to explosives. Nick began to mentally compile the list that Steve had asked for.

'No need for that, Abdul. I'm just the negotiator.'

He entered the house. The porch hallway was small but opened onto a central room, which echoed the exterior of the building: exposed beams and white plaster walls. It was well furnished. There was a minstrel gallery, accessed by a magnificent oak staircase; Nick took in the scene, trying to observe as much as possible.

Standing in the centre, his eyes were immediately drawn to four figures above in the gallery. Two of them were quite obviously Sir Humphrey, with his distinguished silver hair, and his eldest daughter; each was strapped into a harness, which held what must be explosives. Two Asian youths were pushing their captives' heads forward, forcing them against the gallery railing. Sir Humphrey, although dishevelled, looked relatively calm but his daughter was sobbing uncontrollably.

Nick made eye contact with Sir Humphrey. How could he let him know that they were going to do everything possible to get him and his family out alive and that the teams surrounding his home were the best in the business? He could only allow himself a hint of a nod, which he hoped Sir Humphrey interpreted as positive.

Nick was aware that two other men were behind him but continued to stand in the centre of the room, facing the way he had entered. There was no need to aggravate the situation. The two men circled and flanked him from behind, entering his peripheral vision. His first impression was they were all young and typical of the many Muslim men who can be seen in any number of British towns and cities: shaven heads, designer jeans, shirts and trainers. The leader stood out. He was older, perhaps thirty-two, with a shaven head and long beard. He wore a robe that reached the ground. In his right hand was a Browning 9mm automatic.

'Abdul, my name is Nick, I'm here solely as a negotiator, I'm not from the Police or military.' *Better to start with a good lie,* he thought. 'I work for the government; I'm here to see that everyone gets what they want and we end up with a solution that all parties agree to, a happy ending.' Nick pulled back, thinking that perhaps he was being too patronizing. So far the atmosphere had remained fairly calm. From his profile, Abdul appeared to be prone to sudden dramatic tantrums. This had to be avoided at all costs.

'Abdul, all your demands are being dealt with but you must understand that a great deal of negotiating has to be worked through. The main sticking point at the moment is with the American government. I'm sure you appreciate that what we are asking them for is, in their estimation, a lot. We have to convince them it's the right thing to do.'

Nick could hear the sound of his own voice as if he was an outside observer looking in at the scene which was unfolding and concluded that he sounded remarkably convincing. A thought flashed through his head. *So far so good. Keep it up, Nick.* The fact of the matter was that neither the Americans, nor anyone else, had any idea of the drama being played out in this pleasant English backwater.

'Americans are capitalist pigs! Allah will have his revenge upon them!' shouted Abdul. Nick nodded feigned agreement. The negotiating was moving along ok so far, but where were the other four hostages and the two Asians? Abdul was obviously far from dim; he was not allowing all of his cards to be seen. Was this the time for Nick to make his move? He lowered his voice so that the two men closest could not hear.

'Abdul, I would like to talk to you in private; it would be better if the hostages didn't hear this.'

'If you think that you can overpower me, think again! I have no reservations about using this gun. You would also do well to remember that Rashid here has the remote control, which is linked to explosives that will send everyone in this house to their maker. We are all armed and it is our wish to die a warrior's death.'

Given this opportunity Nick took time to study Rashid. The youth was wearing cargo pants and around his skinny right thigh was duct-taped a large red plunger button which was pointing upwards. The youth looked twitchy and nervous. Abdul said a few words to Rashid in Arabic and with the barrel of his pistol, motioned for Nick to move towards the door.

Nick obeyed and walked into the library. It was an imposing room lined from floor to ceiling with shelves of books. The furniture was heavy but functional. Nick noticed two computers and a laptop plus a photo-copier and fax machines as well as other office equipment.

Obviously Sir Humphrey, his wife and daughters, used this room on a regular basis. Nick had read all of their profiles in detail. They were all academics – the family of a senior Foreign Office official would have to be. One of the toughest postings that anyone in that business could have experienced was to be in Iraq during the reign of the late and unlamented Saddam Hussein.

Abdul would have discovered this room as soon as he had taken over the house and doubtless used the computers to maintain contact with any outside accomplices that he might have. Nick turned to face Abdul; they were approximately three metres apart.

'So, what do you want to talk to me 'in private' about, Mr Negotiator Nicholas?' sneered Abdul.

His gun was levelled at Nick's chest; it was cocked. The safety catch was in the off position. Abdul meant business and had obviously been trained to use small arms. He picked up on Nick's eye movement.

'Yes, Nicholas, the safety is off, there's a round in the chamber and the trigger is set to a hair pressure. I feel that for the sake of your health you had better keep your distance. That's if you don't want a neatly-drilled nine millimetre hole in your chest.'

'Don't worry Abdul; I'll stay where I am.' Nick remained calm. Was this the moment to make his move? Every time he had attempted to hypnotize someone it had been successful but there was always a nagging doubt that there could be a time when it might not work or could just go wrong. He had read that there were people not susceptible to hypnotism and Abdul might just be one of them! Or worse. Although Nick's odd coloured eye seemed to give him a great edge on getting his subjects attention focused – what if Abdul was colour blind?

'I've noticed that you are looking tired, Abdul. This must be a stressful time for you.'

'Did you get me in here to talk about my bloody health? What is this Hell?' There was a great deal of annoyance in Abdul's voice and Nick needed him to be calm.

'No nonsense Abdul, I have to look at every aspect of what is happening here and I can see that you really are looking very tired. We want this matter to be dealt with in a way that is acceptable to both sides and as you're calling the shots, it's important that you are as calm and cool-headed as possible. You are under a lot of stress. Just look at me for a second. I can imagine that your eyelids are feeling heavy?'

Nick spoke slowly, taking the conversation to a calmer level. 'Can you feel yourself getting even more tired?' The stage was set for Nick to do his stuff. Just as long as Rashid didn't walk in, Abdul would go under. It just needed a few more soothing words to establish a complete state of hypnosis and then the suggestions could be implanted into his subconscious.

Nick noticed the signs that he had come to know. Abdul's eyes were flicking from left to right. Although standing, his stance took on a more relaxed appearance, the muscles in his neck eased and his eyes glazed. The gun however, remained steady in his hand and continued to point directly at Nick's heart. It was now or never. Suddenly, Nick could see that he was now under his influence and began to implant his suggestions.

'Abdul, I want you to keep a close watch on Rashid. He is an infiltrator and will betray you all. He is being paid by the

CIA and when the time comes he will see you all die before walking away himself. You must kill him if your mission is to succeed. I will give you three words. When you hear them you must shoot him immediately. It has to be done for Allah and the cause. The words that you will hear from my lips only, will be 'Sword of Freedom'. I repeat, when you hear me say 'Sword of Freedom', you must shoot Rashid immediately. Then you will have avenged Allah and your name will be written in the Hall of the Righteous forever.'

Nick allowed himself a brief microsecond, flicking his attention from Abdul to the door through which Rashid might walk into the room at any moment and ruin the whole plan.

Just as calmly and carefully as before, Nick went on:

'I'm going to count backwards slowly from ten to one and when I'm finished you'll be wide awake and ready to send me back to talk to my superiors. Ten ... nine ... eight ... you're slowly waking up. Seven ... six ... five ... you're more awake now and feeling that you're in a winning position. Four ... three ... two ... almost completely awake and ready to move on...one.'

Abdul blinked several times and looked down at the pistol in his hand. He looked like a child reading aloud at school and losing his place in a book. He quickly recovered and regained his confidence. Nick stroked his ego a little to make the transition as seamless as possible.

'As we were saying, Abdul, I am here to ensure that your demands are met but we need a little more time to sort out the details. In the meantime, is there anything that you need?'

'No. Nothing, I have stated my demands. Just go back to your capitalist bosses and tell them that if there is no agreement by 10 am tomorrow we start killing hostages.'

Nick walked out of the library into the main room and looked up at the despairing hostages still hunched over the balcony. He saw the haunting desperation in the eyes of Sir Humphrey's sobbing daughter and, feeling helpless to intervene at that moment, he walked on into the porch. As he left the room, he noticed Abdul looking strangely at Rashid.

For God's sake! Not now Abdul. Wait for the signal, he thought. Walking out into the crisp winter sunshine was a welcome liberation from the desperation that hung like a fog from the walls inside the house.

Nick continued up the drive and turned a corner, out of sight from the house, where Steve was waiting for him.

'Well?' he inquired.

'Yes. It's done,' Nick reported despondently. 'But the next stage isn't going to be easy.'

Inside the stable block there was a flurry of action as Nick began his debrief.

'Here's the picture. We have until ten o'clock tomorrow before they start murdering the hostages.'

'Okay,' said Steve, 'so we hit them at dawn. Did you manage to implant the trigger word?'

Nick nodded. 'Yes, but it will only take out one mark – he's the one with the detonator duct-taped to his leg. He's a nervy bugger, and he really does not like us. I reckon you'll have no more than sixty seconds to hit them before they work out what's happening.'

'No problem,' said Steve. 'We'll have the building swamped in forty seconds.'

'Okay, but there's one problem. If I've been successful in planting in Abdul the instruction to shoot Rashid, we have no way of knowing if he'll make a clean kill. Also, when Rashid hits the deck there's a strong possibility that he could land on the detonator button. It's a hefty brute of a button and could easily be activated by accident.'

Steve shrugged. 'That's a risk we're going to have to live with.'

'Fair enough. By the way, there's a big computer set-up in the library. Make sure that they can't access the outside world with it and alert the whole bloody planet to what they're doing.'

Steve called in his men for a briefing. Those who had been watching the house with sniper rifles and infrared night scopes were replaced by police marksmen, giving Steve a team of twenty men from the Regiment, all of whom had spent years training for a scenario just like this. As well as the forward command in the stable block, there was a rear command post in a commandeered house, far enough away and completely out of sight and sound of the Taggart house. Here the county constabulary and other units were based with direct lines to the Cabinet.

'I want a bomb disposal team ready to move in as soon as I give the signal,' Steve told his men. They'll need six men: two for Sir Humphrey, two for his daughter and a final two to deal with Rashid. Once they've dealt with the walking bombs, I want them to concentrate on locating the fixed explosives and disarming them. We'll need ambulances and the fire brigade at the rear command post. And for God's sake, tell them to approach quietly. No sirens. Repeat: no sirens!'

The SAS men nodded in silence. Consummate professionals, they were an undemonstrative group. Not much in the way of conversation passed between them. Each had a file consisting of photocopied photographs of the hostages and plans of the house and gardens. These they had studied in earnest while sitting around in various corners of the stables. Dressed in black coveralls, they now busied themselves checking and re-checking their equipment.

The SAS men's weapons were individual to each man, their own personal choice, not standard issue. The only time they became more animated was when food arrived. Their food preferences weren't too subtle and tended to consist of the three major food groups of pizzas, McDonald's and Kentucky Fried Chicken, all of which they scoffed with obvious delight, sampling something of everything.

On a central makeshift desk was a scale model of the house with cutaway sections. Occasionally one of the SAS men would go over to the model and scrutinise the layout. Nick marvelled at how this could have been built in such a short time.

As dusk set in, some of the men used Army issue camouflage cream to obscure their faces and hands, then slid off into the darkness without saying a word. Their job was to get close to the house during the night without being detected by the hostage takers. They needed no further orders; each man knew exactly what he would be required to do.

'Okay, Nick,' said Steve, 'this is how it's going to work. I'll lead the frontal assault with three men.' Steve nodded at the three men who were sitting together. 'We'll go in through the front door to grab their attention. At the same time another team will go in through the back.'

Steve gave another nod, this time to a group of men leaning against a wall. 'The rest of our guys will enter from wherever they can, mostly from first floor windows.'

Steve turned to Nick. 'You'll be here to make the call to Abdul. As soon as we hear the shot, we let all hell loose. We'll hit the house with stun grenades and smoke. I can't tell for sure how close the men who have gone out tonight will have got to their fire locations but they are good. By dawn I expect at least three to be on the roof. As soon as you make the call, leg it up to me and follow me in. You have the best idea of the layout and know some of the faces.'

'I'll do absolutely all I can to help.'

'Good. Any bodies, get them outside so we can divide them up. The three who have explosive capacity will have to be taken, dead or alive, to the area I have marked. It's a sunken terrace isolated from the rest of the gardens and the Bomb Squad boys can do their work without hindrance. So, what weapon do you want, Nick? I know that you have a preference for a Glock 17 but there's also a Browning 9mm here if you want it.'

'I'll stick with the Glock, if you don't mind.'

'Fair dos.'

Nick knew there was a very great deal riding on this action. The Home Secretary had added a clause concerning Nick's future career, which stated that if he didn't cut the mustard within his first six months as a special operative, his commission would be terminated.

The stable was reasonably clean and sleeping bags had been sent in at Steve's request. The SAS men appeared to be able to sleep anywhere; their needs were minimal apart from a continuous stream of pizzas, McDonalds and KFC. They didn't so much sleep as rest; all their senses were heightened as the adrenaline flowed. The whole thing could kick off at any moment, so they all had to be ready to go into action at any moment.

There was no heating in the stable and the January night was cold, but the service issue sleeping bags were adequate. Nick slept fitfully, convinced that Steve's plan was sound and there were no soldiers on the planet who were as capable of carrying it out as well as these guys.

Nick had no doubt on that score. He was more concerned whether, when the time came, he'd be up to it.

One hour before dawn, Steve got up – he was already fully dressed except for his body armour. He paced around making final checks to his assembled team. There was no need to rouse them: they were wide awake and raring to get on with the job.

'Okay, troops, cammy up, and then one final briefing in fifteen minutes.'

Nick went over his kit for the final time. He smeared his face and hands with Army issue camouflage cream. Like the SAS men he wore a black jump suit and a dark blue seaman's woolly hat, which was pulled down over his ears.

Nick held an ear defender in his right hand, ready to be rammed into place as soon as he had made the decisive phone call; his left ear was already protected. He had chosen a reverse shoulder holster on the outside of the jumpsuit to carry the Glock 17 and a respirator was slung around his waist on an issue forty-five pattern webbing belt.

If the smoke and stun grenades didn't do the trick they would resort to gas. Hanging from the left side of the belt in a webbing sheath was a twelve-inch hunting knife. A spare magazine of nineteen rounds in his front pocket gave him thirty-eight shots. If he needed more ammunition than this it would be because they had botched it and been forced into a standoff situation. That was deep-Hell, too appalling to be contemplated.

The back door team was in position and apart from the Bomb Squad only three SAS men remained; they would go through the front door with Steve. The first silvery-grey chinks of dawn were illuminating the chill Cheshire morning; perfect conditions for a dawn attack.

'Give me three minutes to get as close as I can, then make the call,' instructed Steve. The door of the stable opened onto the grey early morning light and Steve and his men were gone.

Nick checked his watch and looked around the stable, now empty apart from the six Bomb Squad men sitting quietly, looking slightly dubious. Nick guessed that he looked more than a little terrifying in his latest fashion creation. The second hand of his watch swept to the three-minute mark. He lifted the red telephone receiver and the number rang immediately. There was no answer. Hopefully, Abdul and his cronies were all sleeping.

'Come on Abdul, pick up!' His voice sounded irritated, then...

'What the hell trick do you think you bastards are playing?' Abdul shouted.

'Abdul, its Nick Trevelyan, Abdul, I need you to listen ... *Sword of Freedom*.' Nick's voice was calm, clear and concise; speaking the words that he hoped would drop the key domino and set the rescue plan into action, triggering the commands implanted into Abdul's subconscious.

Nothing happened. Nick's heart pounded. He fixed his eyes on the bomb disposal men who looked at each other, totally confused. Taking the Glock 17 from its shoulder holster he cocked it, hearing the satisfactory sound of a round slamming into the breach, and then he checked the safety catch and replaced it in its holster. Still nothing, then he heard the receiver at the other end hit something hard. There was another pause when in the distance Abdul's voice shouted out:

'Traitor! Bastard! Traitor!'

The next sound was that of three shots fired in quick succession from what sounded like a 9mm handgun. A cacophony of sound broke the tranquillity of the quiet Cheshire countryside: explosions, gunshots, breaking glass, women's screams and ferocious shouting from wild, angry, crazy men.

Nick dropped the handset, kicked the door open and started to sprint the three hundred metres to the house, ramming the remaining ear defender into his right ear as he went. There were more explosions from stun grenades, more gunshots and still the screaming continued.

He covered the first two hundred metres without difficulty but slowed as he hit the gravel drive; he removed the Glock from its holster and flicked off the safety catch. Bounding up the front stairs and through the porch he launched himself into the main room.

What he found was a scene from hell; within such a short time the destruction was incredible. Smoke hung everywhere, the intermittent explosions from the G60 stun grenades and the gunshots were deafening. But worse was the screaming from both men and women. Nick wondered who was doing the screaming. The tactic to create maximum panic was being achieved in a spectacular manner.

Nick tried to make sense of the scene in which he was now a star performer. At the top of the oak staircase an SAS man appeared, manhandling a young woman who Nick assumed must be Sir Humphrey's other daughter whom he hadn't seen earlier; the SAS man's left hand gripped her upper right bicep whilst his right held an Uzi machine gun. He dragged the screaming woman down the stairs, shouting at her all of the way. She was on the verge of collapse; perhaps the shouting was the only thing keeping her going. She was being rescued from a nightmare by a madman. Finesse was not the order of the day. The SAS have a saying: *Maximum force, maximum aggression.*

Where was Abdul and, more to the point, where was Rashid? If he was able to hit the detonator then they were all toast.

Nick had turned starting to make for the library when his question was answered. Rashid was lying on the floor, staring into space. The detonator button looked intact. '*Thank God for that!*' Nick thought. There was a movement to his right. It was Abdul lurching forward like a crazed maniac, his gun blazing but not aimed at any specific target; his thoughts were focused on Rashid's body and the detonator.

The only redemption for him now was to reach it and send them all to Allah. Nick dropped to one knee, reducing his target size, took aim at Abdul and squeezed the trigger.

The Glock barked three times. Abdul spun backwards like a contorted ballerina.

Then silence, uncanny silence. Nick felt a hand on his shoulder. It was Steve. Steve motioned to him to take out his ear defenders, which he did, only to notice that all was not so quiet. There were still the sounds of women screaming and crying. Even with the protection of ear defenders his hearing had been impaired from the power of the stun grenades. But thankfully it was over.

'What's the butcher's bill, Steve?' he asked.

'All aliens dead.'

'No operatives dead or injured?'

'One hostage fatality. A solemn list,' Steve grimaced. 'That's seven dead in all.' His voice showed his revulsion.

'Which one of the hostages bought it? '

'Poor old Postman Pat. He was cuffed to a radiator in an upstairs bedroom. When one of our men came through the window, an alien managed to get off a shot. Pat was in the way and stopped it – a classic case of being in the wrong place at the wrong time.'

A captain from the Bomb Squad arrived and reported that all the bombs had been neutralized.

'Thank you, Captain. Tell your lads well done,' said Steve. The house and garden were filling with police, fire fighters and paramedics.

'Nothing more for us here', he said. More police had arrived and were taking over the situation; Steve handed over responsibility to the senior Officer. The SAS team had congregated in the main room.

'Okay lads, back to the stable for a quick debrief.'

In the stable, all the documentation from the event was being bundled into black bin liners and then thrown into the back of an RAF coach, commandeered from a local air base.

The SAS team had changed clothes and cleaned themselves up as much as they could. They filed onto the coach. Steve gave instructions to the Sergeant Major and the bus moved off, leaving Steve and Nick in front of the stable. Nick was about to inquire how they were getting back to London when the BMW with Tomo at the wheel came around the corner.

Tomo was an excellent driver; the BMW sped along the M6 keeping well within the speed limit, which Nick guessed, was not his normal method of driving.

No need to draw attention to themselves considering the mini arsenal inside the car boot, which would require a lot of explaining if they were stopped. The three of them settled into the journey. Getting back to London by car was going to take a lot longer than getting there by helicopter. Tomo produced an iPod, from which occasional snatches of Santana, Guns and Roses and Meatloaf could be heard. The car was fitted with the latest hi-tech communication gadgetry. Several phones, which Nick knew would be scrambled, rang constantly. Steve was busy debriefing the hierarchy, which was only to be expected in the aftermath of an operation of this magnitude. For his part there was nothing more to do other than sit back and relax. Nick managed to sleep a little, while Steve busied himself on the phones.

His thoughts focused on Steve. Steve really was at top of his game, Nick thought: the British Government was fortunate to have such a dedicated professional man in the team. Nick felt that over the years he had come to know Steve perhaps better than anyone.

Nick knew that but for the break in Steve's life when at the age of sixteen he had managed to join the army's Junior Leader's regiment, Steve would most likely have been thrown onto the scrap heap of British society and like so many others never achieved his full potential. Nick knew that, more and more a new breed of officer was passing through Sandhurst – men who displayed ability over nobility, of which Steve was a fine example.

Finally, as they cruised along the M42 through Oxfordshire the calls to Steve ended and he was able to talk.

'You did an excellent job, Nick.'

He and Steve were great friends; Nick didn't see any need to say any more.

28
Colonel To You

Steve's car wove its way through the hectic London traffic. His personal driver and right hand man, Tomo, was at the wheel mumbling a continuous stream of abuse at all the other road users, and taxi drivers in particular.

'If you keep on like that, Tomo, you'll have a heart attack before you're forty,' Steve said.

But Tomo took little notice and continued to sling incoherent abuse. Steve turned to the other passenger in the back of the vehicle.

'Got a nice little task for tomorrow morning if you're interested.' Steve smiled in a wickedly childlike manner, exposing another side of his character.

'And what would that be?' asked Nick.

'Nothing heavy. Quite the opposite. This could prove to be a light diversion after today's action.'

Steve went on to explain that on the top floor of the twelve-storey accommodation block at Knightsbridge Barracks, located on the edge of Hyde Park, there was a clandestine location, which housed secret surveillance equipment. 'We need to go there and inspect the place. It's a regular bi-annual task and I've volunteered us for the job.'

Nick could see from Steve's face that this was something of a set-up but agreed to go along with the plan.

'Zero eight hundred hours tomorrow morning at Legoland,' Nick added, leaning forward and pulling the earpiece from Tomo's ear.

'Eight o'clock tomorrow morning at Legoland, Tomo!' he shouted into the driver's ear.

'Okay boss, where are we going now?'

'To see the Piccadilly Cowboys at Knightsbridge Barracks. 'Oh by the way, Nick,' put in Steve, 'full number two dress for us; we'll be having breakfast in the Officer's mess.'

Next morning they met at Number 85, Albert Embankment. They were both dressed in their respective khaki uniforms and looked very much the part. Tomo still looked as if he had been mixing concrete.

'Bloody hell, guv! We don't get to see you in the ginger suit too much these days – you look quite respectable.'

'Where's your khaki suit, Tomo?' asked Steve.

'Sold it at a car boot sale. Some young trendy must be walking around dressed as a Grenadier Guard Colour Sergeant.'

'Remind me to have you locked up sometime, will you please, Tomo?'

'Yes, guv.'

As they were from slightly unusual units, the guard at the gates of Knightsbridge Barracks must have been somewhat puzzled. But even so, he flung up a smart salute as they drove in, having seemingly worked out who they were. Nick considered the advantages that his new position was affording him. His insignia was less well known than Steve's but never the less, it impressed.

'Christ, guv, this place stinks of horse ... you know what,' observed Tomo in his own inimitable way when they parked close to the stables.

'Tomo, behave. Go and have a walk around Harrods. I'll call you on your mobile when we're ready to go, and do your best to keep out of trouble. Plenty of eye candy in the perfume department to look at.'

The NCO guard commander had immediately recognized that they were something special. He knew that the light grey beret of an SAS Officer is a rare sight as is the green beret of the Intelligence Corps. The SAS beret badge of inverted wings and dagger commands total respect in any sector of the armed forces. He flung up a smart salute, booked them in and pointed them in the direction of the Officers' mess.

The present Knightsbridge Barracks was re-built in 1970 on the site of the original one. It was a modern building incorporating some of the features from the previous barracks. The Officers' Mess, as would be expected, was lavish. In the entrance foyer, Steve and Nick placed their berets on a long, highly polished antique table. The table had been with the Household Cavalry for centuries and over the years the headgear of kings, princes and generals had adorned it.

Such illustrious characters as the Duke of Wellington would undoubtedly have placed their hats upon it. In more recent times, the Princess Royal would have put her hat there, as the colonel of The Blues and Royals and Princes William and Harry would have done the same as young Officers in the same regiment. Steve and Nick were from units whose officers wore berets.

There were already a dozen or so cavalry officers' forage caps, heavily adorned with gold braid, lying on the table. Next to these, Nick and Steve's berets looked like no more than two pieces of grey and green cloth, decidedly shabby in comparison, emulating a poor relative syndrome. Nick and Steve glanced at each other, a look which spoke a thousand words. The table seemed to epitomize the struggle that together they had fought against for so long. This was one of the inner sanctums of the aristocratic elite.

'The Colonel's expecting us, Nick, so we can anticipate excellent eggs and bacon.'

'I just hope they've got Daddies' sauce,' Nick reported They walked into the dining room. There were about a dozen officers sitting at the long table.

They looked up as they walked in, the insignia on their guest's uniforms causing interest. Steve allowed Nick to walk ahead, a little in expectation of the next event. He wasn't to be disappointed. Nick's old adversary Tristram Wrath-Bonham was sitting at the far end of the table. *Bloody hell!* Nick thought. He knew he should have seen this coming. Steve had set him up, good and proper. Immediately Wrath-Bonham saw Nick he sprang to his feet.

'What the hell are you doing here, Trevelyan?'

Nick allowed time for a pause before answering; he could feel Steve standing two paces behind. There was a total hush in the room. All eyes focused on him.

'You might like to re-think that statement, *Captain*,' said Nick. 'You see, I think you mean, 'What the hell are you doing here *Colonel Trevelyan*?'

The moment was, to Nick, exquisite.

Wrath-Bonham threw down his napkin and, in a fierce tantrum, stormed out of the room. Nick, relishing the moment, watched him leave. Steve took a few paces forward and stood by his side, clearing his throat in a theatrical manner. Nick took a half glance sideways and could see that he was grinning like a Cheshire cat.

The silence was broken by the senior cavalry officer who stood up and welcomed them to the table. They were soon engrossed in conversation. Nick got the distinct feeling that anyone who put Wrath-Bonham his place was welcome in this mess. This was a case of revenge being best served on an empty stomach. Nick sat down at the seat, still warm, so recently vacated by Wrath-Bonham and enjoyed a breakfast that he would remember for a long time.

Nick's words rang through his mind like a merry chime. *What the hell are you doing here Colonel Trevelyan?*

Well, he thought, didn't people always say that revenge was a dish best served cold?

Steve and Nick carried out the inspection, which was the reason for their visit and later walked out into the winter sunshine and onto the Knightsbridge Barracks parade ground. Steve turned to Nick and put out his hand for him to shake, looking him straight in the eyes.

'Well, my old friend, I reckon today we've finally laid to rest the ghost that has been your worst demon ever since I have known you. More good news is that after I reported your part in yesterday's little Cheshire drama to my superiors, I am delighted to be able to tell you that your commission is confirmed and irrevocable, unless that is, you decide to chin the wrong person again.'

There didn't seem much that Nick could say apart from a brief 'thanks', but such was the deep bond of friendship between them that nothing else was necessary.

While Steve busied himself booking them out of the guardroom and trying to locate Tomo, Nick strolled out through the ornate front gates of the barracks, over the road and into Hyde Park. He walked across Rotten Row and stood looking out onto the park towards central London.

Alone, he had time to consider the events of the past.

His future was set, he was doing what he was born to do and it felt good. He was vaguely aware of feeling that he'd found his *raison d'être*, as the French put it so well.

Looking back even further to the crazy series of events that had brought him to where he was now, Nick found it impossible to stop himself from laughing out loud, and he did. The past years had certainly been one hell of a roller coaster. He knew he'd just won a great victory battle over his nemesis, Tristram Wrath-Bonham, but Nick wondered if this was the end of their war or just a temporary ceasefire.

Nick's thoughts were interrupted by Steve. Their visit complete, Steve had checked them out of the guardroom. Over Steve's shoulder Nick could see Tomo nosing their car through the gates.

'Where are we off to now?' Nick enquired.

'Just one loose end to tie up,' Steve replied with his naughty schoolboy grin returning to his face.

The two colonels got into the car and sat in the back seats.

'Where to, boss?' asked Tomo.

'West M4. We're off to Old Windsor.'

'Why Windsor, Steve?' Nick was puzzled.

'I was thinking that whilst we are in the business of ghost laying there's one more we can deal with today.'

'Get on with it,' said Nick, 'I'm beginning to get that uneasy feeling again.'

'Okay, I spoke with you mother and said that we would be dropping by for a cup of tea today.'

If Nick was puzzled before now he was even more puzzled. 'And?'

'My thinking is this, as we're both in uniform – a rather rare occasion for us – I thought that your dad would be delighted that you've got your commission back and now have the rank of colonel. I'm sure he'll understand that what we do is pretty secret stuff and so there'll be a limit about how much we'll need to explain to him.'

Nick felt deeply moved; he felt some dampness suddenly appearing in his eyes. 'Steve, thanks. It's a lovely idea.'

Nick turned to their driver. 'Hey Tomo; my Mum's brownies really are the business; the best in the world, you're in for a treat.'

'Can't wait, boss.'

The car turned left through the edge of Hyde Park, past the Albert Hall and the Albert Memorial skirting the crowds milling around the museums and headed west.

Nick had been so busy with his new career that he'd found little time to visit his mum and dad in recent months. He hadn't told them about his new life, and his new job, because he simply did not believe that – working for the clandestine services now as he was – he was allowed to tell them beyond letting them know in the most general way, which he had, that 'things were looking up career-wise'.

He'd certainly not told them about the circumstances of his new life; he hadn't even told them that he'd redeemed his royal commission. Taking the rare opportunity of seeing him in uniform was to be a complete surprise, which Nick knew would bring them much happiness.

When Nick's mum Annabelle opened the door to him and Steve, and saw them both in the uniform of colonels she just repeated the word 'but' several times, over and over, then called George. The sound of the television continued as George Trevelyan appeared in the corridor.

He just stared.

A moment later he hurried back in to the living room. Nick heard the TV suddenly go quiet.

George Trevelyan, a rather shabby George Trevelyan, who had only ever wanted a successful military career for himself and had never managed to get it, and who had been so totally obliterated when his son had lost his commission, came back into the corridor. He looked hard and long at Nick, then shuffled up to him; smiled, and embraced him.

Annabelle Trevelyan fussed around, making tea and distributing the brownies that she was renowned for. Tomo was a great asset. Apart from consuming an enormous pile of the celebrated cakes, his larger-than-life character bulldozed any negative vibrations that may have been present right out of the house.

All the same, Annabelle's question was understandable and completely relevant.

'What I don't quite understand Nick is how one day you're a soldier and then you're not and today here you are ... a colonel. It's all very confusing.'

'It's a long story, mum,' Nick said.

George turned to his wife. 'I think we should all enjoy the moment, love. I'm sure Nick will tell us sooner or later when the time's right.'

Tomo cleared his throat. 'Might the time be right for another brownie, do you mind me asking?' he asked.

Annabelle smiled. '*Of course,* Mr ...'

'Just Tomo,' said Tomo.

Annabelle went on smiling, then handed the plate of brownies around again.

Nick's father loved meeting Tomo and they jabbered like old colleagues, which in a sense they were. Certainly, there were several locations where they'd both served; they had plenty to chat about.

'I'd normally suggest a glass of the amber nectar,' George said, looking around in delight at his son. 'But somehow, I don't feel I need it today.'

'That's good to hear, Dad,' said Nick. He hoped there'd be lots more days when his father felt the same. 'In any case, Tomo has to drive and we have to get back into London by six.' He glanced at his mother. 'And what news of my little sister?' he asked stopping to explain to Steve and Tomo that his kid sister Sophie was on a gap year tour working in Australia.

'She is in Sydney working and appears to be having a great time.' Annabel answered proudly. 'Her work permit finishes at the end of next month. My only doubt is that she has fallen in love with the place and might want to stay. The house is so quiet without her.'

'I'm sure she'll be back,' said Nick. He went to give Annabelle a kiss on the right cheek. 'After all, Sophie has the best mum in the world.'

Finally, it was time to go and the goodbyes were made. Tomo even managed to secure himself three more brownies in a small plastic bag; Nick knew that his mother was truly flattered by how much Tomo liked her cooking.

Nick kissed his mother goodbye and shook his father's hand. 'Good to see you, Dad,'

'Good to see you, son.'

Nick thought briefly of giving his father some encouragement to stay off the booze, but in an instant reflected that Annabelle gave George daily exhortations on that very subject. Nick just hoped that the delight for George of seeing his son a colonel would bring him a lasting joy and a well needed boost to his esteem that would make him want to steer away from the amber nectar in the future.

Soon the BMW was on its way out of Old Windsor, through Datchet and back onto the M4 heading east towards London. Nick couldn't help feeling slightly sorry for the heavy commuter queue of traffic in the adjacent westbound side of the motorway heading slowly home after a day in the grind and grime of the metropolis. Nick felt a sudden thrill of his own flare deep in his heart. *I'm not part of that world of commuting and kow-towing to the boss*, he thought. *I'm doing what I most want to do, and whatever happens in the future, I just know it's going to be a great adventure.*

Nick thanked Steve and Tomo for their help in Windsor, then settled down to enjoy the ride back into London, feeling comfortably full of tea and brownies. Nick felt that he, Steve and Tomo really did make a formidable team, equipped for most situations. And yes, he just knew there were to be many other adventures yet to come.

Apart from Tomo's occasional blaspheming at fellow road users where the motorway was reduced from three to two lanes at the elevated section, it was a quiet, uneventful drive and Nick allowed himself the luxury of daydreaming a little.

He allowed his thoughts to turn to the women that had featured in his life so far, and who had left an unquestionably indelible impression. Marina, Mercedes and Tamsin. All of these encounters had been spectacular in their own way but none of them could by any stretch of the imagination be regarded as real love.

He wondered if life had that in store for him. He was very much hoping it did. Nick was woken abruptly from his daydreaming when one of the car's phones buzzed.

Steve answered the call, listened for about half a minute in silence, then hung up. He glanced at Tomo. 'Put your foot down.'

'Where are we going, boss?'

'Head for Thames House, Tomo. I'll brief you both on the way.'

'Thames House it is, boss.'

'What's happening, mate?' Nick asked Steve.

Steve smiled at his friend. 'The next adventure.'

Nick gave a nod. 'Are we ready for it, d'you think?'

'I think so,' said Steve.

'So do I,' said Nick.

'You bet we are,' said Tomo. His broad handsome face lit up in an uncontrollable smile. The mischievous twinkle in his eyes betrayed his Irish ancestry. He loved the car and the smile on his face spread from ear to ear at the prospect of being able to turn on the concealed flashing blue lights and cut a swathe through the evening traffic.

Tomo dropped a gear, rammed his foot hard down on the accelerator and the car lurched forwards through the dusk.

29
A Little Self Examination

The British Museum document analysis section was the best there is. They had a new system for dating documents. It's a laser spectrographic system, there weren't too many in the world. There was another in Geneva, and some others scattered around the world. It was the Japanese who invented it. If a historic document needed dating then that was the place to go. Very few universities had the equipment that could date a document at much older than four hundred years. These machines could date a manuscript to within twenty years. Bizarrely it wasn't much good at dating documents which were less than four hundred years old. The process usually took about three days to complete. They shot the sample and then added catalysts. Starting on day one the system slowly aged the sample and by day three the age could be defined to within twenty years. Time on the machine had to be scheduled months in advance.

The enigma of the strange papers he'd discovered – and liberated – from the Vaults over a year previously was eating away at Nick; he could see that the sketches were old and therefore most probably valuable. They could also have historical significance but how could he establish their authenticity? Furthermore, what were they describing? From what he could see, they appeared to be depicting the Earth. There were parallels of latitude and meridians of longitude.

From schoolboy science, Nick recognised the representation of the poles and the earth's magnetic fields. But it was all slightly naively drawn. The text, on the other hand, looked complex: but in what language? Although the spacing between the words was uniform, the actual letters were strange, appearing to be almost inside out. Perhaps they were from a time when little was known about the solar system. Galileo came to mind. Nick looked him up and found that he lived from 1564–1642. The sketches certainly looked as if they could be from that era. This was a riddle wrapped within a mystery.

The spy game turned out to be less intensive than Nick had expected. His training alongside the other operatives was vigorously kept up; they were updated regularly on any new surveillance equipment and weaponry that became available. He was shown the location of all safe houses and other places that might be needed in an emergency. All of this was interesting and allowed him to get out and about but there were also plenty of tedious hours spent in 'The Paper Archives', which were housed in the basement of Thames House.

This was where the pre-computer files were kept and Nick was expected to spend any free working hour mugging up on old cases and contacts. His predecessors had signed hundreds of contracts and set up dozens of spy networks recruiting sleeper agents as far back as WW2. Any of these agents – who were still alive of course – might be of potential use and he was expected to acquaint himself with all of this information.

This for Nick was purgatory. He hated sitting at any desk, let alone one in a basement. Weekly, he could book himself an hour on the ranges where he honed his shooting ability. There was one advantage to spending time in the paper archives, which was that he was mostly alone and contrary to the title, there were computers. This gave him the opportunity to access files that would not have been available to the general public. He looked into everything that he could find on Rudolf Hess and indeed Alfred Horn but his frustration was only compounded by the endless dead ends that he was encountering. He even looked into Leonardo da Vinci and Galileo but he discovered nothing new.

If nothing was happening then his weekends were clear. It was on just such a weekend, a bright sunny day that Nick took his Jag for a spin with the top down. There was something that was bothering him and driving allowed him to focus and concentrate on this quandary with more clarity.

As he headed back towards home, things were beginning to resolve themselves in his mind. His route had taken him out of Windsor to the west and as he returned, his course brought him through The Great Park along the road, which past directly through the centre of the park. He pulled the car over, turned off the engine and allowed the silence to envelope him. In the distance was the castle where he could see the royal standard fluttering on the Round Tower in the light breeze. H.M. the Queen was at home. His mind wandered as he gazed at the gnarled oak trees that lined the main road through the park. These were trees that he had never seen in any location other than in the park. Any one of them would not have looked out of place in a Tolkien story.

Their planting must have been deliberate but for what purpose? No sawmill in the world could have cut a straight plank out of them. He mentally made a note to check out the reason for their existence. Meanwhile his mind returned to more relevant matters. The dilemma, which was bugging him was three fold. Should he go back to the Vaults? Could this somehow implicate Tom Holland if he were to be discovered? He had confided all of his misdemeanours to Steve – all except one – the mysterious papers in the Vaults. Was withholding this fact a betrayal of their friendship?

Inwardly he knew what his final decision would be but he needed to put himself through the mental process of questioning his actions. Tom Holland was an honourable man who had shown Nick total trust and his loyalty to his employer was without question. Nick knew that he had taken advantage of their friendship, something of which he wasn't proud. He could reason with himself that it had been to manipulate Tom in order to get to the contents of the Vaults; but the final vindication for Nick was that Tom's integrity had never in any way been compromised because of what he had done. Not telling Steve about the papers in the Vaults was, he decided, immaterial; after all they could turn out to be nothing, little more than worthless. He was beating himself up on this account for nothing! The sun was now setting behind Ascot to the west and the evening was beginning to get chilly. Nick hit the automatic hood button; the convertible did what it said on the label; folding itself up like something from a Transformers movie. He was cosy inside his sleek roadster. His mind was made up. He would go back to the Vaults.

30
Return to the Vault 31

Tom Holland was elated when Nick called him.

'Hi, Nick! Where the hell have you been?' he asked excitedly.

Nick wondered if there would be any animosity, which might have been caused by the visit he had received from Hugo De Lisle, but Tom sounded genuinely delighted to hear from him.

'It's a long story Tom, which I'd be delighted to tell you all about over lunch if you can find the time to be my guest.' A convenient time was arranged later in the week.

'I look forward to seeing you, Nick, and hearing all about your adventures.'

Tom was waiting on the steps in front of the Vaults. His delight at seeing Nick was obvious and dispelled any worries Nick had about his being suspicious of Nick's long disappearance. They walked out along Chancery Lane heading south towards Fleet Street and on to Tom's favourite restaurant.

Once they were settled, Nick began to tell his story. He would have had to admit that he felt a little guilty that what he was about to relate was a pack of lies but as far as he could see, no harm could come from it.

'So you see, Tom, the call came from out of the blue. An uncle who was a plantation owner in Malaya died suddenly and as I was the only relative whose lifestyle was flexible enough to allow me to go and administer his estate; I was volunteered by the family.' Rather a good story, Nick thought.

'Actually my first reaction was that this was going to be something of a nuisance but in reality it turned out to be a super little adventure.' Since Tom seemed to be buying the story, Nick added a few embellishments.

'The estate was just outside Mersing on the east cost of Malaya, just north of Kuala Lumpur – a really beautiful place.'

He had done his homework but was getting just a little too clever.

'Yes, I know it,' Tom interrupted; 'I was there in the late sixties attached to the Gurkhas.

Oh-no! How unlucky can you get? This was going to need some quick thinking.

'Late sixties eh? You wouldn't know the place now, Tom, and K.L. has been transformed into a modern city in the past decades.'

'Yes I know, I've seen documentaries, not to mention that Sean Connery film which featured the twin towers. It was little more than a tatty village when I was there.'

The panic was over, Tom had accepted his story. Nick could feel that Tom was happy to see him again and remarked that he looked forward to their little chats when he told him that he would be starting work again on his long abandoned stamp collection.

Lunch finished, they walked back to the Vaults and Tom took him down to see Veronica and George who seemed equally pleased to see him again.

'Thought that you had left and forgotten all about us!' Veronica feigned grief.

'How could you think that?' Nick replied, mimicking her grief.

'Know what, Nick? I'm still not smoking. Been over eighteen months now,' she proudly announced.

'I'm delighted to hear it,' was his honest reply because she did look better for having kicked the habit. A sudden realisation hit him; he actually did miss them all.

'Well, while I'm here, I suppose I'd better get on with some work. My stamp collection isn't going to sort itself out.' With this, their little reunion broke up and Veronica went off to fetch his security box.

Opening the box after a year was exciting. Nick knew exactly what was inside but the brown envelope with the mysterious papers had always been in the back of his mind. It was a mystery he couldn't leave alone and was determined to find out just what the extraordinary paper signified.

Saying his goodbyes and promising not to stay away so long in future, he left the Vaults with the brown envelope tucked inside his overcoat. Once again he joined the early commuter rush returning to the suburbs and, in his case, his bachelor flat.

31
Dr Oatley

On the morning of his day off he drove to Oxford. The enigma of the strange papers he had discovered – and liberated – from the Vaults was constantly gnawing away at the back of his mind.

He felt it was high time he tried to deal with this particular mystery.

He hadn't seen the old papers for more than a year, but he remembered them perfectly well. At the very least, the sketches were obviously old and surely had potential historical significance. But how could he establish their authenticity? Furthermore, what were they describing? From what he could see, they appeared to be depicting the planet Earth. There were parallels of latitude and meridians of longitude. Today was the day that he hoped to get some answers.

He walked along Oxford's magnificent Broad Street, a medieval feast for the eyes in stunning beige Cotswold stone, with the splendid Balliol and Trinity Colleges on his left and the fabulous quasi-Grecian Sheldonian theatre up ahead. On the right were obviously long-established antiquarian bookshops in eighteenth-century buildings of Cotswold Stone. Nick chose the most ancient bookshop and went in. The old-fashioned bell on a ribbon of thin metal tinkled above him.

Nick browsed the musty shelves for several minutes checking the place out; then, when he was satisfied, he turned to the elderly looking proprietor, who had only briefly glanced up from behind the counter when Nick walked in.

'I wonder if you might be able to help me,' Nick said. 'You see, I'm trying to authenticate the origin of some papers that have come into my possession,' Nick asked the ancient shopkeeper, man dressed in tweeds, who looked to Nick rather like an antique himself.

He glanced over the top of his bifocals and then around the store in which Nick was the sole customer. Realizing that there was nothing of significance happening, he somewhat begrudgingly agreed to oblige.

Nick produced his photocopies, and images of the Antiques Road Show flashed through his mind. The next few minutes were excruciating. The ancient man said nothing; he grunted many times leafing through the pages until Nick thought that he would crack and shout at the man. *Well what do you think?* But he managed to stay calm until finally the expert looked up from the pages, his piercing blue eyes staring directly at him.

'Mr er …' Tweedy was searching for a name.

'My name's John Bonham,' Nick said.

'Well, Mr Bonham, you've chosen wisely this morning, I assume you took pot luck when deciding which shop to come into?'

'Basically.'

'As I said, you've chosen well. I'm Dr Marcus Oatley. I am, as you have correctly surmised, an expert on antique books and manuscripts, my specialist subject being Leonardo da Vinci. I have to tell you, young man, that in my, may I say learned opinion, these photocopies could be of sketches drawn by none other than Leonardo himself.'

Nick tried hard not to gulp visibly. This was obviously a man not given to joking. He continued, 'I pride myself on knowing all of the da Vinci notebooks and sketches, of which there are many. These sketches, if they are indeed genuine, and I would need to examine the originals myself to confirm their authenticity, would have never been seen before.'

The full magnitude of what Dr Oatley had just said was beginning to sink in.

'Do you have any idea, Mr Bonham, of the potential value of these articles?'

'Well I was rather wondering whether you could tell me,' Nick said.

'The fact of the matter, Mr Bonham, is that, if they're genuine, then the value is, essentially, whatever you would care to ask for them. They would be, to all intents and purposes, priceless!'

The statement hit Nick straight between the eyes like a cricket bat.

'The existing known da Vinci sketches,' Oatley went on, 'are owned by such distinguished places as Musée du Louvre, Paris, The Royal Library, Windsor Castle and the Biblioteca Nacional, Madrid, which might give you some idea of the level of esteem at which this work is held. You might also be interested in the subject matter, Mr Bonham.'

Oatley continued, 'Da Vinci was interested in the solar system and these diagrams depict the rotation of the earth on its axis, the gravitational pull and magnetic poles. He was way ahead of his time as I'm sure you know from your school days.'

This was astounding news indeed and might shed some light upon the Hess connection but that information was not for the ears of the learned doctor at this point.

'Da Vinci was convinced of the negative gravity theory at the poles and these are the diagrams which he used to demonstrate his supposition,' enthused the expert.

'Wow, Dr Oatley, that certainly is a revelation. I'm slightly shocked.' Nick could bring himself to utter nothing but his truthful feelings. He was actually warming to the wily old antiquarian and he guessed from the way he was smiling now that the feeling was mutual.

'Mr Bonham, if that is in fact your name, I'm going to be totally frank with you.' Nick saw a twinkle in the old man's eyes that he hadn't noticed before.

'I would hazard a guess that you have come by these extraordinary artefacts by surreptitious means. That is of no consequence to me. I am now an old man. If I may confide in a stranger for a moment, I have very little by the way of family. My sole true love is Renaissance books and manuscripts.'

Dr Oatley paused. Nick had more sense than to say anything. He felt sure that the old man was just waiting for a moment so that he could build up more of a sense of confidence before continuing with further revelations.

'In all of my years exploring historical literature I've never encountered anything as astonishing as what you've shown me today,' Oatley suddenly went on. 'I've no interest in how you came by these treasures but, please listen; I would beg you to treat them with the utmost care because they could be of immense historical value to the entire world.'

Nick nodded slowly. 'Thanks, Dr Oatley. But I'd still really appreciate some idea of their value.'

Oatley glanced around his shop, as if he feared an eavesdropper might be hiding somewhere, and then said, his voice little more than a whisper:

'You must understand that at a very conservative estimate each of the sketches would be worth a minimum of a million pounds. Altogether, ten million would be considered an extremely low figure.'

Any fear Nick might have had that Dr Oatley would blow the whistle on him disappeared with the last statement. He considered himself a good judge of character and his gut reaction was that Dr Oatley was being totally honest.

'Thanks very much, Dr Oatley, I really appreciate all this. Jolly kind of you.'

Dr Oatley pushed his bifocal spectacles slowly and deliberately from his nose to the top of his head.

'There are of course ways of determining the authentic age of the papers but that I feel might pose more than a few problems for you.'

The learned doctor stroked the greying beard on his chin and explained.

'The British Museum Document Analysis Section is the best there is. They have a new state of the art laser technology there for accurately dating ancient documents. It's a laser spectrographic system, there aren't too many in the world. There is another that I have heard of in Geneva, and some others scattered around the planet. It was the Japanese who invented it, very clever people the Japanese, particularly in laser technology. If a historic document needs dating then that's the place to go. Very few universities have equipment that can date a document to much older than four hundred years. These new laser machines can date a manuscript to within plus or minus twenty years. Bizarrely, it isn't much good at dating documents which are less than four hundred years old. The process usually takes about three days to complete. They shoot the sample and then add catalysts. Starting on day one the system slowly ages the sample and by day three the age can be defined to within twenty years. Time on the machine has to be scheduled months in advance.'

Nick felt that he was getting the maximum information and advice from the good doctor. The more the information flowed, the more naïve he himself came across as being.

'My only wish is that you find a way of bringing them into public view so that they can be analysed and enjoyed by all,' said Dr Oatley. 'Here is my card. I would ask you to please keep me informed regarding the progress you make. Please, do not hesitate to call me should you need help on the matter. I will be more than happy to assist.'

They shook hands and Nick walked out of the quiet mustiness of the shop and into Broad Street in Oxford.

During the drive home, the real significance of what had happened in the shop began, to sink in. He felt very great comfort in the knowledge that the originals were locked away safely in his safety deposit box under the watchful eyes of Tom, Veronica and George.

As the days passed, Nick pieced together what he knew. Firstly, as regards Hess, Nick was aware that Hess flew to Scotland in 1941, that his treatment by the British authorities could only be considered bizarre, and that somehow Hess had managed to stow away the documents in the Chancery Lane Safety Deposit.

As for the Da Vinci sketches, Nick was aware that they depicted:

1. The angle of earth's tilt on its axis.
2. The Earth's magnetic field; object entering orbit, due to earth's gravitational pull.
3. An object leaving earth from the poles, not affected by earth's gravitational pull.

4. The Moon.
5. The parallels of latitude; effects of gravitational pull lessening towards poles.
6. The vortex effect present at the North and south poles.

Somehow these sketches had played role in causing Hess to make a life-altering decision to fly to Britain during the war, but Nick could only guess at the missing pieces of the jigsaw. Germany at that time was making tremendous advances in rocket science. After all, following the war the Americans had basically recruited many of the leading German rocket scientists. The Nazis were also known to have been working on an atom bomb of their own.

If da Vinci's assumption was correct and the negative gravity theory of the poles actually existed, then if the German V rockets could somehow be launched from the poles there would be significantly less fuel required to send them into space and from there to orbit the planet. They would be able to carry a heavier payload, which could potentially be the almost completed atom bomb. All of this added up, but why then did Hess take the papers out of Germany? It would be sorely tempting to take a sample and somehow get the British Museum to analyse the paper but the risk would be too great and far too many questions were sure to be asked.

Nick felt as if he had solved part of the puzzle but there were still plenty of pieces missing. He had made some progress in the paper archives on his Hess riddle but the answers still continued to elude him. He knew that if he were to enlist the services of Orville Skippings, the section computer genius, Orville would come up with the answer. For the time being though, Nick resolved to try to solve the problem himself.

Still, he was pleased he had Orville as a possible resource.

32
Orville

As a new operative in Military Intelligence, Nick had been assigned to Juliet Section, which consisted of himself and five other agents. His first impressions were that his new colleagues were less than obvious 'spooks'. There were three operatives who more or less fitted the bill, i.e., two women and one man, fit, active and more than capable of looking after themselves in a tight spot.

The fifth member of the team was very far indeed from being like James Bond. Orville Skippings was downright scruffy, which was actually a conservative description. Indeed, Orville was bordering on rancid which was particularly evident towards the end of the week – leading Nick to the conclusion that Saturday or Sunday must have been his bath night.

None of this seemed to matter to the Section, for Orville was a genius. He epitomised the absent-minded professor in every detail but none of this mattered when he got behind a computer. It was a joy to watch him practically make the computer sing and dance. Orville could hack into a cuckoo clock and make it bark. This man was a rare asset in the world of digitalised espionage. He could break codes and hack into anything and everything in seconds.

Juliet Section – named after the word for 'J' in the phonetic alphabet, of course – was led by an Irishman called Edward Fitzpatrick. His role involved liaising with the Home Office and heads of security organisations on a global level. Nick estimated that he was in his early sixties, which meant that his service had spanned decades of world conflict, in particular, the Cold War period. All of this made his knowledge base remarkable.

So this was Nick's new group of workmates. Steve was based in the same building but his remit was more at Cabinet level attending all Cobra meetings. When the nasty stuff happened it was Steve who was called for; he dealt with the heavy details and his SAS teams were regularly in action. Nick was a sort of floater between Juliet Section and Steve's unit.

Six weeks passed. Nick was involved in several minor operations but his specialist ability hadn't again been called upon. He was getting used to his new role and enjoying life again. He knew that it was regarded as important that he became established as a part of the West London scene. Terrorism operated at all levels and it was imperative to have operatives implanted into every plane of the social scale.

Starbucks was one of his favourite local coffee venues. He enjoyed walking through Windsor, buying the everyday things that he needed and stopping for a coffee before returning to the flat. His training had covered all aspects of intelligence work including surveillance. He enjoyed living in Windsor; the town really felt like home, but work happened in London.

That day, there was something different. Being a Tuesday, he had made his customary visit to his bank and as it was raining he lingered a little longer in Waterstones looking for something to read; something that he couldn't quite get a handle on was worrying him. Within the depths of his sixth sense, a distant warning bell was beginning to ring.

The coffee house felt warm and cosy after the miserable rainy day outside. He ordered a latte and sat down at a window seat. From here he could observe people coming in and out of the coffee house.

'Hello, Nick.' Tamsin appeared next to the table; she must have been in the building when he arrived.

'Tamsin!' His surprise was impossible to hide. It took a while to regain his composure; 'Or is it really "Tamsin"? Everything else about you was a lie so I imagine your name was, too'

'Yes – you're right, Nick, my real name is Sian. Nick, I'm so sorry for the deceit and what I did to you. I know that you'll never forgive me – but I just had to see you again and tell you that my feelings for you were real.'

Nick felt confused, to put it mildly. Seeing Tamsin again was a shock; she was just as beautiful as ever. During the months that had passed since she so callously walked out, he'd had plenty of time to think about the cruelty of her actions and yet so much had changed in his life since he had last laid eyes on her. He recalled one of the lecturers at GCHQ telling them: *Once someone is recruited into an intelligence agency be it the KGB or CIA or whatever, they will never be allowed to leave.*

And now, Tamsin/Sian was playing him. He could feel it. But what did she want? Did she know what his role in the cloak and dagger world of espionage was now? He needed to find out more. He went along with the game; this had to be checked out, it was all too pat.

'I want you to know that I was being controlled by the CIA,' Tamsin said, very quietly, 'and you were my first assignment. If it's any consolation to you, after that mission I was taken off field duties as it was thought that I had allowed myself to become too deeply involved with my "mark". They put me behind a desk. I stuck it for almost a year, and then resigned.'

Acting as casually as he could, Nick drank the remains of his coffee.

'Sian,' – saying the name made him feel uncomfortable, as in his mind it emphasised her duplicity – 'I have to go. I'm late for an appointment. But I'd love to talk to you more. How about dinner tonight? Are you in town for long?'

Sian nodded. 'Nick, I'd love to. Shall we meet outside here, say at seven thirty?'

They agreed to do just that and they each walked out into the street and parted while the pipes and drums of the Grenadier Guards marched up the hill from Victoria Barracks to change the guard at the castle.

Nick needed to call Steve urgently but couldn't take the risk of calling from his flat, which he now suspected could have been bugged. The sudden appearance of someone with Sian's background was far too suspicious. His cell phone was secure; he sat on a bench in front of the castle and made the call to Steve. Nick explained about Tamsin coming back into his life.

'Steve, were you at the debriefing when I was raided last year?'

'Yes of course I was. After you called me from Paddington Green, I demanded to be there.'

'Did Tamsin ever know the full extent of what I was up to?'

'No, we kept the CIA in the dark as much as we could. Once it was established that you were merely a serial criminal and not a terrorist risk, the CIA immediately lost interest in you and pulled out.'

'So she doesn't know the full extent of my hypnotic ability and what went on in the Vaults?'

'No, they were severely frustrated when their highly sophisticated listening devices didn't work underground.'

'What do you think she's after, Steve?'

'No idea, mate. Could be that suave charm of yours – but I would guess that you're right and that she has a deeper motive. You'll have to play along but, this time, don't get burned, okay?'

'Don't worry, my memory is good. I can still see her face when we got hit; her only reaction was annoyance at having her cover blown.'

He went back to his flat. Steve had sent over a two-man team and the building was swept for bugs. None were found. At the same time, they installed minute surveillance cameras, which covered the living room. Any intruder would have to pass through there.

'All done, guv, no bugs here,' said the operative in charge who looked rather like the senior of two regular GPO engineers.

Nick's admiration for the organization he'd become part of was increasing by the day. Steve's ability to call up operatives and have them on his doorstep within the hour felt very impressive to Nick. Reassured by knowing that the flat wasn't bugged, Nick relaxed, wondering how best to deal with the situation.

He put on some classical music and immersed himself in thought. He realised that he was listening to Nigel Kennedy playing Vivaldi's *Four Seasons,* classical music that Tamsin had introduced him to, in what now seemed like a lifetime ago.

He wondered whether he'd put that particular piece of music on as a subconscious result of meeting her again or was it just a coincidence?

That evening he picked her up in his Jag and drove to a trendy restaurant in Ealing. They decided on a secluded table and took their time eating, enjoying the meal. The wine was excellent, the atmosphere was relaxed and Nick chose his time to make the next move. There was nobody within earshot and the waiters had completed the greater part of their work. It was now time to attempt to hypnotize Sian. He had to be very subtle and, as always, the feeling that this might be the time when it didn't work, was gnawing at his insides.

'Sian, look at me, look into my eyes,' slowly and gently he soothed her into a feeling of calm comfort.

She smiled. 'You know, Nick, I can't tell you how many times I have thought about you over the last year, but the most memorable and lasting image has to be your eyes. I have never seen anyone with eyes like yours. Two separate colours is weird but with you it has a wonderfully haunting effect.'

Flattery is usually acceptable but this wasn't the time or the place. He got her full concentration and continued with his work.

'Your eyes look quite tired, Sian, your legs and arms are feeling heavy too. Allow them to relax. Just let your eyes close.'

Twenty seconds and she was under. Her head slumped slightly forward but to any of the other diners in the restaurant they appeared to be a couple deep in conversation. Nick waited for another two minutes to be sure that she was in deep hypnosis.

'Sian, I'm going to ask you some questions which you will answer completely honestly.'

'Yes,' mumbled Sian.

'What do you think happened to me when you went back to the States?'

'You were caught stealing from the Chancery Lane Vaults,' murmured Sian. 'You weren't a terrorist and so the CIA had no further interest in you. I made enquires and no charges were ever made against you as the whole affair was too embarrassing for the authorities and was dropped.'

Nick felt gratified to know that his cover was intact.

'Sian, why have you come back?'

'For the da Vinci Papers.'

This was a bombshell. Nick knew he had to think fast.

'How... how do you know about the da Vinci Papers, Sian?'

'I went through your apartment, cleaning, when you were in London. Don't you remember, I found your funny little painted toy figures and gave you a hard time over them. Then I discovered the papers. I made photocopies and at first thought nothing of them. Later I researched them and discovered that they are worth millions.' This all fitted, but how did she expect to get the papers from him?

'Sian, what's your next move?'

'Mr Palestroni wants me to gain your confidence and get more information about the papers.'

'Mr who?'

'Caesar Palestroni. He is paying me to do this. He is very powerful. His men are watching everything that I do.'

Nick looked around the restaurant. He suddenly felt worried that he'd been negligent and been detected whilst hypnotising Sian and questioning her? After all, surely she had someone with her to make sure she was safe?

There was no one who looked suspicious but he decided that for now, he had enough information. His sixth sense had been right after all.

'Sian, I am going to wake you up, but before I do, I want you to remember these two words, "Four Seasons". In the future whenever you hear me say them, you will immediately return to the state of trance that you are in now.'

He implanted the trigger words into Sian's subconscious, but before he was able to start the countdown to bring Sian out of her trance, a waiter suddenly arrived at the table.

'Would you like coffee, sir?' Nick glanced nervously at Sian. But the waiter didn't appear to notice anything untoward; he was busy concentrating on the forthcoming tip.

'No thank you, just the bill please.'

When he'd gone, Nick bought Sian out of the trance. She blinked nervously several times and looked slightly embarrassed as if she had started a sentence and forgotten what she was talking about.

Nick smiled inwardly as it appeared that whenever people were brought out of a trance they felt as if they were guilty of a temporary memory lapse. The evening ended on an affable note. Sian gave him her mobile number and they agreed to meet again soon. Nick dropped her off where he had picked her up in front of Starbucks.

Early next morning Nick went to see Steve at Thames House and told him about the previous evening. Once he had, and in the secure, completely un-bugged safety of Steve's private office, Nick finally told Steve the whole story concerning the now authenticated da Vinci Papers.

'When I first discovered them I had no idea of exactly what they were. They certainly looked authentic and were most undoubtedly old but it's only recently I've verified their origins.'

Nick went on to explain about his visit to Oxford and his meeting with Dr Marcus Oatley.

'Bloody hell, Nick, you certainly do have a knack for falling into Hell and coming up smelling like a Chelsea Flower Show garden.'

'Yes, I know all about that but what about this Italian connection?'

'Caesar Palestroni? Yes, we have masses on him.' Steve buzzed through to his secretary Jayne and politely asked her to bring him the file on Signor Palestroni. Once Steve had rung off he glanced at Nick.

'I get the feeling that Sian is acting on her own in this matter. Seems as if she has her own agenda and may well have moved on from the CIA. I can have that checked out.'

When the file arrived, it was huge. Palestroni was wanted by Interpol for a multitude of reasons: fraud, money laundering, political corruption, illegal arms dealing and drugs.

He was certainly not above resorting to homicide in order to achieve his ends. In his native Italy he was extremely high profile – half the country loved him and the other half hated him. He was undoubtedly corrupt but extradition laws protected him. France, Germany, Britain and in particular the United States would all love to get their hands on him but he stayed within the protection of Italian law. He was immensely wealthy, his acquisitions stretching across all spheres of business from mining to technology. His principal residence was a villa in Sabina on the outskirts of Rome, which was said to be extraordinary; housing what must be one of the world's greatest private art collections.

'He's a wily old bastard,' Steve mused. 'There've been plenty of attempts to entrap him and get him out of Italy but he always stays one step ahead of us.

'Listen, Steve, how about this? We know he badly wants the da Vinci Papers. Sian knows that they exist and that I have them. Remember, she took photocopies. She is working independently for her own gain, which has to be why she is here. Palestroni is bankrolling the operation. Steve, we are going to need really high-quality copies: copies so good that even da Vinci himself couldn't have confidently confirmed that they were fakes and he's been dead so long that's hardly going to be a problem. Can the boffins at GCHQ come up with something?'

'I'll get onto it right away.' Steve went off to make the calls. Nick poured himself a coffee from the percolator in Steve's office. He read more of the Palestroni files; this was certainly a dangerous man if only half of the contents of the files were true. Dealing with him was going to be high risk. Steve returned after half an hour.

'While you were away, I contacted Orville and brought him up to speed on the Hess/Horn puzzle,' Nick said. 'He's looking into it and he'll have a report ready by eight this evening.'

'Good call, Nick. If that egghead can't sort it out, then it can't be sorted. Okay, the news from GCHQ is this. They have no problem with making believable forgeries from the originals, which will stand up to high levels of scrutiny. But naturally, they'll need to work from the originals though, not photocopies. The more difficult element in this is that they will have to be made on paper, which is contemporary to the da Vinci period, late 15th century. As you can imagine this is going to be difficult to source but not impossible. The initial tests which Palestroni's experts are bound to run will be on the paper. There is no way that this can be faked, so it has to be genuine.'

Steve relayed the details of his enquiries. 'So tell me, Nick, what are you intending to do?'

'I want good copies of the da Vinci Papers that will keep Palestroni's academic specialists occupied long enough for me to get close to him,' Nick said. 'I'll use Sian to get me into his villa and I will have to play it by ear from that point. My plan is to get him out of the country to England, or, better still, the States where he can stand trial. From what I have read in the files, he has supplied arms to most of the terrorist organizations in the world. He has to be stopped.'

'Just run that by me again, mate. You plan to get yourself invited into the lion's den where you will serve him a set of counterfeit da Vinci Papers and then get him to give himself up?'

'That's more or less the idea, yeah.'

'Nick, you have had some pretty half-arsed plans in your time but this one wins the global prize for them. Once you get inside his villa we will have no way of getting you out. You will be completely alone. No wires, no weapons and no back up. You'll have about as much chance as a mouse in a cattery.'

'Do you have any good news?' Nick asked.

'Yeah! Italian food is great and they do a mean line in wine.'

Nick walked over to the window and looked out onto the drizzly London day and across the waters of the River Thames. What was he letting himself in for? If he were to be brutally honest with himself, he didn't really know. Nonetheless, the plan, such as it was, had been given the green light and was being put into action. Against all of his training Nick had no plan B to fall back on. But then, neither did a mouse in a cattery, he reflected. After all, how many mouse holes would there be in a cattery? Exactly.

There was a knock on the door of Steve's office. It was Orville, the personal hygiene monster. He walked into Steve's office, and plonked two folders onto the desk. A fine fragrance of stale sweat immediately began to waft around the room. Niceties were something that Orville didn't spend much time worrying about.

'It's all there,' Orville said. 'I've hacked into German archives and British World War Two intelligence files and I think that you are going to enjoy reading about Herr Hess and his adventures. It all makes sense to me apart from Hess calling himself Alfred Horn. Alfred Horn, initials A.H. Adolf Hitler, initials A.H.'

'Hess was a long-standing friend of Hitler,' Nick said, after breathing in and wished he hadn't. 'But he was kicked into second place when Goring came on the scene. That must have pissed Hess off very considerably.'

As Orville turned to leave he pulled a half-eaten Mars bar from his pocket, brushed off the fluff, and before stuffing the rancid brown object into his mouth, made a final remark over his shoulder.

'Of course these papers have twice the value now. Double provenance, Leonardo da Vinci and Rudolph Hess.'

Then he was gone.

Steve went over to a cupboard behind his desk, took out a can of air freshener that he kept for Orville's visits and sprayed the room vigorously. He went to open the side-window, but this only opened about twenty degrees, while the main window didn't open at all, hence the need for the air freshener.

Once Nick and Steve felt it safe to breathe properly again they glanced at each other and laughed. Nick picked up the files, shook off a dusting of biscuit crumbs, and then tossed one of the files over to Steve. They settled down to read.

Within four days, Nick had fetched the da Vinci Papers from the Vaults. They were taken to GCHQ where they were brilliantly copied by the boffins onto genuine 15th century paper that had been flown by a M15 operative based in Florence. The original papers were then returned to Nick and he took them back to the Chancery Lane Vaults.

Nick called Sian and arranged to meet her for dinner the following Saturday. She agreed and Nick used his time reading everything that he could on Palestroni, plus familiarizing himself with the part of Italy where the villa was located.

33
Germany 1941

Gravel crunched under the tyres of the sleek Mercedes Benz staff car as it pulled in a long curve and drove up to the heavily guarded crash barrier. An immaculate young SS officer snapped to attention opposite the driver and delivered an impressive salute to the high-ranking occupants in the rear of the vehicle.

The SS officer meticulously checked the identification of each of the car's occupants, even though all of the participants in the two-minute drama knew full well that the senior of the vehicle's passengers was, after the Fuhrer, one of the best-known men in Germany and in fact, the western world.

Rudolf Hess was impatient to leave the confines of Berchtesgaden, the Fuhrer's Bavarian mountain retreat. The weekends when he was expected to attend the Fuhrer's social gatherings always left him feeling oddly frustrated, confused and disgusted.

The frustration that had been steadily growing over the past months had become far stronger in recent weeks, as he realized that his role in the Fuhrer's plan was nothing more than that of a puppet. Hess was of use to Hitler simply as a figurehead. A hero of the First World War when he had served the Fatherland with gallantry and distinction, he epitomized all that was expected of a soldier of the Third Reich.

Hess increasingly felt like – and indeed was – little more than a tailor's dummy, parading in the magnificent uniforms that his rank demanded; making stirring but empty speeches that were actually written for him by the Fuhrer's advisors, to the Fuhrer's requirements; meeting only the people that the Fuhrer allowed him to meet, knowing that his every move would be reported back within hours or even minutes.

The disgust that Hess felt was, correspondingly, increasingly disgust for himself. He knew that his military role was an empty one, as empty as the countless millions of spent shell cases that littered the landscape in the war-torn countries into which Germany had carried the Swastika; all countries now full of nothing but vitriolic hate for the Nazi overlords.

Disgust for himself, too, as he displayed mock admiration for the man who, day by day, displayed the advancing ravings of a maniac, and was leading his beloved Germany to certain defeat, humiliation and perhaps even annihilation. And yet he, like so many others, did nothing to make a stand against this tyrant.

The adulation of the masses was hypnotic and the total admiration of his fellow Officers massaged Hitler's ego and inflated his pride, beyond reason. For Hess, the weekends spent at Berchtesgaden had become increasingly intolerable. Hitler surrounded himself with an inner circle of generals and government ministers, all of whom were forced to agree with, and act upon, his every whim. Otherwise strong men were silent in his presence and acted out the charade that their unhappy fate had made them part of.

The unbalancing of Adolf Hitler's mind was becoming more and more obvious, even to Hess who was hardly too well balanced himself, during these nightmare weekends. Hitler involved everyone present in the making of his home movies, much to their embarrassment except for Eva Braun, who loved being photographed whenever the opportunity arose, and the ever-present children of Himmler, the Chancellor.

The retreat was a fortress, sixty miles southwest of Munich, garrisoned by Hitler's elite guard who were almost all at least six feet tall.

The staff car wound its way down from the magnificent Bavarian mountains to the foothills, where the scenery changed from the ruggedness of the German Alps to spectacular countryside that the Germans liked to call their 'Golden Land.'

Rudolf Hess gazed through the window of the limousine, barely blinking as the beautiful countryside glided past. Here the trappings of the Third Reich and the evidence of war were less in evidence, causing the motorcade of the vice Fuhrer's car and its escorts to bring a dramatic contrast to the otherwise idyllic rural scene.

The only other passenger in the car was Colonel Hann who was Hess's aide-de-camp. He was only too aware of the mood of his immediate superior, and knew from experience that the best policy was to keep as quiet as possible, hoping that Hess would forget that he was even present. He knew from previous visits to Berchtesgaden that, on the return journey, as the kilometres slid past and Hess distanced himself from Hitler, he would slowly return to his former self.

Eventually, Hess broke the uncomfortable silence. He enquired about the coming week's appointments and listened disinterestedly as his aide read out his coming engagements. As he had expected there was nothing of substance. Nothing in which he might be able to contribute to his nation's war strategy. Hitler, as ever had made sure of that.

The sole glimmer of interest was aroused by Tuesday's engagement. Hess had been given the task of supervising the unloading and cataloguing of several road and train convoys which were laden with art treasures that had been brought back to the Fatherland in an attempt to keep them safe from Allied bombs.

This lame excuse appeased any sceptics who were offended by the operation, which amounted to little more than looting in the name of The Third Reich. It was common knowledge that many of the treasures would never reach Berlin but would instead find their way into the numerous private hiding places known only to senior, Reich, S.S. Officers.

Tuesday arrived and Hess was driven to the cavernous warehouse, already stacked high with every form of art treasure imaginable, yet still the lorries rolled in to disgorge their loot. Many of the artefacts had been professionally crated whilst others were simply wrapped in blankets. A team of historians and art experts would start pouring over the treasures as soon as they arrived. Occasionally, something of particular importance would be uncrated or unwrapped, creating a murmur of excitement causing everyone to congregate around the latest discovery.

The civilians present were highly educated academics and for the most part had little interest in the war. They were forced to be party to this twentieth century Aladdin's cave, which was totally alien to their fundamental beliefs. Hess wandered from one group to another. The atmosphere in the warehouse was not difficult for him to detect. All the art experts who found themselves part of the peculiar scenario, disagreed absolutely with the spectacle that was unfolding before them.

The magnificent collection of stolen art treasures, plundered from the greater part of Europe, represented centuries of culture and were now being greedily hoarded and stacked like so many sacks of corn. Hess himself greatly appreciated the beauty of art and was appalled by what he was witnessing. It would have been so easy for him to voice his agreement with those present and to decry the cultural rape that was being carried out in the name of The Fatherland. But to do so would be tantamount to suicide. Instead, he had to maintain a strong façade of superiority, which was to be expected of him, and refrained from being drawn into a discussion, which might move towards disagreement of the matter in hand.

The morning passed while everyone got on with their work. Before too long the novelty of being under the same roof as the Deputy Fuhrer wore off and the art aficionados continued to fuss over the ever-mounting treasure trove.

Lunch was a decidedly morbid affair; with art experts who were lucky or unlucky enough to find themselves seated at the top table with Hess, remaining singularly guarded for fear of incriminating themselves. Hess himself was decidedly uneasy and guided the conversation towards neutral and obscure niceties of polite rhetoric.

For his part, he would have liked nothing more than to make full use of this unusual opportunity and immerse himself in a free flowing discussion with such a gathering of distinguished academics. But he needed to be guarded. All at the table were profoundly grateful when the meal had ended and each could return to their allotted tasks.

Rudolf Hess felt that he was an outcast amongst these people and he knew precisely why. He was a soldier; he dealt in death, whilst the academics were interested predominately in art, history and beauty.

The strange thing was that he was in agreement with their sentiments. He wandered to a quiet corner of the warehouse and lit a cigarette. While enjoying the seclusion that this particular calm corner afforded, Hess casually rummaged through one of the crates. It had already been opened but seemingly abandoned by the academics before its contents had been checked, perhaps for a more interesting find.

Inside the crate, an old leather portfolio caught his eye. Hess noted with some surprise that some sketches within bore an uncanny resemblance to similar work that he had seen once before by Leonardo Da Vinci. The portfolio fitted easily into his briefcase and Hess slipped the package inside. He took the documents with him and later enlisted the services of Prof. Von Rorritz, an eminent historian with whose help the documents were later authenticated.

What he found caused him to abandon his family and country; on the 10th of May 1941, he flew to Britain, creating one of the most intriguing unsolved enigmas of modern history.

In a series of sketches, diagrams and articles, Leonardo Da Vinci described his discoveries which, if published, would without any doubt have a devastating, apocalyptic effect on mankind at that point in the evolution of human history and for the following fifty years.

Man has long known that the earth is spinning on its axis. If any ball or globe is spun, a centrifugal force is created that is much stronger at the outer peripheral or equator than at its point of axis. At the axis or polar points, it is a logical conclusion to assume that the centrifugal and therefore gravitational pull will be far less or even eliminated completely. Da Vinci discovered and analysed this phenomena proving beyond doubt that his discoveries were factual.

The twin invisible vortices, which exist at the north and south poles, magnetic and gravitational, create an area of zero gravity. As Da Vinci explained; if a rock were to be catapulted up into the vortex it would simply continue to go up and up as it would not be returned to earth by the gravitational pull.

Another example given by da Vinci is the eye of a tornado or cyclone, where whatever is in its path is sucked up due to the temporary removal of gravity through natural forces. In Hess' hands, the da Vinci Papers were explosive.

Germany at that time, with the fanatical support of Hitler, was slowly working on developments that would, within a few years, lead to the Nazis developing their lethal V1 and V2 rockets.

Hitler was well aware of the importance of these developments to Germany. If they could be made operational in time, they would give him the power to bring the world to its knees. Hess had been privy to several meetings when the rocket scientists had been subjected to all manner of threats to hasten the preparation of the rockets.

But regardless of the threats, the scientists had argued that breaking free of the earth's gravitational pull was a major obstacle, and the enormous quantity of fuel required in order to achieve this, appeared at that point a seemingly unsolvable problem.

This problem had been anticipated much earlier and a research facility had been set up by the Nazis in Poland to examine the theory of negative gravity. Once free of the gravitational pull, and in orbit, the power required to manoeuvre the rockets or direct them back to earth was minimal. They could be used to bomb any point on the planet that Hitler desired.

Imagine if the da Vinci Papers information were to be delivered into the hands of Hitler's scientists. Launch platforms could be positioned at the poles and a minute fraction of the fuel to power ratio would be required to launch the deadly V2's which would send them out through the earth's gravitational pull to orbit the planet.

From there they could be directed back to deliver destruction on any given point on the planet as decided by the Fuhrer with little effort and deadly accuracy.

The initial response of Vice Chancellor Rudolf Hess was elation, for he alone held in his hands the one piece of the jigsaw that would undoubtedly give Germany the means with which to beat the Allies. And more, once the Fatherland had perfected the atom bomb – which according to Hitler, was just a matter of only possibly months away – the whole world would be paralysed by the grip of the Third Reich, and all this could be achieved with no massive troop deployment necessary, other than defending and holding the vortex sites. The implications and potential of the documents was inconceivable and yet, there was huge doubt in his mind.

The doubt posed by Adolf Hitler himself. There was no question that he was entirely mad but his grip on the country and the military was total. What would he do if he were allowed to achieve his goal of world domination? Hess deliberated over the papers for some days, during which time he was constantly harassed by Von Rorritz who could not understand the reason for the delay in showing the crucial documents to the Fuhrer.

Von Rorritz knew that Hitler's obvious delight in the discovery would undoubtedly mean huge recognition for him personally, assuredly securing him a place in history as the genius academic who first uncovered the secrets of Leonardo da Vinci's work.

A meeting between Hess and Von Rorritz deteriorated into an argument and from there finally to a fight. Hess attempted to make clear his fears explaining what might be the outcome should the papers reach the hands of Hitler. But Von Rorritz could see his opportunity for recognition slipping away and refused to listen. Hess, the soldier and by far the stronger of the two, killed the professor and later disposed of his body.

This was not achieved without arousing some suspicion and after much deliberation, feeling that his time in Germany was running out, Hess made the momentous and epic decision to fly to Scotland on the now historic date.

At 5.45 pm on Saturday 10 May 1941, Hess, a pilot with more than twenty years' experience, took off from the Messerschmitt works airfield at Augsburg, Bavaria, in a twin-engine Bf 110 fighter-bomber.

After a journey of almost a thousand miles lasting four hours, he crossed the British coast over Ainwick in

Northumberland and then flew on towards his objective, Dungavel House, eventually baling out at 11 pm to land near the village of Eaglesham. Detained by the local Home Guard, Hess gave his name as 'Alfred Horn' and demanded to see the Duke of Hamilton, then a serving RAF Officer.

A deal was struck with Winston Churchill who withheld the full extent of the matter from both his American and Russian counterparts, Roosevelt and Stalin. The only three people who knew the deadly secret were Hess, Churchill and Von Rorritz.

Von Rorritz was dead, killed by Hess who was by this time himself showing significant signs of madness, and besides, who would believe such an incredible story? Churchill decided that the only solution to the dilemma was to bury the story as deeply as possibly.

At first, Churchill sent Hess to the Tower of London, making Hess the last in the long line of prominent people to be held in the 900-year-old fortress. Churchill gave orders that Hess, code named 'Jonathan' was to be treated with dignity. Hess remained in the Tower until 20 May 1941.

By the time of the Nuremburg trials, Hess demonstrated just how unsound his mind had become. Finally, the verdict of the trials was reached which resulted in committing Hess to solitary confinement in the Spandau Prison on a life sentence.

Churchill himself carried the burden of the knowledge to his grave, convinced that he had tidied up all of the loose ends to the best of his ability.

For the duration of the initial negotiations with Churchill in London, Hess was given certain freedoms and liberties. Later, during the period prior to the Nuremburg trials, he was held under light guard at Maindiff Court near Abergavenny.

Initially, two Welsh Guard Sergeants were always in attendance and latterly two male nurses from the hospital were charged with the responsibility of his security. This was a strange and inexplicably lenient treatment for such a high-ranking officer from an opposing Army that was determined to crush Great Britain.

Particularly as he was, post Nuremburg, incarcerated for what must have been the most costly imprisonment of one person in the history of mankind. During the period he spent in Abergavenny he was sent to London in a secure army van on several occasions to be debriefed by M16.

By the third visit Hess was being sent in a van with just one guard, and a driver. He had already spoken to the guard, and had found him a co-operative person who was morbidly fascinated by the Third Reich and by the fact that Hess had known Hitler. Hess whose English was fluent had assured the guard that he, Hess, owned a fortune in stolen art in Germany, including a Van Gogh, and in return for a little favour would give the guard the Van Gogh after the war. The guard agreed, and Hess gave him the da Vinci papers and asked him to take them to a safety deposit box in the London Safety Deposit Centre and bring Hess the key.

During that third trip to London, the guard claimed he had a sick relative to visit in London and was granted twenty-four hours' leave after Hess had been taken to meet his interrogators.

The guard obligingly put the da Vinci papers in storage at the London Safety Deposit Centre. Following Hess's directions, he used the name 'Alfred Horn' for the owner of the papers. The guard had to pay for a year's storage in advance, but the price was not high and the guard had plenty of savings, as there was not much to spend money on in Abergavenny during the war and his food and board were provided by the army. Besides, the prospect of owning a Van Gogh after the war was sufficiently enticing for the guard to be happy to make a small investment.

Unfortunately for Hess, after depositing the Da Vinci papers the guard decided to walk from Chancery Lane back to Paddington station because he fancied some exercise and also thought he would save on the underground fare in view of what he'd just forked out at the London Safety Deposit Centre.

The walk went fine until he reached Oxford Street, when two German bombers that had survived fighter attack out of an eight-plane bombing unit unleashed their 500lb bombs. Most fell harmlessly in Hyde Park, but one struck Oxford Street only about thirty feet from where the guard was walking. He hadn't bothered to take shelter; he'd not bothered taking shelter before during air raids and had been fine. *I'm a soldier, after all,* he would say to himself. After all, the bombs could fall almost anywhere in central London.

But this time the guard's luck ran out. The bomb blast blew him into several pieces, and the only consolation was that he was dead in less than a second. The unmarked key for the safety deposit box fell onto the road, and was melted by the ensuing fire. The remains of the guard were incinerated.

A week or so later Hess heard that the guard was missing and as he had not contacted any of his family was believed to have died during an air raid. Hess never knew if the guard had carried out his mission. The secret lay undisturbed until discovered by Nicholas Trevelyan many years later.

As for the Van Gogh, some years after the war it was returned to the German Jewish family from whom Hess's men had stolen it.

34

Preparing

When Nick and Steve had finished reading Orville's report, they looked at each other in amazement.

Orville had done a superb job as usual; his report was highly detailed and to the point.

The extracts came from multiple sources. Some sections read like a novel, which must have been written by someone with inside knowledge whilst other details were compiled almost as a list of facts. Say what you liked about Orville's personal aroma, his research was expansive and detailed.

'I think I need a drink,' said Steve. Nick felt the same, so they went in Nick's car to a pub a little way from Thames House. It was Saturday evening and London was quiet. With two pints set on a corner table, they began to discuss the information that they had just read. Steve opened the conversation.

'That really is one hell of a story and I can see why Rudolf wouldn't have wanted Adolf to get his hands on it.'

'The irony of it is that it's pretty much irrelevant today, since the Berlin Wall came down and with all of that space junk that's floating about in orbit,' he mused.

'I guess enough time has now passed for the implications to be of far less relevance that they were sixty odd years ago. But if the da Vinci negative gravity theory holds up then I had better pass this info onto my superiors.'

They called in another two pints and the debate continued. Much of this was now of little interest to Nick. His sights were set on the infamous Signor Caesar Palestroni; Nick wanted to catch the guy very badly.

The following Saturday evening arrived. Nick picked Sian up from the taxi rank outside Windsor Castle. He had purposely not enquired about where she was staying, not wishing to add more confusion to issues.

They drove to Ealing, where Nick had made reservations at the same trendy restaurant as before. The evening went well, the conversation was kept general and it soon became obvious to Nick that Sian was playing the romantic card. He allowed it to happen and simply ordered more wine, enjoying being seduced by a beautiful woman in the line of duty. What more could a man ask for?

After the meal Sian and Nick went back to Nick's flat and drank some more. What happened was what they both wanted to happen.

They made love again in the morning and later went into the West End and had lunch at a restaurant just off Piccadilly.

After lunch, Sian, a tad exhausted perhaps, made her excuses and left. Nick returned home to watch the rugby on TV feeling rather relaxed and pleased with himself.

Next morning he was at Legoland discussing details of his plan with Steve when a call came in from the surveillance team watching his flat.

'They are just going to patch through some interesting images from your pad,' said Steve. They settled in front of a monitor.

'This was taken half an hour ago,' Steve explained. The surveillance camera had captured two men entering his flat via the patio door.

'That's always locked,' Nick complained.

'Hang on, Nick – there's more,' said Steve.

The two men went on to search the rooms very professionally without disturbing anything. It took them ten minutes and they were gone. The monitor flickered and flashed and then new images settled. The lovely naked body of Sian appeared from the bedroom and walked over to the patio doors. She slipped open the catch which locked the fixed side of the doors so that, although it looked more or less the same, it was locking nothing. The time counter flashed 09.30 on the Sunday morning.

'You certainly do have to suffer so much for your country my friend,' laughed Steve, the images of the delicious Sian still in his head.

'So now that she knows the da Vinci Papers aren't at my home – where it would have been a simple operation to have stolen them – she will have to make a fresh move to get me to bring them out of hiding. She would have expected the deal to be closed after the break-in. If the papers were still hidden in my flat, they would have been stolen and that would have been the end of the matter.'

'Do you think that you will have to suffer more sex with this Mata Hari in order to bring this to a conclusion? You really are a fine example to us all.'

Nick left Legoland early in order to miss the commuter traffic. He arrived home feeling dirty and grumpy from the commuting. He took a shower, dressed in a bathrobe and crashed out on the sofa. He dozed a little until the ring tone of his mobile brought him back to the present.

'Hi Nick, it's Sian, I was wondering if we could meet for a drink tonight?'

'Yes, of course. Tell me a time and a place.'

'Eight at the Castle taxi rank would be fine.'

After hanging up, Nick called Steve to tell him that things were on the move.

'Keep it in your trousers for as long as you can manage,' was his only remark.

'Bollocks,' was Nick's.

'Those too,' said Steve.

Eight o'clock on the dot, Nick pulled up at the Castle taxi rank and Sian jumped into the car. She looked more beautiful than ever. Her black hair, which was usually tied back, was loose and flowing. She wore casual clothes, which were obviously designer and the aroma of her perfume, which he remembered was Opium, caused his passions to be aroused.

'Anywhere in particular?' Nick asked.

'Just a quiet pub where we can be alone and talk.'

They drove along the Thames to Runnymede where Nick knew a secluded pub. It was quite early and the place was only about a quarter full. He went to the bar and ordered drinks while Sian settled at a quiet table in the garden. How was she going to make the next move, he wondered?

When they had settled, she made her opening gambit. 'Nick I have to admit I have been less than honest with you,' Sian opened.

Now there's a surprise. Nick knew he could have made a dozen sarcastic replies but decided to keep quiet and give her a chance. 'And?'

'Nick, I know that you have some very important papers by Leonardo Da Vinci.' He feigned surprise.

'I discovered them by mistake in your apartment when I was tidying up,' Sian explained. I never thought much about them but I have since discovered their true value.'

Just conveniently leaving out the fact that you had them photocopied, Nick thought.

'I have a client who is prepared to pay you a large sum of money for them,' Sian said, coming with uncharacteristic directness to her point.

'Suppose I don't want to sell them?' Nick said, playing her at her own game.

'Nick, I know that what I did to you was unforgivable but I've got myself into a dangerous hole and I don't know how to get out. I have promised my client something which he has now become obsessed by and he won't take no for an answer. I'm really scared, Nick. All that you have to do is sell them to him! He's filthy rich and you will be rich yourself.'

'And how do we pull off this deal?'

'We don't need to worry about anything. My client will arrange everything. The money will be deposited in an account of your choice or my client will open an account for you in Switzerland or wherever you wish.'

'And what do you get out of this, Sian?'

'I get a percentage of the agreed sale price. Surely that's only fair, under the circumstances?'

'And your client, who is he?' Nick knew the answer but reckoned that Sian would be suspicious if he didn't ask.

'I'm afraid I can't tell you that at this point. I can only tell you that he's Italian.'

'Give me time to think about it.'

'Sure, Nick, but please don't take too long. My client is a very impatient man.'

Nick allowed her client to be impatient for two days before contacting Sian again. He phoned her mid-morning.

'Okay, tell your client I want one million pounds sterling for each of the six sketches minus your commission, money to be deposited in a numbered Swiss bank account.'

'Nick, thanks so much. You won't regret this. Where are the Da Vinci Papers now?'

'In the London Safety Deposit Vaults. I thought you might have guessed that.'

Next day the plans were laid out. Sian and Nick would be picked up and driven to Chancery Lane where he would pick up the papers from his security box. They would then be driven to Heathrow; from there they would be flown first class to Rome.

For the final stage of the journey, the client's private helicopter would take them to his estate. Naturally, the documents would have to be authenticated which was not a problem as there were apparently substantial laboratories at the client's villa. Nick could see plenty of problems but he needed to act naively to keep the action flowing.

'Perhaps you'd better stay at my place the night before we go. It will make things less complicated,' he suggested. *And it will give me another great night with Sian*, he thought. At this point she could hardly disagree. It felt rather mercenary but then again it was she who had written the original script.

Sian arrived that evening with a large suitcase. They went out to a Thai restaurant, followed by a play at the Theatre Royal. Nick loved the theatre, which Tamsin, then Sian, had introduced him to. It was a superb evening. The production was Agatha Christie's *Murder on Air,* a play set in the 1930s, which perfectly complemented the musty old theatre. Back at his flat, Sian comprehensively ministered to his and her needs. They slept soundly and awoke refreshed and ready for the adventure ahead.

At soon after ten in the morning, a black Mercedes with smoked glass windows arrived and they were whisked off along the motorway and into the London traffic. The Mercedes double-parked in Chancery Lane while Nick went inside to retrieve the documents. Parking tickets appeared not to be an issue for these people; it took no more than ten minutes. He had purchased a good quality briefcase for the occasion, which now held the precious papers. Nick alone knew that the papers that he had retrieved from his strong box in the vaults were the copies and that the valuable originals were safely tucked up in the vaults.

The Mercedes left the city centre via the Hammersmith flyover, back onto the M4 and on to Heathrow. At the airport they were greeted by what Nick assumed were employees of the mystery client and their cases were checked into first class.

Nick kept a secure grip on the briefcase. Ten minutes into the flight and it was obvious that Sian was nervous. She found it hard to stop talking and constantly repeated herself, asking numerous questions about the Da Vinci Papers. Nick was becoming irritated; he needed quiet in order to think. A solution came to mind, which might kill the two proverbial birds with one stone.

'Sian.'

'Yes?'

'*Four Seasons,*' said Nick. Immediately Sian's head slumped forward. 'Sian, you are going to enjoy a deep sleep until I wake you.' And she did.

How many people would love to be able to silence their partners so easily from time to time? he wondered. The flight gave him the space that he needed plus the affirmation that the trigger word was firmly implanted for immediate activation, when needed. He had no idea that this cautionary action would later save his life.

The flight to Rome took about two hours. Once again, at the airport, they were fast-tracked through customs and another black Mercedes – an exact replica of the last one – took them the short journey to the section of the tarmac reserved for private aircraft and helicopters.

A new character had entered the arena. Waiting for them at the airport, an immaculately dressed man introduced himself as Signor Palestroni's personal assistant. He politely gave his name as Alexis. He was slim, good-looking, with piercing blue eyes and blonde hair. He looked Scandinavian, but from his accent Nick could tell that Alexis must be German.

Nick made another instant assessment of Alexis: this was an extremely calculating and dangerous individual. Nick had the strongest of feelings that Alexis could be perfectly and efficiently violent when he chose to be. A man, Nick decided, not to turn your back on.

Alexis nodded to two guards who were standing close by and Nick and Sian were given a highly professional body search. A smaller Mercedes drove over from the official arrivals building and their luggage was transferred to the helicopter undoubtedly having been scanned for anything suspicious.

The chopper went over exquisite country roads lined with poplar trees, which were flanked by the rolling green terraces of the region's famous vineyards.

Finally, they touched down on the villa's private helipad. Nick noted two other helicopters, each sporting the Palestroni crest. He was impressed. *Time to meet the family,* he thought, as they stepped down from the helicopter and walked across the sweeping lawn towards a magnificent villa.

In truth, 'magnificent villa' was something of an understatement, for in reality, there were three superlative buildings encompassing three sides of a square.

The central, lower and for the most part single storey building must have been Roman. From the outside it was evident that it had been painstakingly, sympathetically and lovingly restored to its former glory.

Nick guessed that this must have been the country estate of a very high-ranking Roman official, at the very least a Senator. To the south there was another magnificent building but from a different period in Italian architecture.

This was a Renaissance mansion rather than a villa. It towered over the Roman structure, rising in the central section to five stories. The third building was again from a completely different period. This was a modern design with minimal architectural embellishments. It was clearly not built as living accommodation, having a far more functional appearance.

In the centre of the three buildings was an immaculately manicured Italian Renaissance garden, which looked as if it would have been laid out at the time the south building was constructed.

At that point in the history of the site, the Roman building would probably have been just a ruin. Nick could not help but be impressed. He brought himself back to reality by reminding himself that all of this beauty had been paid for by deeds that were not only decidedly ugly, but very likely, also murderous.

35
Into the Lion's Den

Alexis led them towards the central Renaissance mansion.

Nick made a mental note of everything that might be useful if he needed to make a hasty retreat. One thing was very noticeable: there were a lot of guards patrolling, they were all armed and most had dogs. He also noted that his exit routes were beginning to close.

The central doorway was just magnificent. Enormous wooden doors opened onto a huge entrance hall. The décor was as fresh as the day the building was first opened. There was far too much to take in during the short time it took to pass through the hallway. Alexis led them to a side chamber where Nick was surprised to see a lift. This modern piece of equipment was so well designed that it fitted in completely unobtrusively with the rest of the architecture.

Sian, Nick and Alexis got into the lift and Alexis pushed the button for the fifth floor.

The silent elevator came to an almost imperceptible halt and the doors slid open with a sound like silk curtains over a Persian carpet. The three of them walked out into a magnificent room.

Once again Nick was stunned by the splendour and opulence of the room, which was oval with a vaulted ceiling. To the front there was a semi-circle of windows that overlooked the formal gardens and beyond, far beyond. Nick made a mental calculation that he might have to run at a fast pace for the best part of an hour just to get off of the property! Standing in the centre of the semi-circle of windows, his back towards them, Caesar Palestroni looked out over his domain.

Nick had done his homework well and knew a great deal about the man who stood there. Palestroni's hands were clasped behind his back. The man of the house was seemingly oblivious that anyone had entered his inner sanctum.

'Signor Palestroni?' Alexis spoke quietly as if afraid to disturb his master. 'Signor Palestroni, here is Mr Trevelyan.'

Alexis, demonstrating his true arrogance, did not bother to announce Sian.

'Ah, yes. Mr Nicholas Trevelyan and the beautiful Sian.'

Nick couldn't help thinking that the dossier on Palestroni back at Legoland had been pretty well spot on. Caesar Palestroni was not a tall man. His file said that he was about five feet six inches tall, but his bulk gave him the impression of being taller.

The dossier suggested that it was likely Palestroni had been under the surgeon's knife on several occasions for cosmetic reasons, the last operation being a full facelift. He was slim and well proportioned which might have been accredited to another piece of surgical intervention: this time for a tummy tuck

Palestroni's hair was thinning. In an attempt to hide this, he'd dyed it black, combed it backwards and slicked it down. But all he managed to achieve was a look, both sinister and seedy, even with his slick wearing of his immaculate dark blue suit with the jacket draped over his shoulders.

Nick knew that Palestroni was sixty-two but the Italian looked at least ten years younger. His English was fluent, and he spoke it almost without an accent.

The semi-circle of windows where Palestroni was standing was a raised area, five steps higher than the main part of the room. In order to get to where Palestroni was and to shake his hand, Nick needed to climb these steps but made a point of staying two steps lower than Palestroni so not to antagonise his host with his greater height. He had noted that Alexis never went up the steps as if this was hallowed ground and not for employees.

'So, Mr Trevelyan, you've brought me the elusive Da Vinci papers?'

'Yes, Mr Palestroni, I have.'

'That is, of course, if they are indeed original.' Nick knew that Palestroni would have seen Sian's photocopies but decided he would not allow himself to be drawn into any argument at this point.

'Mr Trevelyan, it might interest you to know that I have a superb collection of Italian masters from all periods of my country's illustrious history. Later, perhaps tomorrow, when you are settled I will personally take you on a tour of my gallery. But ... there is something which is missing from this magnificent collection.'

'Really?' said Nick.

'Yes, indeed. Something which grieves me deeply. With all of the beauty that I have collected under my roof, I do not have one work by the most famous of all Italian and arguably world artists, Leonardo Da Vinci. One of Italy's most famous sons and yet, in which cities is most of Da Vinci's work to be found?'

Nick did, in fact, know a great deal about Leonardo Da Vinci. He'd taken the trouble to learn all he could about the great man during the past few days but Nick knew that this was neither the time nor place to demonstrate his newly acquired knowledge. More to the point, he didn't know the answer to Palestroni's question anyway.

'I'm afraid I've no idea,' he admitted.

'Let me enlighten you, then. The answer is Madrid, Paris and London. All far from these shores.' Palestroni permitted himself a brief pause. 'And now finally, thanks to you and the beautiful Sian, I shall soon own my own Da Vinci.'

Nick handed the briefcase to Palestroni, who placed it upon a huge Napoleonic style desk. Gently, he opened it. He then opened a drawer in the desk and took out a pair of white cotton gloves. Lovingly, one by one he removed the tissue wrapped documents and placed them on the desk. His joy in what lay before him was palpable.

'The man who drew these was a painter, inventor, visionary, mathematician, philosopher and engineer – but above all he was born in Tuscany.'

Nick could see wet tears in Palestroni's eyes before he recovered his composure. Placing his hand under the edge of the desk he pushed, what Nick, seeing the hand disappearing under the desk, assumed must be a hidden call button.

Within fifteen seconds two guards entered the room. Nick made a mental note of this action. Palestroni reverently returned the sketches to the briefcase and snapped the lock closed.

'Take these to the laboratory and make sure that you give them only to Professor Marietto,' he said to a guard. 'Now, my friends, you must forgive me for my lack of hospitality. Alexis, will you please take our guests to their rooms. You must be tired and will need to refresh yourselves before dinner.'

Palestroni turned his back and returned to his gazing at the tranquil view. It was evident that the meeting was over. Nick considered asking for a receipt but decided that, given the circumstances, it might be considered slightly trivial. He had been granted an audience with Palestroni and that was the best that he could expect for the time being.

Alexis took Sian and Nick to the west wing of the mansion. This was again a contradiction in architectural styles. Externally the building had the appearance of a Renaissance mansion but internally the west wing was much more like an ultra-modern hotel. Palestroni was obviously accustomed to receiving large parties of guests and he dealt with them in an efficient manner.

Sian and Nick were given separate suites. Nick showered, wondering how much of his activities were being monitored. He had never suffered from bashfulness; if he had been, army life would have cured him. He wandered around naked for most of the time before dressing as the time for dining approached. The internal phone rang. It was Alexis.

'Mr Palestroni requests your company for dinner: eight o'clock in the east wing dining room. Oh and by the way,' Alexis added, 'Signor Palestroni does not accept lateness.'

'I'll be there,' Nick replied curtly. 'That's if I can find the dining-room in time in this huge building.'

It had occurred to Nick that the enormous size of the house gave him an opportunity to wander around with a perfectly plausible excuse.

At a quarter to eight, dressed for dinner and genuinely hungry, Nick set off, purposely taking what he knew was the wrong direction. He played the bumbling guest and by the time he had finally found the east wing dining room, he had explored a fair amount of the building. He didn't find anything that looked overly suspicious, but of course he was well aware that Palestroni would hardly have left incriminating evidence in the house.

The dinner guests were mingling; drinks were being offered by uniformed staff and the whole affair had the appearance of a small gathering in a smart hotel. Nick's attention was attracted by the entrance of Sian, who had obviously made a special effort and certainly looked stunning.

Palestroni called Nick over and introduced him to Professor Marietto, the man he'd mentioned when giving his instructions to the guard. Marietto was an elderly, bespectacled, scholar looking man. In a strong Italian accent he explained that the Professor was leading the team, authenticating the Da Vinci papers. Nick shook his hand, inwardly wishing him the very best of bad luck.

'I'll have reached my decision by mid-afternoon tomorrow,' Marietto announced. 'But I have to say that from the data which I have analysed so far, things are looking most promising.'

It was a very good dinner; roast guinea-fowl that had been shot, Palestroni assured Nick, on the estate. Some excellent white asparagus to accompany it, and fresh pasta shells in a delicious sauce made from, Nick divined, tomatoes, basil and cream. The conversation mainly focused on art. Palestroni could be charming, though he also tended to speak to Nick in a patronising way, as if Nick, being English, couldn't know about art and could know even less about Da Vinci. When, finally, the dinner party ended, Nick felt relieved. Pleasant good nights were exchanged and when Palestroni had left the dining room, the other guests gradually drifted away.

Nick walked Sian back to her room; he suggested a nightcap and whatever else might transpire. Sian feigned exhaustion after the events of the day. Nick decided that this wasn't the time and certainly not the place, tempting as it was. He needed to be one hundred per cent alert – as Steve had warned, he was now in the lion's den. He said good night to Sian and went to his suite.

At eight the following morning there was a knock on his door and a maid pushed a trolley into the room that had an abundance of breakfast foods on it from both English and continental cuisines, including fried eggs and bacon, fried sausages, croissants, warm rolls, fresh fruit, various juices, tea and coffee. Nick sampled most of what was on offer, then showered and dressed.

Sometime after eight the phone rang in his room. It was Alexis.

'Mr Palestroni would like you to join him on a tour of his art gallery. Be in the entrance hall at ten o'clock.'

On the stroke of ten, Nick walked into the entrance hall. Sian was already there. They were immediately joined by Palestroni. Walking a few paces behind him was Alexis. The four walked out and down through the formal garden.

The exotic scents of the flowers wafted through the air causing an aromatic invasion of their senses. They walked across the grounds and into the gallery, the interior of which was as hi-tech as any building that Nick had ever encountered. It was also as large as any public art gallery he had ever seen. *All of this for one man and his occasional guests*, Nick thought.

There were even guards walking unobtrusively around in a livery which wouldn't have looked out of place in the National Gallery in London or the Louvre. Proudly, Palestroni strutted around like a peacock in his own Taj Mahal, showing off his treasures.

Nick felt almost guilty for taking little notice of the truly magnificent collection that he was privileged to see, so self-indulgent was this egotistical maniac that his monumental arrogance was becoming more and more evident with each minute that passed.

Once the tour was over, Sian and Nick made all of the polite noises expected and headed back to the tranquillity of their suites. At two-thirty, the internal telephone rang again. It was Alexis.

'Mr Palestroni would like you to join him in the turret room at three pm. Be in the entrance hall at five minutes to three.'

How regimented life is here , Nick thought. *These folk could all do with a little spontaneity.*

'Thanks,' said Nick. 'I'll be there.'

At five to three exactly, Alexis, Nick and Sian met in the entrance hall. Alexis didn't speak but nervously checked his watch, waiting until thirty seconds before the hour when he abruptly herded Sian and Nick into the lift. It arrived at the fifth floor precisely at three pm and Palestroni was standing as before, gazing out of the windows.

Again, he ignored their presence until Alexis gingerly announced their arrival. Caesar Palestroni turned to survey his visitors. Alexis positioned himself by the elevator whilst Sian and Nick walked forward.

Finally, when he decided that the theatrical interlude had produced sufficient dramatic tension, Palestroni spoke.

'Mr Trevelyan, I've some good news for you. Professor Marietto has carried out extensive tests and assures me that the Da Vinci papers are genuine.'

Nick glanced at Sian. She was smiling. He felt massively relieved that one of the highest hurdles had been cleared. But there was something not quite right. In his peripheral vision, he noticed that Alexis had quietly taken the pistol from his shoulder holster and was holding it down to his side. Palestroni continued.

'Unfortunately in the difficult and troubled world that we live in, good news is quite often followed by bad. Today is one such day for you Mr Trevelyan. You have brought to me the finest treasure in the world of art to be discovered this century for which you are to be commended. But in reality your part in the overall affair is as nothing. You are simply the messenger. Even less! You are no more than a common thief. And so, regrettably you will have to be eliminated.'

Palestroni's statement was icy cold and to the point. He was judge, jury but not the executioner. He was now in possession of the da Vinci papers and hadn't paid out a penny. Nick also realised that the drama, which Palestroni enjoyed so much and was about to instigate, satisfied both his dual twisted sense of the macabre theatrical and total greed.

'Come here, my dear.' His attention was now focussed on Sian. She cautiously walked towards him. He opened a drawer of the huge desk and took out a handgun.

Are you familiar with this weapon?' he enquired. 'You should be. As a CIA agent you will have spent many hours practicing with one just like it.' Sian took the weapon and expertly checked it. Nick immediately recognized the gun as a Glock 17, ironically his favourite handgun.

'And now I want you to dispose of Mr Trevelyan. He's become surplus to requirements and is rather a nuisance.'

The order was delivered without emotion. Nick saw the blood drain from Sian's face. She looked at Palestroni and then at him.

'I must also mention that, should you not carry out this request, Alexis will kill Mr Trevelyan and then regrettably, he will kill you too. That would be such a pity for you are a beautiful creature. Sadly, Alexis does not share my love of beautiful things.'

There was a silence.

Nick watched as Sian released the magazine clip, checked to see that there were actually rounds in the magazine, and replaced it, snapping the clip shut by hitting the butt of the weapon onto the palm of her left hand. She then cocked the pistol, loading a round into the chamber and thumbed the safety catch forward. The weapon was now lethal.

Watching the expert way Sian handled the gun, Nick was suddenly aware of a facet in her character that he had never seen. This was a woman whom he thought he knew but obviously he didn't know her at all. There was a cold realization that the woman whom he had so recently had sex with, was now cast in the role of his executioner.

Her eyes glanced around the room. To Nick, it looked as if she was thinking of shooting her way out of what was an impossible situation. Alexis sensed the advanced tension, his gun hand moved from his side to his chest and Nick heard the unmistakable sound of the weapon being cocked. To Palestroni and Alexis it looked as if she was preparing to kill Nick. But what was actually running through Sian's mind was something that Nick would never know.

He knew he needed to think fast. Slowly, trying not to arouse suspicion, he moved to position himself between Sian and Alexis. It appeared as if he was about to plead with Sian. Palestroni was expecting to see a spectacular ghastly drama played out in his exquisite private turret room theatre. He surmised that Nick was simply a weak opportunist who had become out of his depth and would break down, pleading for his life. Actually, this wasn't too far from the truth and Nick needed to dig deeply into his reserves to continue.

He moved closer to Sian. The gun was held in her right hand, which now hung at her side. When he thought that the distance between the four people playing out this drama was right, he whispered to Sian words that only she could hear.

'*Four Seasons*,' came his whisper. Sian's head sank slowly onto her chest. Nick was nervous that it might have appeared suspicious but he needn't have worried. It simply looked as if she were saddened by what she was about to do which added to the keen sense of theatre, flooding the room. Palestroni looked on, perversely enjoying each second of the drama that he had created. The gun was still in her hand and Alexis was in a position to finish him in an instant if Nick made any sudden moves. He whispered.

'Sian, when Palestroni tells you to kill me you will disobey him, raise your gun and shoot over my shoulder at Alexis. You must kill him or he will kill you.'

'Enough!' Palestroni was getting impatient, like a Roman emperor. He had ordered Nick's death and was eager for the execution to take place.

'Sian! Kill Trevelyan.' Sian's beautiful head straightened slowly, her arm came up, the gun hand was rock steady. The point of aim moved from Nick's crotch to his stomach and up to his heart. This was when he closed his eyes. Had he actually done a good enough job in planting the new instruction? Perhaps under stress, hypnotism loses its potency. He had no way of knowing. The gun came level with his eyes, which remained semi-closed. Could this be how it was to end for him? Had Steve been right? Going into the lion's den was a stupid idea, tantamount to suicide.

The first shot rang out, closely followed by two more. Nick spun around to see Alexis on the floor in a heap. He ran over and picked up his gun. Another Glock 17.

Sian was standing motionless, still hypnotized. She had been given no other instructions and her head was slumped forward. Palestroni made a sudden move and hit the emergency button on the corner of his desk. Nick had just enough time to re-position himself. A door at the western corner of the room burst open and two guards rushed in. There had been three shots fired. Alexis was in a heap on the floor, Sian was standing with a gun in her hand.

The guards made an instant assumption and fired. Six shots thumped into Sian's torso. She was dead before she hit the floor. The guards' attention was concentrated on the scene before them. In a split second they noticed Nick but it was too late. He pumped two shots into each of them before they could get off one themselves. Palestroni's Praetorian Guard had been eliminated. There was no time for sympathetic feelings. Nick knew that he had only seconds before the second group of guards would arrive.

He ran towards Palestroni. It was evident that he was not a fighter. Why should he be when he could employ someone else to do his dirty work for him? Nick wanted to tear him limb from limb but needed him unharmed in order to carry out the rest of his plan. Nick charged up the steps like a raging bull, lowered his shoulders and surged forward with his head, delivering a ferocious head butt to Palestroni's sternum. He went down like a sack of potatoes. Nick stood over him and dragged him to his feet. Nick was far taller. He cupped

Caesar's chin in his right hand and stared into his eyes. He needed to control his rage and above all he needed to be quick.

'Caesar, look deeply into my eyes.'

Nick started the procedure to hypnotise Caesar Palestroni who was groaning and whimpering in an uncontrollable manner. He had totally lost his confident aura of power and arrogance. He sobbed like a child and suddenly he looked every year of his usually well-disguised age. The groaning continued but he wasn't responding to Nick's well-tried formula. *What the hell was going on?* This had never happened before. Time was running out. Sirens were wailing all over the building, the turret room was bound to be one of the first locations that the guards would check. His only hope was that the secondary guards would expect their boss to be safe in the knowledge that his handpicked Praetorian Guard was there to protect along with Alexis, the head of security.

They had no way of knowing that all three were lying dead on the floor of the turret room. *Think, Nick, think!* He was too pumped up with anger – that could be it. *Calm down, calm down!* Palestroni was also so scared that he wasn't receptive to anything. S*low the action down, breathe deeply, take it easy.* Slowly the situation calmed. Caesar was still sobbing like a baby but he was calmer. Nick started again.

'Caesar, look into my eyes.' Caesar did what he was told for the first time possibly in his entire life. Now the technique began to take hold and Palestroni's head slid down onto his chest. The sobbing stopped and he relaxed. Nick breathed a huge sigh of relief. Palestroni was under but this was only the beginning and Nick still had much to do.

The door at the western end of the turret room burst open and four guards rushed in. Nick turned towards them, presenting Caesar's back to them. He was his human shield; they could not take a shot without risking hitting their boss. They advanced slowly, maximizing their target and fanning out to improve the angle. The laser beams from their sights flashed across Nick's face searching out any exposed area at which to shoot as soon as the order was given, but Caesar Palestroni remained silent. Nick's forearms were burning with the pain of supporting the weight of his body; Palestroni was all that was shielding him from a hail of bullets. He knew that he couldn't hold on for much longer and as soon as he released his grip and Palestroni slid to the ground, Nick would be dead. The time left was measured in seconds, not minutes. The hyenas were closing in for the kill.

'Caesar! Everything that's just happened will be wiped out of your memory. When you regain consciousness you'll remember I saved your life when Alexis and Sian tried to kill you. They shot your two guards and I shot them. It was me who saved you from being murdered by Alexis and Sian. They've been plotting to do this for months. You know that Sian was a CIA agent. She told you that she had resigned but that was a lie, she was still very active and was in collusion with Alexis. I killed them! I saved your life!'

Nick hoped that the story was preposterous enough to be believable. Palestroni's confidence was returning and growing in strength. 'Caesar you owe me a tremendous favour. I will now be your head of security; you will rely on me for everything, as you did with Alexis. From now on you will not make a move without me.'

'This man saved my life,' he whimpered.

The guards were moving in and were close enough to hear his voice. Nick prayed that they could speak English. 'There is one more thing Caesar, whenever you hear me say the word, *"Caligula"* you will return to this deep state of hypnosis. Remember, Caesar, *"Caligula"*, only from my lips, my voice. Now I am going to bring you back to consciousness.'

The guards surveyed the scene of carnage before them. Their leader was in the arms of a tall man who was whispering to him. Four weapons were trained on his head. Soon they were going to have to make their move and blowing Nick away was the only option open to them.

'Six-five-four. You are feeling relaxed and waking to remember all that I have just told you. Three-two–one. Wide awake and ready to clear up the aftermath of the unsuccessful assassination attempt on your life which I foiled.'

The guards were confused. Was the tall man attacking or helping their boss? It would be too dangerous to shoot, their Boss was far too close to the stranger. The guard leader called to Palestroni in Italian. Nick couldn't understand what he said but his best guess was 'Do you want us to shoot this man?' Palestroni groaned. Nick helped him to stand up.

'Put down your weapons,' he ordered. He walked over unsteadily to survey the scene. Slowly his composure returned.

'Nicholas, how can I ever thank you enough?'

'Caesar, no need to thank me; I'm just delighted I was here when the attempt on your life was made.'

'I knew from your file that you were a superb soldier, Nicholas, but this is phenomenal. Alexis was the best. I never suspected him for a moment. A traitor in my team, right by my side. Nicholas, I want you to take over Alexis' job! Name your price.'

First name terms so soon, Nick was delighted at the way his plan was working out although there were elements that he, in his wildest dreams, never could have expected.

'We can talk about that later, Caesar. For now we have to clear up this mess.'

Palestroni ordered his doctor to be called immediately and slouched down into a huge armchair. Nick could see him rubbing his chest with a confused look on his face. Nick went over to the body of Alexis and checked for a pulse. There was none. He removed Alexis' shoulder holster and put it on. Then he made the Glock safe and checked the magazine: four rounds expended from a magazine of ten. Then he slid the gun into the holster. It gave Nick a feeling of security that had been missing since his arrival at the Villa.

After ordering the guards to check on the bodies of the two guards who had died, he went over to Sian. Even in death she was beautiful. Perhaps, if she had not been hypnotized, she could have fought on and perhaps she might still be alive. Nick felt a massive pang of guilt because it was he who had rendered her motionless after she had killed Alexis. From the way that he had seen her handle the gun, he knew she would have been more than capable of putting up a hell of a fight.

He took the magazine from her gun; three rounds expended and put it in his jacket pocket. He now had over a dozen rounds with which to defend himself if things turned nasty.

The doctor came, fussed around Palestroni and declared him stressed but in good health. He recommended rest. The doctor wanted Palestroni to go to his bed where he would administer a sedative. Before they left, Nick enquired, 'How do you want me to dispose of the bodies, Caesar?'

'We usually just bury them in the grounds in deep lime filled pits. The guards know what to do. Please take care of it, Nicholas. I am feeling very tired.'

How many bodies had been disposed of in this manner? Nick wondered. Who would ever know the full extent of this tyrant's previous exploits? Nick called the guards over. One looked as if he was superior to his colleagues. Nick ordered him to fetch all CCTV tapes of the last day. Caesar watched his efficient manner and Nick could see that he was pleased that he had made such a fine choice of a substitute for Alexis.

With Caesar in bed and out of the way for a while, Nick could move more freely. Word had passed amongst the employees that he was now head of security which gave him free range of the buildings but he dared not allow Caesar Palestroni out of his sight for long. The senior guard returned with the videotapes. Nick explained that the tapes would stay with him and busied them with the disposal of the bodies. For the first time since entering the estate, he was able to use his mobile. He called Steve.

'Hi Nick, thank God. Are you okay?'

'Roger to that Steve. All is well but I have a list of requests before I can deliver the turkey in time for Christmas.'

'Fire away.'

'I want clearance for Mr P's private jet to land at Northolt airport in six days' time. He is then to be given a tour of the best national fine art galleries at the highest level including the Windsor Castle collection. We will need the leading fine art experts in the country to stroke and pamper our guest and massage his over inflated ego. You must send the invitation in three days' time via diplomatic courier with as many official looking bells and whistles as you can think of. This invitation is to be over a two-day period. We have just six days to prepare our mark. Arrange all accommodation and transportation at a minimum five star level. In addition, please inform our colleagues in the CIA that their operative's body will be found tomorrow on the outskirts of Rome. Tell them to pick her up and take her home with minimum fuss. I'll call again in three hours.'

Nick had no intention of allowing Sian's body to be planted in Italy no matter how beautiful the location, where her relatives would never know what had become of her. The body must go home to her family for the grieving process to take its natural course. He owed her that at the very least.

Having taken over from Alexis as the new head of security Nick now gave the orders and was not questioned that night the body of Sian was dumped on parkland on the outskirts of Rome. Not the highest level of respect but the best that he could manage considering the circumstances.

When Palestroni emerged from sedation he busied himself preparing his gallery for the installation of the da Vinci sketches in a place of honour within his remarkable collection. He wasted no time, personally making sure that the art world knew of the spectacular coup that he had achieved in securing the most momentous discovery in decades.

Nick stuck to Caesar like a daemon. Nick couldn't take the chance that his hypnotic implantation might deteriorate or even disappear, allowing Palestroni to remember what had really happened. A couple of times he talked to Nick about the shooting.

'It's all very cloudy, Nick. I can't remember clearly exactly what happened. Why did my chest hurt so much?'

'Ah, that would have been when I knocked you to the floor when they tried to shoot you; it was a very close thing.' Nick was enjoying himself, playing out the charade, embellishing his fabric of lies, deceiving the man who had himself used lies and deceit to his advantage for so long.

On the afternoon two days after the shooting, a special diplomatic delivery arrived for Palestroni. Nick watched as he read the official looking document. He looked unhappy but said nothing. Later when they were sitting quietly alone, Nick activated the trigger word.

'Caesar, "*Caligula*".' The man's head sunk to his chest.

'What was in the documents that arrived this afternoon?'

'I've been invited to London to be the honoured guest of the highest society of art aficionados in the world.'

'So why were you so unhappy about being invited?'

'I can't go and take the risk of being arrested.' Nick looked around. The cameras were off and there was little chance that they would be disturbed. Caesar Palestroni was probably one of the richest and most powerful men in Western Europe but at that moment he was totally at Nick's mercy.

'Caesar, you're considered a supreme authority in the art world, your collection and knowledge of Italian art is well respected. If you go to England you will be completely safe. In addition, you will be accorded all of the honours associated with a man of your eminence. Caesar, go to England and enjoy the glory which is rightly yours.' Nick then turned to some other more rather personal business.

'Caesar, with all that has happened you appear to have overlooked the little matter of transferring the six million pounds into my Swiss bank account.'

This was a debt that Palestroni had never anticipated paying so Nick needed to be subtle. As far as Palestroni was concerned, the da Vinci Papers were in his possession and no payment needed to be made.

'You will give instructions for this to be done today.' Nick thought that he had done enough for this session to alter the man's mind so he slowly brought him out of his trance. Caesar sat gazing out of the window for several minutes and then he suddenly slapped the arm of his chair.

'I will go to England. This is a rare opportunity and too good to be missed. Make all of the preparations, Nicholas. We fly tomorrow.' Nick went off to inform the pilots who would need to file a flight plan for Northolt, which was a specialist airport. Then he called Steve.

'Hi, mate; all systems go for tomorrow! I'll see you at Northolt at midday. Has the circus been organised?'

'Everything's in place. It should be a splendid show.'

Being an integral part of the Palestroni entourage, Nick was privy to view the day-to-day workings of the slick business machine that was Caesar's empire. There was a constant stream of secretaries and accountants continually bringing documents/faxes and e-mails that were ceremoniously laid before their master, which he then read with all the pomp of a Roman Senator. Nick noticed that Caesar never made notes; everything was stored in the remarkable, devious, mind. Before any document was shown to Palestroni it had first to be scrutinized by Gregory who was the chief accountant. During all hours of business Gregory was sewn to his master like a shadow. Everything had to receive his seal of approval before it could be submitted to the master.

The whole scenario, Nick felt, had a medieval feel to it, which was accentuated by Gregory who somehow reminded Nick of the character created by Bela Lugosi in the earliest black and white horror movies. When Gregory moved he gave the impression that he was hovering rather than walking. His elongated pale face was bordering upon frightening. A long, hooked nose pinched at the tip dominated his features with a pair of deep set hooded eyes which darted from person to person creating an impression of mistrust in whoever they fell upon. It was evident to Nick that Gregory did not like or trust him. This was about to be compounded when Caesar gave Gregory the order for a Swiss bank account to be created and six million pounds to be deposited therein. The steam was practically visible emitting from the chief accountant's pointed pixie-like ears and Nick revelled in it.

36
Visit to England

Caesar Palestroni's private Lear jet touched down at Northolt airport on the western outskirts of London. A gaggle of eminent art historians, who genuinely thought that this was an auspicious occasion, were in attendance. Several were considering cornering Palestroni who had triumphantly heralded the news that he was now the proud owner of hither-to unknown works by Leonardo da Vinci; news that had set the art world alight. If they were lucky, he might make a generous loan of the sketches to their respective galleries thereby gaining notoriety and much needed income for them. Among the crowd, Steve mingled with the art fraternity. Caesar was in his glory. Steve came over and quietly shook Nick's hand.

'Bloody hell, mate! This is a great achievement. You really are the man, I have to admit.'

'I appreciate that, Steve.'

'You wouldn't believe the hassle I have had getting the Home Secretary to approve this pantomime, so seeing you touch down with your new buddy has meant that I can keep my job. I could have ended up counting gas masks and pick axe handles in some MOD warehouse miles away from civilization if you hadn't come up with the goods.'

'Thanks for having faith in me, Steve.'

'Oh by the way, does this mean that I will have to give you your car keys back?'

'Bloody right it does. I've handed you Caesar on a platter plucked, gutted and stuffed like a Christmas turkey.' I'm all done here, I'll just hand in my resignation to Mr P then I will be off back to my flat for a well-earned rest,

'Ah, well I wanted to talk to you about that.'

'Oh no! What the hell do you have planned now?'

'Well it's not exactly me, Nick, it's our American cousins. They want you to stick with Palestroni while he is in London and then get him to go to New York. It's all a matter of extradition laws. They can do a far better job on him over there than we can here. You just have to get him to fly on across the Atlantic of his own accord.'

'Bloody hell, I detest the man and now you want me to stick around with him for another week. I thought my part in this charade was over.'

'Sorry, Nick, but we need you. This is a very special case and we can't allow him to slip through the net again.'

'Okay, so what's the plan?'

'Stay with Palestroni while he does his tour of the galleries choose a moment and then hypnotize him so that the CIA can dig out all of the information to put together a watertight case. None of the information extracted under hypnosis would be admissible in a court of law either here or in the States but if we can poke about in Caesar's brain and get as many leads as possible, we will have him bang to rights and nobody will know how the information was gathered.'

'Okay, Steve. I'll do it, but only two operatives plus you. I'll tell you when and where.' Nick gave the matter some more thought.

'Palestroni has reduced his bodyguards to just two; they are with him at all times and even sleep in the corridor outside his hotel suite at night. It might be a problem but as I'm now his head of security I think that I can get around it.

'Whatever you say, Nick. You're holding all the cards. By the way, Sian's body was picked up in Rome and taken back to her hometown. The director of the CIA has sent his personal thanks, he is genuinely grateful.'

'Not the happiest ending but the best that I could achieve under the circumstances'. The unhappy event of Sian's death flashed through his mind like a painful electric shock; she had hurt him immeasurably but he had recovered and the quick succession of events prior to her dramatic departure had helped to ease the pain he had felt. Any animosity towards her had mellowed as the monumental charade moved onwards.

'There's one more thing, Nick, which is massively important and which you need to know about. Whilst Palestroni remained in Italy he was safe and immune from threat but as soon as we get him out of the country there'll be dozens of very, very dodgy people who'll be terrified he could spill the beans on hundreds of illegal and unethical deals that he did with many people from government officials to drug barons over decades. His life will be in great danger. There will be a lot of people wanting to see him dead and who certainly have the capacity to order his demise.'

Steve looked a little apprehensive and Nick knew that there was something more that he was about to reveal.

'There is one last piece on info that I have to pass on to you.'

'Okay spit it out, I know you too well not to recognize when there's bad news on the horizon.'

'The Head Shed has decreed that you will be accompanied at all times by a Professor Norton from the Fine Arts Council. This eminent prof is evidently the dog's cahooneys when it comes to all matters of art and is going to be your shadow for the entirety of the visit, embedded with you and your new boss.' Steve found it hard to conceal his disappointment at being the messenger of such annoying news and had pre-empted Nick's reaction. An outsider faffing about could scuttle the operation without even realising it.

'You're joking mate, please tell me that you're joking. That's all I need. A tweedy musty old codger covered in dandruff, tripping over his shoelaces and screwing things up. Tell them that I don't want him interfering in this deal. It's looking sweet and with luck will all go to plan.

'I'd anticipated your reaction and made a strong case against this interference, making all of the points that you would have made yourself but they are adamant the prof will be moving into the room next to you today and will be stuck to you like a band aid.'

'Bloody hell, just when I thought the plan was set along comes a governmental hiccup. How do they dream up this stuff?'

The assembled group were standing in RAF Northolt's small VIP arrival suite, Steve and Nick were standing slightly away from the main throng of po-faced dignitaries and excited art experts. A small group of journalists had been allowed into the suite where the excitement of Palestroni's visit was evident.

Across the room a tall blonde woman approached Nick and Steve, her heels clicking on the tiled floor. Her long, fine blonde flyaway hair was piled on her head, a pencil stuck into the confusion. Wispy tails of the hair tumbled down, causing the woman to attempt to tuck the strands back into position as she walked, giving the impression that she must have left her home in a hurry that day. She was carrying an armful of A4 plastic folders and papers pressed to her chest; over her right forearm was a satchel-like bag with more documents protruding from the top. With her left hand she struggled with the hair problem until she was about ten feet away from the two men the folders and papers slipped from her grasp cascading onto the floor, scattered themselves before her sliding towards them.

Instantly, Nick and Steve bent down to help her retrieve the folders and papers. The immediate, almost involuntary reaction from both of the men, was to bend down and help retrieve the papers. As Nick and Steve were bending down and gathering the papers the newly arrived woman was standing no more than a yard away. Nick and Steve grimaced at each other as they simultaneously found themselves looking at the most gorgeous pair of legs that either could remember seeing. They regained their temporary lack of composure and stood up. Such had been the chaotic manner in which the newly arrived female had made her entrance that neither of the men had noticed that she was a stunningly elegant woman. The short scene played out like something reminiscent of a bad American High school B movie.

Nick and Steve, having retrieved everything, stood up and handled it back to her.

'Thank you so much gentlemen, please excuse my clumsiness. I'm late for an appointment I'm afraid, and rather lost.'

'Perhaps we can be of assistance?' he offered.

'Well actually I am looking for a Mr Nicholas Trevelyan but I have no idea what he looks like.'

Nick and Steve looked at each other in amazement.

'I'm Trevelyan,' said Nick.

She smiled, a lovely smile, the dimples in her cheeks adding a childlike element to this otherwise sophisticated woman. 'That's so lucky. I'm Professor Norton. But please call me Cassandra.'

'It's good to meet you, Cassandra,' said Nick, feeling this was one of the great understatements of the century. 'Please call me Nick.'

Cassandra smiled. *A wonderful smile*, Nick thought. 'With pleasure,' he said, feeling more tongue-tied than he wanted to feel at that moment.

Steve, not wanting to be left out of the conversation, introduced himself.

'Yes. Colonel, I've been briefed about you.' The professor spoke to Steve in a clipped, self-assured way; yet Nick noticed that her voice was low and sensuous.

Nick made a quick assessment of his new colleague. He estimated her age at about thirty-two. She was tall, extremely elegant with fair skin and very considerable beauty. *Probably a true blond*, thought Nick, and he also thought it would be a wonderful mission to undertake discovering if she really was but he tore himself away from his adolescent daydreaming trying desperately to focus on the job at hand. He was pretty sure, judging from the meditative look that had come onto Steve's virile features, that he was having similar thoughts.

'Nick,' said Cassandra, 'will you please introduce me to Signor Palestroni. We must get on with the visit'

'Yes ... yes, of course.'

Steve moved discreetly in Palestroni's direction while Nick steered Cassandra over to the nucleus of the group, Palestroni himself.

'Signor Palestroni I'd like to introduce Professor Cassandra Norton. The Professor will be accompanying us throughout you visit to England.'

'I can't think of a more delightful companion to have for such a momentous tour.' Palestroni automatically layered on the Italian charm.

There was some more small talk and then Palestroni and his now enlarged and beautifully embellished entourage were ushered to the exit.

Caesar Palestroni was a happy man. Wherever he went, he was the centre of attention. The art world appeared to adore him. Steve, as always, had done a remarkable job at very short notice. The grand tour of all the capital's major art galleries was spectacular and the accommodation first rate. Nick busied himself for Palestroni's approval as an efficient head of security. In reality, he had nothing to do as Steve had security ultra-tight and was always close by keeping unobtrusively in the background. Nick grabbed an opportunity to talk with him.

'It has to be tonight. Be ready for my call in the hotel after 10 pm.'

'Leave it with me; I'll be in the next suite with the two CIA operatives revved up and ready to go.'

The motorcade swept from one gallery to the next. The handmade shoes on Palestroni's feet hardly touched the ground. In the evening there was a dinner in his honour given at the hotel and attended by even more arty folk. Nick was amazed that Steve had found so many appropriate people.

All of the guests were suitably dressed for the occasion giving Cassandra the opportunity to wear something a little more daring than the business suit that she had been in all that day. The cocktail dress that she wore was supremely chic showing her elegant figure off to full potential. Her hair was down and tumbled around her graceful shoulders. She was the focus of attention not only because of her remarkable looks but also for her extensive knowledge of art.

Palestroni was not a late-night man. The fear of wrinkles spoiling his latest facelift was too extreme for him to contemplate. At sometime before ten he bade his guests good night and retired to his suite. Naturally, Nick and Cassandra accompanied him. His personal maid and manservant had prepared everything exactly the way he liked it. Nick told them that their final task would be to arrange coffee and sandwiches for the two guards outside the door and then they could leave for the night and go to their room in the hotel annex. Taking the opportunity to talk with the guards he explained that three newspaper journalists would soon be arriving to do the final interview of the day and that they would be staying for about an hour.

Palestroni sat in an armchair talking with Cassandra. Nick brought a brandy as was his nightly ritual accompanying a sleeping sedative. Cassandra took the opportunity to go to her room and change from the formal clothes that she had been wearing for the dinner and do the repairs, which all women are inclined to make when the opportunity arises.

'I'll be about an hour as I have reports to write on my laptop.'

She made her apologies and left.

'Nicholas, I am so happy that I decided to come here. The threat of arrest was probably all paranoia on my part. I wouldn't have missed this for the world.' Nick sat down in a chair adjacent to Palestroni.

'Palestroni, I want you to listen carefully "*Caligula*".'

Palestroni's head slumped forward onto his chest. Nick took out his cell phone and called Steve. Before he had replaced the phone in his pocket there was a soft knock at the door. He walked over and opened it. He explained to the guards that these were the journalists he was expecting and they were allowed in.

With Steve there were two other people, a man and a woman. Neither looked anything like agents. They were more like lawyers, which was probably exactly what they were. No introductions were made, for none were expected. Nick checked them for the conditions that he had agreed with Steve earlier: no cell phones, no excessive smells like perfume, no aftershave and definitely no smoking. There could be no mistakes.

'Ask him whatever you want but do it through me. Keep your voices low.'

The woman asked if the conversation could be taped and she produced a small recorder from her bag. Steve positioned himself at the door and the bizarre interview began. Just short of an hour later, Nick decided to call the meeting to a halt. He had never held anyone in a hypnotic trance for anything like this period of time before. Silently, the trio left the room. Nick waited for a while and then brought Palestroni out of his trance. He looked very tired.

'What time is it, Nicholas?' enquired Palestroni sleepily.

'Midnight. I'm afraid you fell asleep which is not surprising after the day that you have had.' There was a gentle knock at the door and Nick let Cassandra into the room. He took the opportunity to talk with the two guards who were sitting in easy chairs outside the door of the suite explaining that Signor Palestroni was about to go to his bed for the night. Cassandra looked relaxed wearing a T-shirt and colourful baggy Ali Baba pants. Even in this very dressed down outfit she still looked lovely. Nick was beginning to feel the tell-tale signs of a growing affection for this amazing woman.

Palestroni said goodnight and wandered back to his bedroom. Nick and Cassandra were finally alone. Each could feel a growing attraction towards the other they both knew that it was totally unprofessional and would undoubtedly lead nowhere - but the attraction was vast. The conversation bounced around from art to family and a glimmer of an expectation that this could actually progress into a passionate interlude was growing in both of their minds. Nick was about to move in a little closer and join Cassandra on the sofa where she was sitting when there was a knock at the door. *Bloody hell! I'm homing in about to make my move on the most beautiful woman I have ever see and now what?*

He knew that Steve would have called him on his cell phone if he needed to talk and came to the conclusion that the two guards needed his attention. Looking into Cassandra's eyes he got the impression that she was equally as disappointed as he at their rare private time being interrupted. What might have turned into a magical moment. He reluctantly walked to the door and opened it slightly.

There was a tremendous crash. The door was flung violently open, knocking Nick to the floor. A man surged into the room closely followed by another. They had pistols in their hands.

The first man who had exerted the massive energy on the door was taking aim at Nick who was on his back on the floor. There was a thud from a silenced pistol and Nick thought that he had met his end. The enormous effort that the first man had expended on the door had put him off balance reducing his accuracy. The bullet slammed into the floor inches from Nick's head. Nick had no time to consider what a close call it had been. He drew his Glock from the shoulder holster and before the assailant could squeeze off a second shot, which would certainly have found its mark, he fired the required triple tap into the attacker.

The problem was that the first man was blocking Nick's shot at the second man who was turning to fire his pistol at him. There was then a further single unexplained shot, the bullet passing between the teeth of the second assailant severing his spinal cord at the junction to his skull; the two attackers lay dead on the floor. Still lying on the floor himself Nick looked across at Cassandra, who was motionless, frozen in a classical shooting stance two arms pointing forwards, a wisp of smoke curling from her pistol. Cassandra sat quietly down on the sofa where only seconds earlier she had anticipated a romantic embrace and perhaps more. She looked visibly stunned. Nick got up pulled out his cell phone and called Steve.

'Contact! Get here now.'

'Roger.'

Nick went out into the hallway where he discovered the two Italian bodyguards slumped dead in their chairs, each shot cleanly between the eyes.

He walked back into the room only to be confronted by Cassandra rushing towards him wearing only a bra and panties. *What the hell!* She flung herself at him wrapping her arms around his neck and gave him a passionate lingering kiss on the mouth. Nick was nonplussed, *what in the name of god was going on.* Then he realised. From where she was sitting on the sofa Cassandra had a view of the corridor, which led to the bedrooms. She had seen that Palestroni, woken by the commotion was coming to investigate. He shuffled bleary eyed into the room looking old and bewildered. The two bodies were obscured from his view but what he did see was two people involved in an extremely passionate embrace.

'Oh I see,' he muttered to himself, shrugged his shoulders smiled and wandered back along the corridor to his bedroom.

Steve arrived with two operatives. He stepped over the two bodies, looked around the room and walked over to where Nick was standing.

'Jesus mate I leave you alone for an hour and all hell breaks loose.'

Cassandra quickly recovered her clothes and dressed.

Steve was busy on his phone arranging for the bodies to be removed and a clear up to get underway.

Nick took Cassandra into his bedroom and they both sat on the bed.

'Okay, prof who are you?'

'I'm out of the same stable as you Nick, M16. It's just that there are many facets in that building that our paths have never crossed.' She was looking shaken by the experience and it was beginning to show.

'I have read your file Nick and I don't mean your general file I mean you closed "eyes only file".' By this time she had starting so shake visibly.

'I'm sorry Nick but I haven't actually killed anyone before and – would you mind just putting your arms around me for a just few minutes while I gain my composure.'

They sat on the bed in an embrace, which lasted for twenty minutes or more. Cassandra sobbed a little. Nick stroked her hair. It wasn't a passionate gesture, it wasn't sexual, it was just one human being, needing the support of another human being and Nick was more than happy to supply it.

Finally, she thanked Nick and said that she would be fine. They walked back into the reception room where Steve was sitting nonchalantly on the sofa. Everything had been cleared away and nothing was out of place. There was not a sign of the drama that had played out right there less than half an hour ago. Steve and his men had once again worked their miracles.

Cassandra made her apologies and went off to her bed.

Steve and Nick talked for another hour and he explained what Cassandra had done and who she was. Surprisingly, Steve didn't find it too alarming.

'The world of spooks is like that; they don't always let the right hand know what the left hand is doing.' he mused.

'The next question?' Nick enquired. Who the hell were those guys?' Steve scratched his chin thoughtfully.

'Could be a team sent from dozens of former clients of your friend Caesar. During his multi-faceted career the esteemed Palestroni has severely pissed off an extremely large and violent group of people, most of them wouldn't be on your Christmas card list. Steve considered the question, both as an answer to Nick and an ongoing problem which would have to be unravelled. 'They were obviously very professional and will be hard to trace. You are going to have to keep your wits about you Nick, there could be others who know that Palestroni is vulnerable for the first time in years by being away from his home turf.' Nick was thoughtful.

'I'll bare that in mind but I can sleep a little more soundly knowing that your guys are in the building.' Steve continued.

'Our American friends are delighted about Palestroni going to New York, they have enough to send Palestroni away for the rest of his days', Steve informed Nick enthusiastically.

'So all that we have to do now is get him through tomorrow and convince him to continue the grand tour in New York.'

'That'll be tomorrow's agenda.'

'You need to find a convincing American art aficionado who will make the offer of a continuation of the wonderfully successful tour. Someone from the Smithsonian or the Paul Getty Museum and all of that by tomorrow afternoon. A bloody good actor might be the answer. I will add my weight to the story to make it believable and now that we know that Cassandra is working with us she will be very useful.'

The next day was, if anything, more intensive than the first. Palestroni and his entourage were whisked around gallery after gallery. Cassandra was completely herself again as if the dramatic events of the previous night had never happened. By lunchtime even Nick's head was spinning and he was relieved to go back to the relative calm of the hotel where they had lunch.

'Nicholas, our hosts appear to have saved the best until last. This afternoon we will be taken to Windsor Castle where a unique collection of da Vinci's work is housed. Can you imagine a more fabulous location for an art gallery?'

Nick smiled inwardly. Palestroni had achieved most things in his life but royalty had so far eluded him. Before they set off they were presented to the President of the *American Fine Art Foundation*. Walter Skorjefski was a stereotypical art critic from his goatee beard to the leather patches on his brown tweed jacket.

'Mr Palestroni, I am here on behalf of the Fine Art Foundation of America. We have been following with great interest your truly amazing UK tour and in the wake of the phenomenal success we would like to invite you to continue the tour in the United States as a guest of the American Fine Art Foundation. Naturally, all expenses will be met by ourselves and we are considering a two day visit along the lines of what you have graciously agreed to here in London.'

Initially, Palestroni looked delighted but as the full repercussions settled in his mind he backed off a little.

'Mr Skorjefski I'm deeply honoured by your generous offer which I have to say is somewhat sudden…'

Skorjefski interjected. 'Please don't make any immediate decisions Mr Palestroni. I realize that this is an offer made at very short notice and that you are of course, an extremely busy man but our thinking is that as the success of your British tour has been so well received by the art world, an immediate continuation would be advantageous.'

'You are most kind; please give me time to consider the offer. I will call later with a decision.'

With that Skorjefski left and the motorcade set off for Windsor. So believable was Skorjefski that Nick was left wondering if he was in fact the real thing or just someone that Steve had set up for the occasion.

Windsor Castle's art treasures were astounding but the Da Vinci section focused Palestroni's attention. He appeared to be close to tears; such was his admiration of Leonardo. Nick walked towards the Rolls Royce that was to take them back to their hotel. Palestroni was some distance behind basking in the waves of adoration, which were being lavished on him by who knows who. As Nick neared the Rolls Royce he did a double take.

'Tomo, what the hell are you doing here?' Sitting in the driving seat was Steve's wingman looking uncharacteristically neat and tidy. 'Bloody hell Tomo, I hardly recognised you. Someone's done a good job. You've scrubbed up quite nicely, you look almost human.'

'The boss said that I had to look the part. Any special requests?'

'Yes, I need time to work on our Italian friend so keep an eye on me as I might want some extra time. Could mean a few extra turns around the block might be in order.'

'Roger that guv.'

In the back of the car, driving back to the hotel, Palestroni was deep in thought. This thought was greatly enhanced by the shapely legs of Cassandra who was sitting opposite allowing the Italian to see just as much as she thought necessary.

Eventually, he confided: 'Nicholas these past days have been supreme. The invitation to America would give me double the pleasure but I cannot take the chance of going to the United States. It would be far too dangerous.'

It seemed to Nick that every time he used his hypnotic influence on someone, the circumstances were always different and slightly unusual. Here he was sitting in the back of a Rolls Royce. He was not facing the subject; both of them were looking ahead. The limousine had been supplied by Steve and, at Nick's request; the glass partition between the driver and passengers was soundproof. How was he to know that Tomo was to be the driver?

There was another new element, Cassandra was present and witnessed the scene first hand, which gave him cause to think that perhaps it wouldn't work considering the attention Palestroni was paying to Cassandra's legs.

He gave a slight nod to Cassandra.

'Caesar, "*Caligula*".' The much cosmetically enhanced Italian's head slumped onto his chest.

Nick hazarded a glance at Cassandra who gave a small nod of approval. Nick began the information embedding procedure.

'Caesar, you must go to America tomorrow. You were worried about coming to England and nothing awful has happened. You will tell Skorjefski that you will accept his generous offer and you will fly to New York tomorrow.'

Nick could see that they were almost at the hotel. Tomo's eyes flashed from the rear view mirror to the road ahead. Nick held up five fingers and the limousine glided past the hotel on a five-minute trip around the block. Nick finalised the data implantation, rounded up the hypnotic session and gave the thumbs up to Tomo.

'Caesar, I will now waken you from this trance and when you are fully awake you will start making plans for the flight. You will tell me to give orders to all of your staff to prepare for the US.' Nick commenced the countdown sequence and slowly Palestroni came out of the hypnotic trance.

Throughout the whole bizarre sequence Cassandra looked out of the window doing her best to blend into the background.

'Cassandra please get me a drink. I must have fallen asleep. The last days have been exciting but tiring in the extreme.' Cassandra poured tonic water from the drinks cabinet and Palestroni returned to his daydreaming, Cassandra politely re-adjusted her position slightly showing more leg thereby giving Palestroni even more to daydream about.

As the journey to the hotel was coming to an end, he began to give Nick orders, saying that he had decided to take up the offer of going to America.

'Nick, please tell my pilot to file a flight plan for New York, leaving midday tomorrow.'

'Yes, of course, Caesar. Leave it with me.' Cassandra flashed a secretive smile at Nick and even more leg at Palestroni.

That evening there was a final dinner at the hotel. Cassandra was wearing another stunning dress; she really was a woman with taste. Steve bobbed about among the guests and when the opportunity arose, Nick and he talked.

'All set. He will be leaving for New York sometime tomorrow afternoon', Nick reported.

'Well done, Nick.'

'So when do I get to go home?'

'Not until Palestroni's jet has touched down in the Big Apple and you have handed him over to the CIA, I'm afraid.'

'I'm beginning to think that this could all be a ploy on your part. I'll be getting deep vein thrombosis from all of the flying around, or is this how you intend getting your hands on my car?'

'We'll fly you and Cassandra back first class, airline of your choice. Stop bellyaching.'

Later when dinner was over, Palestroni retired to his suite.

'This has been a wonderful experience for me, Nicholas, one I shall never forget.'

'Mr Palestroni, I have a feeling that you may be right.'

As planned, the next day at noon, the Lear jet took off for the east coast of America. The flight across the Atlantic was uneventful. Palestroni busied himself with the computers and fax machine in the on-board office, which spat out a continuous stream of documentation. Occasionally, he chatted to Cassandra about art in general and specifically his collection. He was happy in the knowledge that the capable Gregory was holding the financial fort back in Italy. He had become exceptionally calm over the preceding few days.

Nick sat in a deeply cushioned leather chair and considered the situation. When he reckoned that they were closing in on the final approach to New York, he made his way to the flight deck and started a conversation with the pilot and co-pilot. It appeared that the jet had sufficient fuel to reach its destination but not much more in reserve. Refuelling would be necessary as soon as it landed.

The time was right for Nick to have a little chat with his boss. Something that he had been waiting for since the first moment that he had the dubious pleasure of meeting the illustrious Signor Palestroni.

Palestroni was sitting in the main cabin sipping a Martini with Cassandra opposite. Nick sat down in the adjacent seat. He had noticed that the stewards had remained remarkably inconspicuous throughout the flight entering the cabin suite only when necessary. Almost magically, one appeared and advised Palestroni that the captain was about to make his final decent into JFK airport.

'Well Caesar, I guess that this is the end of the line', Nick relished this moment.'

'What do you mean by that, Nicholas?' quizzed Palestroni.

Cassandra looked on in bewilderment.

'I thought that this would be a good time to tell you of a few truths, Caesar,' Nick said.

Palestroni suddenly looked bewildered. Nobody had spoken to him like that for many years and it took a little while for the reality to sink in.

'Am I missing something here, Nicholas? What are you saying?'

'Shall we start with the da Vinci Papers?' Nick asked.

He allowed a pause for effect. Palestroni just stared at him.

'What? What do you mean, Nicholas?'

'They're all forgeries,' Nick said. 'Top-quality forgeries, yes, but forgeries all the same. '

Palestroni just went on staring at Nick, who wondered whether the Italian's brain was simply unable to take in the news that had just been imparted to it.

'By the way, Caesar,' Nick went on, 'I'm sincerely grateful for the six million pounds you've so kindly deposited in Switzerland for me.' Nick allowed himself a hint of a smile. The truth was beginning to hit home and Palestroni's mind went into overdrive.

'My scientific team authenticated the papers.' Palestroni delivered this as a statement of fact.

'Yes, but your boffins were fooled, Caesar. Believe me, your da Vinci Papers are nothing but elaborate forgeries. The real ones are safely locked away in my safety deposit box in London, waiting for my return.'

This was turning out to be more fun than Nick could ever have imagined. 'And as a special bonus to me they're sure to be worth at least four times as much as soon as this little pantomime hits the Press.'

'I can call Gregory and have the Swiss bank account terminated.' Palestroni was still supremely confident.

'I have to admit that could be a distinct possibility apart from one problem.'

'Ah! And what could that possibly be?'

'Well, Mr Palestroni – that problem would be me!'

Palestroni laughed out loud. 'You – what can you do to stop me?'

'I control you, Caesar! Difficult as it might be for you to believe, it's a fact.'

'What do you mean?' Palestroni demanded.

But Nick just smiled. He twisted the knife a little more.

'Caesar, we're on the approach to JFK airport. When the plane lands you'll be arrested for a range of crimes that would have made Al Capone's head spin.'

The veins in Palestroni's neck were clearly visible; blood was pumping at high pressure into the brain of the man who was one of the most wanted on the planet.

'No need for a coronary at this point, Palestroni. I want to be able to deliver you in good condition. "*Caligula.*" '

The Lear jet touched down at New York's Kennedy airport. A cavalcade of limousines was waiting on the tarmac to escort Palestroni – but not to visit art galleries.

Nick glanced at the woman he cared about so very much.

'Cassandra?'

'Yes?'

'Have you been to New York before?'

She smiled faintly. *Even her faint smiles are momentous*, thought Nick. 'I think it's time that you called me Cassie and yes, I have been here several times.'

'I was thinking how do you feel about you and I spending a week here together, Cassie? I think MI6 can stretch to that don't you?'

Her smile was suddenly as bright as a midsummer morning.

'That's a really lovely idea, Nick. I can't think of anything I'd rather do.'

The Lear jet's engines had hardly stopped turning before a dozen CIA men swarmed aboard and swept through the cabin. Nick explained who he and Cassie were. A big crew-cut dark suited CIA officer sat down beside them and introduced himself as Agent Riley. He was slightly confused as to why Palestroni was taking a nap when so much was going on.

'Why's Palestroni asleep?' he asked, 'Have you drugged him, do I need to call the Paramedics?'

Nick and Cassie looked at each other and smiled knowingly.

'Just give me a minute please, agent Riley.' Riley walked over to the kitchenette and got himself a cup of water.

'Caesar, I am going to wake you and when you are wide awake you will be delighted to be in America and looking forward to your visit.' Ten-nine-eight.'

Cassie was watching the scene, intently enjoying every moment.

'Seven-six-five-four, more and more awake and happy to be in New York. Three-two-one, wide awake and looking forward to a wonderful day'

Palestroni was awake looking drowsily out of the aircraft's window.

'I hate flying, Nicholas,' he murmured. 'Best thing is to sleep as much as you can and arrive fresh.'

'I agree, Caesar. Yes, I do agree.'

'Cassandra please get me a cup of water; my mouth is dry.'

'Mr Palestroni you will have to ask one of these other gentlemen for that I'm afraid.'

'Other gentlemen?' Palestroni turned his head and could then see that the back of the cabin was filled with agents in dark suits.

'Palestroni we'll be off now, lots to do but we'll leave to in the hands of these capable gentlemen.'

Nick and Cassie stood up and walked to the back of the plane where the steps were already in place. There seemed no real reason to say goodbye, they simply walked away having done their job.

There was a debriefing later by the CIA and they were accorded the VIP treatment.

Riley dealt with everything efficiently.

'What do you intend to do now Nick,' he enquired?

'Might spend a few days here, I was thinking. Maybe even a week.'

'We'll supply you with a car and driver for the duration of your stay', Riley said.

'Very generous of you. Thanks very much. Oh, and could you please arrange a call to Colonel Heligan in London?'

Riley immediately arranged Nick's request. The call was answered by Steve who had already been briefed by the CIA on how the mission had gone.

'Well done, Nick and give my congratulations to Cassandra too.'

'Steve do you think that the machine could continue to run without us if Cassie and I were to spend a week here in NY?'

'Yes, I don't see why not.'

'And do you think MI6 could stretch the budget to paying the hotel bill?'

There was a huge laugh from the other end of the phone.

'Nick, have you forgotten that tucked away in Switzerland you've got six million smackers earning you a bloody fortune?'

'Hell, I'd actually forgotten. Must be Cassie. She distracts me.'

'I bet she bloody does. Okay. Nick take a week and call me as soon as you get back.' Steve paused. 'Oh, and whilst we are on the subject of the six mil, the six items that you "sold" to mister P were manufactured by GCHQ and therefore the money belongs to them. Enjoy it while you can because as soon as you get back here they will be looking to transfer your loot to a MI6 account.'

'Thanks buddie; you really know how to spoil a guy's fun.'

'I can't feel too sorry for you Nicko as you do still have the originals bogeyed away in Chancery Lane. Have a good day.'

'Roger that mate. And thanks.'

'You're welcome, as they say in America.'

Nick pondered the fact that he could actually afford any hotel in the town that he wanted but decided to go back to the Phoenix Plaza where he felt at ease.

'Cassie I've booked the presidential suite for us. If you are uncomfortable with that I can soon arrange separate rooms.'

She smiled again, one of her smiles he knew he'd never forget. 'No need Nick, I'm fine with your plans and wouldn't hear of anything else.'

And so the scene was set.

Nick Trevelyan was about to enter into another relationship and felt that this was something very, very special. Perhaps, he thought, contemplating the earlier unhappy endings to his previous relationships, that was all somehow necessary, preparing him for something wonderful. Maybe the pain was all part of the growing up process.

And he had grown up. And he would be growing up more, but for the time being he knew he had become the person he had to be.

Nick Trevelyan, the former army officer who lost his commission and himself, who went to Portugal and grew to understand himself better there, and who returned to the world of action and found himself again.

Nick Trevelyan, a man who loved his country, the wonders of history, and who was a friend who would stand by those who stood by him.

Nick Trevelyan, a man who loved women, who believed in love and who knew, all too well, that he would always be susceptible to the splendour of women and to the infinity of what love could be.

Nick Trevelyan, an officer ... and a gentleman.

The Da Vinci Papers as photographed by the RAF in 1941

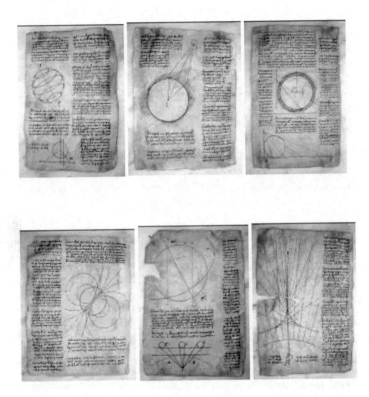

The Da Vinci Papers as they were when taken from the Chancery Lane strong box

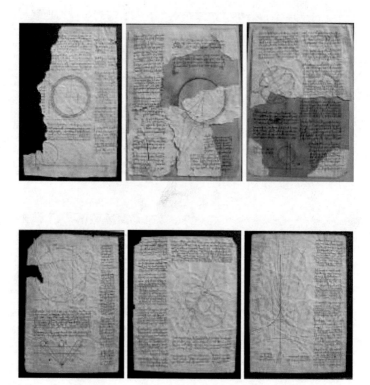